LADY OF THE SKIES

THE COMPLETE BOUND BY DRAGONS SERIES

ALISHA KLAPHEKE

Cover Illustration by Julia Dea

Map by Soraya Corcoran

***No AI used anywhere on or in this book

Formatted by Vellum (not Vellum AI—two different companies)

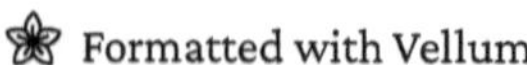
Formatted with Vellum

BOUND BY DRAGONS

SHROUDED MOUNTAINS
REALM OF LIGHTS
Vineyards
Hunting Lodge
Caer Du
Gwerhune
The Fae Forest
FJORDBOK
The Veil
Border River
Veilbury
Midhampton
SAXONION
Isernwyrd
White Sea
Strykeford
DEIGS
Masdam
Glass River
Leptis
LAQQARA
Luxurium
Skull Desert

CHAPTER 1
TAHLIA

At twenty-one, Tahlia still had plenty of time to change her fate. She would do anything, sacrifice all, work until her fingers bled to make it happen. Even though she was a half-breed and didn't have the right blood or the proper ancestors, she was determined to become a Mist Knight and ride dragons into battle.

Rubbing her cold hands together, she smiled and imagined the feel of the high-altitude wind on her face, the way it would clean the filth from her cheeks. She'd heard people say rank and money weren't the keys to happiness, but those folks had never had to go without food for days on end or been trapped inside the house with the pigs all winter long.

Somehow, she would fly her way out of the life of a lowly squire who picked up after others and away from the poverty she'd lived in since she was a child.

Failure was not an option.

Her friend Fara held their lady knight's mare, Daffodil, by the reins. She raised a dark eyebrow and set one purple hand on a hip.

"Tahlia, I don't like that look. That's the look that says you're about to drag me into trouble."

A cold breeze blew through the snow-laced pines and pulled a strand of Fara's hair from behind her dramatically pointed ear. Fara was a full Fae—unlike Tahlia, who was half-human and half-Fae.

The horse stomped the ground, nostrils flaring, as if she could sense Fara's disapproval. Tahlia brushed the mount's right flank, removing the dried mud the mare had picked up during the journey through the mucky pass into the lower reaches of the Shrouded Mountains.

"Oh, you love trouble. Don't try to deny it." Frustration itched under Tahlia's skin. She longed to move this fate of hers forward more quickly. But so far, no opportunities had shown themselves.

"I like fun trouble," Fara said, "and Tahlia-style schemes are less joyful and more *we nearly died*."

"Well, you have time to prep yourself because I don't have the plan quite figured out yet."

She snorted. "That has never once stopped you."

Tahlia chuckled as Fara looked down the trail toward the town gate, where their lady had gone an hour ago.

"What's taking her so long?" Fara asked.

Tahlia brushed a cluster of burrs from Daffodil's back leg. "You don't think she could be seeing him, do you?"

Their lady had a former lover in this small mountain town. They'd had an affair when she was much younger, before her father arranged an engagement to a male of his choice. The moment that fellow died from a fever that ravaged their town, their lady informed her father that she would be taking part in the dragon tournament. The lady wanted to become a dragon rider and to be free of her father's machinations. Tahlia didn't blame her one bit, and she only hoped the lady's rise would make her own dream come true that much faster.

Fara glared at the town walls as if she could see through them with enough concentrated effort. Neither she nor Tahlia possessed such magic, so all of this was guesswork.

Fara groaned. "I think maybe so. She's never taken this long at market."

"Did you get a glimpse of that message?" A dove had dropped a note at their camp two days ago.

"No, but her flushed cheeks pointed to some naughty contents. Stones, do you think she's left us for good? I can't handle another day without a meal. I'm not built for this!"

Tahlia blew out a breath. "Eh, it's all right. We will figure this out."

But if their lady decided against heading to the Shrouded Mountains for the event, Tahlia, too, would be stuck in this small dull town for as long as it pleased her ladyship.

Tahlia put the mare's brush in a saddlebag. "I'm going to find out."

"You can't just walk in there and start asking where she is," Fara said.

"Why not?" At the end of the right fork in the road, two guards stood at the city gate.

"Because it could take you hours if not days to find her."

"I doubt that. How hard can it be to locate a female who's six feet tall and dressed in tourney leathers?" This place would be abuzz with the appearance of a lady knight. Not only was she a noble, but she was female and most knights were male.

Fara looked to the sky, her face flushing. "I'm going to kill her if we find her alive."

"I will be back in an hour."

"No, you won't. Not a chance." Fara muttered angrily at the ground, lost in her usual spiral of worrying thoughts.

There was one way to get her friend's head out of the spiral. She had a weakness for gambling. "I bet you half my rations."

Fara lifted her head. "You're on."

~

Two hours and three inns later, Tahlia had found their lady locked in a chamber with her former lover.

She knocked for the second time. "But, my lady, if you don't go to the tournament, won't your father find out and come after you?" The door at this particularly cheap inn was thin enough to allow sounds of their kissing and more to carry to her ears.

"I don't care!" the lady shouted. "Be gone! You're free to do as you like. I am a lady no longer. I am now the smithy's wife, and I care not for anything my father says."

Pressing her forehead against the door, Tahlia exhaled. This was a problem. A big problem. Without their lady, she and Fara were out of a job. They maybe had one tiny sack of coins between them. Not nearly enough to live on while seeking new employment. Especially since it seemed highly unlikely their lady would be doling out references as to their skills and character.

But the lady would not change her mind. Tahlia knew her well enough to be certain of that sad fact. Running her hands through her tangled black waves, Tahlia left the lady and her lover to their new life path.

Now to figure out hers.

As she maneuvered through the crowded market, Tahlia's past rose up in her mind. She'd lived with her family in a crumbling merchant's home for a few years when her father tried out another of his *grow rich quickly* schemes. That idea had failed like his others. Her father ended up drinking their savings away while Tahlia and her mother worked extra jobs at a nearby pig farm just so they could eat once in a while. She remembered her older brother coming home frustrated from his job, eyes bloodshot and his fists coiled and prepared to hit someone. He never actually raised a hand against Tahlia or their mother, but Tahlia had kept her distance anyway. She knew an animal ready to fight when she saw one. It had been the worst time in her life, spent dodging her brother and suffering the pangs of an empty stomach. Her mother was kind, but Tahlia never connected with her in the way that some did with their mothers. Tahlia had spent the majority of her life thus far hungry and lonely.

But she was finished with that life. As Tahlia made her way toward the gate, dodging a gorgeous family of silver-skinned full Fae with ram horns and a lovely couple with pale skin and tails, she permitted herself to dream big. If you didn't let it all go and just wish hard once in a while, how could you know what might actually be possible?

By the time she reached Fara, she was determined that her time had come.

"Our lady will not be returning."

Fara began stammering, her fangs showing and her lavender lips pulling into a grimace. "Then why are you grinning?"

Tahlia held up a hand. "This is a golden opportunity."

"Please, can't we just head into the town and wait? She might change her mind." But even as she said it, Tahlia shook her head and Fara began nodding, knowing their lady had loved this fellow for years and wouldn't be leaving. "Do you think she had this planned? That the message was from him?"

"It had to be."

Turning the exact shade of a ripe aubergine, Fara handed Tahlia Daffodil's reins and started kicking the bags they had carried on their backs during the journey up to this point. She let loose a string of curses that would have made even Tahlia's horrible brother blush.

"Don't attack our only belongings, Fara. We'll need every bit of bread and dried meat in those bags to survive the rest of the trip to the tournament."

Fara whirled. "What do you mean?"

"I mean that I am going to compete in her place."

"No. We are not going. They'll put you to death."

"Why?"

"Because you're half-Fae. Because your blood isn't gold enough, Tahlia. You know I personally believe that is a stupid measure of ability, but I'm not one of the judges."

"I can use your blood for the testing if they demand a sample."

"And when they catch us, we both die," Fara said.

"If you don't want to risk it, I understand. You can go with my good wishes."

"Well, thanks for that, but you're all I have in the world." Fara's throat moved in a swallow.

Tahlia's chest ached. She took Fara's hands. "You're all I have too, sweet friend, and I want more for us. So much more."

Fara started to pull away, but Tahlia held her friend's fingers and locked eyes with her. Fara's eyes were more slitted than Tahlia's but not by much. Since high Fae skin tones, features, and ears varied so much, no one could tell Tahlia was only half-Fae. But those Fae whose ancestors rode dragons from the beginning of time had a bright gold shimmer to their blood—a byproduct of dragon power seen when a Bloodworker applied certain chemicals. That particular Fae blood was called Mistgold.

"We can do this. I'll be Lady Tahlia of... Lady Tahlia of Northwoods. We can use the isolation of the Mist Knights as a tool. They don't know of far-off small estates. They will believe it if we show confidence."

"You have too much confidence."

Tahlia's grin was untamable. "Maybe, but I can use it to fill our bellies and clothe our backs."

"I don't know..."

"Dragons are just larger horses."

"Ha!" Fara pulled away. "Sure, they're just horses as large as castle stables who breathe fire."

"Who is the best rider you've ever met?"

"You, you arrogant arse."

"Exactly. I was born for this, Fara, even though I have only the slightest hints of Mistgold in my blood. We will be a part of the most glorious culture. The Mist Knights." The name of the group who guarded the Realm of Lights' coastline practically sparkled in her mind's eye. "Once I make my way into the order, you'll have the coin to do exactly as you wish. Stay, leave. Continue to help me or take on a different position. Whatever makes you happy. You can't find that kind of freedom without gold and silver to your name."

"I hate to admit it, but you're right, of course."

"I am, and we can do this."

"Where will you get tourney leathers?"

"I don't know, but I bet you already have an idea."

"They sell sets at the base of the Mist Road," Fara answered begrudgingly.

"Do we have enough to buy one?"

"If our lady doesn't come after that sack." Her gaze flew to the brown bag tied to the horse's saddle.

"She's too *busy* to worry about coming back. To her, that sack is nothing. She has a full purse with her already and a smithy who will make enough to please her." Their lady had never been materialistic like the rest of her family. Tahlia had always respected her for that.

"Fine. But if there is even a hint of the judges being onto you, we leave immediately."

"They won't find out," Tahlia said.

Fara's neck went red, a sure sign of her notorious temper rising. She lifted a finger and shook it under Tahlia's nose. "But if they do..."

Tahlia took her hand and gently lowered her finger. "I was born for this. My blood has gold in it."

"Not enough to pass the Bloodworkers' test."

"Like I said, I can use yours. We're clever. We can get around that. If you're up for it."

Exhaling and breaking away, Fara spun.

She had to agree. Tahlia didn't want to admit it, but she truly wanted Fara at her side. With Fara's support and her blood, this wild plan was actually plausible. Without her, it would be lonely and far more dangerous.

"Please, Fara. Consider it. Let's change our fates. We can do this."

Grasping clusters of her hair and muttering, Fara stared at the sky. "I never should have given you that apple."

Tahlia laughed, remembering the day they'd met when Tahlia had been a slip of a thing—fourteen, half-starved, and desperate. Fara had given up her breakfast so Tahlia could make it to their lady's military event in Seelie King Lysanael's city.

"You know you want to do this with me just a little bit ."

Fara growled and waved a fisted hand at the gathering clouds. "Fine. Let's go before a storm rolls in and makes me even more irritated. But stop smiling."

"You didn't even look at my face."

"I don't need to. I can sense that smile. You're not allowed to have fun doing this. I'm still against it."

"What's life without some risk?"

"Comfortable. And it usually includes cats, which I approve of."

"Dragons beat cats any day."

"Not in my book."

Tahlia chuckled. "Have it your way. No fun on this adventure. Zero. Got it."

But she couldn't help but feel more alive than ever. This was a real chance to grab the life she wanted, to snag her fate from the greedy hands of the Old Ones. A thrill zipped through her blood and she grinned at the sun shining through the breaks in the clouds.

CHAPTER 2

MARIUS

Marius finished tying back his long Fae-white hair as he strode across the foyer of the Mist Knights' castle, a structure that had been carved from the mighty cliffs of the Shrouded Mountains and specifically the peak called Dragon Tail. The pale light of pre-dawn streamed through the stained-glass windows. The click and knock of his boots echoed off the domed ceiling, where powerful crystals half the size of his dragon refracted the windows' glow to scatter complicated patterns over the stone floor. Morning exercises would begin soon.

He pursed his lips and adjusted the whip coiled loosely around his shoulder. The place was empty. Was he the only one awake and prepared for the day's schedule? It wasn't as if he wouldn't rather have a nice lie-in with a hot cup of tea and a novel that he wouldn't want anyone to know he was reading, but now wasn't the time for relaxation.

The ever-present mist of the Shrouded Mountains dampened his cheeks as he left the half-open doors of the foyer and hurried to the tournament grounds. The grounds were devoid of any activity.

Frustration lanced through Marius. Could no one follow a schedule?

He threw up his hands and headed out of the tourney grounds and toward the stables just outside the inner gates of the cliffside castle. It was one thing for the knights to sleep in after a festival or during a holiday, but the tournament was days away. There was no time to waste.

The dragon stables were also cut out of the mountain and not even Marius had fully explored all of the inner pathways of the labyrinthine structure that housed the entirety of the Mist Knights' dragon herd.

Outside the large doors, Marius's squire, Remus, was polishing a saddle. The young lad's straw-hued hair hung over his freckled face. He was just nineteen and though he was too jovial for Marius's taste in assistants, he did seem remarkably brave and intelligent.

At Marius's appearance, Remus stood, shoved his hair behind his ears, and bowed. "High Captain, I have your saddle ready. Would you like me to gear up Ragewing?"

Marius wanted to tell the lad to tie back his unruly hair, but he didn't want to be too harsh quite yet. The lad had only started working for him a week ago when Marius's former squire had been promoted to knighthood.

"Thank you, Remus, but you know I prefer doing that myself."

The squire nodded and handed the saddle over. "Ragewing finished his morning meal, sir."

The saddle's smooth seat and straps gleamed in the rising sun's light. The scent of the leather and the smoky odor of the dragons combined to calm Marius and chase away his frustration with the other knights and knights-in-training.

"If I may ask..." Remus swallowed.

Marius grunted. Remus was always asking the most inane questions.

"Why do you need a whip or a bow on the back of a fire-breathing dragon?"

Breathing out through his nose, Marius attempted to be less surly. It was a challenge he wasn't sure he could conquer.

"Because dragons at their best can blaze maybe five times in a day. When they are injured or battle-fatigued, that capability decreases."

"I would have thought one or two blasts of fire could end any fight."

"Sadly, no. And fire should always be the last resort anyway. It isn't a kind way to kill and should only be used when there is no alternative."

Remus's eyes widened and his lips parted.

"Why do you seem so surprised to hear that?" Marius asked.

"Because you are High Captain Marius Leos Valentius, defender of the Realm of Lights, Shadow of the Shrouded Mountains—"

Marius's cheeks warmed at the praise and he held up a hand. "Please. It's ridiculous to give me all the credit. Every battle was won by a unit of Mist Knights and our dragons. I am only one male and I do nothing without Ragewing and my knights."

"Humble too." Remus whistled quietly and shook his head. "You might hate it, but you're my hero, High Captain."

If the lad knew all Marius had done during those battles, he might feel otherwise. Marius didn't regret his actions, but not all of them felt heroic upon reflection. More like desperation and panic laced with ingrained military skills.

"If that's all, I need to get moving," he said wryly.

The squire bowed. "I'll meet you out here when you are ready, sir."

"Very good."

The entryway to the stables had just enough space for three dragons to pass side by side. Torches blazed along the rough stone walls, lighting the way. Marius walked the familiar path to Ragewing's cave and stopped outside the smaller gate. The cave was dark, lit only by the ventilation holes cut into the ceiling, but the shuffling of a tail along the sweet-scented rushes let Marius know his dragon stood inside.

"Ready to fly, my friend?"

Marius leaned on the waist-high gate and extended a hand. It was never smart to just march into a dragon's cave without first gaining permission from the beast. More sounds issued from the dim enclosure and then a warm snout found his hand. Marius's eyes adjusted to the low light and he gave Ragewing a smile. Ragewing was a Heartsworn, a dragon known for loyalty and intelligence. They were large and fiercely loyal to their riders. Stories had been told of Heartsworns sacrificing themselves for those they loved—other dragons and riders alike.

Ragewing's scales held all the shades of red from scarlet to a color that was nearly pink. His dark orange eyes were slitted like Marius's. The fiery eyes glittered in the low light and the second lid —the one that protected a dragon's sight from fire damage— slipped up then back down again. Ragewing's throat had a golden sheen that swept down his belly and ran along the underside of his spiked tail. He was a gorgeous creature and far larger than the other Heartsworns on the mountain. He was their alpha. Marius sometimes worried about that fact because Commander Gaius's Heartsworn should have been alpha. But dragons were not high Fae and they didn't really respect the Fae ranking system. They had their own way of determining pack leaders.

Running a hand down Ragewing's snout, Marius whispered, "Good morning, my proud monster. How did you sleep? I hope it was a good night for you because we have a host of idiots to deal with this morning. Every last one of them will be late to the grounds."

Ragewing snuffled into Marius's flying leathers and he rubbed the animal's long neck, checking a wound that he'd suffered in yesterday's air sparring with the commander. Dragons healed quickly and the cut appeared nearly mended already. Swinging the gate wide, Marius went inside the cave and began to saddle him. Marius threw the saddle over the dragon's back, then bent to retrieve the rope attached to the girth. Pulling the rope, he found the end of the strap. He untied the rope from the strap and buckled the girth to an appropriate tightness. Ragewing bumped his shoulder and threw a wing over his head.

"Yes, I know. You need a day off. You'll get one very soon. I swear it."

Ragewing truly did deserve a break. He was the hardest working dragon on the mountain, and probably in the world. Normally, they'd be training half days only this time of year, when the pirates had left the coastline due to storms and the commander had no missions for them. But it was a tournament year, so the work just kept coming.

Only one new Mist Knight would be named at the conclusion of the tourney, just one individual who showed the prowess and keen mind of a would-be expert military dragon rider. It was up to the commander to pick the winner from the combatants, but Commander Gaius would ask Marius his opinion.

At twenty-five years of age, Marius was the youngest person ever to be promoted to High Captain of the Fae Mist Knights. He wasn't about to screw up this appointment by failing to rouse those under him to train thoroughly enough. The only one higher in rank than him was the commander, and someday, Marius would take over that position.

It was all part of his plan.

He would marry the commander's daughter, Ophelia—another dragonriding Mist Knight and a great one to boot—and carry on the grand tradition of his people. His blood was nearly all Mistgold, and he and the commander's daughter would produce young that were even stronger. His skill with the dragons was matched only by the commander, but Marius's offspring would be better than either of them.

Your sacrifice won't be for nothing, Bellona.

After his parents had died, his older sister had given up her chance to leave for the healing arts academy and handed over all of the inherited coin to support Marius's training efforts.

Bellona had died shortly after his arrival here.

The courier Marius had paid to deliver his wages to Bellona had informed him that an invading party from the nearby seaside had ripped through the town and killed many. Marius squeezed his eyes shut, recalling the words as they'd spilled from the courier's mouth, those terrible words. *"...horrible tragedy, High Captain..."* Marius pressed a hand to his chest. *"...only a handful of survivors..."*

He still couldn't believe she was gone.

Bellona had valued Mistgold blood and the traditions of their people even more than Marius at that time.

Old Ones bless her wandering soul.

He would make her proud, he thought as he worked Ragewing's bridle into place. If he failed in this, it would be akin to stomping on her grave. No, he refused to be anything less than excellent as he lived out his dream and hers for their family's bloodline. With every pirate he killed on missions, he avenged Bellona's death.

Once Ragewing was saddled and had finished the pear slices Marius had brought for him, the two met Squire Remus and started toward the arena.

"Pears again, hmm?" Remus's lips twitched.

Marius pulled at the gold-embroidered collar of his uniform with one hand and held loosely to Ragewing's reins with the other. "It's not silly to give a dragon a treat now and then. They trust those who offer fine gifts. It's in their nature."

"Aye, Captain. I'm sure you're right. You probably know more about the beasts than anyone alive."

"The commander knows more."

"All right. Maybe so. But you rode earlier in life, didn't you? He didn't start riding until age thirteen, if the rumors are right," Remus said.

"I rode my first dragon at five."

"Old Ones, but that was young! How did you ever manage that? Who taught you?"

This new squire talked too much. His appreciation of Marius's talent and dedication was nice though.

"My mother and father instructed me at first." Marius didn't care to get into his entire family history right now. "Let's focus on the task at hand, shall we?" He raised an eyebrow at the squire.

The young lad nodded and went quiet.

Three of Marius's fellow knights stood in the arena and a few more were making their way in with their dragons. Ophelia stood ready—he was quite glad his future mate was punctual—while others soared toward the tournament grounds to land beside her and the others.

"Except you three," Marius said, nodding to Titus, Maiwenn, and Morvan, "you are late. You will clean stalls after our morning flight and give your squires an hour off."

"Aye, High Captain," the knights said in chorus.

Ragewing's reins were a soft, familiar texture in Marius's right hand. "Justus, your uniform is wrinkled. Go." He pointed to the castle keep then eyed the rest of the knights. "We can't be less than our best, especially considering the king and queen might arrive soon to watch the tournament. Remember, your tidiness speaks to the attention you show your dragon and your position here. When I see unkempt clothing, I wonder if your tack has been checked properly and if you checked your dragon's scales and their food. Dragons deserve the best care we have to offer."

Justus handed his dragon's reins to his squire, then hurried away to follow Marius's orders.

"First, we will fly in formations. Once I give the signal," Marius said, "Ewan will move out, turn, and fly as our enemy."

"High Captain?" A female Mist Knight named Claudia raised a finger.

"Yes?"

"How many dragons do the pirates have now?"

"At last count, only three. But three very capable full-sized Green-flanked Terrors."

The knights murmured, their wary gazes going to the one Green-flanked Terror in the Mist Knights' herd. Ophelia held that dragon's reins, her blue-green hair rippling behind her. Though she was beautiful, neither his body nor his heart longed for her touch. Only his mind wanted her as his mate because she was a part of his plan. This wasn't about love, but about upholding and protecting the Mist Fae's way of life.

Ophelia glanced at him and her lips shifted into a subtle smile. She never smiled for anyone else. That did please him because perhaps she was indeed willing to go along with his plan.

"Double check your tack now and then we will fly," Marius ordered.

The knights obeyed him, tugging girth straps and running hands over bridles and buckles. Squires prompted the dragons to spread their wings so they could do a last moment look for any injuries or disease.

Justus returned in a properly pressed uniform and as soon as he seemed ready, Marius climbed into Ragewing's saddle.

"Bow and arrow formation to begin!"

Marius patted Ragewing and they burst into the sky. He would never stop being astounded by a dragon's take-off capabilities.

CHAPTER 3
MARIUS

The dragon expanded his great ruby-hued wings, and then they were flying through the mist and toward the blue sky above.

The rest of the knights followed him into the air and soon the formation was complete. Marius eyed Justus. He kept dropping back too far.

"Stop tugging at her reins, Justus!" Marius shouted over the wind with the power of his Mistgold blood. Those who had strong blood were usually gifted with the ability to send their voice much farther than other Fae.

The rest of the knights kept nicely in formation, and once they'd flown over jagged Sunthrone—the second-highest peak in the Shrouded Mountains behind the castle's perch—he raised his arm and locked eyes with Ewan. The knight dropped below the formation, wheeled around, then came back at the group blowing third fire, a flame strength only a third of the power his dragon possessed. That level of flame was harsh enough for serious sparring, but not so fierce as to maim anyone if things went wrong.

The formation split into two and sandwiched Ewan and his

Spikeback mount. The dragon's pale blue scales and wings made him nearly invisible against the sunlight. Ewan had his dragon drop low and it took Marius a second to notice the shift. Titus and his Spikeback and Atticus on his Heartsworn dove to meet him with mock attacks of third fire.

They missed their target as Ewan, great rider that he was, had his dragon tuck his wings and dive. He knew exactly how to use the color advantages of his mount. Marius and Ragewing shot toward him, then increased speed and looped up under Ewan to drive him back into the tight spot between the formations. Ewan swore as he veered left, taking a flame on his dragon's chest. He steered his dragon away, adopting the movement for a false injury.

"Titus! Morvan! Come around the back of unit one!" Marius tapped Ragewing's shoulder and the dragon whipped himself into formation with unit one.

The two mock enemies flew as ordered then rushed the back of the unit, sending flames in quick bursts.

"Star maneuver!" Marius shot upward, taking the northernmost point of the group's practiced position.

The others darted in all directions, spanning out like stars on a clear night. The mock enemies, Titus and Morvan, went after Ophelia and her Green-flanked Terror, knowing that she was the greatest threat.

Ophelia steered her mount around and let loose a bit more than third fire. Titus's Spikeback wailed and roared. His right wing tip was singed.

"Ophelia! Too much fire. Maintain practice power or you're done for the day!"

And if she showed cruelty to her dragon again, he would punish her as he would anyone else.

She shot him a glare, but the next volley of fire was truly just that and not flames.

Marius glanced at Maiwenn, who rode her Seabreak, a cyan dragon with four wings that could also swim if the need arose. She was his secret attacker in today's practice. Maiwenn gave him a nod and wove her way through unit one, taking out two at a time with the lesser mock fire strikes.

Lifting his arm, Marius made a circle in the air before pointing to unit two, who flew around Morvan and his Heartsworn, surrounding the rider and dragon while they were distracted in their attack on Ophelia.

But none of the riders could catch Maiwenn. Seabreaks were known for speed just as Heartsworns were, but this particular Seabreak had been blessed with a quickness Marius had never seen in a dragon.

Trailing Maiwenn and driving her toward Ophelia, he drew his whip from his shoulder and snapped it toward Maiwenn and her mount's tail. The tip nicked the dragon's last spike, a spot most dragons wouldn't feel unless they were Seabreaks. Maiwenn's mount yowled and turned, eyes flashing with rage.

Leaning over his dragon's neck and winding his whip around his upper arm, Marius aimed his voice at Ragewing's ear. "Wait..."

Maiwenn's dragon opened its maw to breathe fire—maybe to blaze full strength considering how angry she appeared to be.

Marius whispered, "Now."

Ragewing shot upward and the wind blasted Marius's face. He had to hold tightly with both his legs and his arms to keep from falling. He looked over his shoulder to see Maiwenn's flames shooting at Ophelia. He'd turned the two mock allies on one another and they'd been marked enough by lesser flames to show a loss.

Marius led the two units back to the arena.

Maiwenn landed near Marius. "High Captain! That was clever."

"Thank you." Marius hopped off of Ragewing and opened the top of the water trough near the side of the public stands so the dragons could drink.

"I think we should increase our tolerance for fire, High Captain." Ophelia's voice cut the air as she led her Green-flanked

Terror to the second trough, where Titus and Ewan were wiping down their dragons and checking for any serious wounds.

"The tournament calls for more aggressive training exercises on the final day. You'll have your moment to show your fire, Ophelia."

He studied her features, trying to get a read on whether or not she was angry or if she had indeed given in to his command. Though he outranked her, it was a delicate situation. Her father was the commander and she had sway due to the familial link even though it was not at all proper. He shouldn't even worry about having to reprimand her, but the commander had shown her favoritism in the past, so he had to watch himself. Marius would have much preferred a unit with clear rank procedures so there was no question as to what actions were permitted. Ophelia's gaze was flat, but she released her dragon's reins and came closer.

She looked him up and down, then almost smiled. "I look forward to the tournament festivities. Will you be accompanying me?"

He inclined his head. "Of course. If you'll have me."

"I *will* have you." Her smile grew teeth and he wasn't sure he liked that tone.

"Good." If she thought she could control him, she was wrong. He would wed her for the sake of Mist Fae blood and tradition, but he would not be cowed by her. They would be equals. Partners. Hopefully, she would be amenable to that situation.

The dragons lapped the water like massive cats, splashing so much that he had to step back to avoid being sullied. Ragewing stopped drinking and eyed him.

"Yes, I know what you are waiting for." He scooped a handful of water from the trough and poured it over the back of Ragewing's lowered head.

When Marius turned back around, Ophelia was already on the far side of the arena, leading her dragon back to the stables. He needed to tell her how he felt about their future and see what she thought about it. She'd shown interest through body language and finding him at meal times, but was she serious about their impending relationship?

He blinked. He shouldn't think of their potential marriage as impending like one did a sense of doom. No, he didn't feel like that. It was exciting. Correct. A good thing. Yes.

A shudder ran down Marius's back and he froze. What was that?

"You look like you're about to spontaneously combust, High Captain." Remus was standing right beside him, offering a cup of mint water.

"Did you feel that?"

"Feel what, sir?"

A wave of energy had pulsed through the air. Or perhaps he was simply excited for the tournament. "Nothing. Never mind."

"Are you upset about something? You seem pretty distracted."

Marius took the offered cup and drank the cool beverage down in three swallows. "Thank you. And I'll thank you also to mind your own business."

"You are my business, Sir Marius."

"You know what I mean."

"Do you want me to take Ragewing back?"

The other knights were on their way out of the arena. None of them seemed taken aback by...by whatever that feeling had been. They walked and chatted as if nothing had happened. The next session would take place in the afternoon after the dragons had rested and then flown individually with their riders. All was as normal.

"No, I'll tend him here," Marius said, "and then I'll put him back in the stables myself. You can take an hour off."

"Thank you, sir."

Remus said something else before leaving, but Marius couldn't be bothered to listen. Ragewing lifted his head and eyed the gate leading to the market and the homes beyond the castle keep.

"Is there something on the air right now, Ragewing? I felt odd for a moment." It wasn't as if the dragon could actually answer, but oftentimes, Ragewing found a way to communicate if he was motivated enough.

The dragon bumped Marius's side and snuffed a hot breath of dragon smoke. The black circles cloaked Marius's view of the arena and gate for a moment. He set to washing the spring pollen from Ragewing's wounded area and tried to let go of both his worries about Ophelia and the strange feeling.

King Lysanael and Queen Revna would arrive soon. He had to remain focused.

CHAPTER 4
TAHLIA

The road leading out of the lower mountains lived up to its name—the Ghost Path. Not only did the mist that always hung heavy in the Shrouded Mountains cover this area, but also the elaborate tombs of fallen Mist Knights walled the snaking line of cobblestones.

Tahlia glared at a tomb topped with stone dragon wings. "These Mist Knights must be a humble sort." She snorted and set a finger on the writing. "Here lies the majestic Julius, master of the clouds and stars. Wonder what one commands the clouds and stars to do? Get you a cup of tea? Or perhaps a back massage?"

Fara laughed. "Check this one out. Here lies Magnus, bane to pirates and master of the art of love."

"Oh, wow. Can you imagine him requesting that phrase on his stone? Hello, Master Tombcarver. I like to slice and dice bad guys and have seen plenty of action, if you know what I mean," Tahlia said in a stupid, low voice as she elbowed Fara. "Can you word that in your fancy style?"

"I can practically see the Tombcarver's eyes rolling. I'm surprised he doesn't play jokes on these arrogant arsehats."

At the bottom corner of the next tomb, a tiny carved creature caught Tahlia's eyes. "Is that a mule?"

Fara bent to look closer. "It is definitely an ass." Her finger traced the long ears.

"Maybe he did have his own little jokes on these haughty knights and nobles."

Chuckling, Fara jogged to the next tomb while Tahlia held the horse's reins. Purple hair lifting in the wind, Fara knelt at a tomb that had suns carved all over it and pointed at the bottom, in the center. "This one has a rooster crowing so hard its eyeballs are popping out."

Tahlia barked a laugh and Daffodil jumped. Tahlia set a hand on the mare's neck to calm her. "I want to meet this Tombcarver. He seems like our type of Fae."

"I'd buy him a drink if I had any extra coin."

"We are going to have so much gold that you'll be able to buy him the whole tavern."

"Sure, Tahlia. Sure."

"Don't fret. I have enough faith for the both of us."

Waving a hand in dismissal, Fara shook her head. "Just come on. Let's get this over with."

They'd arrived at a small market at the base of the main climb to the Mist Knights' castle and training grounds and tournament arena. Banners painted to show the various mountain dragon subspecies fluttered from poles. Most of the banners showed the massive Heartsworns with their scarlet scales while a few held images of the vicious and blood-thirsty Green-flanked Terrors. Banners with Spikebacks the color of the clouds and sky stood to the right. Some displayed Speedy Seabreaks with their four ocean-blue wings. Leather bags and belts lay stacked on tables and jugs of wine and mead lined a stall under a pale green awning. Merchants hawked their wares with their impressively loud voices. Mist Fae like Fara could truly shout if they wanted to. Tahlia really hoped that didn't come up during the tournament. Younglings ran underfoot through the market, bumping into fist-waving old males and jostling customers with items clutched in their arms. Across the chaos, a table laden with tourney leathers sat like a big, fat present for Tahlia.

"Come on." Tahlia urged the mare to hurry.

Fara came up beside her. She was licking her lips and had one hand on her stomach. "I would beat someone to nothing for a bite of those meat pies." Her hunger was legendary.

"We should have some coin left after this. I think. Maybe." Tahlia gave Fara a look that was half grimace, half smile.

"If you let me do the bartering."

Tahlia shook her head. "Not a chance. Your cute joke about beatings will turn into reality. Your job is to mind the mare." She handed her the reins as they approached the table.

The merchant's back was to them, his blue skin shining in the golden light that passed through the airy mist. "Do you have the coin for this?" he barked out. "If not, don't waste my time."

"We do."

He turned and looked Tahlia up and down. "How about you meet me for a drink at sundown instead? You're only going to get your little self killed in that tournament."

Fara lurched forward, the veins in her neck and forehead standing out. Tahlia put a hand on her wrist and kept her voice calm.

"Thanks for the offer, but I'm ridiculously determined," Tahlia said.

"Ridiculous is accurate. Well, at least you're aware of it. That'll be forty-nine gladecoins." He produced a string marked with black lines here and there and proceeded to lean over his wares to measure her torso and waist lazily.

Tahlia raised an eyebrow. "Take your time."

"It's not easy over this table with you so small and everything. You're lucky your chest isn't overly sumptuous."

"Gee, thanks."

Fara snorted and Tahlia elbowed her roughly, though she couldn't help but snicker.

The merchant went into a tent behind his table, then appeared again with leathers in tow. He shoved a vest, a helmet, and trousers. She handed over the coin and a thrill hit her chest.

"It's happening," she whispered as she dragged Fara behind a stall with a black awning and curtain to try on the purchase.

"It is whether I like it or not. Do we have enough for food or did you give it all away? I'm absolutely starving." Fara's stomach growled and she lifted her eyebrows as if to say, *See?*

Tahlia wrangled the vest over her head and Fara began jerking the tough leather into place. The vest snared on Tahlia's shoulder.

Fara snorted. "Fits perfectly." She growled and pulled harder.

"Hey, easy there," Tahlia grunted out. "I may not have a lot going on in the chest vicinity, but what I do have, I'd like to keep intact."

By the time they had it on and laced, they were both red-cheeked and laughing. Tahlia worked off her boots and put on the trousers. They didn't fit well—big and small in all the wrong places—but they would do. She replaced her boots, and then held out her arms for Fara to examine her.

Fara stood back and crossed her arms. "You look the part at least. Well, you're too short to appear threatening, but other than that, I'm impressed at what an outfit can do."

Tahlia spun with her arms wide. "I am never taking it off."

Fara dragged her toward a table where a fellow with orange skin was selling meat pies. "Two please," Fara said to the pie seller. She turned to Tahlia. "Do you want one?"

"You ordered two," Tahlia said.

"One for this side of my stomach and one for the other."

"Three please," Tahlia said to the male.

The male handed out the pies. "You competing this go around?"

Fara had one unwrapped and half eaten before Tahlia could

blink. "No," Fara said through her mouthful, "she's just wearing the outfit because it's so comfy."

The merchant ignored Fara's sarcasm. "You don't have a pound to spare, lass. Sure you can handle a dragon? You must have Mist-gold blood so bright it burns the Bloodworker's eyes."

Tahlia swallowed around a lump in her throat. "Definitely. Yep. Loads of gold in these veins." She set her jaw and stared back at the merchant, attempting to ooze confidence. It gave her an immediate headache.

"Aye, I see that ferocity in your eyes. Hope it's enough!"

"Thank you." Tahlia turned away and headed toward the Mist Road.

Fara caught up, crumbs falling as she walked.

"We need to focus now," Tahlia said. "Maybe go over my backstory and yours."

"Mine can stay what it is," Fara said.

Fara was a full Fae and had grown up not an hour's walk from here, so she was likely right except for one thing.

"What about your mother?" Tahlia asked.

"I'll use a different surname."

Tahlia tucked her pie into the small bag tied to her belt to save for later. "She won't show up to watch the tournament, right?"

"No way." Fara licked her fingers. "She's too old for that now. Has to be."

"You don't sound one hundred percent positive."

"I am no Seer."

"Good enough. Now, I am Lady Tahlia of Northwoods. I'll keep most of mine the same so we don't have too much to remember. One brother. Left Northwoods to gain work as a squire even though my brother was against it. I might have to claim that both of my parents fell out of favor and died years ago."

"Smart," Fara said around a mouthful. "That way they won't be encouraged to figure out if they have met your kin at court or area festivals. What are you going to say of your experience with dragons? You know they will have a Mist Knight interview you. It is a casual affair from what I've heard, but those folks don't miss much."

"I'll just claim I was at Grimsbrook for six years."

The mare tossed her head at the increasing steepness of the path. Tahlia rubbed her neck and whispered encouragement to Daffodil as Grimsbrook passed through her mind.

The period when Tahlia had trained at that old keep during her thirteenth year had been tough. The dragons though—they had been amazing. Tahlia had taken right to riding, but the other Fae in attendance had bullied her to the extreme. After a few broken ribs and a knockout that made her forget her name for a full day, her mother had pulled her out of the academy. She'd only been there for six months. If she were there now, she would fight them, but she had been young and small for her age.

Fara wiped her mouth with the back of her hand and folded the meat pie parchment. "Do you have a family sigil to use when you sign the book?" She put the parchment in her trouser pocket and rubbed her greasy hands on her knees.

"I'll use a tree and a dragon's tooth as a sigil. It's common enough that I can blend in, right?"

"You're the boss," Fara said.

"No, we are a team."

Fara stopped. "No, Lady Tahlia. At this point, I need to be seen as your squire." She reached for the reins. "Now, give me these."

Tahlia released her hold and chewed her lip. "All right. That's probably for the best. Promise you don't think I'm an arrogant witch?"

Fara led Daffodil ahead. "Oh, you are, but that's what it takes to ride dragons."

True. She grinned at Fara's back. The Old Ones had certainly blessed her with a good friend.

After a half hour of walking the punishing incline through the wet, cold clouds of the Mist Road, the gate of the Mist Knights' castle rose like a stone giant crowned in sparkling gold and blue crystals the size of Tahlia's arm. The crystals were the reason the dragons lived in these mountains—they gave the creatures power and strength.

"Tourney competitor?" a voice said through the mist.

They continued on a step and the mist cleared enough to see the two males in Mist Knight livery—black and blue crystalline shapes surrounding a dragon with wings spread across the guards' chests.

"Yes. I'm competing." Tahlia impressed herself by not allowing her words to shake.

"Good luck, dragon rider." The other guard swung one of the double doors wide.

A shiver ran from Tahlia's head to her toes. Her heart beat double time. "Thank you."

Fara was grinning at her as they entered the outer bailey of the Mist Knights' home, the place Tahlia had dreamed about her entire life.

CHAPTER 5
MARIUS

At the end of the tournament grounds, Marius dismounted and walked around to Ragewing's head. The dragon trilled and Marius rubbed the beast between the eyes, then under the chin. The smooth warmth of Ragewing's scales and the scent of the dragon's fire-smoke breath loosened the tightness in Marius's shoulders and neck. Ragewing's flame-like eyes studied Marius, intelligence flickering in their depths. The dragon snuffled against Marius's scar, the one that ran all the way from hairline to chin on the left side of his face.

"It doesn't bother me anymore. I swear it."

Ragewing tucked him under a wing and the creature's protectiveness warmed Marius's heart.

"You did very well today, Ragewing. As usual." He ran both hands down the dragon's lower neck and chest, then began loosening the girth. "I don't want to head back to the stables at the moment, friend. It'll be packed with everyone rubbing down their mounts. Plus those noisy younglings your sister just bore..."

Raising his snout to the air, Ragewing let out a low, proud growl.

"You are such the doting uncle, hmm?" Marius smiled and rolled up the dirtied linen he'd used on the dragon's scales and tossed it into the laundry bin.

The quiet here on the far side of the stands was pleasant and the angle of the wall created a nice shelter from the wind. He could see the grounds and the open gate at the other end, and perhaps was less noticeable—although hiding with a dragon was near to impossible. He was so tired of answering tournament questions. Yesterday, everyone and their mother had been querying him about how many competitors would be in this year's event, what the chances were of someone dying, and who was the favorite. The enthusiasm of the newer knights was commendable, but he wished the commander or even Ophelia would speak up more often. He pushed his worries away and worked on Ragewing's tail and feet, removing debris and applying dabs of the herbal unguent he kept in a small leather-wrapped vial in his belt bag.

A female with tan skin and wavy, shoulder-length dark hair strode into the arena, her head swiveling and her eyes wide. If he didn't know better, he'd have guessed she was here to watch, but she wore a set of ridiculously out-of-date riding leathers. She must be a competitor in the tournament. She spun, her arms wide, and a laugh like chimes rang from her mouth. His lips lifted. Most competitors were far too terrified to enjoy the beauty and majesty of the tourney grounds or to show such joy at simply being here. But fear was the wiser reaction. Stopping mid-spin, the female stared in his direction. He and Ragewing had been spotted.

Marius growled. "Oh, goodie. More questions."

Ragewing bumped his shoulder.

"I'll be polite," he whispered, "but she needs to be informed of the danger. Obviously she is clueless. And quite small for this task."

"Good morning," she said, her voice bright as she approached.

Her eyes were a dark golden brown, like the honey gathered in the valley at the base of the mountains. She was incredibly petite, barely reaching the midpoint of Ragewing's foreleg. Her gaze slid over his face and body. He swallowed. What was she thinking?

She eyed Ragewing, full lips parting as she studied his tucked wings and the two spikes on his head.

Marius bowed shallowly. "Morning. I assume you plan to compete for the new Mist Knight position?" Her uniform was actually a set of mock leathers some of the market merchants sold to children. He didn't think she knew that.

"Yes." She set her slender hands on her stomach, then patted herself down. "Is there something wrong with my armor?"

He gritted his teeth. She'd be seriously injured wearing those ratty, ill-fitting strips of poor material. "Don't you have a sponsor?"

"I am independent."

Of course she was. Serious contenders took the time to find noble families that would team up with the dragon rider's kin to pay for gear. Fighting the urge to shake his head, he blew out a frustrated breath. "If you pass the interview and blood test, then I will see to it you receive proper gear."

She'd fisted her hands at his mention of the steps to enter the tournament, but now her face cleared and she smiled like a sunrise. "Really? You'd do that for me? You are so kind! I bet you're really highly ranked what with your purple tassels and all. You must know High Captain Marius." Coming close, she leaned toward him and eyed the arena. "Is he as tough as they say?"

He pressed his eyes shut. There wasn't enough patience in the world...

A squawking sounded and suddenly a youngling dragon barreled across the arena. Ragewing launched himself toward his nephew by blood. The female Fae's eyes widened and she ran—surprisingly quickly—toward the youngling, getting between the dragons. Marius's heart shot into his throat and his head pounded as he sprinted to catch up.

She held out her arms and spoke up to Ragewing. "He's not intending to threaten your rider."

"Back away," Marius commanded. "Ragewing, she means no harm. Back away!" he shouted at the female. "That youngling is his kin."

The female glanced at Marius, then slowly moved away from the dragons. Ragewing loped forward and set his wing over the yowling young beast.

"Aww, look at them." The female was grinning and had her fists tucked under her chin like she was witnessing the most wonderful thing in the world.

Ragewing licked the youngling's head, cleaning the small dragon as if he were his own. It was rather adorable, but also dangerous.

"You could have been killed," Marius said to the female. "That was incredibly reckless."

"There's no need to shout at me. I realize I made a mistake. Is this how the High Captain trains you to respond when someone is trying to help? No wonder everyone is scared of him."

He stared, waiting for her to figure it out. She was the most infuriating person he had ever met.

Her gaze slid to the whip curled around his shoulder, then her fingers flew to her full rosy lips and her cheeks pinked.

Warmth coiled low in his body and he cleared his throat.

"Old Ones save me," she whispered. "You *are* the High Captain!"

Inclining his head slightly, he glared. "Indeed."

Shadows had bloomed across the arena, and a dark-haired, purple-skinned female leading a horse walked up to the south entrance of the arena. It was past time to finish this and get Ragewing back to his stall.

"I... I didn't realize..." she stammered.

For the first time, she seemed at a loss for words. A miracle.

"And you are late to the sign-ups," he said tightly. "Is that your squire? You must turn in your vial of blood immediately."

"Thank you. Yes." She gave him a grin and bow, then ran to

meet up with the other female that he assumed was her squire. They hurried out of the arena, horse in tow.

At least she had listened to his warning about time. Foolish thing.

He ran a hand down Ragewing's shoulder. "Surely, she won't make it past the interview. We can't let more of these fools enter and get themselves killed. Some just do not have the proper respect for our work..." Grumbling, he tried to focus on herding Ragewing and the youngling back toward the stables, but the female with the dark honey eyes and the pink cheeks never really left his thoughts.

CHAPTER 6
TAHLIA

High Captain Marius Leos Valentius. She had actually met him. Spoken to him. A stuttered breath left her. Just with his gaze, he'd given her lovely shivers.

"I lost you at the bend in the road." Irritation clipped Fara's words.

Tahlia held up a hand. She hadn't meant to worry her friend. This place was just so incredible that she could hardly focus on doing anything. The sights and sounds and smells drew her attention back and forth and around again like she was watching a pitchball game.

"I'm sorry. I noticed the arena and just had to see it for myself immediately."

A reluctant grin crossed Fara's mouth. "Fine."

"Did you ask what we need at the sign-up table?" Tahlia asked. "I assume you found it past that crowd?"

"I did. They want your blood for the test right now and they say if we don't have it turned in by the next bell, you can't compete."

A grimace tugged at Tahlia's mouth. "I had no idea there was a time limit."

"Where are we doing this?" Fara was already fingering the hilt of her dagger.

Tahlia dug around in the bag strewn across her body. There had to be a bottle in here somewhere.

"How about over there?" she whispered.

Fara curled her lip. "Near the public piss pots?"

Finally, a cool, curved item touched Tahlia's fingertips. She drew out a green vial, one that their former employer used to gather seeds of medicinal plants. "Yes, come on."

She dragged Fara into one of the curtained toilet tents, leaving Daffodil chomping on a clump of weeds outside. Thankfully, this particular tent was empty. Uncorking the bottle with her teeth, Tahlia let loose a horrible groan.

Fara's eyes went wide. "What is your problem?"

"If everyone thinks someone is sick in here, they'll leave us alone."

Nodding, Fara pursed her lips and gave a cough and a groan too.

Knocking the rest of the seeds from the vial, Tahlia grinned. "That's the spirit."

Fara used her dagger to make a small cut about halfway up her arm and Tahlia held the bottle up against the wound. Fara's Mistgold Fae blood flowed into the vial.

Tahlia found a bandage at the bottom of the sack and helped Fara tidy up her arm and roll her sleeve back down. Tahlia took Fara's face between her hands.

"Thank you for doing this."

Fara grinned, her cheeks puffing around Tahlia's fingers. "Just don't die on me."

"I'll do my best to live on and annoy you forever."

. . .

Back at the sign-up table, Tahlia handed the vial over to a barrel-chested, blue-skinned male. "My blood sample." She gave him what she hoped was a winning smile as her heart rate increased and her hands grew clammy.

His features held no emotion. He took the offered bottle and set it beside a long sheet of parchment. "Name?"

"Lady Tahlia of Northwoods."

"Experience in years?"

"With dragons?"

His gaze snapped to her face and he just stared.

"Oh, of course." A nervous laugh bubbled from her. "Six years at Grimsbrook."

The male's grip tightened on his red feather quill. "Really?" He looked her up and down.

She tugged at her leather vest and raised her chin defiantly. She was so lucky the human half of her allowed her to lie. "Yes."

He jerked his head in a nod and inked her name onto the parchment. "Sigil?"

"Tree and dragon tooth."

Waving a hand to indicate he needed more detail than that, he paused in writing.

"The tooth sits longwise above an oak's silhouette."

"Ah." He jotted down some unreadable notes, then set his quill down and cracked his knuckles. "Your interview will be at the Brass Lantern with High Captain Marius." He handed her a scroll shut with a waxed blue and silver seal.

"But..."

"You're lucky. With that level of experience, you will have plenty to discuss with him."

Tahlia's neck heated and she gripped the tiny scroll tightly. "Of course. Yes. Thank you. What time?"

"At sundown. You can eat together if he is in the right mood."

Fara leaned over Tahlia's shoulder. "Right mood?"

Tahlia imagined that Marius would be in a foul mood considering he didn't agree with how she behaved with the youngling dragon. But she would win him over. Somehow.

The male chuckled knowingly. "You'll see." He shooed them on and began asking the male behind them the entry questions.

Fara urged the horse around a cluster of children trading painted stones. "You didn't ask when we'll hear the results of the blood test?"

"I am sure they'll let us know at the interview if there was any issue, which there won't be." Each of the children's stones had a sigil on it, perhaps of their favorite knight or dragon...

"It's nearly sundown now. Tell me about that knight in the arena."

They walked the winding path that wound through a market and along the higher cliffs that stretched into the peachy late-afternoon sky. Stairs ran along the cliffs and numerous Fae walked here and there. They lived in the caves carved from the mountain's face and each cave boasted a crystal above its arched entrance.

"It was the High Captain." Tahlia grimaced at Fara.

Fara gripped Tahlia's arm. "What?"

"Yes, I didn't recognize him. He seemed too young to be the male everyone talks about." And too good looking. That whip on his shoulder made her mind whirl with thoughts that were decidedly unknightlike...

Fara's grip on Tahlia's arm went slack. "We are as good as dead."

"Why?"

"Because." Fara shoved her hands in her hair and turned in a circle. "Now he knows your face and you didn't know who he was. A terrible first impression. He'll know you're sneaking in here," she whispered in a hiss, "and that your blood is false and he'll come looking for us and will have his dragon roast us for his supper."

"Fara."

"I don't want to be someone's supper." Fara's eyes were wild—a sure sign of her losing it. "I want to have a meal, not be one!"

Tahlia grabbed her by the arms and stared her in the face. "Fara. You must stop yelling." *Especially yelling about our secrets,* she tried to say with her eyes.

Fara's gaze took in the crowd around them. "Right."

"But you didn't let me tell you the best part," Tahlia whispered as the crowd stopped paying them any attention. "He was tending to Ragewing. That dragon is glorious. The colors, the scales, the fire-bright eyes... And High Captain Marius wasn't too bad himself with his immense height and that fierce stare. He has this powerful presence..."

"Yes, yes. Attractive and dangerous male. Just every idiot's type. Now, can we go find our lodgings?"

Tahlia leaned close. "We don't have the money for that."

"They provide lodging to those who have one of those." Fara jerked her chin toward Tahlia's hand—where the small scroll was gripped in her fingers.

"Ah. All right." The street branched out, and down at the end of the western route, an archway made entirely of crystal sparkled above the crowd. "I'm guessing that is the entrance to the inner bailey."

The crowd thinned as they approached the archway and one of the four guards in Mist Knight livery standing at the entrance raised his sword.

"I swear on the Old Ones' greatest crystal," the guard shouted at the gathered folk. "If you don't back up, I'll lop the heads from the lot of you!"

"Calm down, Severin. They're just excited," another guard said.

"Only competitors! No rabble!" Severin said, glaring at the people straining their necks to see through the arch.

The second, more level-headed guard shook his head and waved Tahlia forward. "You have your mark?"

She held up the tiny scroll. "You mean this?"

He took it, cracked the seal, and read it over. "Yep. You're in. This your squire, yes?" He was looking behind her at Fara.

"Yes. Where do I find our lodgings?"

"Straight through there." He pointed down a side street inside the archway. "A stable hand will take your horse at that second archway. Then you'll come to an unmarked door where competitor lodgings are given out. Remember, be on your best behavior. There is always a dragon watching the castle." His smile was sharp. He elbowed her. "Just kidding you, knight. Get on in there and make your hometown proud!"

Tahlia's heart thudded and her smile turned absolutely feral. She was more than ready to do just that. Fara shut her eyes—she was probably praying—and they passed into the legendary castle of the Mist Knights, the very heart of the Shrouded Mountains.

CHAPTER 7

TAHLIA

Fara paced the chamber the Mist Knight's servant had given them for lodging during the two-day tournament. "I hope Daffodil isn't stabled beside a dragon."

Tahlia gave her a look from where she lounged on the bed by the door. "They know we didn't bring her as a midnight snack."

A strangled noise came from Fara. "I can't believe you're going to jump onto a dragon tomorrow! Are you certain about this? Can't we just set up a nice little table here and sell arts and crafts?"

"You've never made anything crafty in your entire life."

"That's beside the point."

"It isn't."

"No, but Mist Knights can be cruel. They test you when you're up there," Fara said, pointing at the ceiling but presumably meaning the sky, "and if you fall, they will just let you die. Ack! I'd forgotten! You met the High Captain! Tell me everything. Was he covered in blood?"

"Stars, Fara, no, he wasn't coming back from war."

"You don't know that."

"I doubt they'd be holding a tournament if we were suddenly at war."

"Fine. Now, how did he act?"

"Polite. His dragon was amazing. And his dragon's nephew made an appearance. Cutest thing I've ever seen."

"Did he scold you for being in the arena without permission?"

"The dragon?"

Fara's nostrils flared, so Tahlia ceased the teasing.

"He was a touch grouchy looking but he didn't say anything negative," Tahlia said, the High Captain's storm-gray eyes and deep, stony voice flashing through her mind. "Maybe his face is just like that."

Fara lifted the blanket on the bed and examined the sheets underneath. It was her usual spider check.

"He said if I pass the interview," Tahlia continued, "he would find me some better riding leathers."

Dropping her bag on the bed, Fara spun. "He what?"

"And the fact that he is the one assigned to give me the interview, I bet I'll have a brand-new set by tomorrow morning."

"You actually feel good about him interviewing you? I'd be a puddle of fear on the floor. Plus, you didn't recognize him at first, right? He has to be irritated."

"There's more chance he is annoyed with the way I slipped between his dragon and the youngling dragon."

"What?" Fara looked ready to keel over.

"It's okay. I put myself between his dragon and the youngling because I was afraid the big guy was going to attack him. The youngling was running straight at the High Captain."

"You did what?"

"Your voice is doing that squealy thing again."

Making claws of her fingers, Fara glared.

"I was trying to help and the High Captain didn't think that was a good idea. But he knew the youngling was his dragon's nephew and I didn't. An honest mistake."

"You got between the dragons? Seriously? That wasn't some sort of slang idiom I am not aware of? Like 'oh, today I was between the dragons. It was a hellish afternoon.'"

"No. Not an idiom."

Fara covered her face with her hands. "We are doomed."

"I choose to believe he isn't mad at me. He isn't that horrible. He was gentle with his dragon and I think he's a good person. Truly. Maybe everyone just believes he is cruel because of his grouchy face."

"But what about the high number of foes he has killed and the great number of knights-in-training that he has kicked out of the castle?" Fara asked.

Tahlia shrugged. "We don't know what stories are true."

"I wonder if that one about him chasing a stable hand off the mountain with his whip is true."

"I doubt that. He could probably have scared the fellow away with just his glare."

Fara laughed, her shoulders relaxing away from her ears a bit. "What are you going to wear to the interview?"

"Not this?" Tahlia patted her leathers.

"You are supposed to wear civilian clothing, I believe."

"I'll see what I can do with our lady's green trousers and that scarlet tunic of hers."

Nodding, Fara pulled them from the saddlebag. "I'll shake them out and smooth them as best I can while you go to the baths."

"Ooooh, the baths."

"I've heard they are the best in the land besides King Lysanael's."

Thoughts of hot steam and lavender-scented soaps were already making Tahlia swoon.

Fara grabbed her arm before she could leave. "But be careful. You must go to the trainees' bathing area, not the knights' area."

"Or I'll be in hot water?" Tahlia wiggled her eyebrows.

Fara rolled her eyes. "Go on."

Tahlia whistled as she left the chamber and headed down the corridor. There was only one way to go, as the corridor dead-ended the other direction. At a fork, a chalked sign hung from the ceiling. One arrow was marked GREAT HALL and the other said BATHING CHAMBERS. Simple enough.

The bathing area's high ceiling let in the sunset's orange glow. A few males and females walked this way and that, mostly wrapped in bathing sheets and carrying folded stacks of clothing. Some had tall cups of something that smelled like mint. Multiple rooms branched off of the main area, and without signs, she had to guess which one was for her.

Tahlia ended up in a smaller room with a deep circular pool of steaming water and a set of shelves stocked with sheets as well as a pitcher and three of those tall cups. Had there been a sign as to who was supposed to use this bathing room and she had just missed it? She went back to the arch she'd passed through but didn't see a sign anywhere.

Well, no one was here anyway, so it had to be fine. She set to peeling off her road-stained clothing and boots. Three steps led into the water, and the feel of its heat was dream-worthy. Sinking all the way in, she let the water cover her head. It was incredible. She was in good shape and could handle a lot, but that climb up the mountain had made her muscles sore. The hot water loosened them up and helped her relax.

Everything was going to be wonderful. She'd be clean and ready to meet the High Captain after this. In fact, she'd be so nicely tidied up that he probably wouldn't remember seeing her covered in road dust in the arena. Yes, she would get a chance at a better first impression.

Rising up out of the water, she ran her hands over her hair to slick the moisture out. She opened her eyes and lost the ability to move.

High Captain Marius stood at the far end of the bath.

His hair was fully wet as if he too had been underwater. Droplets fell from his strong brow to black and gold inkings that curled across his large chest muscles. The inking snaked down his wet side to his hipbone and further, though the water obscured the rest. Inkings were for those who had suffered a great loss. Who had he lost?

Her heart was a ringing bell in her ears. She lifted her gaze, cheeks blazing like a thousand dragons aimed their fire right at her. A lovely heat gathered low in her belly. "I'm guessing *I'm* the one in the wrong chamber."

The corner of his lips twitched as if he almost wanted to laugh but his eyes said he was too irritated to give in. His gaze never strayed from her face. "You certainly are."

"I..." She swam toward the stairs and he stepped fully into the deeper center of the pool, avoiding her. "I'm sorry. I'll go now." A laugh bubbled inside her, but she fought it back as she glanced at his scowl once more. "Feel free to enjoy the show," she joked, "but if you want to turn around, I'll grab my clothes."

Facing the shelving, she heard the water moving around him. Was he turning around? Why wasn't he saying anything? Had she really upset him that badly?

Quickly, she dried and dressed. Heading for the archway, she looked his way. He stared at the wall opposite the shelves, his gorgeously muscled back to her.

"Sorry again!" A chuckle bounced out of her before she could exit the area. As soon as she was in the main bathing chamber, her snickering turned into a full belly laugh. Only she would end up naked with the legendary dragon rider within hours of arriving in the Shrouded Mountains.

"Control yourself, competitor." A female with blue-green hair and blue eyes glared down at Tahlia. Her thin but strong-looking arms were crossed and she wore the full regalia of a high-ranking dragon rider, just as the High Captain had in the arena. Small purple tassels hung from the shoulders of her white leathers, and a wreath of golden laurel leaves wove through her tightly braided hair.

"Laughing is not allowed?" Tahlia twisted her hair and squeezed water from the ends.

The female's nose wrinkled and she stepped back. "Buffoonery isn't a characteristic of a Mist Knight. You'll learn soon enough who does and who does not belong." Her gaze cut Tahlia before she marched away and joined a group of three half-dressed females standing in front of another steaming chamber.

Tahlia smiled at the female's retreating figure. "I belong. Don't worry." She said it more to herself than anyone.

The female whirled and glared for a moment before going back to her associates.

"Could you maybe tell me which chamber I am supposed to use?"

The females continued their chat and ignored her question. Shrugging them off, Tahlia strode past the group and entered the chamber they seemed to be claiming. Several females bathed in the pool and a few were dressing by a torch-lit alcove. They had riding leathers, but no fancy tassels or wreaths of honor.

"Are you my fellow competitors?"

"We are." One of the females in the water nodded.

There was no more talk as Tahlia finished the washing she'd started in the high-ranking male chamber. *Guess that's another rule.* The list in her head was getting quite long...

CHAPTER 8
TAHLIA

The Brass Lantern stood in the outer bailey of the castle among the houses and shops of the common folk and craftsfae. Though the sign looked ready to drop from age, the inside was rather pleasant. A fire crackled on one side of the large main room and tables in all shapes and sizes sat in clusters to create a pathway for the servers bringing trays of food and drink. Everything smelled delightfully of bread.

Tahlia had no time for bread at the moment though—stones, wasn't that a sad thought? Bread was the stuff of dreams. But so was seeing the High Captain and his inkings in the bathing chamber.

She tugged at the neckline of her tunic. "Is it overly warm in here?"

"I don't think so. I'm freezing. As usual." Fara eyed her. "You're red. What's wrong? Are you sick? Was anyone coughing in the bathing chamber? I've heard there is an ague going around. I'll go get you an herbal tea. My grandmother used to say—"

Tahlia snagged her arm. "Fara. Breathe. I'm not sick. Just... nervous." She hadn't told her friend about the wonderfully horrible mistake in the bathing chambers. Fara would have exploded from fret. "I'm fine."

But what would Marius say about the fact that she had seen him naked from the waist up? And why was she thinking of him as Marius? It was a nice name though. Just as nice as the way that water had slid down his body to that place near his hip... A shuddering breath left her.

"He isn't here," Fara said over Tahlia's shoulder. "I wonder if they know about the blood. They've found you out," she whispered.

Tahlia waved her worry away. "Don't catastrophize. He's here somewhere. If they had discovered our secret, the mountain guard would already be dragging me to prison or whatever horrible thing you were afraid of."

"You might think your little pep talk is helpful, but I assure you, it is not."

In the far corner behind a group of green-skinned males who all had the same nose shape, Marius sat at a table alone. His brow furrowed as he read through a stack of parchment. He grabbed a small scarlet book beside the stack and scribbled something inside. His quill bobbed and he paused to touch his chin as if in deep thought. The light of the tavern's sconces, candles, and fire drew out shining lines of gold in his moon-white hair. He'd pulled it back into a queue.

Tahlia took an unsteady breath. He was really far too lovely to be scary. Even the scar that ran all the way down his face worked to make him alluring. "I see him."

"Uh, yeah, I can tell you do."

Tahlia whipped around to look at Fara, who was grinning.

"Don't let him muddle your mind, Tahlia. He may be as hot as his dragon's fire, but he is also just as dangerous considering the trick you've played on him and his associates to get here."

"I'll be smart. Try to stop worrying."

"Sure. Next I'll stop my heart from beating. No problem."

Tahlia chuckled. Giving her friend a quick tap on the arm, she walked away and toward Marius's table.

He looked up as she approached and his stern expression faltered, lips parting slightly and eyes widening a fraction. "You?"

Oh, he hadn't known he was assigned to her. Should she apologize for barging in on his bath? Or just let it be and forget it happened? His expression showed contempt. He hated her. She'd have to change that.

"Yes, me," she said. "I hope they gave you all the potential competitors' information there." Glancing at the parchments and book, Tahlia slid into the chair across from him, folded her arms on the table, and smiled as she looked into his storm-gray eyes. "I'm thrilled to have been assigned to you for my interview."

"You shouldn't be. I'm the toughest interviewer on the mountain."

And the best looking in the baths. Swallowing, she cleared her throat. "Well, what would you like to know?"

"I'll be the one asking questions."

"Of course, sir. As you wish."

He sifted through his parchment until he found what he was looking for and held it aloft. "Potential competitor five. Hmm."

With a grunt, he studied the written lines. He looked like someone had poked him with a sharp stick. What did that *hmm* mean?

"The committee," he said with that gravelly voice of his, "states here that you spent years at Grimsbrook."

"I did."

His gaze whipped across her face. "Say that in full, please."

He wanted her Fae blood to stop any deceit from spilling from her lips. But he didn't know she was half-human and could lie fairly well.

Meeting his gaze, she said, "I trained at Grimsbrook for six years."

Blinking and nodding, he went back to his page. "What sub-breeds did you work with there?"

She had worked with several kinds even though she'd only been at Grimsbrook for a short time. Most of what she knew of dragons, she'd learned from books and scrolls.

"Green-flanked Terrors, for one," she said.

"What did you learn about the greens?"

What did he want to hear? "They eat twice as much if you let them, but they don't need that much to be healthy. Their flame travels farther than any other breed's. They were originally nocturnal and are prone to eye strain, so they work better longer if given protracticol before a day flight."

"What are the risks involved with that concoction?"

"Lethargy if given too much. And addiction. They enjoy the feel of the herbs in their bloodstream."

He set both hands on the table. They were easily twice the size of hers. For the thousandth time, she wished she were bigger. It would make riding easier and would keep so many from underestimating her.

"Tell me about another sub-breed you rode at Grimsbrook."

"I rode a Heartsworn that was a bit smaller than your dragon." She waited for him to comment, but he remained silent. She cleared her throat. "She didn't want me on her back because Heartsworns are loyal to a fault and she was bonded with a male there. I wore his cloak to give her his scent, but she bucked me off almost immediately." Maybe she shouldn't have told him that. "I also rode a Spikeback and used its shorter bursts of fire in close sparring."

Cocking his head to the side, he studied her face. Was he about to order her to leave the mountain? Was it over already?

"What would you command your dragon to do if you were surrounded by three enemy dragons and their riders?"

The questions went on and on from there until Tahlia's stomach was growling with hunger. She coughed to cover the sound and prayed this interview would end before she died of starvation. The whole tavern smelled like bread and meat and it was such a torture. Fara would have already perished.

"Well, you do know your dragons," Marius said. His voice was powerful even at this low volume. It was obvious that he had Mistgold to spare in his blood. "Now, tell me," he commanded. "Why do you want to do this? Why leave a safe life on the ground for one in the sky surrounded by fire and pirates' iron?"

Tahlia's heart lifted and thudded in her ears. "I wouldn't be who I am if I chose the safer route in life. Flying on dragonback is the only time I truly feel like myself."

A smile tugged at one side of his mouth, the most she'd seen of a happy expression in the male. Warmth filled her chest and ran up into her cheeks. It was fun getting him to let go of that sternness. Plus it was an interesting challenge trying to please someone so steely and generally disgruntled.

"As soon as I get the approval from the Bloodworkers," he said, "I will put your name in for the lists."

Squeezing her hands in her lap to keep from leaping up like a maniac to celebrate, she listened to his list of questions concerning Fara's squire-like qualities as well as inquiries as to what skills Tahlia had besides riding.

"And what weapon do you choose on the ground?" he asked.

"The gladius."

His glance hooked her sharply. "A longer sword would be better for one as short-limbed as you."

Tahlia pursed her lips. "I'm pretty good with it."

He nodded and jotted the word down under her name in his scarlet book. Was that his personal record of competitors or was that some official book?

"In the sky?"

"Bow."

"Have you tried a whip?"

Her gaze went to his shoulder. His whip was no longer curled there, but she remembered its tidy braid and the sheen of the well-oiled leather.

"I haven't. Will you teach me? That would be amazing."

"No, I don't have time. You don't have the luxury of additional training either. The events will begin at dawn tomorrow with the Presentation of the Competitors, and I have word King Lysanael and Queen Revna will be in attendance. After that, you will be tested on ground weapons and flying. A short break will be provided in the early afternoon before the mock sky battle. If you are still alive at that point, you will be required to attend the announcement of the one who has earned the open position."

"I can't wait."

"That answer only shows ignorance."

"I'm not supposed to be excited about the tournament?"

"It's a deadly challenge. Some don't make it through."

"No one has died in the tournament in years. Actually, none that I've heard about since you were given your current rank." He might have seemed cold, but he ran a good show here, if the stats were any indication.

He waved off her attempt at subtle praise. "You should temper your joy. It will make you reckless in the clouds. I know. I've seen it."

"Temper your joy. You're even worse at pep talks than me." Tahlia couldn't help herself; she chuckled.

Marius just glared.

"High Captain?" A male in Mist Knight livery bowed beside the table.

"Yes?"

"I have blood test results you should see."

Tahlia's veins ran with ice. This was it. Would her and Fara's trick fly?

"Thank you," Marius said as he took a sealed scroll from the messenger.

The seal was the same blue as the livery, but the image in the wax showed a whip and a crystal—had to be Marius's sigil.

"Don't you use your family's sigil? Did your father or mother also use the whip?"

"I chose my own sigil when I arrived here."

"But why not carry on your family's sigil?"

"Has anyone ever told you that it's rude to pry into people's pasts?"

"They have tried." She grinned and tried to make that glare fade. No such luck. "Sorry. I'll let you keep your secrets."

"I doubt you've kept a secret your entire life."

"You don't know me."

He cracked the seal but kept his stormy gaze on her. "I know you are intelligent, reckless, and you run your pretty lips like a drunken bard playing a lute."

Pretty? Her face went hot.

Sniffing, he focused on the scroll's contents. Someone with a lantern passed by the outside window and their light spread over Marius's throat and his upper chest where his shirt gaped a little. A curve of his inking showed.

Marius frowned and she dragged her gaze away from the smooth skin of his upper chest.

"Do you want to know what the Bloodworkers say of your blood?" he asked.

She held very still. "Yes."

"You have a high rating of Mistgold in your veins as well as a hint of human."

Her jaw unclenched and she took a full breath. Thank the Old Ones.

"You must come from an old line of dragon riders," he continued, "because no one up here has a human in their ancestry."

Fara's blood showed she had at least one human ancestor? Tahlia didn't think her friend knew that. Now, if the workers had been studying Tahlia's blood in truth, they'd have seen basically no Mistgold and a load of human ancestry...

Nodding, she tried to appear confident. She relaxed her hands on the table and leaned back. "I don't know of any humans, but I suppose someone could have kept it secret."

"It's certainly nothing to be proud of."

"Humans aren't that bad."

"Aren't they?"

"The queen is a great ruler." It had been a shock when King Lysanael had married and mated with the human, but it was so far, so good with her on the throne.

"True," Marius said, "but she is an exception."

"How many humans have you known?"

Why was she arguing? She needed to shut her mouth and end this thing as quickly as possible before she messed up.

Marius's nostrils flared. "We're finished here. I know what I need to know."

Her pulse stamped against her neck like an impatient horse. Holding her tongue was more difficult than her moments spent on that Heartsworn's back.

"I should fail you," he said. "I should save your life."

"You don't think I can do this." She realized she had leaned forward and was fisting her hands on the table. Relaxing her fingers, she tried to slow her breathing.

"I do not. You are too small, too rash around dragons, and ignorant of the risks in the life you are attempting to begin."

"But you said *should*. That you *should fail* me. That means you are only considering it."

"The most important trait for a dragon rider is courage. If you prove that you aren't as ignorant of the risks, then you might be the bravest person I've ever met. The way you leapt in front of Ragewing..." The spot between his eyebrows wrinkled and he shook his head slightly, his gaze going wistful. "The youngling alone could have ended you before you could shout *I'm an idiot*."

"I know that."

"Do you?"

"Yes. I've seen riders scorched to ash during the bonding period. I lost two friends at Grimsbrook and I wasn't even—" Tahlia stopped herself. She'd almost told him the truth about not being there for very long. "I have seen the dark side of riding dragons. But what kind of Mist Knight would I be if I didn't risk my life to save a youngling? There are so few! Have you read up on the latest report of breeding in the wilderness beyond Sunthrone?"

"I..."

"It's terrible. We must make younglings and breeding a priority. There are worse ways to die than for a cause one believes in."

Tilting his head, he studied her, and his gaze was like a touch on her cheeks, her forehead... He wasn't meeting her eyes. Quickly, he began studying the parchment he'd been reading when she'd walked up.

"You are in. For now," he said without glancing her way. "I will send a Leatherworker to you for a fitting immediately. Meet her in your chamber. The guards will know where to find you. Dismissed."

Tahlia stared, her body frozen. She was in. She was allowed to compete for a place in the Mist Knights. This was no dream. It was real. True. Mentally stirring herself to action, she grabbed his hand to shake it.

"Thank you, sir..." The feel of his warm, calloused hand on hers sent heat simmering up her arm. Blinking, she licked her lips. His gaze snagged on her mouth and remained. "I mean, High Captain. Thank you! You won't regret this decision."

She released his hand and slid out of the chair. Without a backward look, she strode into the tavern crowd to seek out Fara. They had to get back to the chamber for the fitting and for sleep. Tomorrow, it all began.

"I was born to ride dragons," she whispered to herself, "and no one can steal my fate."

CHAPTER 9
MARIUS

Marius raised a hand and one of the Brass Lantern's barkeeps came running.

"Sir, how can I help?"

"Will you have one of your trusted fellows to take this message to the Leatherworker at the end of Rumbling Lane?" He handed over a note he'd written about Tahlia and her needs with regard to new riding leathers. He'd promised a king's sum for a quick job overnight. It wouldn't be more than the male had managed before for Marius.

Finishing the ale he'd ordered after Tahlia's exit, Marius gathered his materials and set off for the commander's chambers. Tahlia's fierce defense of her actions in the arena rang through his head despite his best efforts to stop thinking about her.

The commander's palatial chambers spread across the very top floor of the Mist Knight's castle. A platform operated by staff who worked an elaborate pulley system deposited Marius at the door rather quickly. A servant let him in and Marius awaited the commander and Ophelia for an evening drink they had arranged earlier. The foyer of the lodgings was set with crystalline floors in a mosaic pattern, and the windows looked over the cliffs to distant peaks ringed in fog and ripe valleys illuminated by the moon and stars. The commander's chambers brought truth to what the newcomers called the Mist Knights' castle—the castle in the sky.

But even all the beauty couldn't calm his nerves.

Tonight, he would ask for Ophelia's hand in marriage.

It begins now, Bellona. I will make you proud. Your sacrifice will not be wasted.

His chest ached still for his long-dead sister. He would forget the loss for a day or so, and then, just when he least expected it, the grief hit him like a trebuchet's stone.

"Ah, Marius, so good to see you." Commander Gaius walked into the room. He had slicked his blue-green hair—the same shade as his daughter's—away from his face and his gaze was as cool as it ever was. This male was always very in control of his feelings and he never let anyone see more than he wanted them to see.

Marius stood from the pillowed stool he'd been provided and bowed curtly. "Commander Gaius. I hope this evening finds you well."

"Ophelia says you have something to ask me. She will be here shortly. Her new valet required a bit of a talk."

Marius honestly didn't want to know why Ophelia had yet another new valet.

"Yes, should we wait for her?"

"Of course." Gaius called for crystal wine and had Marius join him in sitting by the snapping fire at the far end of the room.

The wine was exquisite, just like the commander's clothing and chambers. All was in its proper place and in the best condition. Gaius did everything the way Marius endeavored to do. If Marius played his cards right, he would be just like Gaius someday. Marius's father, Aloysius, had been a good male, but not the type one looks up to. He'd been messy and forgetful. And he'd made one terrible mistake after another. In low moments, Marius believed Aloysius had brought death upon himself and upon Marius's mother as well. If he'd been paying more attention to detail, Aloysius and Marius's mother wouldn't have been visiting a fever-stricken town.

Gaius sipped his wine from a rare Murrina cup. The carver's resin applied to the purple, green, and pink fluorite was known to give the contents a unique flavor. "How did your interviews go?"

Stomach tightening with nerves, Marius drank most of the wine from the Murrina cup Gaius had given him. "Good. I only sent one away. An older male who didn't have the experience necessary."

Nodding, Gaius motioned for the servant to pour more wine for Marius. "How many competitors do we have this year?"

"Eleven."

"Have any bets on who will win the position?"

"Not yet. I've only seen those I interviewed."

"You didn't eat with the others?"

Mealtimes with his fellow knights provided not just food, but information on the goings-on. "No, I was early to the Brass Lantern and ate there."

Ophelia strode into the room wearing a heavily embroidered dress and her golden laurels. "I hope I didn't keep you waiting long."

Her gaze found Marius's and she raised an eyebrow and parted her lips. She was a handsome woman and many suitors had knocked on her chamber door over the last two years, but thus far, she had only paid attention to Marius. He was proud of that fact, but he wished his body stirred when she came near. Surely, at some point he would find her physically attractive.

He stood and kissed her cheek. She smelled of the thyme honey lotion she used daily. Gaius handed her a cup of wine from the servant's tray. She sipped and joined them by the fire.

"What have you two been discussing? The interviews, I'd guess?"

"Yes," her father answered. "We only lost one in the process."

"Odd that we only had twelve attempt to compete. Everyone is scared of our High Captain." She nudged Marius with an elbow. "Don't you ever stop being your vicious self, darling."

Gaius eyed Marius. "I don't think we need to worry about that. Marius is as predictable as the sunset."

"Unless he is in the air." Ophelia's eyes went hazy, her attraction to Marius obvious.

Marius realized he was frowning. He worked his features into a less severe countenance. "I think it's the weather more than anything. Those late snows kept some from travel." It was springtime in the mountains now, but the realm was large and travel wasn't easy for everyone even when they were only a mountain or two away.

"He's too humble, our High Captain is," Gaius said, raising his cup to Ophelia.

She raised hers too.

Marius grumbled and finished his wine. He'd grown up on watered crystal wine, so it didn't hit him like it did newcomers. He'd forgotten to warn the interviewees about that particular danger... He would need to send messages out tonight before anyone ended up completely hammered from the special drink.

"So, Marius." Gaius leaned forward and rested his elbows on his knees. The edges of his eyes showed his years. "You had something to ask me?"

His stomach twisted. Would Gaius say yes or have him thrown out?

"I have come to ask for Ophelia's hand in marriage."

Gaius smiled warmly. Ah, he'd already known. Of course he had. The male knew everything that happened or was even about to happen on the mountain.

Standing, Gaius raised his cup. "I give my blessing to what will become the most powerful couple in any realm!"

Ophelia kissed Marius fully on the lips, and he pulled away, not wishing to display so much affection in front of her father. A scowl shadowed her face for a second, but soon she was smiling again.

"Thank you, Father. I agree. We are going to rule this mountain."

Her eyes glittered like a snake's and Marius's stomach knotted. Was he making a mistake? Surely not. He mentally shook off the worry and raised his cup, toasting to Gaius's good health and Ophelia's prowess in the sky.

Gaius excused himself to talk to a servant, leaving Ophelia with Marius.

What would Ophelia have done in Tahlia's place when the youngling ran free? Ophelia smoothed her gold-threaded dress and sat beside Marius. No, she wouldn't have risked her life for the dragons. Unless glory would have come from the action. But that was wise; that was basically what he'd told Tahlia—that her actions had been foolish. Why could he not stop wondering and thinking about her?

"What's wrong, darling?" Ophelia touched his shoulder as a servant approached Gaius and asked about instructions for tomorrow's event.

"Nothing. Thank you. I'm simply tired. I might go soon. Would that disappoint you?"

"I'd rather you stay for a while. We should burn a dragon lavender to commemorate our engagement."

Something about talking to Ophelia now felt hollow when compared to his tension-filled interview with Tahlia. He studied Ophelia's face and the look she wore when glancing over at her father. Who was she really? He had never asked her many personal questions about courage and why she rode dragons. How could he wed someone simply based on their blood?

"Yes. Let's do that," he said finally.

He walked with her to the small garden that grew outside the balcony doors. The moonlight scattered over the dragon lavender's dark purple blooms and patterned leaves. The lines in the leaves resembled dragon scales. Together, they plucked a leaf and a bloom each and started back inside.

Marius stopped Ophelia with a hand to her arm. "Can I ask you something as your intended, not as your High Captain?"

"Anything."

"Why do you ride?"

"It was my destiny to ride dragons. Could I have been anything else with a father like mine?"

He lifted his eyebrows and watched Gaius through the uneven glass of the balcony window. "Probably not. But really, what do you love about it?"

Ophelia's lips bunched and she looked out over the cliffs. "I can't say I love it any more than other exciting pastimes like dancing, gambling, or even dazzling my intended with seduction." She faced him and ran a hand down his torso, then along the inner side of his thigh. Her lips found the crook of his neck and she kissed him there. The scent of her lotion made his head pound.

She drew back and eyed him warily. "Don't you like me touching you?"

"I do. Of course I do."

She crossed her arms. "You'll have to do better than that to persuade me to spend all my years in your bed."

He forced a chuckle, his stomach turning. Why didn't his body respond to her? She was beautiful. Strong. Smart. He wanted her. Leaning close, he swept his hands up to her face and cradled her jaw. The lavender wedged between his fingers touched her ear.

"How is this?" He set his mouth to hers and slowly licked her upper lip.

She moaned and pressed against him. "Let's go to my chamber."

"Your father is here. I'd rather wait until...a better time." He stepped back, wishing his heart had been beating as quickly as Ophelia's.

Her lips became a flat line, but she nodded. "I understand. I was just carried away." A rare smile softened her face.

Was he being silly? They were adults. They were engaged. But it felt wrong to be so emotional in front of the commander even if he did approve of their relationship.

THEY WENT BACK INSIDE and joined Gaius. At the commander's crystal altar, Marius and Ophelia placed their dragon lavender into the rose-hued bowl and Gaius lit the offerings. As the sweet and smoky scent laced the air, Marius started to speak the ritual words, but Gaius beat him to it.

"Bless these two in their coming union and in the joining of two great minds and hearts. May their lives be long and fruitful, filled with the rage of dragons and the defeat of their enemies."

Marius and Ophelia knelt for a moment, then stood up again. They set their fists to their right temple each, a sign of understanding and the final step in this small ritual.

After another glass of wine by the fire, a heated discussion arose about the competitors.

"The Bloodworkers have four samples with significantly high amounts of Mistgold," Gaius said. "We should pull from that small group instead of keeping it open to lesser bloods."

Ophelia stared at the fire and ran her finger over the edge of her cup. "I agree."

"But why not test all those who passed the first steps?" Marius asked. "The ones with the best blood might be terrible on dragonback."

Gaius brushed some lavender ash from his sleeve. "But their training is noted, and with that much Mist Fae blood, they wouldn't have been able to lie."

Marius moved his cup from hand to hand and back again. Why

had he even said that to Gaius? All the best dragon riders had extremely high levels of Mistgold in their veins.

"True," Marius said. "Do you want to change the tournament process now? For tomorrow?" It was too fast, but if Gaius demanded the change... That would be chaotic at best and terms for a small revolt if things went south.

"No, not for this one. But next time, I think you should see to that."

"Me?"

"Once you are wed to Ophelia and your life is settled, I'm going to step down and suggest you as my replacement."

Marius gripped the cup so hard that his forefinger knuckle popped. This was what he'd always wanted. So why was his head pounding and his stomach twisting? Perhaps he was afraid of failure.

"Thank you very much, Commander. I'm flattered."

"It's not flattery. You lead better than I ever did and you're an ace in the air. I want only the best for you," he said, turning to face Ophelia, "and this male is the best."

Ophelia tilted her head and regarded her father. "Are you certain you're ready to step down?"

"I'm ready as soon as you are."

As soon as Marius and Ophelia were ready to wed, he meant. This was good. So good. Wasn't it? They would marry very soon and Marius would become commander.

Marius stood. "I'm afraid I have a headache. I need some rest. We can set a date for the wedding after the tournament. Does that work for you?"

He examined his future wife's features, wishing she had truly answered his earlier question about dragon riding.

"I say we wed exactly one week from today."

"So soon?" Marius's palms grew damp. "Why rush? We can plan a proper feast and gathering if we have more time."

Gaius rubbed his chin and glanced from Ophelia to Marius.

"No reason to wait for a party you wouldn't even wish to attend, Marius."

It was true. Marius was not the festival type. He much preferred a book and an early bedtime—so much the better for early morning riding and training.

"No," the commander continued, "the wedding will be held in one week. Prepare as you see fit and I will call in my steward to handle the larger details."

"All right." Marius bowed to each of them and left quickly.

He would be married this time next week. Shaking his head, he rapped the outer door to call up the moving platform. The pulley squeaked quietly and soon Marius was back in his room, lying on his bed and wondering at the untamable storm inside his heart.

CHAPTER 10
TAHLIA

"Are you sure I don't look fully ridiculous?" Tahlia examined her reflection in the mirror. The new leather armor had arrived before sunup. "I had no idea they would fit so much more tightly in the legs."

Fara lay on her bed, one arm slung over her forehead. "And they work so much better with your up top assets. You look amazing."

"I look naked."

"It's just that you have more curves than most riders. These fine leathers were literally made for your shape."

"I feel a bit exposed though." Tahlia turned and grimaced at her arse in the reflection. It wasn't that she didn't like her body, but she'd never worn anything so revealing in the way it fit every line and angle of her body. It was making her uncharacteristically shy.

Sitting up and rubbing her temples, Fara let out a groan. "Why did you let me drink that terrifying crystal wine? I forgot how strong they make it for the Mist Fae."

"I wasn't even around when you were enthusiastically imbibing."

Fara spread her purple arms wide. "I was just worried about your interview."

"You didn't need to worry. I told you. It went well...I think." Tahlia knew she could be overly optimistic. Was she wrong? No, he had approved her admission to the tournament and he had sent her this armor.

"Well, now *I'm* telling *you* to stop fretting for once," Fara said. "The Leatherworker assured me this was proper and ordered by the High Captain himself."

Tahlia pulled at the bottom of the vest. The armor was actually incredibly comfortable, far less stiff than the set she'd used to gain entrance to the mountain as a potential competitor. But she felt like her body was being exposed as sensual rather than tough.

"I can be attractive and tough, right? Even though I'm shorter than I'd like?"

"You definitely are. Attractive and tough, I mean, not short. But you *are* that too. Stop fussing. You look astoundingly glorious, like a war goddess come down to the mountain."

Tahlia laughed. "Thanks, friend."

"You're going to drop jaws and then you'll awe them with your riding skills. If they don't find out about your blood and put you to death by dragon fire."

"You were doing so well there for a moment."

Fara collapsed back on the bed and shut her eyes. "I hate to tell you this, but you're going to have to attend the Presentation of the Competitors without me. Unless you like a whining vomiter at your back."

Tahlia dampened a washing cloth in the basin sitting on the small table between their beds, set it on her friend's forehead, and let it fall over her eyes. Fara let out a sigh of relief.

"You sure?"

"Am I sure I don't want to heave last night's dinner all over your fancy new outfit? Yes, I'm quite positive about that. You won't fire me for this, will you, boss?"

Tahlia chuckled. "It's only your first offense. I'll allow at least two mistakes."

"Gee, you are kind." Fara smacked her leg lightly. "Now, go. Or you'll be late and they might not let you into the hall. I heard the king and queen were already seated and taking supplicants' questions."

"Heal up quickly. I'll need you in an hour. I can't go out there alone."

"You could, but you won't have to." Fara moved the cloth to wink.

With a deep breath, Tahlia nodded and stood. She picked up her new helmet with its red plumage.

It was tournament time.

~

LIGHT from the long windows sparkled across the dragon-sized crystals that adorned the great hall's ceiling and walls. Rosy pink, ocean-toned blue, and deep indigo spread over the gathering crowd of Mist Knights in their pale leathers and red-tufted helmets, velvet-wrapped nobles of the Shrouded Mountains region talking animatedly, and a good number of common folk in home-spun wool looking on with wide eyes.

Holding her helmet under her arm, Tahlia took a spot near the front of the crowd, beside the other Mist Knights and competitors, with the nobles to their right and the common folk to the left of the room.

On the dais, Seelie King Lysanael, and his mate, Queen Revna of Isernwyrd, sat on tall black-stained wooden thrones. Beside Queen Revna, a shadow materialized and became a forest dragon. Like all forest dragons, he was much smaller than mountain dragons and the power of invisibility ran through his veins. The dragon—Arkyn, Tahlia thought she'd heard him called—currently had his snout in a large copper bowl of something that was staining his snout a dark blue.

Beside Arkyn, a man in a helmet with blue tuffs rather than red stood stiffly, the ends of his blue-green hair showing. Commander Gaius. He honestly scared Tahlia more than any dragon could. Hands clasped, he leaned toward the king and queen. King Lysanael's dark crown glittered atop his head of obsidian-dark hair as he nodded at something the commander had said. Queen Revna eyed the crowd like she was measuring each person up for a fight. Her hand went to her dragon and she slid her palm down his neck. Arkyn shuffled his wings and settled himself on the ground beside the queen with his tail extended behind the commander. It reached all the way to the steps on the side where two more Mist Knights approached. Ah, it was Marius and that foul, high-ranking female from the baths. Marius held his helmet and searched the room with his stormy eyes.

His gaze stopped on Tahlia. He tripped and swore loudly, glancing backward at Arkyn's tail, which was slapping the dais like a happy dog's might. Was Marius all right? Maybe he was hungover like Fara. Marius looked up and his focus locked onto Tahlia. A flush darkened his cheeks and she bit her lip to keep from chuckling.

He spoke in the female's ear and she turned a glare on Tahlia. What were they saying? Had they found out about the feigned blood sample?

CHAPTER 11
MARIUS

Marius cleared his throat, straightened, then bowed to the king and queen with as much dignity as he could manage after tripping over a dragon. Ophelia curtseyed alongside him.

Queen Revna smirked. "A legendary dragon rider who trips over the beast's tail? There must be something truly interesting in the crowd to have distracted one as experienced as you, High Captain."

Only recently had the royals been taking part in festivities on the mountain. Marius wished they'd never come.

Gaius's intense stare was practically scorching Marius's cheek. Marius did his best to act as though nothing was amiss and the mere sight of Tahlia's arresting curves hadn't swept his feet right out from under him. There had been a dragon tail involved, but he never would have tripped so easily had it not been for the shock of desire that had hit him upon seeing Tahlia.

"I didn't sleep as much as I would have liked, Your Majesty," Marius said to the queen. It was true and tasted so on his tongue, but it wasn't the whole truth.

The queen raised an eyebrow. Her eyes were so odd, completely human and icy pale. "Right."

King Lysanael smiled at his wife, then his eyes drew downward and he pursed his lips. "I'd like to mention my fallen brother as we open. Would that break any cultural norms, Commander Gaius?"

"Mist Knights always honor our fallen," the commander said, bowing slightly. "Please, feel free to express your respect for your loved one."

King Lysanael rose from his temporary throne and extended a hand to his queen, who took it and stood with him. "Greetings, knights, nobles, and folk of the mountains."

The crowd bowed and curtseyed, their gazes locked on the dais as they studied the king and queen, the commander, Marius, and Ophelia.

"What is wrong with you?" Ophelia hissed.

"I tripped."

"I noticed, but you seem flustered."

Ophelia's glance went from his face to the crowd.

Marius didn't want to know if she saw Tahlia and could read anything from the way he had looked at the competitor. He focused his gaze on the back wall.

King Lysanael was recounting the history of the older brother he'd lost to the weather here in the Shrouded Mountains. "All he wanted was to be one of the knights of legend, to ride into the clouds to glory." The king bowed his head and his chest moved in a deep, slow breath. Queen Revna took his hand in hers. He smiled at her, then regarded the crowd once more. "I honor him by attending this year's tournament. In his name, I will give the next Mist Knight named a parcel of land near my winery, a place dear to my heart."

The crowd let out a cheer of excitement.

The king raised a hand to quiet them. "Now, I believe it's time for the Presentation of Competitors!"

Another shout of joy went up and filled the great hall with

noise. Marius wished this pageantry was over because the sooner they flew with the competitors, the better. The breeze this morning smelled of a storm.

Gaius went to the other end of the dais and called up the competitors as the king and queen took their seats.

"Lord Renwall of Turnlington," the commander called out.

Renwall stalked up the steps to Marius, who was required to kiss both the male's cheeks in a ridiculous old tradition.

"What is the deal with the kissing?" the queen whispered as Renwall walked away from the dais.

Ophelia gave the queen a polite smile. "At the very first tournament, the High Captain of that time kissed his lead rider for luck. The rider ended up abed with a fever while the rest went flying to drive back pirates coming inland up north. All of the dragons and their riders died that day except for the one who had been ill. That's why the High Captain's kiss is known to be good luck. It's an odd tradition, granted. But we are used to it."

Queen Revna shrugged. "I'm all for more kissing." She winked at Marius, then cut her eyes in the direction of the crowd.

He knew where she was looking and forced himself not to follow her gaze to Tahlia. Ophelia would notice and there would be more questions.

Marius twisted slightly to look at Arkyn, Her Majesty's dragon. "Is your dragon feeling under the weather?" He mentioned the dragon to get the queen's focus off of him, but Arkyn did seem a bit lethargic.

The queen snorted. "He ate too many of those fine blueberries your staff provided."

Gaius called out another competitor.

"Serves you right, little monster," the queen whispered to the dragon.

Well, she wasn't the queen he had expected. Far too relaxed for a public appearance.

Marius kept kissing competitors until the moment he had been dreading arose.

"Lady Tahlia of Northwoods."

He stared at the back wall like it held the answer to every mystery in life.

And then she was standing in front of him. In those body-hugging leathers. With that pouty mouth of hers.

He swallowed, looked at her perpetually smiling face, and shifted to the left to kiss the first cheek.

"Thanks again for the armor," she whispered.

Stiffening, he leaned right to finish the job. She needed to keep that to herself. If Ophelia heard that... Her father probably already knew about the kindness he'd shown Tahlia, but it wasn't all bad. They had helped out competitors with lighter purses in past tournaments. But Ophelia would have serious questions if she found out.

"I said *thank you.*"

He grunted. Tahlia's scent enveloped him—something like lemon and spring leaves—and he kissed her second cheek. Her skin was so soft. She said another couple of words, but his heart was beating and he was so worried that he didn't hear any of it. She was gone from the dais in what felt like both the shortest and somehow the longest moment of his life thus far. Well, perhaps not as long as that one day in battle with the pirates, but still...

He forced himself not to watch Tahlia leave the dais as Gaius called another competitor's name.

"Marius." Ophelia's voice was a whisper. "What was she thanking you for?"

"I interviewed her." Not a lie...

"So it went well."

He clenched his jaw. "She knows more about dragons than I did when I first competed for my place."

Ophelia nodded.

"She is reckless, but I'm hoping it isn't a constant with her," he said, tightly.

"None of it matters if she can't fly or fight better than the rest."

"True."

His gaze disobediently strayed to where Tahlia now stood with the knights, their families, and their staff. Maybe she would fail the first trial and his life would go back to normal. He took a deep breath and forced his focus back to King Lysanael and Queen Revna, who had stood.

"Thank you for welcoming us so kindly," the king said to the crowd. "We look forward to a day of what you do best—dragon riding!"

A cheer rang through the hall and though a few of the competitors wore wide smiles, a couple looked ready to spill their breakfast onto the ground. He wouldn't look at Tahlia, but he could guess she was one of the smiling ones.

"Are you thinking about our engagement announcement?" Ophelia eyed him, a bit of what seemed like genuine joy in her eyes.

"When should we tell everyone?" he asked, carefully avoiding her direct question.

The presentation was over and the knights, commoners, and nobles began to disperse, heading out the main doors.

"At the announcement of the winner maybe?"

He nodded and imagined his life as a checklist. He had gained the rank of High Captain. Helped the order grow stronger. Bonded with a dragon successfully. And now he had the promise of the commander's daughter's hand in marriage. Everything was progressing according to his long-term plan.

Ophelia took Marius's arm and they followed the crowd. Excited conversations were broken by the occasional roar of a dragon. Earlier, the squires had assembled the mounts in the arena. Onlookers could enjoy the sight as the first trial—ground weapons—started.

Inside the now packed and chaotic arena, Marius gave Ophelia's hand a kiss and they broke away, each heading to their judging position on opposite sides of the two rings set up at the northern end of the arena. Competitors and their squires practiced in dirt tracks along the sides of the public seating. Nobles and the common folk filled the public seating on the raised sets of benches arranged on both sides of the tournament grounds. King Lysanael, Queen Revna, Arkyn the forest dragon, and Gaius climbed into the royal box to watch the proceedings.

The first knight to arrive in Marius's ring was, of course, Tahlia with her short gladius sword in hand. Palms sweating, he swallowed and maintained an emotionless expression that was proper for judging.

"Hello again!" She waved like children did, so enthusiastic and witless.

This was a deadly tournament and a serious possible appointment to the Fae military. She needed to stop acting so damn happy. It was going to get her killed.

Her opponent entered the ring. Twice her size, muscled like an ox, and wearing well-oiled and tidy armor, this male was the perfect competitor. A likely winner. The male showed calm, attention to detail, and the correct level of sober attitude. Good. Tahlia would lose immediately, and it would be the beginning of the end for her here on the mountain. He should never have helped her with new armor or passed her through the interview. He couldn't wait for her to be gone.

CHAPTER 12
TAHLIA

The giant male's sword crashed toward Tahlia's head. But where she'd thought maybe he'd be a bit lumbering due to his impressive size, he was sadly quite quick. She lunged sideways and a lock of her hair fell to the sandy earth.

"Thanks for that," she said, panting. "It was getting in my eyes. I thought we were supposed to be using the flat of our blades." She glanced at Marius. "High Captain, isn't that the rule here?"

She spun and thrust her gladius toward the giant male's kidney, turning the sword so it would just smack him and not pierce the leather vest.

"Flats, yes," Marius said, his arms crossed and his stormy gaze locked on her opponent.

Though he agreed, he didn't seem overly concerned with the giant male nearly slicing her in two.

They fought on, her going low mostly and him high. Once she had him lulled into a rhythm, she threw her blade at his chest, timing it so it would hit hilt first. The hilt bumped the male and he stumbled back a step.

Marius cocked his head, then looked toward the three scribes jotting down points. “Death hit. Lady Tahlia of Northwoods is the winner.”

The scribes agreed, and Tahlia was announced as moving on to the next round. Fara jogged up and handed Tahlia a small bucket and a ladle. Tahlia tucked her gladius into its sheath and scooped a serving of mint-scented water. It tasted divine.

“Thanks, squire.”

“Of course, my lady.”

“You still look green around the gills.”

“I feel like death, but I’m not going to fail you.”

Tahlia returned the small bucket. “You’re the best squire in the world, Fara.”

“I’m really not.”

“You put mint in my water.” Tahlia exhaled, enjoying the fresh feel on her tongue. “That’s fabulous.”

“No, I didn’t.”

“But it smells like mint,” Tahlia said.

Marius lunged forward and grabbed her arm. “What did you say?”

“I said it smells minty. How is that bad?”

Swallowing, Marius held her in place. He shouted a question, but he sounded like he was underwater.

“What did you say?” The arena began to spin. “I can’t hear you.”

Tahlia rubbed her face with numb hands.

“Tahlia?” Fara’s voice was pitched too high.

What was happening?

“Sit down, competitor,” Marius said. At least that’s what it sounded like.

“I don’t feel quite right.”

The arena tilted sideways and night fell.

~

Tahlia woke in Marius's arms. Very strong arms. His hand cradled her head as she blinked and dots swam in front of her eyes. What was happening? He was shouting at someone.

"...and I said immediately and don't bother with Felix. Only bring me Albus! I swear, if you don't get back here in one minute, I will—" His warning broke off as he looked down at her. "You're awake. Thank the Old Ones." His thumb stroked the top edge of her cheek and part of her ear. "Can you hear me? Sometimes ghostmint steals your hearing for a day."

"I can hear you." Her throat felt like it was made of sand.

His eyes pressed shut, then he opened them again to study her face and body. "Does your stomach cramp?"

"No, I just feel... I'm a little beat up but that's probably more from the giant sword-wielder than from... What happened? What is ghostmint?"

The scrabbling sound of feet on the ground and the raging torrent of Fara cursing like a pirate covered whatever Marius tried to say in answer. Tahlia attempted to sit up, but the arena spun and Marius urged her back down.

"Who is Fara destroying?"

"She tried to take Remus's arms."

"Who is Remus?"

"He is my squire and not guilty of this crime. Someone poisoned you and we have yet to find out who. I guess the why is the favor I showed you by gifting you those leathers. Yes, the Leatherworker didn't keep his tongue and now all know that I did you a kindness."

"Another competitor wanted me out of the tournament?"

"Yes, so they poisoned you. Or had someone else do the deed. We will find the culprit and I will see them weep on their knees before you."

"Fara is just trying to annihilate Remus because she needs to murder someone."

"Seems so."

"That's her typical response. Attack and ask questions later."

"So when you say you've been around dragons for a long time..." He studied Fara.

Tahlia chuckled and pain lanced through her throat.

"Just be still," Marius said. "Our best healer is on his way. He has a tonic that will help."

"I won the first bout."

"Yes, and you lived through a poisoning."

"I didn't miss my second match, did I?"

"No, I called a stop to the tournament for the moment."

A male with deep wrinkles and a nose like a crow's beak hustled over and knelt. He pulled a vial from his cloak and gave it to Marius. "Drink that, Lady Tahlia. It will drive the rest of the poison from your pores and set you to rights. You did quite well considering you smelled the ghostmint before drinking. The High Captain told the messenger that you could scent the mint odor."

"What do you mean?" Tahlia imbibed the bitter contents of the vial. The fluid made her lips pucker but cooled her throat nicely.

"I am Healer Albus. I have had experience with ghostmint plenty of times. The herb possesses a very subtle scent. There had to be a rather daunting dose in your water bucket for you to smell it."

A thought about the poison touched Tahlia's mind, then slipped away before she could actually pay attention to it. Hmm...

"Now," Albus said taking her forearm firmly, "hold still."

He flashed something small and gold across her skin and she felt as if she had been bitten.

"What was that?" she asked.

Albus and Marius traded a look full of narrowed eyes and male know-it-all-ness.

Marius helped Albus smear a dab of something sticky over her forearm. "Albus is just taking care of you. Don't worry."

"I'll test it to be sure the dose isn't hiding," Albus said quietly.

Marius raised both eyebrows. "Like it did with Honorus?"

They whispered on, and Tahlia shook her head to try to hear better. Her vision cleared further and she moved her jaw to pop her ears. The strange feeling the ghostmint had caused passed.

"Can I get up now?" Tahlia asked. "I feel all right."

Fara broke from the two squires who had been holding her away from Remus and his blackened eye. She ran to Tahlia and practically snarled at Marius.

"What happened? Do you know what happened to her?"

"A poison." Tahlia really needed Fara to stop shouting at the High Captain in such an accusatory tone. "But I'm fine."

Albus nodded. "She is remarkably strong, this one."

"My lady is the strongest!" Fara said, taking Tahlia's arm and helping her up.

"Maybe you should rest for a while longer," Marius said.

Tahlia frowned. "I can't hold up the tournament."

The severe female who had snapped at Tahlia in the baths and had stood beside Marius at the presentation walked up. The wind lifted the braided ends of her blue-green hair. "No, you can't. High Captain, it is past time we continue."

"Lady Ophelia, we will resume the tournament when I see fit."

Ophelia's eyebrow twitched and she stared at Tahlia like she was a bug about to be squashed beneath her boot. "The commander says we must begin now."

Was Commander Gaius this female's father? They had the same color hair, so it wouldn't have been surprising.

Marius glanced at the royal box and the commander gave him a quick nod. "Indeed," Marius said with an unreadable look at Tahlia. "Prepare for your next sword fight, competitor."

Everyone but Fara left Tahlia's side of the fighting ring. "You're well enough to do this now?"

"I am," Tahlia said. "I have to be."

Fara handed her sword over. She must have picked it up when Tahlia fell. "Your opponent isn't quite as big this time. That's one small mercy. I swear, when I find out who poisoned you, I'm going to disembowel them right in front of that Ophelia hag."

Tahlia had to laugh. "Calm down. We knew this tournament would be dangerous. I survived and now I'll be extra careful about what I take in and who is around."

Chest puffing in a deep inhale, Fara shook her head. "I wish you had more time to recover."

Tahlia clapped a hand on Fara's shoulder. "I'm fine." She lifted her gladius and faced her second opponent.

Her vision was still foggy, but she could see well enough to fight and her muscles were moving like normal.

The male across the ring from her also fought with a shorter sword and his grin said he knew very well how to use it.

Tahlia widened her stance and waited for him to attack.

CHAPTER 13
MARIUS

Marius finished reporting to Gaius, who had wanted every detail about what happened to Tahlia.

"Thank you, High Captain." Gaius sat back in his chair beside the king and queen. "You should return to your judging because I don't trust Sir Titus as much as I do you."

King Lysanael leaned on the arm of his chair. His gaze scanned the arena as the competitors continued their ground-fighting trials. "Who do you believe is responsible for the poisoning?"

"We have no leads on that as of yet," Marius said.

Queen Revna scratched the underside of her dragon's chin. Ten seats had been removed from the public seating to allow for Arkyn's size. "I've never heard of ghostmint."

"It can be used for healing if given in the right doses," Marius said. "The herb is common in these altitudes."

"I'll have to get a sample of that," the queen said, her icy eyes glittering with fascination.

Marius remembered she used to be an assassin for the human king. "I will see to it, Your Majesty."

He bowed and returned to the arena. Tahlia was clearly winning, her opponent sweating like a fevered dog and kneeling on the sandy ground. Titus called the result, and after two more rounds that ended in a similar fashion, the ground trials were over and the scribes were tallying points.

Tahlia was in the top five, and Marius wasn't getting his wish that she would be leaving the mountain.

MARIUS LED the competitors to the dragons assembled at the other end of the arena. "Now you will meet each dragon and they will choose one of you for the next trial."

"They choose?" A male missing an ear looked at the mounts with wide eyes.

Marius grunted. "Do they not choose their riders at Grimsbrook?"

All of the competitors had trained at one of the dragon riding schools around the realm. Most had the same policies, but differences did arise here and there.

"They used to." Tahlia's voice was brighter than it should have been after her terrifying day. "But they are running low on dragons, from what I heard."

"It is a concern, certainly," Marius said. "Now, walk past the dragons in a slow and steady line. Allow them to scent you. You will know when you have been accepted or rejected."

The competitors did as ordered. The male first in line ducked as a Seabreak lashed its head at him. A rejection. He strode past a Heartsworn and two Spikebacks who acted like he wasn't even there. Finally, a juvenile Green-flanked Terror lowered his head to the male.

"The Terror has chosen you," Marius explained. "We can only set new riders on a Terror when they are young. You must remember this dragon doesn't have much rider experience at all and he may dive too quickly during exercises. Keep him in check. If you are capable of doing so. If not, well, you might not last the day."

The male paled slightly but grabbed the Terror's reins and led him toward the spot where everyone would takeoff for the flying trial.

More dragons chose more riders and finally it was Tahlia's turn. The Spikebacks growled in unison as she passed them. Interesting. What didn't they like about her? Perhaps she still smelled of ghostmint. Dragons loathed the odor of that herb. She came to a stop at the one Seabreak and looked up at the dragon's ocean-blue head, seemingly unafraid. The dragon lifted its snout and roared, causing a few youngling Fae watching past the fence to scatter.

Tahlia set her hands on her hips. "Come on, gorgeous, I know it's you."

"How do you know?" Marius asked.

"I've always had an affinity to water. Plus, she feels...right."

"That's either incredibly powerful intuition you have, competitor, or you are simply good at pretending. I hope it's the first or she might strike you down."

"She won't."

Tahlia stepped closer to the Seabreak and the dragon flapped its set of four wings. The shell-shaped, pearly-white stripes along its neck and sides caught the sun and made Marius blink. She was a beautiful dragon.

The Seabreak sniffed Tahlia's head, then set its snout against her stomach. Tahlia turned, grinning from ear to ear. "See? We are meant for one another!"

"For today's trials only. You can't bond unless you win this tournament. She will get over you when you leave. Don't think she is as loyal as the dragons in the old tales. Bonds like that take years to form and solidify."

Tahlia rubbed the Seabreak's neck and cooed at the creature.

"Grouchy High Captain thinks you don't really like me, but we know the truth, don't we?"

Marius rolled his eyes. He waved at the squires and stable lads standing nearby, then left for the takeoff point.

Remus led Ragewing from the far end of the arena to the point to meet him. Tahlia's ridiculous conversation with the Seabreak continued behind him.

"Do not attempt to name that dragon, Tahlia."

He stopped and looked at the ground.

"You mean Lady Tahlia?" she said, her tone joking.

Damn. He hadn't meant to use her first name without a title. Why did she throw him off so much? Stones, he wished she would just give up this tournament and leave him in peace.

He hurried to Ragewing and mounted up. "Quickly, competitors." He gave each of their dragons a number, one through seven —all that were left of the competitors after the ground trial.

The other Mist Knights stood at attention near their dragons, present for the pageantry. They didn't ride in the flying trial. It was all competitors with Marius giving the commands in the air.

Once all the tournament participants were seated on their dragons, Marius waved for them to launch. Ragewing joined the group, spreading his wings and shooting into the darkening sky.

The sword-like perfume of a coming storm rolled through the churning clouds. The dragons cut through the tattered ends of those clouds. They would have to fly low at first so Marius could judge the riders.

Someone let out a whoop and zipped past. Tahlia. Of course. Her eyes shone with joy and she wasn't even holding on to the reins. He tried to unclench his jaw...

"Slow and in a tight angle formation!" he called out using his powerful voice to be heard over a rumble of thunder.

Would she obey orders or act reckless as she had on the ground?

Tahlia turned her Seabreak and led the rest in forming behind Ragewing and Marius.

"Nice lead, five!"

He could almost feel her smiling. The corners of his mouth twitched and he shook his head. Raising a hand, he led the group on a breathtaking dive. Riding low and close to Ragewing's neck, he turned to glance at Tahlia. She was just a little mound of white and black on the Seabreak's back. Numbers six and four were dragging behind. A point from each of them.

Ragewing responded to Marius's double pat on his scales and pulled up sharply. Tahlia nearly passed him on the right but managed to rein in her dragon and hover in a lovely show of control. She really could ride. Half the others mimicked the movement while the last half were still trying to stop their diving dragons. Number four went into a deadly spin.

Tahlia shouted, but the rising wind stole the words, and then she was launching toward the ground again.

She was going after number four.

"Stop!" he called out.

But Tahlia didn't look back and her dragon kept on. Young dragons sometimes grew so dizzy they couldn't stop spinning until they smashed into the ground. Tahlia urged the Seabreak to fly faster than number four and his Spikeback. Tahlia drove her Seabreak under the other dragon, who shrieked in panic and flipped, halting his downward, deadly spiral. The Spikeback rolled and shook his head while number four held on, pale-faced. Spreading his wings, the Spikeback found his direction and soared upward as his rider regained his position in the saddle.

Tahlia returned to Marius, hair ripped from her braids and her cheeks pink. Number four rose up and joined them and the rest of the competitors, who had finally gathered close to hover.

"Thank you, number five," four called out.

Tahlia waved a quick hand in acknowledgment and looked to

Marius. “I apologize for ignoring your command.” He could barely hear her.

“If you had failed,” he said, “you would be out of the tournament. Since you saved a rider, you remain. Let us continue.” Barking orders, he had the competitors and their mounts fly in tight spirals below the lightning-touched gray clouds. He commanded them to fly in a triangle formation, a double square, and then he ordered them to soar into the storm.

CHAPTER 14
TAHLIA

Lightning cracked the mist, and Tahlia set a hand against the Seabreak, directing the dragon to swoop past the Spikeback that Marius had ordered them to encircle. Only the Spikeback's tail was visible in the churning clouds, but the creature and its rider were hovering, so her spot in the circle wouldn't alter much. The wind rose and howled in her ears and rain lashed through the mist. How was it both misty and pouring? These mountaintop storms were incredible!

"Why are you smiling?" number two, a male competitor on a bright red Heartsworn, called out to her over the wildly beautiful weather.

"Why *aren't* you smiling? This is amazing!" Tahlia and the Seabreak took up the far spot in the circle of dragons around number three.

Marius's voice boomed in an echo of the thunder. "Well done. Now, drop in a spiral. Number order. Use your instincts to avoid lightning and pay attention to your dragon's natural inclination to avoid being struck as well!"

Fara would die if she knew what I was up to... Tahlia grinned, her heart soaring. The taste of the storm, metallic and green, touched her tongue. Marius looked like one of the Old Ones with his whip curled over his big shoulder and his hair lashing about his chiseled cheekbones and jawline.

His gaze slid to her and his lips parted like he was about to say something.

Looking away quickly, Tahlia focused on her task. Dropping behind number four, she urged the Seabreak to spiral downward. Glimpses of the arena showed between the black and silver clouds —the purple paint of the wooden trim around the walls and the waving arms of the cheering crowd.

Below Tahlia and the Seabreak, competitor two was having trouble. The Heartsworn's wings struggled against the wind. He was holding her reins too tightly.

The tiny hairs on the back of Tahlia's neck stood on end.

"Move!" she shouted.

She turned her dragon left as light washed the world and thunder gripped her ears and ripped into them. Blinking, ears ringing, she held to the Seabreak and whispered words the dragon surely couldn't hear.

"Thank you, love." Tahlia blinked, still trying to see through the spots in her eyes.

The other competitors had scattered with the close strike. Two, seven, nine, and one were gathering themselves into spiral formation again. Tahlia and her Seabreak flew toward them, gaining speed and aiming for their proper position. Others joined in, faces paled—no doubt as pale as hers considering how they had nearly been fried—and soon they had all but one competitor.

Marius and Ragewing were nowhere to be seen in the sky either. Worry pinched at Tahlia's stomach as they flew through another bank of clouds. Surely the High Captain wouldn't have had trouble. She imagined his storm-gray eyes shuttering and his body falling through the clouds. She bit her lip and forced the image out of her mind.

"Where is four?" she called out to the other competitors. Four was the same rider who had nearly fallen earlier. "Anyone seen the High Captain?"

But Tahlia might as well have been mute for all that she was heard over the lashing rain and rolling thunder. She should have learned the hand signals for communication. They were rarely used because those with strong Mistgold in their blood didn't usually struggle to be heard.

The clouds cleared briefly, and Tahlia looked down to see the arena stretched out below the spiraling dragons.

On the ground, Ragewing stomped impatiently and Marius crouched beside a splayed rider. Next to them, the rider's Spike-back roared in pain and rolled to his side.

But Marius and Ragewing were alive and well. The relief that rolled over Tahlia had her trembling in her saddle. She slicked some wet and fallen hair from her face and readied to land.

The spiral of competitors landed in order, splashing mud everywhere. Tahlia leapt from the Seabreak's back and rushed toward the fallen dragon and rider. Her heart thundered as loudly as the continuing storm. The crowd had gone still and their worry was palpable. The rider's eyes were shut, but his chest moved as Marius spoke over him to Albus, the healer who had helped Tahlia with the poison. Thank the Old Ones, the rider was alive. She turned toward the dragon, who was surrounded by a host of squires and Mist Knights.

"Give him space," Ophelia demanded as she spread a glossy concoction over the blackened scales on the Spikeback's side.

The dragon heaved a deep and shaky breath and his wings shuddered, half open and terribly vulnerable on the muddy ground. One Mist Knight guarded the dragon's head as Ophelia and her squire worked the unguent onto the wounded beast.

"The rider is talking to the High Captain now." Fara's voice was suddenly at Tahlia's shoulder.

"Good."

"They say he was simply knocked out. He wasn't hit like his mount," Fara added.

Tahlia slicked her wet and mussed braids out of her face and looked from rider to dragon and back again. "Poor thing. But dragons handle this sort of thing from time to time."

"Fire, yes, but lightning? Have you heard many stories of them living after a direct hit?"

"I am sure there are cases."

"I hope your optimism is truly on target this time, friend." Fara put a hand on Tahlia's shoulder and Tahlia gripped Fara's fingers, appreciating the support.

She was shaken, more so than she'd ever been. Not that she would let anyone know, especially Fara, who would likely drag her away from the tournament for fear of her dying.

"You're certain you want to continue?" Fara whispered.

"Completely."

Blowing out a breath, Fara ran her purple hands through her wet hair. "I can't wait until this is over. I just hope I'm not alone at the end of it."

The rider groaned and sat up and the crowd cheered as Marius helped him to standing. The Spikeback huffed and got his legs under him. Ophelia leapt back and the other Mist Knights followed her cue, giving the dragon room. The king, queen, commander, and the onlookers in the stands let out a cry of "Huzzah!"

Tahlia bumped Fara with her shoulder. "You won't be alone. I did well up there."

They hurried to Tahlia's Seabreak, who seemed to be happy, nibbling a bit of greenery that decorated the wall of the arena.

"I want you to do poorly up there," Fara said.

"What?"

Fara held out her hands. "But only so badly that you're kicked out of the lineup, not kicked out of life."

A laugh bubbled from Tahlia amidst the continued cheering. The injured Spikeback was led away and Commander Gaius raised his hands to quiet the masses. Fara helped Tahlia get the Seabreak's reins over her head so Fara could lead her back to the dragon stables.

"We break now for rest and food," the commander said. "The sky battle will commence one bell before sundown. Time is kept on the water clock in the great hall, where all competitors are welcome."

Tahlia shivered with excitement. The sky battle. She had waited her whole life for this.

But first—food. And perhaps a little conversation with the handsome High Captain...

CHAPTER 15
TAHLIA

Loud conversation and the clanking of plates and mugs filled the great hall. The crystals gleamed with magical light overhead—the sage-colored one aided in the dragons' health, the rose-hued crystal encouraged mating when numbers were low, the massive clear crystal formations were said to enable the bonds that formed between dragons and their riders, and the purple and gold ones lent courage to the dragons. They were beautiful, and Tahlia imagined she could feel their benefits even as a non-dragon. She smiled and energy simmered down her back. She always did have a strong imagination. A few Mist Knights, a squire, and a couple of competitors also looked up at the crystals while their neighbors held up mugs in toasts to the day's feats and the coming challenges.

"To number five!" Tahlia's fellow competitors stood and gave her a cheer. Number four remained in the healing wing of the castle keep, but reports said he was well on his way to good health and might even be able to rejoin the tournament.

Tahlia waved at the cheering folk and walked with Fara to a

table near the back of the hall, where servants poured in and out with heavy-laden food and drink trays.

Fara inhaled noisily and took a seat beside Tahlia on the bench. "Finally, some real food."

"I don't know if I can eat. I'm too excited."

"But there is cake." Fara raised her eyebrows at a tray a servant was sliding into place at their table.

The cooks and their assistants had set cakes in all the colors of the crystals into ordered concentric circles. Iced images of the dragon subspecies marked the cakes' tops and lacy rings of yet more icing lined the edges of each one.

Fara grabbed two purple and gold ones. "I wonder if these will taste like courage."

Tahlia nabbed a rose-colored one. "What does romance taste like?"

Fara laughed. "Please don't answer that. I'm afraid of your dirty jokes," she said around a large bite.

The rose cake was soft on the tongue, the perfect type of texture to go with the more sturdy icing. The taste was a blend of white chocolate, rose, and cinnamon. Delicious.

The servants filled their mugs with watered wine, and a piper and a lute-player began a jaunty tune. Three of Tahlia's fellow competitors found an empty area beyond the first set of tables and started to dance.

Fara swirled her mug and sniffed. "There's barely any wine in here at all."

"I suppose they don't fancy the rest of us falling off our dragons."

Glaring, Fara took a drink. She wiped her mouth with a linen napkin and eyed the other people at their table. "Please don't even joke about that."

Tahlia snorted a laugh and enjoyed a white cake that had a pleasant herbal taste to it like a sweet mint with a hint of basil. She washed it down with the watered wine, which somehow complimented the treats in the most lovely way.

The clatter of dice and bones sounded at the table behind them.

"Ah," Fara said dreamily, "the siren song of gambling dice."

Tahlia turned to see Marius engaged in a game with another Mist Knight. The marble gaming board bore a sigil—two lions flanking a dragon's head.

Fara joined Tahlia in staring. "Mist Knights must have even more money than I thought if they have their own marble gaming boards. Look at those carvings."

"I overheard number one saying the knights are given a higher stipend than they previously received due to the increasing threats on the eastern coast." Tahlia wiggled her eyebrows.

Curiosity had Tahlia up and walking over to Marius and his gaming partner. She sat beside the High Captain on the bench. Fara muttered something about "pushing her luck in too many directions," but Tahlia ignored her.

"Is that your board?" she asked Marius.

"It is Titus's." His gaze cut to her then away.

Her heart beat a little faster. He smelled like fire and the stormy air they'd flown in.

"That's a lovely fritillium." She smiled at the wooden dice cup that Titus upturned over the marble board. The surface was a deep rosy hue.

Titus inclined his head. "Made from dragonwood, of course."

"Of course."

"Want to play?" Titus asked. "I've been rolling dogs. Marius has already beat me soundly. He could use some better competition."

"It's only luck though," Tahlia said.

"Oh, don't tell our High Captain that."

Tahlia looked at the side of Marius's handsome face. "Why?

Don't you agree?" His scar caught the light for a moment before he turned toward her.

"If you keep track of the numbers your partner rolls, you can choose which numbers you keep for your count on your rolls," Marius said.

Tahlia winced. "That's a lot of numbers to jam inside your head. Sounds painful."

One of his moon-white eyebrows lifted and he watched her with those stormy eyes of his. Stones, but he was beautiful. And scary. It was a perfect combination. He pursed his full lips and she wondered if they would taste like the drink sitting beside his hand? How would a male like the High Captain kiss? Would he be slow, torturing her with the tip of his tongue as she ached for more? Or would he be aggressive and claim her mouth as his own with a demanding embrace? She cleared her throat and pushed those thoughts away.

"Games are meant to be fun, right?" she asked, frowning at Marius. "They're not supposed to be a lesson in mental tallying."

Titus laughed and covered his mouth with a fist. "Apologies, High Captain. I didn't intend to disrespect you, I—"

Marius waved his apology away. "We are off duty. Relax."

Tahlia snickered and gave Titus a friendly wink. "Oh, really easy to relax with that face of his turning you to stone over the game board, isn't it, Sir Titus?" She froze. Why had she just said that? She decidedly did not look from Titus to Marius. Was she trying to anger him and ruin her chances?

"Your cheeks flush at the slightest thing, don't they?" Marius said.

She slid her gaze to the right. He was studying her face.

Please let the table grow a mouth and eat me whole.

"It's just those stormy eyes of yours," she said quietly, grinning with all of her teeth and hoping to all of the Old Ones that he wouldn't kick her off the mountain right now. "They are just, um, incredibly stern."

Why was she still blabbering? *Shut up, me.* She bit her lip, and Marius's focus narrowed to her mouth. Under his body-clinging leathers, his broad chest shifted in a quick breath.

Titus was shaking, obviously holding in laughter with his pinched lips. Marius eyed her coolly, but though his expression was cold as a Saturnalia morning, she found herself feeling like she'd stumbled into the blazing hearth across the hall.

"I'm not going to eat you alive, Lady Tahlia."

An image of the High Captain setting his sharp teeth against her thigh flashed through her naughty mind. She imagined the feel of his hot tongue on her skin and the slip of his hair through her fingers. Growing far, far too warm between her legs, she coughed and pulled at her undershirt's neckline and prayed for a breeze.

"Of course not," she said nervously. "Let's play, shall we?" She grabbed the dice and bones and tossed them in the fritillium, nearly elbowing Fara, who had appeared suddenly. Tahlia upturned the wooden cup and watched the numbers appear. "Fara!" she said in an overloud and ridiculous tone she couldn't seem to hold back. "Where were you? We were just having a great conversation!"

Fara winced and pulled at her ear. "I was making you a plate of oysters and venison." She slid the plate toward the gaming board.

"Wonderful! Thank you!"

Tahlia paused in pointing out which numbers she chose to keep as her score and shoved an oyster into her mouth. Spicy heat seared her tongue and ravaged her throat. Sputtering, she managed to get the oyster down.

Marius patted her on the back, his expression less cold now. "Are you quite all right?"

Fara offered a fresh mug of what smelled like clean water. "Sorry, my lady. They must have a hot sauce over them. I didn't know. The staff didn't say anything when they set the tray on the table."

"It's delicious, actually. I just wasn't prepared."

Fara stood, hands fisting at her sides. “I’ll take care of this.” She stormed away.

Panicking, Tahlia pointed at the two and the five. “That’ll be my choices. Forgive me, I need to stop my squire from murdering an innocent seafood server.”

She started to stand, but Marius took hold of her wrist with an iron grip. With a gasp, she stopped. What was he doing?

He blinked, seemingly confused by his own actions. “Apologies. Do go. So sorry.”

Tahlia nodded and took off, scanning the crowd of servants for one who was being destroyed by a well-meaning maniac.

But her mind was elsewhere, playing a game with a handsome, dangerous male she had no business thinking about.

CHAPTER 16
MARIUS

Marius left Titus to the gaming board, giving some lame excuse about needing to speak to Remus concerning a saddle issue. He was feeling... All wrong. Irritated. Agitated. Frustrated. Hot. Confused. He rubbed a hand over his face and tried to decide where he was going.

Outside. Yes. Some air would help.

The lowering sun gilded the outside of the keep and turned all the crystals into mirrors for the sky's tattered clouds. He braced his forearms on the half wall that opened to the area leading to the cliff's edge, the spot where they often took off at the start of a mission.

A hum of energy rolled over his shoulders, down his torso, and then lower. He frowned. What was that? He'd felt something odd in the arena this morning too. Even Ragewing had noticed it, so he wasn't completely losing his mind. Or was he going mad, and the dragon had simply been humoring him? After all, one small female with an overactive mouth had completely discombobulated him.

What was that shade her cheeks turned when she blushed? It

was almost the color of autumn crystal wine... He shook his head and finished his mug of watered wine. So foolish.

A subtle wash of light caught his eye. He looked toward the cluster of varied crystals that grew in the rock over the keep's entrance archway. Had they lit up? Surely not. That would mean their magic was working...

A light, feathery sensation danced down him and brought his body to a version of alertness that was highly unacceptable at the moment.

"I am sorry for saying what I did about your face, High Captain."

His heart slammed into his ribs. Stones and snakes and everything in between, it was the female. Why was she following him? And why did her leathers fit her unlike how they fit anyone else?

"If you stare at my waist for much longer, I'm going to think you appreciate it more than my ability to ride a dragon," she said, grinning like an Unseelie.

His body thrummed with want. What was happening?

She sidled up to him and leaned against the half wall. Her golden amber eyes almost appeared glazed.

"Did you have stronger wine? I assure you that the sky battle to come is no small thing. You must be in top shape if you plan to display your talent on the dragon and with fire commands..."

Her gaze snared him, and his words of warning fizzled on his tongue. The world tipped a little.

He reached out and tucked a loose strand of her ebony hair behind her gently pointed ear. She shivered and her eyes half shut.

"You're fascinating." He was in a daze... "So fearless."

A grin slicked across her wine-damp lips and he longed to taste the drink on them. Another wave of desire lashed through him.

Her eyes snapped open wide and her grin broke into a bright smile. "Ah, no. I do feel fear. But my passion overrides it. To feel the wind as we fly... The dragons are miracles! The way they work with us instead of eating us whole. They could and well we know it. And their ability to turn and soar and dive. Don't get me started about their beautiful flame!"

Her joy suffused him. She understood what he felt for dragons and for the sky. She, unlike anyone, displayed the happiness he felt quietly inside...

Suddenly his hands were tangled in her wavy hair and he was pressing his lips against hers. She tasted like spice and wine and warm summers. He gripped her waist—so small in the circle of his hands. His blood roared and he shoved her against the half wall. She laughed, low and sultry, against his mouth and twisted her tongue with his. Sensations like sparks lit up his skin at every point of contact.

"Oh, no..." Ophelia's voice cut through the fog stirring Marius's mind. "I guess you two didn't get the warning in time."

Jerking backward, he clasped Tahlia's hips tightly. Stones, he had kissed Tahlia, and Ophelia had seen them.

Tahlia quickly stepped away from him and shook her head. "I'm sorry. I don't know what happened. I promise you that—"

Ophelia held up a hand. "Calm yourself, competitor. It's the crystals. A series of small earthquakes in the valley lit up the ley lines, and the breeding crystals activated. They have been flashing off and on since this morning, though only one guard noticed and he thought he was mistaken."

Tahlia was still flushed and a tangle of hair hung over one luminous eye. "Activated. Without a dragon's touch?"

"Yes," Ophelia said. "They warned us inside, but I guess you two missed the announcement... Anyhow, be careful. If you felt the effects that strongly, the magic will likely give you some tempestuous imaginings. They mean nothing."

Marius felt like he was under a scribe's eyeglass. "Yes, I was getting some air and, well, I, it was certainly disconcerting." He took a breath to steady himself, then bowed once to Ophelia and once to Tahlia. "Though the explanation makes this incident understandable, I remain apologetic. To you both. Now, I must meet with Remus before the sky battle preparation begins."

He spun on his heel and strode through the courtyard toward the gate, his mind on the wrong pair of lips.

The sunset's light and mist blurred the view of his pathway. Dizzy, he wound his way toward the southern wing's side entrance.

His thoughts refused to be tamed as he imagined a disrobed Tahlia lying on her stomach at the edge of the cliff, near the takeoff point. Moss cushioned her naked body and he couldn't stop staring at the way her legs curved up to her...

He blinked and tried to dispel the daydream as he climbed a curving set of stone steps. But his mind wouldn't obey and instead showed him Tahlia.

In the moss at the edge of the cliff, she glanced over her shoulder, her pouty lips swollen from kissing him. He covered her bare body with his and whispered in her ear.

"Wild one, I have caught you now."

She moaned and shifted one smooth leg so that he was positioned to fully mate with her. Pressing her hands to the earth with his fingers laced in hers, he held her in place and drove into her warmth. A groan escaped him and he forced himself to go slowly, though the feel of her was breaking him into glorious, blissful pieces. She called his name and he lowered himself—nearly losing his control—to nibble the tip of her ear. She shivered beneath him.

"More, Marius. More. Now..." She turned and he savored the side view of her face, her shuttered eyes and dark lashes. Her sweet tongue touched her bottom lip.

His body tightened and he almost finished then and there, but he kept himself in check, arms shaking as he thrust strong but still slow, drawing her into a fury of mewling sounds and gasps.

"Please."

Her pleas were a tonic stronger than any wine. He couldn't believe he had this courageous, beautiful, sun ray of a female...

She cried out, hips bucking as much as they could, pinned as he had her, and he increased his pace until all was pleasure—and the only good kind of pain—in a breath-stealing release.

Marius blinked and opened his eyes. Somehow, he had made it back to his bedchamber. He stood, slightly dizzy, with his cock in his hand. He pressed his forehead against his bedpost. It had been a daydream. He was the biggest fool ever to fly a dragon, but he couldn't quite bring himself to regret the imagining.

"You're pulling me apart, Tahlia of Northwoods," he whispered to the empty room. "Absolutely destroying me."

CHAPTER 17
TAHLIA

Certainly disconcerting? Tahlia marched across the courtyard and pushed through the great hall doors. The rest-time festivities were ongoing like something insane hadn't just occurred. First off, what kind of phrase was that —*certainly disconcerting*? She growled and rolled her eyes. Second, that kiss had been far more than disconcerting. It had been...heart-rending. The way his arms had felt around her, the honey and clove scent of him, the urgency of his hands, and how he'd looked at her like she was the center of his world...

But Ophelia had spoken the truth, and now that the crystals had calmed and Tahlia could draw her mind away from that energy, she felt that truth. The kiss had been only a product of the breeding magic of the rose-hued crystals. It hadn't been real. And it was good it wasn't a true kiss. If the rumors were true, Marius was engaged. To Commander Gaius's daughter, no less!

Tahlia rubbed her face and tried to forget the feel of his breath on her cheek and the press of his hard body against hers.

"Where in all the realms have you been?" Fara rushed up,

wringing her hands. "After that announcement, I worried you'd run off with a stable hand."

"Would have been a better choice, believe me." Tahlia hurried toward the corridor that led to the baths. She had to clear her head and wash all of that distraction off of her.

"What are you talking about?"

"We kissed," Tahlia whispered as they turned a bend.

A colored-glass sconce flickered with fire on the wall beside them.

Fara made a sound that made Tahlia wonder if she was about to turn inside out. "You, you what?!"

"You heard me." Tahlia took another turn and began to descend the steps to the lower levels of the keep.

Fara was on her heels. "The High Captain?"

"Shh!"

"Shh is right!" Fara grunted, gasped, and muttered a string of curses. "Does this mean that his engagement is off?"

"Hush, please. No, it doesn't. The crystals were the reason."

"Oh. Right."

"Lady Ophelia saw us."

"May monkeys fly from my—"

Tahlia spun and clapped a hand over Fara's mouth. She smiled to soften the attack. "Please, let this go. I shouldn't have even told you. It was nothing."

Fara's eyebrow twitched. "Your look says it was definitely something," she mumbled through Tahlia's hand. "He's going to kick you out, isn't he?"

Rolling her eyes, Tahlia continued into the bathing chambers. They were delightfully empty. "No, he wouldn't do that. He's a good male. I mean, I think he is. That whip is somewhat concerning... But I'd say he is a very good person."

"And you know that because you two are so close?"

"I am not in love with your tone."

"I'm not in love with you risking that scary female's wrath for a quick roll in the hay with the most dangerous male on the mountain!" Fara whisper-shouted.

"Please with every cake in all the realms and every cherry created in the entire universe on top, stop talking."

Squeezing her eyes shut momentarily, Fara nodded. "Fine. But if anyone tries to hurt you, I'm going to...to rip their heads from their shoulders and kick them off the cliffs and—"

"Fara."

She swallowed and took a breath. Pinching her lips with thumb and forefinger, Fara acted as if she were turning a lock and key.

"Thank you," Tahlia said quietly. "I don't think beheading Mist Knights should ever be on the to-do list."

Fara grumbled but kept her threats mostly silent.

The female competitor chamber was also empty and Tahlia was soon in the hot-spring-fed water, attempting to wash away the event. Fara kept quiet as she too washed up, but the looks she cast Tahlia were loaded with fears. Her friend saw too much.

THE SKY WAS a haze of sundown-hued mist. The Seabreak under Tahlia flew like she was swimming, her spine rolling as she maneuvered within the formation of their battle team.

"Don't let him blaze me!" Ophelia shouted at Tahlia.

Ophelia was only on Tahlia's side of the mock sky battle because the commander had drawn names in the arena before takeoff. Perhaps it was a stroke of luck instead of the catastrophe the dark side of Tahlia's mind suggested. Ophelia was amazing on her Green-flanked Terror, all confidence, decisiveness, and smooth maneuvers. But the way she directed her dragon was not good, and Tahlia had bitten her tongue more than once already, wishing she could tell her to stop with the harsh treatment.

Ophelia hammered a fist into the Terror's shoulder. She had on these spiked gloves that even a dragon such as hers would suffer from. At some point, Tahlia would have to figure out a way to get those things from her when they landed and toss them off the side of the mountain.

The Terror shrieked but obeyed the command, turning sharply among the red-tinged clouds to face their mock enemies flying toward them in the distance—Marius, Titus, and numbers three, four, six, and seven.

Tahlia and Ophelia's team consisted of the rest of the competitors—one, two, eight, and nine. Ten and eleven had dropped out quietly after seeing their flying scores. It was surprising that four and his Spikeback had returned. Admirable, certainly.

"Remember," Ophelia called out to their team with her Mistgold voice, "five goes in for short bursts of flame to break their formation."

Tahlia leaned over her Seabreak's cyan-colored neck, aiming her voice for the dragon's ears. "You ready, darling?" The dragon shuffled its second set of wings. "You're gorgeous, you know that?" The Seabreak lifted its snout in recognition.

"One and two," Ophelia continued, the wind tearing at her blue-green plaits, "you herd the half on the right side lower down while eight and nine herd the other half to a higher altitude. Keep them busy until I can blast them each with a mock stream that would take them out in a true fight."

They were permitted to use sparks or third fire, a lesser flame that would wound but not kill in most cases.

Ophelia's bright blue gaze found Tahlia, and Tahlia felt the look like a jab to the throat.

She swallowed. "Aye, Captain!"

The rest echoed Tahlia's call and they increased speed, heading toward Marius and his team.

Ophelia gripped her dragon's sides with the gold and copper claw-shaped tips of her terrible gloves. That had to hurt. Why did she feel she needed to control the dragon like that? Weren't they properly bonded?

Oh, they weren't. That brought reason to all of Ophelia's behaviors—the striking and clawing and extreme vicious tone in her commands. Ophelia was afraid. Did the High Captain know? Was her father, the commander, aware?

"Stop daydreaming and get to it, five!"

Ophelia's harsh shout shook Tahlia from her thoughts and she urged the Seabreak into a flight path just slightly above Marius's team.

Marius's gaze was steely and unblinking as she flew over his head.

"Merchant's purse with a goat!" Marius called out to his team.

What in all the realms did that mean?

Before his team could react to the command, Tahlia had her Seabreak shoot sparks at Titus and his Spikeback. Titus and his dragon veered away from the formation as the others on the opposing team began breaking into three groups with one rider falling back—it was number three, a male on another Seabreak.

Turning her dragon, Tahlia urged the Seabreak to rain sparks in Marius's direction.

He moved like a lightning strike, uncoiling his whip and lashing it toward Tahlia. She gasped and drew back, and the Seabreak reared in the misty sky. The tip of the whip had been mere inches from Tahlia's face before she'd moved. He either had perfect aim and was careful not to cut her, or he had missed.

She didn't think the great Shadow of the Shrouded Mountains tended to miss a target. So she winked in thanks for his mercy before blasting him—third fire only, of course. His eyes widened briefly before he steered his scarlet Heartsworn out of the way, flying low to face members of Tahlia's team. Sparks filled the fighting area and lit the misty clouds as Tahlia drove the Seabreak toward another male on another Spikeback. It was number six, not number four, thankfully. She would feel bad attacking four after his and his dragon's injury, but if she had to attack eventually, well, the situation was what it was. This was hardly a happy picnic up here and the weak had to be culled from the group no matter how tough that was to swallow.

The attacked Spikeback roared and Tahlia's Seabreak lunged for the other dragon's throat.

"Mock battle!" Tahlia called to the Seabreak even as her heart thundered in her ears.

But the Seabreak didn't listen. She bit down on the Spikeback's throat and soon both dragons, and their riders, were tumbling through the fighting. Tahlia gripped the saddle with every ounce of strength she possessed. Sparks singed her exposed forearms and her cheeks. Her stomach rose into her throat as they spun over and over.

She had to stop this.

"Call her off!" number six yelled from the Spikeback's saddle.

"Trying!"

But she knew she had to do more than shout commands. She slid off the saddle and used the Seabreak's slender neck spikes to climb along the dragon's neck, her legs wrapped around the beast as best as possible. They didn't have as many spikes as a Spikeback, but they had enough for this terrifying job. The dragon jerked. Tahlia lost hold with one hand. She gasped and clasped tightly with her legs, getting another grip on the dragon's spikes. Once she reached the pressure point in the dragon's throat, she pressed her fist into the Seabreak's softer underside scales.

The dragon shrieked and fell back and Tahlia's legs lost their hold. She dangled off the rearing Seabreak, grasping tightly to the spikes.

"I'm sorry! I had to. You forgot it was a mock fight. Come on, love. Calm down!"

The wind tore at Tahlia's limbs and stole her breath as the Seabreak launched itself above all of the others.

"I have treats if you let me live through this, darling! Cake! So much cake!"

A snarl pealed from the dragon's mouth and she tipped herself to the right. Tahlia scrambled onto the saddle and righted herself. Panting, she grasped the lashing reins and managed to steer the Seabreak back to the sky battle.

"You are getting so much cake!"

Tears of relief and joy burned Tahlia's eyes. This was living. She could never go back to simply cleaning tack and trailing Fae with better blood around the Shrouded Mountains. No, she was well and fully hooked on the life of a Mist Knight.

Number six waved a thanks, his face haggard with fear.

"Get in front of me, five!" Ophelia crowed from the back of her Green-flanked Terror. "We only have Titus and Marius to beat now!"

Her dragon roared and blasted Titus with a spray of third fire intermingled with at least a smattering of fourth fire. Ophelia was pushing the boundaries of the mock status of this fight.

Marius and his Heartsworn rose from a bank of thick clouds and blazed sparks at Ophelia and Tahlia. Tahlia urged her Seabreak to fly below Marius and then had the dragon whip its tail upward to smack the underside of the Heartsworn. Marius's dragon let out a broken snarl. A flurry of movement blurred before Tahlia's eyes and suddenly Marius and his dragon were flying alongside her and her Seabreak. Marius's whip slithered through the space between them and wrapped its end around Tahlia's wrist.

Her blood ran cold. Did she truly know him? Of course, she didn't. Fara had been right. He could rip her from her seat and toss her to the earth in a moment.

Keeping her legs tight on the Seabreak, Tahlia used her free hand to grab the whip and she twined it around her saddle's pommel.

"Dive!" she ordered her dragon.

The Seabreak dove like a falling star toward the arena, dragging Marius and his Heartsworn with them.

Marius released the whip, and the handle bounced along the wind currents to lob the Seabreak in the side. She snorted and Tahlia pulled the dragon out of the dive and urged her back toward Ophelia. Marius, without his whip, had his dragon surge after Tahlia and the chase was on.

Heartsworns and Seabreaks were the two fastest types of dragons, so they were matched there. Heartsworns could only blaze flame a few times a day, while Seabreaks could blow fire twice as often even if the flames weren't as powerful.

Since she had far less experience with tactics, this was Tahlia and her dragon's only advantage.

Surely, Marius's mount was out of fire for the day. In the rules read before the mock battle, she'd learned that the riders had to mimic true abilities. Marius couldn't have his dragon blaze them if the dragon would normally be out of fire for the day.

Tahlia tugged a rein and pressed her leg into the dragon, turning sharply in the bracing wind. She bumped the Seabreak's shoulder five times and the dragon let loose a shower of sparks that just kept going.

Marius's Heartsworn was forced to fall back and act as if he had been seriously injured.

Ophelia cheered from above as she flew beside an obviously defeated Titus and the rest of the competitors still airborne.

Marius flew downward, toward the arena, but he glanced at Tahlia over his shoulder. "You owe me a whip!" His voice was harsh, but the corners of his lips twitched as if he was fighting a grin.

She wanted to be hopeful, but had her loss of dragon control ended her dream of becoming a Mist Knight? Controlling one's mount was the most important part of the job, and number six's Spikeback bore the evidence of her failure in a nasty, ragged bite along the beast's throat. Granted, the dragon was still flying and the wound wasn't bleeding too much. But would that be enough to claim the loss of control wasn't significant? Though Tahlia was a determined optimist, even she knew that was doubtful.

They landed and Commander Gaius stormed toward Tahlia.

CHAPTER 18
TAHLIA

Was he going to run her through right here for all to see? Well, that was better than being roasted by a dragon, wasn't it? Perhaps not. It would have been interesting to see the inside of dragon fire before death.

His features unreadable, Marius swallowed and stepped closer to Tahlia. Was he going to attempt to shield her from whatever was headed her way via the commander's sword or fist?

"You are a wonder!" Commander Gaius grabbed her shoulders and gave her a shake.

Shock almost stole her voice. Almost. "I am?"

He shook her again, grinning like a madman. Her hair fell further out of the tight braids Fara had worked into her hair after the bath.

"You are."

The assembly cheered from the stands and the king and queen addressed them as the Mist Knights and the other competitors gathered around the commander and Tahlia. Noise covered their conversation and the crowd seemed happy enough to shout well wishes to the royals, who headed toward the festivities that would begin in the outer bailey now that the tournament's events were complete. Only the announcement of the winner had yet to happen.

"She left formation," Ophelia said quietly, gaze on her father. Their hair was an exact match. "She lost control of her mount."

Tahlia held out a hand toward Ophelia. "She speaks the truth. I can't deny that."

"Oh, yes," Commander Gaius said, "you were terrible during most of the battle. But the stones you have, Lady Tahlia!"

"You mean breasts, maybe?"

He glanced down and frowned before waving off her words and throwing an arm around her shoulders. "The type of courage I just witnessed, well, that is what we need up there, and if I were a gambler, my gladecoin would be on you winning this thing. I am quite glad that I don't need to make the difficult decision as to who wins the tournament. That job belongs to my future son-in-law."

So it was true—Lady Ophelia and High Captain Marius were engaged. A strange twisting sensation ran through Tahlia's stomach. The other Mist Knights and competitors murmured congrats awkwardly and continued complimenting one another's flying and talking excitedly about all that had gone on up there in the misty sky.

The king and queen made their way through the bowing and curtseying crowd.

Tahlia curtseyed alongside a bowing Marius, who had joined her and Gaius.

King Lysanael's green eyes flashed with delight. "Wonderful match."

Marius nodded. "Thank you, Your Majesty."

Ophelia strutted over, making eye contact with everyone except Tahlia. She took Marius's arm.

Commander Gaius rubbed his hands together and raised his eyebrows. "How about we get cleaned up for the announcement feast? A great many festivities await us tonight. High Captain, do you have a winner set in your mind yet?"

"Not yet. There is much to consider."

"Yes, of course. Always practical and stern, our Marius is," the commander said quietly to the king and queen. He clapped Marius on the shoulder.

Marius's squire, Remus, broke through the ragged group of riders and bowed low. "May I speak with my lord?"

Queen Revna smiled at him. "Rise and do as you see fit, squire."

Remus whispered quickly in Marius's ear. The High Captain's expression went blank.

"Remus, wash down Ragewing," he ordered quietly, his gaze distant, "and give him two scoops of the gold meal." He pressed his eyes shut for a moment.

"Aye, sir."

He gave Remus a nod then hurried away.

Fara slipped through the group and up to Tahlia as Albus and the other healers broke the party apart and began tending to cuts and minor burns. The dragons were being tended to behind them and the crowd had mostly dispersed.

"I'm so glad I was in the latrine during what people are calling your courageous act," Fara whispered.

"Why were you in the latrine? Tell me you weren't so worried that I would die that it made you sick. Tell me it was the asparagus they served during rest time."

Fara snorted. "I would if I could, my lady, but asparagus never gave me Tahlia-level anxiety."

"Asparagus is good like that. Eh, do you have any idea what Marius's squire just told him?"

"No. What happened? Where is the High Captain? Maybe it's something about the queen's dragon, Arkyn."

"Why do you say that?"

"Arkyn took the last hour of the tournament to invade the kitchens."

"Oh, dear."

"More like *oh, blueberries*. Even part of the great hall is tracked with dragon footprints."

Tahlia politely declined a healer's attention and tried to be excited for the coming pronouncement. Would it be her? Could she dare to hope?

"Do you have any cake?" she asked Fara.

"How did you know?" Fara pulled a small pink circle from her pocket. "Never mind. Dumb question." She handed it over. "I've had more than enough, so eat the whole thing, Lady Tahlia. Please."

"Oh, it's not for me."

Tahlia hurried to where the stable hands and healers were tending to the dragons. Her Seabreak tossed her head and snorted at Tahlia's approach. Fara took the Seabreak's reins from one of the hands and held the dragon loosely as Tahlia offered up the treat to the dragon.

"I promised," Tahlia said to the Seabreak. "And I don't break my promises."

The dragon sniffed the cake and glanced at a stable hand, who was eyeing them judgmentally.

Tahlia rubbed the Seabreak's cyan side. "Ignore him. You compromised up there with me and I insist you enjoy a special dessert."

Finally, the dragon nibbled the cake from Tahlia's palm. The beast's lips tickled her skin and she felt as though her face might crack from grinning too much. She set her forehead against the Seabreak's and both of them exhaled.

"Thanks again for not dropping me to my death. I know my inexperience was an issue."

The great creature snuffled against her neck, blowing back her messy black waves.

"Wish me luck in there, all right?"

The Seabreak huffed a hot breath that smelled of fire, and that was about as good as one could get for a well-wish from a dragon.

"...and if she wanted your opinion, she would give it to you!" Fara was waving a fist at the judgmental stable hand.

"Will you bring her back to the stables?" Tahlia asked Fara. "I'll meet you inside."

"As you say, my lady." Fara gave the stable hand a glare and led the Seabreak the same way Remus had already directed Ragewing to go.

Tahlia looked around as she began the short walk to the great hall. Marius was still notably absent and most of the Mist Knights and competitors had already left for the announcement. Heart beating in her mouth, Tahlia walked on, heading closer and closer to the moment that would either make or break her dreams.

CHAPTER 19
MARIUS

In his chamber, Marius flexed his hands at his sides as his valet unlaced his leather vest. His valet quickly dressed him in a dark blue tunic trimmed in gold thread, black trousers, and black boots. His valet brushed his hair out and tied it back in a simple queue.

"That's fine. Thank you." Marius urged his valet to take the rest of the night off. He had no patience for any more fussing. Plus, there was little time for it.

His mind threw out images of Tahlia flying, her small body poised expertly on her dragon like she'd been born in the saddle. The light in her eyes that turned to fire when she focused on the mock enemies... She was a wonder. Gaius was right to be awed and to make note of her courage.

His mind wove images of memories that had never happened. He threw Tahlia on his bed and she let her knees fall open. Her skin glimmered in the candlelight and the soft spot halfway up her thigh tasted like salt and sugar. A surge of want cascaded through him, heating him to an unbearable degree. He imagined crawling on top of her and binding her wrists to the headboard with his whip. Swallowing, he could almost see the way her head dropped back as she moaned and closed her eyes as he drove into her, showing her that she was his and his alone.

Smashing a fist into the plaster between the stones of his bedroom wall, he snarled.

His mind was a terrible master. Those things would never happen. Of course they wouldn't. But he had to break his engagement with Ophelia. It was quite clear he couldn't be loyal to her. Not after the way Ophelia had begun treating her dragon. She never would have done that when she first signed on. He'd spoken to her about the rough behavior toward the creature numerous times. And also, he couldn't ignore the way his body—and his heart—had been inspired by Tahlia. Even if the worst happened, the engagement had to end.

Crashing into the chair at his desk, Marius leaned forward and gripped his head. His chest shuddered. He would fail Bellona, his beloved sister.

I just can't do it, Sister. Can you forgive me? I will still be the best Mist Knight I can, but this, I can't do this. Ophelia's bloodline is ideal, but the situation is not what I'd thought... Nothing is as I had thought it was. His throat was thick and he gritted his teeth.

Nothing was going according to plan. Absolutely nothing.

I'm so sorry I have failed you, Bellona.

Marius went to his desk and reread the message that Remus had reported. He crushed the parchment in his fist and growled. *Damn it, Tahlia.* He pressed his fist against his forehead and wished there were some way out of this. But rules were rules for a reason. And he had dedicated his life to the Order of the Mist Knights.

Shaking his head, he threw the note to the floor and stormed out of his chamber.

CHAPTER 20
TAHLIA

Tahlia gasped as Marius showed up beside her, silent as death. In line for a refill of the dark wine pouring from the crystal fountain, she nearly dropped her goblet. Fara was already saving her a seat in the middle of the table near the western-facing hearth.

"Yes, High Captain? Aren't you supposed to be up there?" She nodded toward the front of the hall where the king, queen, and Commander Gaius ate at a small table separate from the two other long tables.

"I must speak to you. Privately."

"You look even stormier than usual." She was teasing him, but the steel in those eyes made her shiver. It was not an altogether unpleasant sensation.

He didn't rise to her barb and instead took off out the door, not even watching to see if she would follow. Of course, she did trail him. What was happening? Was this good or bad? She tried to glance at Fara before leaving the great hall, but there were too many servants going this way and that, blocking her view.

Outside, the half-moon had risen like a scythe in the black sky.

The heads of the Seabreak and two other dragons showed in the area between the courtyard and the arena. The stable hands were giving the dragons one last walk before sleep, most likely. Marius led Tahlia to a shadowed corner between the keep's western face and the wall that ran along the courtyard to the arena and the cliff launching point.

Not thirty yards away, he had grabbed her and kissed her hard. Just there. Where the moonlight now cascaded across the rock wall and over the hand-trimmed grass of the courtyard. She could almost feel his fingers digging into her hips. A pulse of warmth between her thighs made her stop before joining him fully in the shadows. The moon's silver luminescence cut across his cheekbones, and his brow shaded his unblinking eyes. Hands fisted at his sides and body coiled, he looked ready for a fight.

A chill wrapped her in a frosty cloak of doubt.

"Tahlia. I know..." His focus dropped to her boots, and then he looked up again and met her gaze. "...about your blood."

Her heart hammered in her ears and she dropped back a step. "What?"

"When Albus cut you to test for ghostmint hiding in your veins, the Bloodworkers examined your blood." His eyes squeezed shut, then opened again, and he pinched the bridge of his nose. "That's how you were able to lie. Did you lie about how long you trained at Grimsbrook? I can't believe I was so foolish. You lied to me. I thought we understood one another. I thought I'd found someone that actually felt the same way I do about..." He gestured to the sky and shook his head, his jaw clenching.

He meant about flying and dragons, about the life of a Mist Knight. "You did. I do. You can't be angry."

"Oh, really? I can't. How does that work out? Actually, don't bother saying anything. Every word from your lips could be a lie, human."

"I'm half-human and it doesn't matter because I am meant for this. You know it as well as I do."

"I know nothing about you."

"Did that taste sour? That had to be a stretched truth. You know everything important. I can fly with the best of them. You, Ophelia, Titus, the other Seabreak rider I saw up there taking scores."

"Maiwenn."

"Yes, I'm as good as her too. You know that about me. You know that I care about the other riders on my team and I care about the dragons. That's more than I can say for your intended mate."

Wincing, he looked away for a moment. "I have seen those new gloves of hers. She has always been too rough on her dragon. I will confiscate the gloves. Now, stop. Stop talking. We aren't discussing Ophelia."

"Are you going to sentence me to death?"

He lifted his head, exposing his throat. "What choice do I have?"

"Does that mean you don't want to?"

Shifting his focus to her face, he stared, silent. She wondered again how he had received the scar that ran along the side of his handsome visage.

"I'm not the one who did the testing. The Bloodworkers know the truth about you. This cannot be kept secret. Not for long."

"What do you mean?"

"I mean, you must flee, Tahlia. Run back to wherever you call home. Or somewhere else. Anywhere but in the Shrouded Mountains."

"I was born in the valley. I'm not human in any real sense of the word. All I know is Fae. And dragons." Unshed tears burned her eyes and they turned her foul blood to flame in her heart. "I will not run from who I am. I am a dragon rider and I am your next Mist Knight."

"All you will be is a pile of ash if you don't escape this place within the next hour." His gaze had turned pleading, his eyebrows lifted and his hands almost reaching for her, though he kept back just inches from touching her.

"Knights don't run from a challenge. They fly toward it."

He lunged, startling her, and he grabbed her arms in a viselike grip. "You must go, Tahlia. Please. I'm already breaking my oath by telling you this and giving you this one chance. I have never, ever broken a rule of the Knights. You with your wild joy and your ridiculous courage have bent my resolve like a storm tosses a willow."

"You're the storm." Like her fingers belonged to someone else, her forefinger found his scar and traced its path from temple to jawline.

He shivered and shut his eyes. "And you light the skies like a second sun and grow happiness in the cold ground of my heart."

Her soul ached. Her heart beat hard and slow—once, twice. She put her palms over her chest and tried to breathe evenly. She would fall right into the storm that was Marius Leos Valentius, Shadow of the Shrouded Mountains, and delight in every shock of thunder and lash of rain...

When his slitted, gray-black eyes flashed open, his lips parted.

She imagined him crushing her to him. His kiss would taste like his scent—of cloves and honey—and he wouldn't set his lips on hers gently, but like a powerful male who wanted to claim her as his own. His hands would cup her face roughly; his tongue would tangle with hers.

At just the imagined scenario, fierce longing shot through her like a bolt of lightning. What was it about this proud, stern male that attracted her so? But she knew already. It was the way he treated his dragon, how he had helped her quietly along this extraordinary journey, and the fatherly protectiveness he displayed for his knights in the sky. Even if it was madness, she wanted this male.

If they could be together...

Every inch of her would hum with desire. She imagined the

many sensations she'd feel in his arms... The turn of his shoulder muscles under her fingers. The groan slipping from his mouth as he kissed his way down her neck to her chest. They would fall to the ground and he would take her here in the shadows with desperate movements, like touching one another would save them both somehow from whatever consequences this connection threw at them as well as the very real danger that awaited her inside the hall.

But all of that was only in Tahlia's head. He stood gripping her arms hard enough to bruise.

With a growl, he pushed away from her. His hair was wild and his eyes wilder. "Go, Tahlia. Please. Just leave. I can't..."

She couldn't leave this place or give up. If she did, the fire inside her would die and she would be a husk of her former self. She wouldn't be Tahlia any longer.

"I will face the consequences. Do what you must do, High Captain. Now, I have an announcement to attend."

He shut his eyes once more, and she glanced at him one last time before leaving him in the moonlight. His hands flexed at his sides and his breaths came too quickly. Forcing herself to keep on walking, she found the door, swung it open, and prepared to meet her fate, whether it be fine fortune or death by a dragon's blaze.

CHAPTER 21
TAHLIA

Tahlia found Fara wielding an eating knife and threatening an elderly male. "I told you I was saving this seat. Now, back off. I don't care what kind of military background you have, you old cod! I'll cut it right out of you!"

Lowering her friend's weapon, Tahlia eased Fara away from the table. "Eh, I need to tell you something."

Once she had, Fara's purple skin turned nearly gray. "I knew this would happen. I can have Daffodil ready in fifteen minutes. Meet me by the outer bailey gate."

"I'm not running, Fara."

"Of course you are."

"Am I a fearful sort?"

"No, but this is no time for your brand of courage, which I deem madness even at the best of times and this isn't that."

"What?"

"Nothing. You are leaving. We are leaving. We will keep our flesh unsinged and call this a grand adventure. I hear the human settlement of Deigs is an open-minded city where two Fae could find a way to live."

"I'm not leaving. You go. I want you to go and be safe. I'm facing this. I would rather die than flee. I am meant for this. I am a Mist Knight."

Fara twisted her hands and spoke close to Tahlia's face, so close that she could smell her friend's wine on her breath. "You have the heart of one, but sadly, you don't have the blood. We can't change their minds. It's a rule and Mist Knights are more obsessed with rules than they are their dragons."

"Go. Please," Tahlia said. The echo of Marius's warning gripped her heart, a trembling hold that threatened to shake her into pieces.

Not waiting for Fara to argue, Tahlia pivoted and strode to the front of the hall where the other competitors were lining up for the announcement.

Commander Gaius walked in from a side door with Ophelia. The commander raised his arms to quiet the hall.

"I've asked Queen Revna to announce the winner since our High Captain is not in attendance. Please stand."

The queen broke away from her dragon and the king. They had been talking closely with a group of liveried stewards. She walked slowly to the center of the line of competitors, her gaze measuring each of them.

Did she know already?

Tahlia's stomach rolled and she breathed through her nose to keep from being sick all over the queen's fantastic scarlet high-top boots.

"The winner is..."

The queen's gaze traveled over each of the competitors. Number one scratched the scar where his ear had once been. Two and three held as still as statues. Four glanced at Tahlia and nodded—whatever that meant. The rest shuffled their feet or pursed their lips.

"Our new Mist Knight of the Shrouded Mountains, noble

protector of the Realm of Lights and the northern coast, is Lady Tahlia of Northwoods!"

Tahlia's heart soared. She felt like she could take flight like a dragon, spreading wings and breathing flame into the clouds. The Bloodworkers hadn't come forward. All was gold and happiness.

I did it. I am a dragon-riding knight. Even if it doesn't last, I did it.

The hall erupted in cheers and most of the competitors gave Tahlia encouraging smiles while a few grimaced, their disappointment understandable.

Commander Gaius and Ophelia stepped forward, and King Lysanael whispered something in Queen Revna's ear. She whispered back and they seemed to have a nearly silent argument, complete with hand-waving and scowls and a growl or two.

"I'm afraid there has been a mistake," the commander said. "Tell us what you found, Head Bloodworker."

Tahlia swallowed. This was it. The end. A sheen of sweat covered her forehead and she fisted her hands to keep her fingers from shaking.

An ashen-faced Marius came through a side door and stared at her. His hair was mussed and his eyes had a feral glaze to them.

A male in Mist Knight livery cleared his throat and read from a parchment. "Competitor five's blood has less than point four percent Mistgold—"

The crowd gasped, but they hadn't even heard the worst of it. Sweat rolled down Tahlia's back, but she remained standing, holding her head high. She was a Mist Knight, even if her blood wasn't what they wanted it to be.

The Head Bloodworker held up the parchment and the room quieted once more. "Her blood also shows that she is half-human."

Angry shouts burst from several Mist Knights as well as competitors two, three, nine, and seven.

"Mist Knights must be Fae and Fae alone!"

"Mountain dragons don't bond with humans. It's a simple fact!"

"Aye. It would never work."

"A disgrace!"

"Must humans stick their greedy hands into all of our traditions?"

This last bit was whispered by a squire close to Tahlia. The coward would never say such a thing loud enough for the queen and king to hear.

Ophelia locked eyes with Tahlia and grinned.

Tahlia's not-good-enough blood boiled in her veins. She clenched her fists and longed to become the dragon she had felt she was only a few moments ago.

Commander Gaius's eyebrows bunched and his lips turned down at the edges. He motioned at two guards standing at the main doors of the hall. "Based on the evidence, sadly, competitor five is sentenced to death by dragon fire."

A chill swept down Tahlia's body and she fought a shiver. She hoped Fara was long gone, safely away from here.

After more shouting and calls for proof and bumping and shoving, the guards had Tahlia and were roughly escorting her out of the great hall.

The competitors, knights, and some of the squires and servants trailed them out of the keep, across the courtyard, and beyond the wall where Marius had kissed her. The manicured grass of the area leading to the cliff's edge was too lovely to be a place where people died. Faeberries grew along the border of the arena wall and mistblooms with their delicate white petals nodded their heads in the breeze.

Suddenly, Fara was beside Tahlia. "You're looking at the flowers, aren't you? You truly are mad." Tears gleamed in Fara's eyes.

Panic sewed Tahlia's throat shut. She coughed and the guards gripped her arms more tightly, shoving Fara out of the way.

"What are you doing here?" Tahlia whispered. "You must go."

The guards rotated Tahlia around to face those filtering into the grassy area to watch her death. The taller of the two guards began to tie her wrists.

"I'm not leaving you, my lady," Fara said.

Tahlia memorized the slant of Fara's nose and the intense love in her gaze. "You must. I love you, my friend. Go. Now."

Fara wiped a tear with the back of her hand and growled. "No. I won't."

The guard wrapping the rope around Tahlia's wrists paused. "You'll go or you'll be burned alive too, squire."

"I..." Fara sniffed loudly and took a deep breath. "My lady is a true knight and I pledge my loyalty to her."

"No, Fara. Please." Tahlia's heart snapped and pain spread like a crack through her chest. Fara couldn't die. Not yet. Not now.

Marius walked up and clapped the guard on the shoulder. "You're dismissed." He took up the job of tying Tahlia, gently knotting the rope. Then he stood beside her.

Now, Fara and Marius flanked her on either side.

"What are you doing?" Tahlia asked him.

"I, too, believe you are a true knight."

Tahlia's mouth fell open, and though her heart pained her, joy suffused the agony.

Marius's gaze cut to her face, then back to the rope. "Even though you used that half-human tongue of yours to lie to me, I am likewise loyal to you. As a fellow Knight of the Shrouded Mountains."

"Marius, I..." She met his gaze as her mind tried to find the words to explain her absolute satisfaction at earning his loyalty and the horror at him standing by her side in this terrible moment.

"Marius?" Ophelia's voice cracked. "Why?" She stared, her gaze wide and unsure. She looked younger.

He glanced at her, eyes as steely as ever. "I'm no longer your concern."

"But..."

"I won't let a knight suffer this punishment without a show of defiance."

Commander Gaius walked around the crowd to join Ophelia. "A show that will leave you dead. Give this up, High Captain. You've lost your head over this half-human."

The king and queen stood atop a rise of earth at the back of the crowd. An aspen's leaves fluttered over their crowned heads. They were deep in discussion again.

"Marius," Tahlia whispered. "Thank you for believing in me, but please take Fara and go."

"Stand strong, Lady Tahlia," Marius said.

Fara put her hand over Tahlia's forearm. Her fingers were like icicles. "We are with you. No matter what comes."

"Fire is what's coming, Fara." Tahlia's resolve trembled under the weight of these two standing beside her.

A stable hand brought out a dark green Terror. The dragon looked as old as the mountain itself, his scales the dark green of shaded leaves and his eyes like rain-darkened stones. There was no spark of connection in that dragon's gaze as there was in most dragons'. This one had been born deadly and had been bridled to do the worst tasks the Mist Knights required. Trying not to tremble, Tahlia stood her ground. This dragon wouldn't hesitate.

"Go, please. Both of you. Marius, you just met me three days ago. You can't possibly care that much."

"When you face death in the skies together, an hour is enough to feel the bond between knights and I know you are already aware of that fact. Your mercy and courage continue to amaze me and I won't let you die alone. This is wrong, and hopefully, by your actions, your squire's, and my own, the commander will see that before it's too late."

"And I doubt he'll fry his daughter's intended mate," Fara said.

"I am no longer that person."

"You broke it off?" Fara asked.

Tahlia shut her eyes and prayed to the Old Ones. Her heart

thundered and cracked. "You have to go. I can't let you die for me." She opened her eyes and bit her lip, wishing with everything inside her that this had all gone differently.

"I ended a relationship that was started for the wrong reasons. I'll explain everything either here if we are spared or in the afterlife if we are so lucky as to be given it."

"Tahlia of Northwoods," Commander Gaius said, his voice monotone, "you are stripped of your false title and deemed a lying human traitor, a blemish on the mountain, undeserving of your time in our ranks." He came closer and rubbed his hand over his face. "Marius," he whispered, "stop this nonsense."

Marius raised his chin and all the emotion left his features. He could have been carved of marble.

A whispering sifted through those gathered to witness Tahlia's death, and then Queen Revna stood beside Ophelia. King Lysanael nodded to Titus and Ophelia and joined his mate.

The stable hand holding the Terror looked to Commander Gaius, who nodded and stepped back, his shoulder brushing his daughter's and his eyes squinted as if he barely wanted to watch.

The stable hand set a fist on the Green-flanked Terror's left foreleg and bumped the scales twice. Blinking and focusing on Tahlia, the Terror raised his head and opened its great maw.

Tahlia held her breath. Fara and Marius took her hands in theirs. Tears pricked at her eyes and her pulse beat the rhythm of a funeral march.

I'm sorry I couldn't send you gold or help you eat like kings, she prayed silently, thinking of her mother and even her less-than-fantastic father. *Old Ones, please bless the souls of these two who stand with me...*

A roaring sounded and the Seabreak Tahlia had ridden flew over the courtyard wall, a stable hand calling out behind her. The cyan-scaled beauty pushed her way past the Terror, who growled low in his throat. The Seabreak put herself between the Terror and Tahlia.

"Stop!" Queen Revna's strong and accented human voice echoed across the courtyard. Why was the king nodding at his mate?

The Terror's stable hand set an open palm on the dragon's shoulder and the beast lowered his head.

"The Seabreak has bonded to her, hasn't she?" The queen gestured toward Tahlia and the female dragon. "You can't deny that. Why would a mountain dragon choose a lesser rider? Mountain dragons are known to be quite particular about their bonds, aren't they?"

"A mountain dragon wouldn't bond with anyone they didn't consider the finest rider," King Lysanael said from where he stood. The cadence of his words said he would brook no argument.

The queen nodded. "And as it turns out, we are privy to information about Lady Tahlia's bloodline that none else here knows. Our informants have discovered that Lady Tahlia's blood comes from a previously unknown Mistgold line."

The ground seemed to shake under Tahlia's boots. What was the queen talking about? That wasn't true. What was she doing? Why was she lying?

Fara glanced at Tahlia. Fara mouthed *keep on praying*. Tahlia did exactly that as the Seabreak leaned over to bump Tahlia's shoulder with her snout.

The Head Bloodworker raised a finger. "Forgive me, Your Majesties, but the testing performed during Healer Albus's work clearly showed there is very little Mistgold in her blood. We do not simply *eye* the blood and guess."

King Lysanael let out a low growl. "Watch your tone with my mate."

The Head Bloodworker lowered his head and stepped back.

"As I was saying," the queen continued, "the Mistgold in her blood reacts differently than most dragon rider blood. It remains subtle and sometimes mimics that of human blood. They were a line of spies for the royal house. My mate and I, king and queen of this realm, decree this as truth."

They were rescuing her.

Tahlia, despite always being the penultimate optimist, couldn't believe it.

"Your Majesty?" she asked, her voice cracking. She wasn't even sure what she wanted to ask.

Fara grinned wildly, and Marius squeezed Tahlia's fingers, his steely gaze betraying nothing.

The queen smiled at Tahlia. "Release this knight and honor her as the newest member of your order. This is a command, just in case you weren't certain." Queen Revna was human. Was that why she'd saved Tahlia?

Tahlia released a long breath, let go of Fara and Marius, and went to one knee. "Thank you. I will endeavor to make this order and Your Majesty proud."

Queen Revna set a hand on Tahlia's head, and just like that, the moment was over.

The Green-flanked Terror and the Seabreak were taken away and Tahlia was left, wide-eyed and unbelieving, as Marius, Fara, and most of the other knights surrounded her with cheers and well wishes. Marius had disappeared in the crowd, but his voice rumbled through the noise here and there.

Commander Gaius shook her hand, a grim smile on his face. Did he know that Marius had broken off the engagement with Ophelia? It wasn't really her fault, but somehow she felt that it was.

"Welcome to the order, Lady Tahlia," the commander said. "I'm glad your bloodline was found to be suitable." His tone said he knew very well his human queen had been lying through her pretty teeth. "I won't take it easy on you though. Know that."

"Of course not, Commander."

"The king and queen will be gone tomorrow and then I will be fully in charge once more. I do not tolerate deceit or give mercy to those who fall behind in training."

"I understand. There will be no deceit from this day forward."

The commander chewed the inside of his cheek and glanced over her shoulder like he was thinking something through. He seemed less happy by the moment. If pressed, she'd have guessed he was glad such a good rider was in the order but infuriated that she was human. And a liar.

"I'll have to learn to trust your word," he said. "It will take a long while, I imagine."

Tahlia didn't know what to say, so she just gave him a winning smile. He shook his head, seemingly as shocked as she was at the turn of events, then he nodded and walked toward the lights of the great hall.

Fara hugged her tightly as the grumblers who didn't appreciate the queen's interference wandered back into the hall to commence the feasting.

"You did it, Tahlia. You actually changed your fate."

Tahlia squeezed her back. "I couldn't have done it without you." She gazed into her friend's face and Fara's smile echoed her own happiness. "I'll be saying thank you for the rest of my life."

"Seeing as how you like to play with dangerous creatures and their masters, I doubt that you'll be around for very long, but I'll take what I can get."

Tahlia scowled jokingly and hugged Fara again.

Marius strode past a cluster of Bloodworkers speaking to the commander. He held out a hand.

"May I speak to you, Lady Tahlia?"

His tone was cold as usual, but his voice was just like that. It didn't mean he was angry or unfeeling. He was simply...a storm cloud made into a male Fae.

But he had just finished a quiet chat with Commander Gaius, so perhaps he was upset about something aside from the other terrifying events of the day. Ophelia must have left because Tahlia didn't see her anywhere. She had to be livid. Perhaps he had his former intended on his mind?

Despite the shock of how close Tahlia had come to shaking hands with Death, she couldn't help but admire the lovely night. Stars glittered like dragon eyes above them and the wind held the promise of summer. They walked away from the stragglers still in the grassy area, leaving the last of the noise as they entered the empty arena.

"I want to apologize for kissing you."

She shook her head. "It was just the crystals."

"Yes, they were quite powerful at that moment and we both must be susceptible to such magic." He swallowed and looked away.

"I was definitely susceptible." Still was. But it had nothing to do with crystals.

Clearing his throat, he kept himself a step away from her. "Regardless, I will be certain to refrain from any such behavior in the future."

Tahlia leaned on the wooden fence surrounding the area where she'd fought with her sword.

"Unless I ask for that behavior?" She raised an eyebrow.

A gentle blush covered his sharp cheekbones. "I... Yes, yes. That would be fine."

"So you'd be all right with kissing me right now if I asked you to?"

His gaze cut across her mouth and her breath caught at the ferocious look in his stormy eyes.

"I was just pardoned by the queen and king. That's a pretty good trick, right?" she whispered. "I think I deserve a kiss."

Dimples appeared in his cheeks and he chuckled softly. His hand swept from her shoulder up the back of her neck, giving her wonderful chills. He gripped her head and looked down into her eyes.

"You need to understand what behavior is and is not permitted when interacting with your High Captain, Lady Tahlia."

"Is this not allowed?" She stood on her tiptoes and brushed her lips over the corner of his jaw.

His throat bobbed in a swallow. "Not at all permitted," he whispered huskily.

Her body warmed. Undoing this stern male was absolutely delightful.

"How about this?"

She slid her hands down his muscular chest and across his flat stomach. His tunic did little to hide the fine lines of his body.

His stomach pulled in as he gasped quietly. "You will be punished for that."

The heat inside her pooled low. "Oh, will I?" Her pulse kicked up, her blood racing.

He slammed her against the fence and kissed her hard, tongue tangling with hers and his fingers in her hair. Tahlia's blood caught fire. She gripped his hips and tugged him close, kissing him back, tasting the honey and clove taste of his mouth and thrilling in every sensation. He pressed into her and she could feel every bit of him. The stars behind his silhouette appeared to spin as he nibbled his way down her neck. She was more than ready for him to toss her down to the arena's sandy ground. Maybe his mouth would find her breasts as she threw a leg over his back...

Someone cleared their throat.

Marius broke away quickly and wiped his mouth. "Yes?" His color was high, but she had no doubt her face was redder.

It was Fara. "I'm so sorry to interrupt, but the knights are asking for you, my lady. The king is looking for you, High Captain."

Tahlia inhaled slowly, trying to stop wanting to throw herself at Marius again despite Fara's presence and the fact that there was a room full of people waiting on them. "Thank you, Fara. We will be in shortly."

Marius gave Fara a nod of thanks and Fara returned to the great hall's pink and golden light.

Tahlia touched Marius's arm and he turned to face her. "Let's enjoy the festivities. We can delight in our own pastimes later this evening."

His eyes glittered dangerously, but the ghost of a grin passed over his mouth. "Agreed."

He looked like a dream she'd had come to life.

"Thank you for believing in me. It's not enough to say *thank you*, but it's all I have."

Taking her hand, he kissed each knuckle. "I'm honored to have aided you, my lady."

Under the blazing stars, Tahlia walked with him into the Mist Knights' great hall. True, she had yet to find out who had poisoned her and there would be hurdles to leap between today and tomorrow, but finally, at long last, she had a home in the place where she truly belonged.

KINGDOM OF SPIRITS

CHAPTER 1
TAHLIA

In the wide expanse of the sunset, wind blasted across Tahlia's face and her braid whipped against her back. Her cyan-hued Seabreak dragon tucked her four dragonfly-like wings and dove through a cloud bank before transitioning into a roll. The dragon's right eye was sore from a scratch received in training yesterday, and an echo of that irritation made Tahlia blink repeatedly. As the dragon completed the roll, Tahlia's stomach tightened, and she whooped, the thrill too much to keep inside. As her dragon zipped by the floating target, Tahlia reached out a hand and smacked the red circle. They had won the day's last training contest. The victory lifted her heart.

"We did it! You're amazing, you know that?" she said, leaning over her dragon's neck and peering through the scattered spikes that defended the creature's spine against attack.

Horns sparkling in the last glow of the day, the Seabreak trilled and blew a puff of smoke. To say that Tahlia loved the dragon would be a severe understatement. When the dragon had a sore leg, a ghost of that pain echoed in Tahlia's body. In the air, they seemed to share a mind. Tahlia had fallen off a few times during difficult spins and sudden turns, but it was only a lack of physical training that had caused the errors. She had known the Seabreak's coming moves. After more practice, they would be as one, and the dragon wouldn't have to worry about making a dangerous catch with her talons when Tahlia slipped off the saddle.

Titus and his pale blue Spikeback caught up. The Fae male shook a fist and grinned, pretending to be angry that Tahlia had beaten him to the floating target.

Maiwenn and her Seabreak—a male dragon larger than Tahlia's female—soared overhead. Maiwenn's glare wasn't visible at this distance, but still, it burned like a brand.

Ah, well, she'd win Maiwenn over eventually. It had only been fourteen days since Tahlia had earned her place in the Order of the Mist Knights and some of the other dragon riders had yet to truly accept her, mostly because she was half-human.

Tahlia leaned on the dragon's neck. "How about a quick inverted spin?"

With a grunt of approval, the Seabreak spun and flew in a tight coil of movement that had Tahlia holding on with legs and hands both. Her blood sang with the joy of being alive.

"Enough playing around," High Captain Marius Leos Valentius called out, his voice carrying above the wind and the flap of dragon wings.

Tahlia's dragon evened out among the wispy clouds while Tahlia kept staring at Marius.

Gods, he was glorious.

He'd tied back his moon-white hair, showing off his proud nose and jaw. His ears were fully pointed because he was wholly Fae, and his dramatically slitted pupils also spoke to the powerful blood in his veins. He had eyes like a true predator—dangerous, flashing, and altogether impossible to look away from.

And he was hers. Or he would be. They'd had one wild night together, then he'd been called up by the commander to go on a mission for six days. During that time, Tahlia had been thrown to

Maiwenn for beginner training. Tahlia already knew a good bit about Marius from the tournament and from the time since he'd returned from his mission, but she wanted to learn everything. And she was more than ready for some one-on-one time with the High Captain.

Biting back a sigh at his beauty, she tapped her dragon's neck and prompted her to land.

All that gorgeous muscle beneath Marius's pale leathers was delectable, and every ounce of that ferocious passion, as well as his lightning-like presence, lured her like the best bait—yes, she had completely fallen for him. Who could blame her?

Tahlia smiled at him and wiggled her eyebrows, knowing his full Fae blood made his vision astoundingly fantastic.

He tilted his head and gave her a good scowl, but she was close enough to see his hand flexing on his reins. It was a tell he had, a movement that meant he was torn between one feeling and another. After hours together in the sky—in the time between her awful training with Maiwenn—she'd seen that particular tick several times.

Her gaze snagged on his hand again and a memory of their night together wrapped around her mind. The heat of that hand of his between her legs. His scent of cloves. The weight of him over her. Whispers of what their future might be...

She shook off those lovely thoughts and prepared for landing, focusing on the job she had to do. The Seabreak spread her four ocean-blue wings wide and caught the wind. They dropped gracefully into the arena. Titus and his Spikeback landed beside them, and then Marius and his Heartsworn dragon alighted in front of the three gathered units of knights.

Marius dismounted his dragon, a handsome scarlet fellow named Ragewing, and he regarded the knights. His gaze barely snagged on Tahlia, but it did indeed snag. She smiled. He might have been quite the stern warrior, but she knew he was falling for her too. Had to be. It was too early to call it anything, but he had stood with her during her struggle to join the knights, and the sparks between them were undeniable.

"Good work up there today, units one and three. Two, you need to keep a tighter line when in the triangle formation. Maiwenn, you still feel up to the position, yes?"

He had named the other Seabreak rider the new captain of unit two after the old captain retired. Maiwenn was a powerful rider, very skilled. Maiwenn and Titus were the best riders after Marius.

Marius served as High Captain of all three units and particularly led unit one, the one Tahlia was in. She was determined to be the best rider in the skies by the end of the summer.

"More training at that level and we will be sure to smoke the northern pirates come autumn," Marius said, almost smiling.

A cheer rose from the knights and Tahlia joined in.

Raising his arms to quiet the gathered knights, Marius said, "Let's celebrate today's training at The Brass Lantern. We can toast our progress with our new recruit." He glanced Tahlia's way, his eyes sparkling with praise that made her stomach flip. "And strengthen our bonds with one another. A tight-knit community is key in times of danger. We must rely on and trust one another despite any differences."

"Aye, High Captain," Titus called out, several echoing him.

Everyone began dismounting and leading their dragons to the water troughs near the public stands of the arena.

"We have to come up with a name for you, darling," Tahlia said to the Seabreak.

The first stars of the early evening glittered across the dragon's ocean-colored scales. Their light cast a veil of silver across her four folded wings, making them sparkle like jewels. As the dragon drank beside Titus's Spikeback, Tahlia splashed water over the Seabreak's head. The dragon eyed her, love shining in the depths of those fire-hued beauties. Tahlia would never stop being amazed that such a massive and dangerous creature could be gentle with her, a tiny half-human, half-Fae female.

Trilling with satisfaction, the Seabreak extended one wing to nudge Tahlia, a show of affection.

"No name yet, hmm?" Titus glanced at Tahlia as he wiped his dragon down with a cloth.

"Nope." And until she and the Seabreak agreed on a name, the bonding wasn't fully formed. Dragon magic was a subtle and prickly thing. Names were as important to them as to their Fae riders. Each dragon had a name that their bonded rider used as well as a name that only belonged to them. How riders knew that second fact was a mystery. Most believed dragons imbued their riders with knowledge through their magic somehow.

"It'll come to you," Titus said. "I have no doubts about your bond." He studied the Seabreak and nodded. "She cares for you already. It's obvious in the way she doesn't shield the underside of her chin from you."

Titus was Marius's second in unit one, the rider who gave orders when Marius was elsewhere or when he was working with another unit. A meaty hunk of a fellow who was quick to laugh, Titus felt like the older brother Tahlia had always wished she'd had. Her real older brother had been borderline abusive. She was glad she'd never lay eyes on him again.

"How about Gertrude?" Tahlia whispered to the Seabreak. The dragon snorted and Tahlia laughed. "Just kidding. Not that. How about Stormwave?" With a growl, the dragon wiggled her snout until Tahlia's arm was slung over the back of the Seabreak's head. "Really? I liked that one. It was Fara's idea." Fara was Tahlia's dearest friend. She served as Tahlia's squire, though she had no plans of working her way into the Order of Mist Knights. "Maybe Coral?" Tahlia suggested. She and the dragon sighed in unison. "Right. Too basic. Well, we will think of something."

"Lady Tahlia." Marius's deep voice startled Tahlia and she spun with fists raised. He lifted an eyebrow at her stance. "That could be construed as an offense to your High Captain, rider."

Tahlia felt light enough to fly without a dragon beneath her.

She fought a grin and lowered her arms. "You can't just pop up behind me like that."

Moving toward her, Marius nearly closed the distance between them, and Tahlia looked up at him, craning her neck to do so. The breath of space spreading from his body to hers filled with a simmering tension. He leaned close to whisper in her ear.

"I thought you liked me behind you, my lady."

Heat shot through her and she swallowed, forcing herself not to climb the male here in front of all three dragon-riding units. She met his smoldering gaze and she could almost taste the salt of his skin on her tongue.

"I'll be at the tavern early," he said. "If you'd like to talk before the others arrive, I'd enjoy that."

Her face hurt from the massive smile spreading over her lips. "Of course. I'll clean up and be right over."

CHAPTER 2
TAHLIA

Tahlia hurried to the assigned bedchamber she shared with her squire, Fara. When she swung open the heavy oaken door, Fara was gripping a tunic and swearing at it. A bowl of water sat on the table under the high window. Soap suds glistened in the light of the wall sconce.

"I don't think you can actually strangle fabric, my friend." Tahlia flopped onto her small bed and toed her boots off.

"It will not release this wine stain and I'm a failure as a squire. You need to go shopping. You can't go around the castle grounds during your off hours looking like a drunken sot."

"I don't care what anything thinks. I'm a knight now. They won't kick me out for a stain."

Her purple face screwed up into a scowl of frustration, Fara threw down the tunic and helped Tahlia unlace the sides of her stiff leather vest. "I didn't plan to be your squire, but I like this position. I don't want anyone to think I'm terrible at it. Your mess reflects on me."

Tahlia chuckled. "Oh, right. Sorry. I'll try not to spill tonight."

"I do have another interest though."

"Other than the dragons and working as a squire?"

Fara nodded. "In addition to being your permanent squire."

"Let me guess. Baking."

Snorting, Fara shook her head. "I could be talked into that. Especially testing our bakes, but that isn't what's on my mind. I have been talking to Healer Albus. He gave me a book about all the medicinal herbs, flowering shrubs, and trees in our kingdom. I've been reading it when you're being insane in the sky."

"But you're not serious about becoming a Healer, are you?"

Fara shrugged.

Fara tended to shift from interest to disinterest in a subject very easily. This was likely just another fleeting moment of curiosity.

"Where are you headed?" Fara asked. "I thought it was an eat-in-your-room night."

Most nights, they dined in the great hall with everyone in the keep. Some days, the staff took time for their families, and the knights and squires made do in their chambers with a tray left by the castle cooks.

"The Brass Lantern. The knights are going to celebrate our day of training. I won the last feat, by the way."

Fara nodded, smiling. "Of course you did. Did it tick off Ophelia?"

"She wasn't in practice again today." Marius had ordered her to take some time to reevaluate her relationship with her dragon because she'd been using these awful spiked gloves on the poor beast.

"Ah, too bad. I would have liked to have a good story about her rage."

"Her rage is pretty legendary from what I've heard."

"Has Marius found out anything else about your poisoner?"

Tahlia chewed her lip, thinking of that day during the tournament. A shudder rippled through her. "He agrees that Ophelia would make a good suspect, but there is no proof. We can't accuse her unless we find some. I'm trying to let it go. I need to focus on training and getting the other knights to feel good about me being here."

"You're just going to let murder go?" Fara raised an eyebrow.

"Sure," Tahlia said, pulling her tunic off. "I'm not dead. Whoever it was failed and now I'm a knight, not just a competitor. They won't try it again." She went to the second bowl of water on their shared table and splashed her face.

"I wish I was as delusionally optimistic as you."

Tahlia dried her face and moved on to her underarms. "Is delusionally a word?"

Fara took Tahlia's second pair of boots from the corner and set them down in front of her. "It is now."

"All right, then. Will you help me with this?" She pointed to her tangled mess of hair.

Fara drew an invisible circle, indicating that Tahlia should turn around. Tahlia did so and Fara went to work on a new braid.

"You need to grow it out so we can have more fun with styles," Fara said, her fingers moving quickly over Tahlia's head.

"I might have black hair like you, but when mine grows past this point, it's a nightmare. Not all of us have silky locks, my friend." Tahlia's hair brushed her shoulders at this length, but it was long enough to tie back.

Fara made a humming sound and sectioned the front of Tahlia's tresses. "I could help you with that."

"Thanks," Tahlia said, "but I like it short."

"Fine. But you could catch an ague up in the cold air without a heavy braid wrapping that head of yours."

Tahlia tried to turn and give Fara a look, but her friend tugged gently on her hair to keep her head straight.

"I don't think that's a real threat, Fara."

Fara's hands paused in their work. "I know dozens of people who have died of an ague!"

"Dozens?"

"Well, all right, just one. My cousin's great aunt."

"You're comparing my ability to fight off sickness with a random great aunt's."

A "humph" came from Fara. "If you are fine with dying, then so be it."

Tahlia rolled her eyes. "If I promise to grow it for the winter, will you stop pestering me?"

"Maybe."

"Probably not, though?" Tahlia asked, elbowing Fara a little in the thigh.

"You need my warnings." Fara bumped Tahlia's arm with her knee. "You don't take anything seriously enough."

"At least you've moved on from warning me away from dragon riding."

"I recognize a lost cause when I see one." Fara's voice softened. "It's truly amazing, what you've accomplished." She finished the braid with a few pins.

Tahlia faced her, touching the tight coils. "Thank you. For everything." She hugged her, not just for the praise and the braiding, but for the way she'd stood by her every step of the way up this mountain. Literally and figuratively.

THE BRASS LANTERN wasn't too loud yet. The night was young and most ate later on. Tahlia walked in and the warmth of the fire across the room cocooned her immediately. Severin, one of the gate guards, played dice with two others at a round table near the front windows. Good thing Fara had stayed back. She'd be over there losing their new income as quickly as it came in.

Two servers moved around the tavern with trays of mead and bowls of stew. Five males and one female huddled at the bar top, their laughter loud.

Marius was sitting at the table where he'd interviewed Tahlia before the tournament. She paused just to watch him, standing behind a cluster of maids enjoying some time off.

Marius held that same scarlet writing book—a tidily bound collection of parchment—he'd been jotting notes in that day. His brow furrowed as he wrote something down, then crossed it out. He switched his quill to his other hand and stretched his wrist. He had his hair down, and a sheet of it draped over his shoulder as he scribbled more lines of black ink. Her fingers longed to touch his smooth skin, to feel the heat at the crook in his elbow and the underside of his strong jaw.

CHAPTER 3
MARIUS

Marius finished his mead, the honey flavor pleasant—unlike his mood. Tahlia would arrive at any moment and he had yet to finalize the questions he wished to ask her. Of course, he wouldn't sit here and read them aloud, but he needed to see them listed out before launching into conversation. If he didn't have a plan, they'd wander into talking about riding and missions. He longed to know her more deeply than that. Lists tended to calm him, but this time, he was far, far away from a peaceful state of mind. His palms were sweating and he couldn't stop fidgeting.

1. If you could change one thing in your past, what would you alter?
2. Do you long to travel when you're on leave? If so, where and why?
3. ...

Three was the problem. He'd written and rewritten it a dozen times and couldn't get the wording right. He'd wanted to ask her about having younglings, but it was a question that could give him away. If he asked that directly, she would see how serious he was about her. He wasn't certain she felt even close to the same way. Perhaps she'd only enjoyed their night together for the physical pleasure of it. Perhaps her heart wasn't affected as his was. Perhaps she would reject his attempts to make her his mate.

"Oh, and what is the subject for tonight's scarlet book of secrets?"

Tahlia's voice sent a thrill through him, and he braced himself to look up and meet her gorgeous dark honey eyes. When he did, she smiled and set a hand on her hip. The feral side of him wanted to pick her up and throw her onto the table right here, right now. Why did she drive him so mad?

"What has the Shadow of the Shrouded Mountains running his hand through his hair and nibbling his quill like a raccoon?" she asked.

Tahlia leaned to peer at his list. He snatched up the little book and slipped it into the soft leather pocket of the simple vest he wore over his tunic. A part of him wished he could wear battle leathers all the time. He always felt too exposed in civilian clothing.

He gritted his teeth. "It's nothing." Damn. He'd practically growled at her. Taking a deep breath, he gestured to the seat across from him. "Please. Thank you for coming before the others."

"I'm glad you asked me to," she said. "Now, what did you want to chat about?"

Marius motioned to the passing server. "What would you like to drink?"

"Is the mead good?" she asked Marius.

He tapped his empty cup. "Very."

"I'll take one, please," she said to the server.

The male nodded, his gaze sliding from her full lips to her breasts. "Anything else?"

"Just the drink," Marius snapped viciously, a snarl following his words.

Tahlia and the server both stared at Marius, then the server inhaled, blinked, and scurried away like the rat he was.

"You didn't have to scare the poor thing to death just for eyeing me up."

"It's not appropriate," Marius said.

Tilting her head, she lifted her pert nose. She seemed to be peering down at him even though he was a few heads taller. "Because I'm a knight or because of some other reason?"

He fought a growl that tried to crawl up his throat. "I, well, both."

"Both what?"

"Damn it, Tahlia."

"Whoa." She spread her hands. "What is happening?"

He shook himself. "I'm sorry. I'm just..."

"You're nervous, aren't you?" she asked.

"Stop looking like that pleases you so much."

She acted at wiping the smile from her rosy mouth. "Sorry. I'll try."

He swallowed and looked at the grain of the table. "Let's start over."

"All right. Are you Marius now or High Captain?"

"Marius."

She touched his hand briefly, then tucked her hands into her lap. Her smile was back and the beauty of it made his heart ache.

"You weren't nervous about flirting with me in the arena," she said.

Her cheeks flushed, but she didn't seem concerned. His mind, however, was a storm. His thoughts whirled, the questions he'd planned and his plans to murder the server with the roving gaze tangled into a grand mess.

"What do you want?" he spat out, immediately irritated with himself for acting like a troll.

"Umm. You'll have to give me some details about what you mean."

Gods, she was laughing at him. Silently, but still. Her eyes said it all. "If you could change one thing about your past, what would you alter?"

Her bottom lip stuck out a fraction, and her eyes focused on the space above his head. "Oh, good question." Her face cleared and she met his eyes. "Nothing."

"Nothing?"

"Every rough experience I've been through has worked to make me the dragon rider I am today. I don't regret the challenges. I would be a marshmallow without them. I know I would. I adore the pleasant things in life a little too much."

Had he heard her correctly? "What is a marshmallow?"

"A square of fluff made from sap and honey and, well, it's a piece of the dessert afterlife if there is such a place. But you must burn the marshmallow to a crisp. Only way to eat them," she said.

"I feel like I've had ten meads rather than one. What are you talking about?"

Tahlia waved off his confusion like one does a cloud of gnats. "What I meant is that I am fine with my past as is. How about you?"

She must have had an easy life before coming to the mountain.

"I can tell from your expression that you think I'm naive. Let me assure you that I'm not. My family life growing up was not pretty. At all."

Pain tightened the edges of her eyes and her hands had balled on the table. He wanted to cover her fingers with his and comfort her, but was that too much?

Needing something to do with his hands, he tapped his cup in a steady rhythm. "I do believe you're right about difficulties in life, but I couldn't give up the chance to have my sister back."

Her open look said she was listening, patiently waiting for him to speak. His chest tightened and he cleared his throat.

"Pirates ravaged our home and killed her," he said. "Bellona was her name. She is the reason I am here. She gave up her place at a healing arts academy to fund my training with the money we inherited when my parents died."

"I'm so sorry you lost her. It's all the more impressive that you managed to rise to the rank of captain after suffering that loss."

"Thank you." It hadn't been difficult telling her about Bellona. Was the only difference that he was confiding in her instead of trying to pluck information from her? He had to laugh silently at himself. He had been treating her like someone he had to question for order business.

"What else do you want to learn about me?" she asked.

"I'll stop questioning you. I didn't intend for this to be some sort of strange interrogation. I'm just, well, I'm not the best at intimate relationships."

She grinned. "No surprise there, big fella."

"What do you mean?"

"You're not the cozy up-and-chat type."

He wished he was.

"But I like you just how you are, Marius. So ask me whatever you had planned."

His heart did a quick triple beat. "You knew I was mapping out our conversation?"

"I guessed." She jerked her chin and eyed the vest pocket that held his notebook.

It was a relief that she was fine with the way he operated. "All right, then, little salty, where would you travel if you had free time to do so? Or are you more of the type who wants to read by the hearth at home?"

Her eyebrows lifted. "Salty?"

"There is a plant that thrives in the harsh, salt-dense soil of the flats outside my hometown. Its true name is the *schrenkiella parvula*, but we always call it *salty*. You enjoy flourishing in difficult scenarios, so the nickname fits in my mind."

Tahlia laughed, and it was the loveliest sound in all the realms. "Fine. I'm salty, but if you're going to nickname me, I get to do the same to you."

"I already have too many ridiculous monikers," he said.

"None from the one you are considering to be your mate."

He stared.

"Don't look so shocked. Why else would you be giving me a rundown like this? It's so you. You like order. Control. You make weighed decisions. Never reckless. It only makes sense that you would want to find out more about me if you plan a repeat of our night together."

"But it was only one night of passion." How would she react to such a pointed statement?

"Oh, no, it wasn't. I felt a connection with you and you felt it too."

"How can you be so sure? We risk disturbing the order by considering one another as a potential mate."

"You considered Ophelia. Is this only more of a problem because I'm half-human and new?"

"Yes. That's exactly why."

"Maybe tonight will help smooth things over? Do you think my whole unit will come?"

He nodded. "I do."

"Because you asked them to," she said, cocking her head to the side.

"Yes."

"The order is lucky to have you," she said. "Do you think you'll be the next commander?"

"It would be arrogant for me to say yes."

"But silly for you to say no, right? You have to be Gaius's choice."

"Commander Gaius," he corrected. Gods, she had to start using the proper titles.

"I thought we were just Marius and Tahlia at the moment."

He was torn between wanting to be casual and easy with her and teaching her the proper way for a Mist Knight to behave. "Still."

She held out her hands. "Fine. Sorry. Commander Gaius's choice."

"He hasn't said anything yet."

"Do you want the position?" she asked.

He took a slow breath. "Yes, but I will be in the sky, unlike him. I would have to run the order in my way, not his. He knows that."

She ran a fingertip from his elbow to his knuckles. His skin pebbled in the wake of her touch and heat poured through his veins.

"Are you certain we need to spend the evening with the other knights?" she asked. "Because I have some pretty solid ideas on what we could do instead."

He chuckled, surprising himself. She made him feel lighter than anyone else. "Can you wait an hour?"

"I suppose." Her smile was the brightest fire in the room.

CHAPTER 4
TAHLIA

Marius opened his mouth to say something, but the tavern door swung wide and the three captains walked in. Titus's bulky form momentarily blocked Maiwenn and Ewan from view. Titus seemed to be finishing a story.

"The dragon took two fingers before the pirate relented and gave up the sack of grain. I told him he was lucky he'd chosen those particular appendages."

Maiwenn snorted. "True." She had a willowy build and moon-white hair like Marius. When she crossed the room, almost every male gazed her way.

Ewan smoothed a hand over his bald head as he grinned. The oil lamps suspended from the rough-hewn ceiling beams flashed in his eyes. Their unique purple-blue color was even more striking against his dark skin.

Claudia and Justus appeared out of the growing tavern crowd too. Claudia had skin the color of the sunset and a long tail. When Tahlia was a youngling, she had been envious of the Fae who ended up with tails. Claudia's whipped around behind her, making her look like a wild forest creature. All right. Tahlia was still envious. Tails were just fantastic.

Justus was a mess as usual. His tunic had a tear at the shoulder and he'd somehow splattered mud all up his tall boots even though they hadn't had rain in days.

Titus, Claudia, and Justus made up the rest of unit one, along with Tahlia and Marius. Though Marius, of course, didn't function as a regular member of the unit since he was High Captain. He just usually flew with unit one.

The barkeep hurried over, his face sweating, but his smile genuine. "Greetings, knights! We will arrange the seating as you see fit and I'll have my best server right over to take your orders."

Marius thanked the man and the group settled on chairs, stools, and benches near two tables drawn together. Soon, they had meads all around, a plate of olives and cheese, and three large loaves of fresh bread.

Tahlia was grateful that her whole unit had come, even if it had been because of Marius's request. She wished all the knights were here, but at least they had the unit two and three captains. She had to get Maiwenn on her side.

"I haven't forgotten about the cliff climb training tomorrow at noon," Tahlia said, leaning past Titus to speak to Maiwenn.

Maiwenn's eyes were ice. "Good."

"How is the training going?" Marius asked Maiwenn.

Turning away from Tahlia, Maiwenn set her jaw. She took a breath. "Very good, despite my misgivings, High Captain."

"And what misgivings are those?"

Maiwenn picked at a flaw in her mug's handle. "I'd rather not say at the moment."

"We can't clear away problems by ignoring them, Lady Maiwenn."

Tahlia wiped her sweaty palms on her trousers. "Just tell me. I'm not afraid of constructive criticism."

"I thought you'd be worthless in the feats of strength and endurance, human."

Everyone froze, Titus with his mug halfway to his mouth and Marius's hand hovering over the olives.

Maiwenn's nostrils flared. "I only speak the truth. She is human. Though she has done well flying and in many of our training scenarios, there is no way she will be as useful as a full Fae when it comes time to fly north."

"You believe Queen Revna and King Lysanael made a mistake in pushing for her survival?"

"No, of course not. But that doesn't prove she belongs in the order. Humans are weak. Selfish. They are not dragon riders."

The silence at the tables rang in Tahlia's ears. Gods, she hadn't thought the female's attitude toward her was that terrible. How wrong she had been...

"I agree with Lady Maiwenn," Claudia said, looking into her mead. "She can lie."

Tahlia struggled to take a breath. "That doesn't mean I will. I can prove to you all that I am worthy."

Marius flattened his palm on the table, then curled his fingers into a tight fist. "You don't have to. You already have. Once you are a knight, you are a knight."

"Unless you defy orders," Maiwenn said.

Claudia nodded. "Or betray another knight."

Maiwenn stared her down. "Both things that Lady Tahlia, with her human blood, could do without batting an eye."

Tahlia stood, pushing away from the table and looking at each of them in turn. "All I have wanted my entire life is to be here, riding dragons. Ask Fara. She has more Mistgold blood than most of you and can't lie. She can tell you. Why would I ever risk losing my place? Can you believe I would endanger the bond with my dragon?"

"You aren't completely bonded yet," Justus said. At least he had the heart to look sorry for bringing it up.

Enora and Atticus arrived during the tense silence.

Enora's freckles stood out on her fair skin. She glanced from Marius to Maiwenn, who was her unit captain. Atticus bent his head in greeting, his silver horns reflecting the light of the oil lamps.

"What did we miss?" he said, crossing his silver arms.

Breathing out slowly and giving Enora and Atticus a nod to say hello, Tahlia reclaimed her seat. "Listen, if you still feel this way at the end of the season. Any of you. If you want me to leave then, I will."

Enora grimaced, her pale red eyebrows bunching. She squeezed in near Ewan on the bench, and Atticus leaned on the half wall beside her.

"No, you won't," Marius said. "You are a knight now. You cannot simply leave. We must work out our differences and grow trust as we fly together."

"Knights have been dismissed though, right, High Captain?" Justus said.

Titus leaned back in his chair, his sharp-edged jaw working like he was gritting his teeth. "It would be dishonorable."

"For her." Maiwenn drank the last of her mead.

"For us," Titus corrected. "Dismissal is a dark spot on the order's history. We choose. We train. We hold fast."

Maiwenn stood up and glanced at Claudia. "We are admitting humans now. Our order is changed. We have altered the rules. The moment our king lowered himself to marry one of them," she said, giving Tahlia a flat look, "the whole realm has gone to shite."

She strode away, Claudia joining her.

Sweat trickled down Tahlia's back. She'd thought the other riders, except Maiwenn, were coming around, but obviously Claudia and Justus were less than thrilled at her presence. She was pretty sure Titus was on her side and maybe Ewan. But what about Atticus and Enora? What about the riders who hadn't even shown up tonight? Marius had led her to believe it had only been a secret order to unit one, so the others weren't in defiance of the High Captain or anything, but they weren't here and their absence spoke volumes.

Titus whistled through his teeth quietly. "Well, that was dramatic."

"Treason usually is," Ewan said. "Will you report her, High Captain?"

Enora hummed. "That wasn't really treason."

"It was close enough," Atticus said. Then he exchanged a whisper with Enora and they both glanced at Tahlia.

Marius's eyes flashed with restrained rage. "I'm not reporting anyone."

Tahlia felt a tiny bit bad about how much she loved how angry he was on her behalf.

"We need time to heal this order," he added. He took a pull from his mug, then set it back down and eyed her over the rim. "We will be stronger for it when we are through this challenge."

Ewan nodded as Enora, Justus, and Atticus murmured words of agreement.

Tahlia had to improve the mood. She hated conflict like this. "If that's done for this evening, can we play some dice?"

Ewan clapped his hands once and laughed loudly. "Aye. Now, this is what I came here for."

A ghost of a smile crossed Justus's mouth, but his eyes were cold.

Marius gave Tahlia a measured look. He had more to say on the topic if she had to guess, but he seemed all right with letting it go for now.

Taking the dice from one of the small bags tied to her belt, Tahlia looked over her shoulder to make certain Fara, who had a serious weakness for gambling, hadn't slipped in. "Let's start the pot at two gladecoins."

"Can we play the night version of Fly or Die?" Atticus asked, grabbing another stool to sit on.

"Sure. Threes are wild?" Tahlia wasn't certain how they played the basic dice game up here on the mountain.

Atticus went over the rules, politely addressing everyone, even though all knew it was only for Tahlia. She felt more of an outsider than ever. She knew so little about the culture here. Maybe she needed to talk to Fara about it. She knew more.

The game went on, everyone taking a turn, losing and betting as they went. The tray of food was polished off. The barkeep brought out bowls of stew and a bottle of crystal wine.

"Ewan, you must have some sort of blessing from the Old Ones." He'd been rolling pretty much perfect numbers. She leaned toward Marius. "You should bet big against him on this round. He's due for a fall, surely."

Marius glanced at her, amusement brightening his eyes. "I don't do *reckless*."

That voice. The low sound of it in that whispering tone turned her stomach into a thunder of tiny dragons flitting from side to side.

"Not even in a game?" she asked.

"Never."

She drummed her fingers on the table. "What if recklessness was the only way to win?"

"I do sometimes act in a way that is not likely to succeed," Marius said. "It's oftentimes required in battle. But I always consider every angle first, therefore avoiding reckless action."

The way she wanted to see him lose control... She licked her lips, blinked, and took another drink of mead.

"Now Ewan," Marius said, "he is more like you, Tahlia."

"I am?" Ewan tossed the dice and watched them land, eyes like a hawk. A one and a five. "Damn." He pushed a gladecoin into the pot at the center of the table.

"You delight in taking risks and perhaps enjoy games a fraction more than the usual knight. Would you agree?" Marius asked Ewan.

Ewan shrugged and grinned at Tahlia. "I guess so."

"Definitely," Titus said.

Marius nodded and slid the dice toward himself. He gathered them and threw his roll. Two sevens and a three.

A cheer went up and Marius collected the coins. "Patient application of probability and reason always win in the end."

"That line isn't as rousingly inspiring as you might think," Tahlia teased.

Marius narrowed his eyes in her direction, but his lips twitched like he wanted to laugh like everyone else was. Well, except Justus, who had gone quiet after Maiwenn and Claudia's departure.

The evening was fun. Marius relaxed and their conversation wove its way through favorite pastimes as younglings to first loves. The riders shared stories of victories and of their first flights.

"Ragewing tried to kill me the first time I rode him."

Tahlia laughed along with the others as she rolled the dice. Ugh. Another set of singles. "Really?"

"He was rather dedicated to my death, yes," Marius said.

"But why would he choose you and then want to be rid of you?"

"Maybe it was a matter of instinct versus desire. His dragon soul called to my soul, as it does in a strong bond. But he desired to remain independent. He was torn."

They played three more rounds, gobbled down a plate of spiced nuts, then everyone broke off and headed to their chambers for sleep.

Marius led Tahlia along the dark streets and through the firelit corridors of the keep.

"I lost some money I didn't know I had tonight," Tahlia said, laughing.

"I might have pushed a silver your way a time or two."

"How naughty of you, High Captain."

He took her hand as they climbed the staircase to his floor. "Would you like to stay the night with me?"

"I thought you'd never ask."

His hand ran up and down her back and her breath lodged between one rib and the next. She swallowed, her body warming.

"Once we get there, you should take charge," he said, his voice silky and achingly alluring in the darkness.

"We will take turns."

They rounded the corner, and he kissed her temple quickly. "Already comfortable ordering me about, I see."

He dismissed his guards and unlocked the chamber door. The scent of Marius along with the perfume of lemons—possibly from cleaning—drew her inside.

"Will you make me a drink?" she asked, giddy with nerves, her body humming with desire.

"Of course, little salty."

CHAPTER 5
TAHLIA

Marius's chambers boasted a grand view of the starry sky. She stood looking out at the silver sparks of light as Marius poured her a crystal goblet of watered wine, then made one for himself. She drank it all in one go, enjoying the slight burn of the liquid down her throat.

"Titus is so good at those mock dives," she said thinking of training. "I need to work on that."

"You'll get there. And you'll get there faster than Titus ever could have dreamed when he was a recruit."

"Thanks, but I don't know." Tahlia ran a finger over the rim of the goblet. "I find it tough to focus on that movement when I have to watch my surroundings."

"You don't quite trust your unit yet. That's understandable."

"I do. Well, except maybe for Maiwenn."

"You don't truly trust the other riders." He drained his goblet and put it on the square table by his ridiculously massive bed. He tapped Tahlia's forehead. "Up here, yes, you trust them, but in here," he said, placing one large finger above her heart, "you aren't there yet. It'll take a battle or a difficult mission for your heart to believe fully in your fellow riders."

"And that's normal?"

Taking her goblet and setting it beside his, he gave her a rare smile. It stole her breath. Sunrises had nothing on a Marius smile.

"Completely typical of a new knight." Taking her hand in his, he kissed each one of her fingertips. Then he pulled her close and held her. She melted into the divine warmth of his arms and the feel of his strength.

"You fly like a goddess," he whispered, his breath hot on the shell of her ear.

Satisfaction curled like a cat around her heart. "You're not so bad yourself."

A quiet hum of amusement echoed in his broad chest.

"Now," she said, stepping back a little and looking him over. "I seem to recall someone telling me I could take charge."

He bowed his head and held out a hand, so courtly and full of restrained power. Want crashed over Tahlia and she took an uneven breath. He lifted his head and gave her a heated look.

"What do you wish of me, my lady?"

"Remove my clothing, one piece at a time. But we will take turns."

With a wicked grin, he began unlacing her stiff leather vest. When it was loosened sufficiently, he tugged it over her head. He reached for her tunic, but she held up a finger to stop him.

"Ah, ah, ah. We are taking turns, remember?" She started working on the laces of his vest while he ran his hands through her hair, undoing her braids and sending the tie and pins fluttering and clicking to the floor. Every sweep of his palm against her scalp sent wonderful shivers down her neck. Together, they maneuvered his vest free.

Next, he unbuckled her belt and threw it down. He slipped her tunic off, his eyes glittering with want. She hadn't worn any upper undergarments today exactly for this surprise moment. She knew her breasts weren't the most luscious in the kingdom by any stretch, but they seemed to do the job, and she was proud to bring out that feral look in such a disciplined male.

"Tahlia..." Marius's voice had dropped to a gravelly tone that usually meant he was losing patience.

"Now yours." She pointed to his tunic.

Growling, he ripped his in two and threw it beside her hairpins. "My lady." His words sounded like an order and a plea twisted into one.

"And the belt. Oh, and go ahead and remove those boots and trousers. Maybe put the boots back on after? Hmm." She tapped her chin, delighting in the way he violently discarded his belt, tugged off his trousers and boots, shed his short pants, then slid his boots back on. He was following her orders, but tension rolled from him in waves that made Tahlia's thighs clench in anticipation.

Another growl issued from the High Captain as he stood before her in nothing but his boots. "You have tested me enough, my lady."

His body was worthy of all the gossip surrounding him. Black and gold inkings trailed down the hard-wrought muscles of his chest and abdomen. It was wild how narrow his waist was considering how incredibly large he was. She ran her hands down the smooth, warm skin of his torso, and he pulled in a quick breath, his head falling back.

"My lady," he begged. "Please."

Cheeks and chest flushing, she set her fingers along his sharp hipbones. Heat flooded her body, her bones going liquid. She eyed one of his more...fascinating areas. "Are all males with Mistgold blood this, umm, blessed?"

He snarled and lunged, lifting her and landing on the bed in one breathtaking movement. His weight sank into her. It was the greatest sensation. He pinned her to the cloud-like duvet with his hips; the pressure from his obvious desire for her threw sparks of pleasure over her flushed skin. A moan escaped her. Gods, he felt amazing.

His lips claimed hers. Then he bent his head to kiss her chest. His tongue flicked over the peak of her breast and around and under, here and there, making her squirm beneath him. She gripped his moon-white hair in rough handfuls. Arching against him, savoring the friction of his body on hers, she whispered his name.

With surprisingly careful movements, he moved on to taking off her boots and leather trousers.

He stopped, inhaling sharply. She hadn't worn any undergarments below the navel either. His mouth came down on her hip, his tongue touching the hot skin there and lower. Pleasure simmered in her blood and her heart pounded so loudly she knew he could hear it. But she wasn't overly worried about it. He cared deeply for her, and while they weren't mated yet, she dared to hope. A little overexcitement on her part surely wouldn't ruin the whole thing.

Kissing a trail between her thighs, his hands wandered around the back of her knees. He shifted her up, closer, and her breath caught. His hair fell over her hips and stomach, tickling her as his mouth drew pleasure from her body like a bard draws music from a lute. She could die now and be happy forever, honestly. His hands slid down and he gracefully took off her socks. His thumb circled the center of her heel and moved upward, eliciting a gasp from her.

"I order you to take command now," she whispered, feeling powerful and incredibly grateful for finding him—her friend, her shelter, her challenge.

A smile like a sword's edge glimmered along his lips, showing his fangs. He bent and lifted something from the floor. He held it up and raised his eyebrows. His whip.

CHAPTER 6
TAHLIA

The milky light of pre-dawn streamed from the high window and poured over Marius's well-muscled chest. Tahlia skimmed her fingertips across his body, her head full of delicious dreams. She lifted her cheek from Marius's shoulder, and he smiled down at her, looking like a completely different version of his normally stern self. His hand cradled her face, his skin warm and perfect. She had definitely perished and moved on to a glorious afterlife.

A knocking sounded through Marius's chambers, and Tahlia growled, sitting up.

"You sound like me," Marius said, laughter in his storm-gray eyes. He slipped out of bed and drew on a pair of linen trousers he had folded by his armoire. "I'll take care of it. You rest."

Tahlia rubbed her face as Marius left the bedroom. "Punch that person for me, please."

A chuckle echoed from the outer chamber, then the door creaked open. Low voices spoke in quick sentences.

Tahlia scrambled out of bed, pulling a small woolen blanket around her and peering out the half-open bedchamber door. The male at the door wore the commander's sigil of the crescent moon and sword.

"Commander Gaius requests your presence immediately. Both of you, High Captain, Lady Tahlia."

Marius faced Tahlia and gave her a meaningful look, pursing his full lips slightly.

She waved a hand. "It's all right. Let's go. I don't want to cause any more problems that might result in you standing in front of a dragon and waiting for the flame." She still could hardly comprehend he had risked that for her.

The messenger nodded to Marius and left.

Marius shut the door and eyed Tahlia. "Yes, you do."

"Do what?" she asked.

Marius passed her, dropping a kiss on her forehead. "Cause more problems. It's your favored pastime, I believe."

Tahlia giggled. "It really is."

Shaking his head, Marius dressed in his leathers and Tahlia did her best to keep her hands off him. Once she was dressed as well, they walked hurriedly down the corridor, past a few other knights and staff.

"So he asked for me too?" Tahlia smoothed her hair back—a lost cause. It was tangled into a knot at the back of her skull. "Do you know what this might be about?"

"No. It could simply be mission information and he heard we were together last night."

"Together." Tahlia grinned and rubbed the spot where Marius's whip had been wound around her wrist. "In so many ways."

He gave her a very Marius look, cold and formidable. She shivered, delighted.

"Lady Tahlia, I must insist you hold your tongue."

"On your—"

Fara and Remus, Marius's squire, rounded the corner and nearly mowed them down.

"Apologies, sir, lady!" Remus bowed low.

Fara's purple face flushed. She grimaced and curtseyed repeatedly. She thought Mist Knights walked around constantly on the verge of murder. Courage wasn't her strength. But loyalty was and Tahlia couldn't have become a dragon rider without her.

"All is well." Marius lifted a hand, dismissing their apologies.

"We were at the stables working and heard you were called to see the commander, so we wanted to check if you needed us to do anything or to accompany you," Remus said.

Marius glanced at Tahlia, who shrugged. "Walk with us," he said, facing Remus and Fara again. "We'll see if the commander requires specific actions."

The males dropped back to discuss the plan Titus had suggested yesterday concerning the upcoming pirate raids in the north.

Fara popped her knuckles and looked at Tahlia, the whites of her eyes showing all around her slitted irises. "How was the tavern? Please only tell me the good parts. And slow down and let me do something with this hair of yours."

"The tavern was good. Except for a few grouches."

Braiding and pinning Tahlia's locks. Fara bent close to her ear. "Are you still certain you want to be a Mist Knight? Because I truly believe we could open up a vicious Leatherworker shop in town."

"Exactly how could making purses and satchels be vicious?"

Fara patted Tahlia's finished braid, then came up beside Tahlia. "We would slay the competition."

Tahlia snorted. "Not literally?"

"No, you blood-thirsty miscreant. With our high-quality skills."

Tahlia tilted her head and clicked her tongue. "Skills neither of us have."

"We will have them."

"I'm not giving up dragons for arts and crafts, Fara."

"Come on. It's cozy in town. Less wind. Fewer things that want to eat you."

"Bluewing doesn't want to eat us," Tahlia said, thinking of yet another possible name for her Seabreak dragon.

Fara wrinkled her nose. "I don't think that's the name. Did you ask her about Stormwave?" She meant had Tahlia asked the dragon. The Seabreak did have a way to communicate with Tahlia. Because they were almost fully bonded, just a head nod or a snort could tell Tahlia what the Seabreak was thinking.

"She didn't go for it."

Fara narrowed her eyes. "Maybe your dragon should try to be less picky."

Tahlia leaned closer to Fara and whispered, "I'm not sure what this little meeting will entail."

"Maybe he uncovered information about who poisoned you?" Fara glanced at Tahlia as they kept on down the corridor where the sunrise was just beginning to cast pink and orange over the windowsills, the walls, and the floor. Fara's pupils were fully slitted because her blood was almost completely Fae, like Marius. Tahlia's were not quite the same shape because she was half-human. During the competition to become a Mist Knight, that human blood had resulted in someone poisoning her and had landed her in front of the execution dragon to be roasted. Thankfully, she had come through after a twist-turn of events.

"I would love it if the commander had some information." An uneasy feeling crawled through Tahlia's stomach. She wanted to find out, but if it hadn't been a competitor who was now long gone, off the mountain, then the poisoner was still here.

The corridor opened into the keep's foyer. The home to the Order of the Mist Knights was more mountain than hand-built structure. Towers rose from rough stone and massive crystals—some as clear as a summer day and others of rosy pink, sage green, ocean blue, gold, and indigo—crowned the castle at various entrances and balconies.

The stained glass and crystals scattered light across the foyer's tapestries and wide stone steps. The rose-hued crystals had given Marius and Tahlia some delightful trouble toward the end of the competition. An earthquake in the valley had activated them. Since Marius and Tahlia had a natural attraction to one another, the crystals' mating magic, which was usually reserved for dragons, had poured over Tahlia and Marius, bringing them together more quickly than was normal.

Tahlia didn't regret it one bit.

Beyond the keep's foyer, the great hall bustled with activity. The water clock chimed the hour as they crossed the tiled floor and headed for the first of three corridors. Two guards opened double doors leading to the platform that worked on a pulley system to reach the commander's chambers.

The guards nodded in respect to Marius and Tahlia. The taller of the two glanced at Remus and Fara. "Only the High Captain and Lady Tahlia have been invited."

"I'll see you at the stables?" Fara asked Tahlia.

"Sounds good," Tahlia said.

Fara gave them each a curtsey, then left.

Remus gave Marius and Tahlia a bow and followed Fara.

As soon as the squires were gone, Tahlia asked the question burning her tongue. "Do you think the commander has information about the poisoner?"

Light from the passing floors blinked across the small space.

"That is my dearest wish, I assure you," he said. "It would make sense considering he has invited you."

"But it could be about..." Tahlia wiggled her eyebrows.

"Perhaps," he said, looking straight ahead as the platform trembled slightly and lifted them higher and higher.

He had his serious face on again, back to being the High Captain.

She slid a hand over his thigh and watched the next floor pass by. He tensed, and in her periphery, he shot her a reprimanding look. It was only encouraging really. She dragged her palm higher on his leg. His large fingers closed over hers, sending sparks up her arm, then he moved her hand to her thigh. She fought a smile. Breaking through his orderly way of life was her second-favorite activity. Of course, dragon riding was number one.

A memory of the first time they'd met flashed through Tahlia's mind. Marius had been standing with Ragewing in the arena, his Fae-white hair lifting slightly in the breeze, the muscles along his exposed arms rolling under his sun-touched skin. His gaze had been that of a hawk's, focused and deadly serious. Immediately, the urge to ruffle his feathers, to break that concentration, had surged inside her. She'd wanted to see him undone a little and that was even before she knew that he was the great Shadow of the Shrouded Mountains, a figure that meant death for anyone who dared to cross the border without good cause and the male who had ripped apart scores of pirate crews and their ships with his exacting strategy and fierce courage. Once she'd realized he was the High Captain, that urge had only grown stronger.

The memory of the first time they'd shared a bed shot heat from her heart to her core. Closing her eyes briefly, she pulled in a shaky breath. Images of his hawk-like gaze near her inner thigh flickered behind her eyes. *I promised punishment for your impertinence,* he had whispered teasingly over her skin as a spark of mischief lit his stormy eyes.

A shiver of desire had crashed over her like a wave. *And what did you have in mind, High Captain?* she had said back. The warmth of his hand sliding up her stomach to cup her breast had been divine, and the way he'd cradled the back of her head and spoken ever so softly into her ear...

The platform came to a stop. Two more guards stood at the door. They bowed their heads as Marius and Tahlia exited, leaving the platform and its echoing shaft. Tahlia glanced at Marius, who gave her a quick wink. She couldn't fight the wide smile that tugged at her lips.

The guards, dressed in Gaius's crescent moon and sword livery, opened the commander's door and stood back for Marius and Tahlia to enter. Tahlia removed her gladius and sheath from her belt and stowed them by the front entrance near a decorative amphora mounted into a wooden frame. Sitting for any length of time with a sword attached to one's waist was awkward. Marius kept his on. Of course, he was used to wearing it since he'd been in the order for years.

Commander Gaius sat in a low-backed, velvet-upholstered chair by the thick glass of his large window. The window looked out on the grounds—the courtyard beyond the foyer, the wall where Marius had first kissed Tahlia under the crystals' influence, and the manicured lawn that led to the cliff edge that the knights sometimes used for takeoff.

Gaius stood as they approached, and they bowed and curtseyed. The commander's normally flushed face was oddly pale, but his hair was still as full as ever, mostly covering his dramatically pointed ears. He nodded to them.

"I understand today is your free day," he said, "so I won't take up much of your time. To put it bluntly, I have a personal request."

Personal? Tahlia glanced at Marius, but his focus was on the commander.

Gaius paced, the sunlight washing over the black tunic he wore when not on duty. "It's Ophelia."

Tahlia's gut twisted. Ophelia, Gaius's daughter, rode in Tahlia's unit, but she'd been out of action ever since Marius reprimanded Ophelia for using spiked gloves on her Green-flanked Terror. And there was also the whole Tahlia-inadvertently-broke-up-their-engagement thing. Tahlia shifted on her feet, but Marius remained as still as stone.

"My daughter still hasn't properly bonded with her dragon, but that moment is not far off."

Marius's eyes and mouth twitched like he wanted to argue, but he held his tongue.

Gaius halted his pacing and stared Marius down even though he was shorter than him. “She remains unhappy with the way your engagement ended, Marius. I can’t say that I blame her.”

“I apologize for the way I handled that,” Marius said to Gaius, his tone sincere.

Marius then glanced at Tahlia, but she wasn’t about to say anything close to sorry.

He must have been able to tell she wasn’t going to apologize because he squeezed his eyelids shut. The muscle in his jaw worked the way it did when he was frustrated, but his eyes opened to show the smallest twinkle of amusement.

She hadn’t planned to fall for Marius, and Ophelia had done her best to keep Tahlia from the order. Ophelia was probably the one who had poisoned her, though Tahlia had zero proof of that. Plus, Ophelia had been cruel to her dragon. Anyone who treated animals poorly deserved to die in Tahlia’s not-so-humble opinion.

“I accept your apology,” Gaius said to Marius, “but I request that you two keep yourselves, how should I say this… I request that you hold off on your potential mating bond until Ophelia has had time to work through this difficult time.”

Potential mating bond. Tahlia wanted to jump in the air and sing a song. But did Marius feel that way toward the idea of their future?

It was silly that Gaius was asking her and Marius to keep a distance. Ophelia was no delicate flower. Was she truly struggling? Tahlia couldn’t imagine the proud full Fae female who rode one of the most terrifying creatures in the world being broken by anything.

“Of course, sir,” Marius said.

“As you wish, Commander,” Tahlia said.

“I must ask,” Marius started, “have you gleaned any information about who poisoned Lady Tahlia from your informants?” His nostrils flared, his quiet rage trying to burst through his disciplined exterior. He didn't seem to be too keen on Gaius's request either.

Gaius pressed a fist against his mouth, then let his hand fall as he gazed at Tahlia. "I thought we had a lead on who meant you harm, Lady Tahlia, but I'm afraid I don't yet know. I will send you any information I gather the moment it arrives."

"Thank you," Tahlia said.

"I appreciate this. Both of you, thank you very much," Gaius said.

They nodded in unison, then left the chamber and entered the now empty platform shaft.

"Oh, wait," Tahlia said, recalling her gladius. "Hold on. I forgot my sword."

"I'll go on." Marius studied her face like he was gauging how she would respond to the order they had been given.

"How long do you think he will ask us to stay apart?"

Marius lifted a hand like he wanted to reach for her, but he let his arm fall. "Not an extensive period, I'm sure."

"All right. Fine. I'll see you later, then, I guess."

"Tahlia, you are the light in my day. We will get through this to whatever waits for us on the other side." He took her hand and rubbed the back of it with his thumb.

A smile tugged at Tahlia's frown and a shiver danced over the place where he touched her. "And you're the storm I like to rouse just to see the lightning, High Captain."

He smiled in full, rang the bell for the guards below to work the pulley, and disappeared.

Tahlia returned to the commander's chamber, hoping to slip in and out without notice. She didn't want any more awkward chats with Gaius about Marius or Ophelia. The guards nodded to her and permitted entry.

Inside the front entrance, she bent to retrieve her gladius. A shadow flickered in her periphery. She glanced up to see Ophelia emerge from another room, blue-green hair tightly woven around her head. Ophelia headed toward the back corridor of the apartment. She didn't seem to have noticed Tahlia, thank the Old Ones. Dark swirls and star-white sparks spun along Ophelia's left hand, and an odd floral scent wafted through the chambers. Tahlia blinked and rubbed her eyes. When she looked again, the swirls and sparks were gone. Had she just hit her head too hard in training yesterday? Surely. There wasn't any magic that appeared like that, was there?

She attached the sheathed gladius to her belt and took her turn on the platform, her mind whirling with thoughts of Ophelia, poison, and the fact that she wouldn't get her hands on Marius anytime soon. Gritting her teeth, she headed toward the dragon stables to find Fara and update her on all the goings-on before they had to start on their laundry.

Maiwenn caught her at the entrance to the stables. "Since we are free today, you're going to train with me."

Damn it. She had hoped Maiwenn had forgotten. "Unfortunately, I have laundry to do. I know, so domestic."

Unblinking, Maiwenn didn't crack a smile. "We aren't doing the cliff climbing. I have something else in mind. Meet me in the arena. Now."

Ugh. And this day had started so nicely...

CHAPTER 7
TAHLIA

Tahlia climbed onto her Seabreak's shoulder, holding the edges of the dragon's scales as she moved toward the saddle.

Maiwenn was already mounted on her male Seabreak, Donan. He flapped his four wings, a larger version of the female's set, and huffed into the air. The show of dominance was wasted on Tahlia's dragon. She pranced past him, head high and wings extended like she didn't see him as any sort of leader.

Already sweating, Tahlia took the reins and wished with everything her dragon would curb her rebellious nature for the afternoon. Maiwenn was already going to be horribly mean. She'd proven that in their other training sessions. Tahlia didn't need anything making Maiwenn even less pleased with Tahlia's existence.

"Follow me," Maiwenn said, her Mistgold blood raising her words' volume so that her voice echoed through the arena.

Tahlia and her dragon took off as ordered. A bank of clouds soaked Tahlia's face and made the saddle slick beneath her. She should have kept her bottom firmly set, but it was tough when

Donan flew so fast and Tahlia's dragon was trying to display that she had no problems keeping up.

"You'll lose me if you fly like a maniac, darling," Tahlia said to the Seabreak.

The Seabreak broke through the bank of cover and the sun glittered across her lovely horns.

"First," Maiwenn said as Donan wheeled around to face them, making Tahlia's mount rear and list to the side, "we will run a triangle with an imaginary third. On my count... Three, two, one!"

Donan was a slash of ocean blue in the pale wash of the sky. Tahlia's dragon roared in frustration that Tahlia felt like an itch just beneath her skin. They were not in formation no matter how Tahlia imagined said third rider and dragon.

"She can't fly that fast, Maiwenn. She's trying!"

Maiwenn had Donan turn sharply and they flew overhead, their shadow throwing Tahlia and her dragon into darkness. "Sorry, I can't hear your weak human voice," Maiwenn called out, using that power that only those with hefty amounts of Mistgold in their blood possessed. "Shout louder maybe?"

Tahlia wanted to flip her off and fly away, but she bit her tongue and tapped her Seabreak's neck, urging the dragon to take up one point of the triangle formation.

Before they flew in the right position, another rider burst from the thick strip of clouds.

Tahlia's heart stuttered, and she drew the reins back to slow her dragon. Maiwenn had Donan pause too; her face was unreadable.

Ophelia.

The female's blue-green hair whipped in the wind. "Good afternoon, riders."

Her Green-flanked Terror snarled and flapped its ratty-edged wings to hover in place.

"Lady Ophelia," Maiwenn said, nodding respectfully.

Gods, how Tahlia wanted to strangle Ophelia. She'd sleep better at night, that was for sure.

And why was Maiwenn acting like they needed to show extra respect for Ophelia? They were all of the same rank. Was Maiwenn behaving that way simply because Ophelia was Commander Gaius's daughter?

Tahlia jerked her chin in a reluctant greeting. She'd be damned if she bowed her head to the one who had likely poisoned her.

Ophelia's grin sent a shiver through Tahlia. "Let's see that triangle formation you were sadly attempting again, shall we?" Ophelia called out.

"No problem." Tahlia's throat burned from trying to shout as loudly as possible over the wind and across the distance between the three riders and their mounts.

Ophelia cocked her head. "I'm so sorry. You'll have to say that again. Didn't catch it."

Tahlia waved her off.

Ophelia shrugged. Maiwenn's Donan took off like a shot. Ophelia's Green-flanked Terror took up the lead spot in the formation with ease, but Tahlia's Seabreak flew hard and couldn't quite hit the right mark. The dragon's sides heaved as she struggled to speed up.

"It's too fast," Tahlia shouted out. "She's not big enough."

"Or is her rider too clumsy?" Maiwenn called back.

So they could hear Tahlia, at least some of the time. She gritted her teeth. It was one thing to bully Tahlia, but they were treating her dragon poorly too.

"You are perfect. They are just being ridiculous," Tahlia said, doing her best to aim her words toward the dragon's ear. The Seabreak twisted its ear toward her, so hopefully she heard and understood.

"Order a new formation, Tahlia!" Maiwenn commanded.

Would double square be a good one? They would still be missing a rider, but it was one they practiced less, so perhaps that would be a good challenge. Or bow and arrow? Then she could call out a drop, which would be easier on her smaller dragon.

"Bow and arrow!"

Maiwenn and Ophelia remained in triangle formation as if they hadn't heard her. The wind had risen, so maybe they weren't just being pricks this time.

"Bow and arrow, then drop on a five count!" Tahlia shouted, trying again.

Ophelia turned her way and blasted forward, taking up the arrowhead point. "Bow and arrow, drop at five!" she shouted in Maiwenn's direction.

Maiwenn steered Donan and soon they were parallel with Tahlia and her mount.

"One, two, three, four..." Tahlia whispered to herself.

She pressed her palm against the Seabreak's scales and the dragon dove. The blue beauty tucked her wings tight and she zipped toward the arena, outpacing Ophelia and forcing the Terror to adjust his head and wings to decrease the influence of the wind on his speed. Ophelia looked over her shoulder and gave Tahlia a smile full of threats. Tahlia swallowed and focused on the quickly approaching ground.

"And up now," Maiwenn ordered.

Tahlia's and Ophelia's mounts moved in sync, drawing their wings wide and using the airspeed to flip directions. Tahlia's body lifted from the saddle, wind whooshing under her and trying to pull her away. She forced her heels down in the stirrups and tightened the hold her legs had on the dragon's mounded spine. The Seabreak turned her head to eye Tahlia and they lost altitude.

"Go on! I'm fine!" Tahlia smiled in what she hoped was an encouraging spirit even though it probably looked like she was about to vomit, which she was.

They caught up and ran three more formations and simulations. Justus and his Spikeback, Longfire, joined them. Every time Tahlia was ordered to run a mock scenario, she had to use hand signals. They either truly couldn't hear her or they were trying to prove the point that half-humans shouldn't be in the sky with them. She could have sworn all three of them were getting her directions wrong on purpose. At one moment, Justus had Longfire blow third fire—a lower level of flame but still rough and not at all what Tahlia had commanded. The fire nearly scorched her Seabreak. Tahlia's blood boiled.

When Maiwenn at last called for landing, Tahlia and her dragon were winded and gasping. On shaky legs, Tahlia dismounted. She leaned against the Seabreak and ran a hand down the dragon's quickly moving ribs.

"I am sorry they are acting like fiends. It's my fault, and I hate that you're being dragged into this."

The dragon twisted and snuffed into Tahlia's hair, blowing her wind-tangled braid even more out of its pins and ties. Tahlia reached up and scratched the Seabreak under the chin. A deep trill vibrated through the softer scales there and Tahlia's anger and frustration fled in the wake of knowing this majestic creature cared for her and didn't blame her for anything.

Footsteps sounded behind her, and Tahlia turned to see Maiwenn, Ophelia, and Justus looking at her like she was a piece of dragon dung.

"You see?" Maiwenn put a hand on her hip and shook her head. "The fact that you don't have Mistgold blood and aren't even fully Fae means you are a weak link in our unit. I am not trying to hate on you for fun. It's not your fault you're tainted with inferior blood. You can't choose your birth. But it's a fact. And it will get some of us killed. I'd swear on it."

Ophelia's gaze traveled up and down Tahlia as if she was sizing her up for a physical fight. "Where are you from? Don't lie this time, human."

"Northwoods was a lie?" Justus asked.

"It was," Tahlia admitted. She'd indeed lied when she'd competed for her place. She'd told them she was the Lady of

Northwoods, a completely imagined name and title. "I was born south of the capital."

Justus's eyes widened.

Ophelia held out a hand. "So you weren't even born near the Shrouded Mountains."

"That doesn't surprise me," Maiwenn said.

"But some of the other riders weren't born here," Tahlia argued.

"They had parents who were and were only temporarily relocated because of their landholdings."

Nodding, Ophelia continued, "You can't possibly fit in with the order. You know nothing of our culture or our ways. The order must function as one body. I am sometimes a fist while Titus is our eyes and Maiwenn serves as a wing."

Tahlia frowned. Ophelia was very good at being horrible, but not so great at metaphors. "Right. It's true. I'm learning. I mean, it's only been fourteen days or so..."

Her glare said she didn't care about the short timeframe. Of course not. That would have been reasonable.

"What festival do we celebrate silently at the end of the year? What sacrifice is required during said festival?"

Tahlia had no clue. She had been studying the Shrouded Mountain culture, a niche community in the Realm of Lights that did indeed do things differently from everyone else. But she hadn't had enough time to learn everything. "I don't know."

"I appreciate you being truthful," Maiwenn said, her tone painfully reluctant. "Do you have any clue about our great library and the ancient magic and history stored there? Have you studied any of the archives yet? Or are you spending most of your free time—"

She abruptly cut herself off, glancing at Ophelia and appearing to decide not to mention Marius. At least, that was Tahlia's guess.

"I thought the only magic came from the crystals and the

vaguely understood power stirring in the dragons' blood and in yours," Tahlia said.

Justus raised an eyebrow. "We used to work Unseelie magic here."

"You did?"

"It was outlawed and for good reason," Maiwenn said. "But you need to know these things. Our sacred days. The proper way to behave as a representative of our mountain. The dangers hiding in our history."

She was mean-spirited, but Tahlia couldn't fault her logic. Ignoring Ophelia's insanely creepy stare, Tahlia addressed Maiwenn. "You're right. I am trying."

"Try harder."

Tahlia glanced at Ophelia who was now looking at her own hand. A red scar, like something she'd received recently, marred her palm.

"Can I go now?" Tahlia asked, directing the question to whomever was really running this show.

Maiwenn gave Ophelia a frown, then faced Tahlia. "Yes, but don't get comfortable. I might send for you."

Justus glared, his gaze like a burn.

Fantastic. Tahlia would probably be in the bathing rooms when Maiwenn popped up again to torture her. Surely, the riders who weren't thrilled with Tahlia's presence would all get over it soon, right?

DURING TAHLIA'S laundry time an hour later, alarm bells rang through the castle grounds.

CHAPTER 8

TAHLIA

In Tahlia and Fara's bedchamber, Fara threw down the tunic she'd been folding. "What is happening?"

"How would I know?" Tahlia asked, tossing a neat stack of socks onto the bed before rushing to the door. "I've been with you, dear friend. Or did you forget I was here in the excitement of our laundry party?" She squeezed out her damp hair with a square of linen as they hurried into the corridor.

Most knights had a servant in addition to a squire, but Tahlia didn't have the funds. Payday hadn't come up yet, as she'd only been a knight for a handful of days, so they had to do their own chores either before sunrise and training began, well after the dinner hour, or during the rare instance of free time.

Fara ran beside Tahlia, her dark lavender face flushed. "I thought maybe you would know something about the emergency through your dragon."

They pounded down the stairs.

"Sadly, no," Tahlia said.

"Maybe it's only a drill. Just to see if we can exit the keep quickly and safely."

"Sure. The order is usually all about keeping everyone safe and cozy."

Fara let out a groan that was part whine as she grasped Tahlia's arm. "Slow down. I'm not as fast as you."

"You should be," Tahlia said. "If you consider your blood versus mine."

Fara narrowed her eyes and cocked her head. "Your training is already showing. Plus, I think bonding to a dragon makes you faster."

"Huh. I had no idea." That was fantastic.

The trumpets sounded again and Tahlia's happy mood dropped away.

They hurried through the foyer, jostled by others doing the same. In the courtyard, all the other knights, squires, and castle staff had gathered. Heads were close together and the buzz of worried conversation was nearly as loud as the wind that buffeted the greenery growing along the walls.

Marius stood at the opening in the low wall, talking to two Healers—one of whom was Albus, the male who had saved Tahlia from the poison and who had discovered she was half-human. Tahlia tried not to resent the fact that Albus had reported her. It was his job, after all.

Tahlia and Fara went to stand by the rest of unit one.

"What is this all about?" Tahlia asked Titus, whose arms were crossed as he studied Marius.

Titus glanced at Tahlia and Fara and nodded in greeting. "The High Captain hasn't said anything yet. But it can't be good."

Dread slithered up Tahlia's spine.

Marius cleared his throat and clasped his hands behind his back. "I have terrible news to report. I never thought this day would arrive so soon. Our Commander Gaius is dead."

Tahlia gripped Fara's hand as a chill swept down her back.

No. They'd just seen Gaius a few hours ago. He had been upset, maybe a little pale, but he had seemed as healthy as anyone.

"It has to be a mistake," Fara said quietly. "Right?"

The other knights grew eerily silent, a mark of how shocked they were.

Marius showed not an ounce of emotion as he addressed the crowd, but Tahlia knew he was crushed. The commander was a father figure to every knight in the Order of the Mist Knights.

Fara chewed her thumbnail and looked wide-eyed around the hushed crowd. "...has to be a mistake."

"High Captain Marius doesn't make mistakes," Claudia said from the other side of Titus.

Marius touched the ring of black adamant he wore on his smallest finger. His steely stare found Tahlia. Her heart jumped, and she expected him to give her a meaningful look, but he grimaced and turned away as if the sight of her hurt him.

He cleared his throat and addressed the crowd again. "Our Healers say that his death happened mid-morning. They don't know the cause, only that there was no obvious wound despite the blood found at the site. Lady Ophelia reported his door was locked and that he wasn't answering her knocking or shouts from outside. She called out, and..." Marius's hand strayed to that ring again and he covered his mouth and cleared his throat once more. "And the castle guards worked the door open."

A twinge of unease bit at Tahlia's heart. Ophelia hadn't been able to get through the door? But she had been there already when Tahlia and Marius had met with Gaius. Had she left and then been unable to return? The commander's door had been unlocked when Tahlia had been there, the chambers open to those people the guards permitted onto the platform.

Titus stepped away from the others and weaved through the churning group of Fae, no doubt heading for Marius.

Tahlia looked around the crowd on tiptoe. "Where is Ophelia now?" she whispered to Fara. "Do you see her anywhere?"

The wind whipped across the courtyard and the scent of rain filled the air.

Fara began searching too, craning her neck to see past Justus's wide frame. "I don't. But she hasn't been around lately anyway, right? She hasn't yet returned to training?"

"Not regular training," Tahlia said, "but she showed up for my session with Maiwenn."

"Why didn't you tell me?"

"I honestly didn't want to dwell on it."

Fara clicked her tongue and pursed her lips. "Laundry is preferable to those two, yes."

"Exactly."

"But why are you asking if I saw her here?"

"Because earlier, before our terrible and oh-so-special training, I saw her in the commander's chambers."

Fara frowned. "You did?"

Marius had started laying out the plans for the funeral, his voice strained with cloaked grief. "...and we will host a Blessing Procession here for the town as is called for considering his position."

Tahlia tilted her head toward Fara. "I'll tell you more later," she said quietly.

Fara's eyes widened, then she nodded. "Understood."

Tahlia had to talk to Marius. He needed to know she'd seen Ophelia in the commander's chambers. That Ophelia had somehow, in some Fae trickster way, lied about not being able to enter her father's rooms. Granted, that deceit didn't mean she'd killed him... After all, Commander Gaius was Ophelia's father. He had cared for her. She didn't have any reason to murder him. Did she? Could she truly be that unhinged about Marius and the breaking of their engagement? And even if she was, why would she take that out on her father, the male who had respected her enough to ask Tahlia and Marius to hold off on their relationship just for Ophelia's sake?

Tahlia tried to meet Marius's eyes, but he had a crowd around him—Healers, Bloodworkers, Remus, Maiwenn, Ewan, Titus...

Everyone wanted to give their condolences and needed his input on what would happen next.

Fara scowled at the crowd mulling around Marius. "He should have announced the new commander. It would have been in the death documents sealed in Commander Gaius's lock box."

Tahlia's mind whirled. She climbed onto a boulder embedded in the courtyard lawn to get a better look at Marius.

Who would lead the Mist Knights now? The most sensible choice would be Marius. Tahlia thought of her lock box and how empty it was. She had one small note that whatever money she left when she died would be split evenly between Fara's and Tahlia's mothers, but that was it. She had no grand declarations to include and seal up with wax as the notary watched on. That part of her becoming a Mist Knight had been comically simple and quick.

"It'll be Marius as the next commander," Tahlia said, more to herself than anyone else.

Ophelia's blue-green hair appeared in the crowd. A chill wrapped around Tahlia's body. Stone-faced, Ophelia approached Marius, Titus, Maiwenn, and Ewan—all the unit captains.

Maiwenn's eyebrows rose at Ophelia's approach, but why? Was it because Ophelia wasn't showing grief? But Ophelia was a Mist Knight, a trained warrior who could most likely hold back emotions until she was granted privacy. Also, she was a cold hag who probably only ever wept for herself.

Ewan crossed his arms, face unreadable. His dark skin was a stark contrast to Maiwenn's pale complexion. He leaned toward Titus, who had fisted one of his big hands over his mouth, assumably to keep anyone from reading his lips.

Ophelia spoke to the small group of leaders, holding out a slip of parchment.

Marius stiffened and blinked as if surprised by the parchment's contents. His lips tightened into a line and he nodded once, curtly, before stepping back and letting Ophelia stand in front of him to face the gathering.

Titus, Maiwenn, and Ewan moved away, whispering among themselves, their gazes tied to Ophelia.

Ophelia folded the parchment and tucked it inside the pocket of her vest. She raised her arms to call for attention. Conversation halted and everyone—riders, squires, and castle staff—stilled and went silent. The only sounds were the distant growls and mewling of young dragons that carried on the wind from the stables.

"We will mourn my great father at dawn," she said, her voice nearly as powerful as Marius's. "Mist Knights, I am your new commander."

A shiver ran down Tahlia's back and she gripped her sword's hilt. This was the worst outcome possible.

"Surely this is a mistake," Tahlia whispered to Fara. "Marius should be next in line."

Fara's gaze cut to the knights around them and she took Tahlia's hand in the way she did when she wanted Tahlia to hush.

"Meet at the southern barbican one hour before dawn, Mist Knights. Wear your best. My father deserves your respect."

The knights raised whatever weapons they had on hand. Bows, daggers, and swords were lifted high and shouts went up. "Hail, Commander Gaius! Hail, Commander Ophelia!"

Tahlia unsheathed her gladius and joined in belatedly, sweat beading along her upper lip. With Ophelia in charge, she would have to be very careful about talking to Marius concerning Ophelia's presence earlier in the commander's chambers.

When the chant died down, Tahlia dragged Fara beyond the courtyard and into the arena.

"What are you doing? Don't you need to talk to the High Captain?" Fara asked, tugging at Tahlia's hold on her arm.

Once behind the arena wall, Tahlia checked that no one was within earshot and pulled Fara close.

Then she told her everything—about Ophelia sneaking around, about the dagger in her hand, and how it didn't fit with the story of how Ophelia had been barred from Gaius's rooms.

Fara chewed her thumbnail. "If you falsely accuse a commander publicly, you'll be back in front of that death sentence dragon again before you can say 'I'm new here.'"

When Tahlia had first arrived to compete for a place in the order, her half-human blood had set her on a path to death by dragon fire. There was an old Green-flanked Terror whose job it was to end the lives of riders who committed serious crimes. Tahlia shuddered, recalling the dragon's dead eyes. With the help of the king and queen, as well as Marius, Tahlia had barely escaped that fiery fate.

"I'll just tell Marius," Tahlia said. "Do you really think Gaius named his daughter as the next commander?"

"It's an unusual choice, but I suppose it's possible. It would be a tough thing for Ophelia to fake that he had chosen her, seeing as the other captains would have to approve the sealed death document written in Gaius's hand."

There were plenty of ways to deceive without directly lying.

Fara's gaze intensified. "I do not like that look, Tahlia. Seriously, even if they don't put you to death for the accusation, they will banish you from the mountain and you'll be cut off from your dragon."

Tahlia's throat went tight. Separation from the Seabreak would feel akin to losing a limb. No, worse than that. It would be like having her soul scraped out of her body.

Shoving her fear into a dark corner of her mind, Tahlia started to walk away. "I'm going to find him."

Fara stopped her with a hand. "Now?"

Tahlia swallowed. "Yes."

"Be careful," Fara said. "Promise me you won't do anything insane."

"Your definition is different from mine," Tahlia said.

"We are using my definition here."

"I can't always be careful, Fara."

"You are never careful. I'm just asking for you to give it a whirl in this mad situation."

A dark laugh rose from Tahlia. "I'll do what I can."

Fara hugged her close, then released her. "I'm going to eat my way through the market and try to pretend this isn't happening."

"Good plan."

Fara started in the direction of the arena's main entrance, waving a hand in the air as a farewell.

Tahlia knew exactly how lucky she was to have Fara in her life, but Tahlia had to risk telling Marius everything she'd seen. He needed to know. Now.

CHAPTER 9
TAHLIA

The corridors were oddly silent and Tahlia hurried through the passageways toward Marius's chambers, which were situated above the great hall. A stone staircase wound its way up to the next floor of the keep and arrow slits set into the walls let in rectangles of the morning sunlight.

Marius's oaken door boasted a scene that had become familiar. A view one could only see from a dragon's back, the door's carving depicted the keep, the two rings of stone walls that surrounded it, the main waterfall that Tahlia couldn't recall the name of at the moment, and the jagged peaks that ran from Dragon Tail like a dragon's spiny back.

Tahlia lifted the bronze knocker—formed to look like a dragon's tooth—and let it bang down, heralding her arrival.

Marius answered quickly, swinging the door open. His eyes held the darkness of grief, but one corner of his mouth flicked upward as he looked at her. He stole her breath with his rough-edged good looks.

"Lady Tahlia."

His voice was a balm, easing her busy mind and anxious heart.

He stepped back, and she entered his rooms. The scent of beeswax candles and Marius's scent of cloves tickled Tahlia's nose. He offered her a pillowed chair by a small round table that held a decanter of water. She took it and looked up at him.

"I am so sorry about Commander Gaius. He was very important to you."

"To all of us." He poured two cups of water and set one in front of her.

Oh, the way his words broke on the last syllable... Her heart ached for him. "But especially to you, I think."

"It's true." He drank down a swallow and studied her face. "You already know me better than most, my lady."

The sorrow in his eyes pressed against her pulse points, making it hard not to hang her head and weep with him.

Maybe she should, but...

"I have some uncomfortable information," she said, keeping her tone even.

Frowning, he sat in the chair opposite hers. "I'm listening."

"First off, I'm here as your, um, friend, not as your warrior."

"Tahlia, just tell me."

She cleared her throat, hoping this wasn't an incredibly terrible mistake. "Earlier, when we last saw the commander..."

Marius's gaze strayed to a window set high in the wall and his chest moved in a slow, deep breath. "Yes?" Grief shadowed his every small movement.

"I left my gladius at his front door, and when I returned to retrieve it, the door was unlocked."

"But Commander Ophelia stated that it had been locked. Perhaps not yet?"

She held up a hand. "That's not even the strange part. Ophelia was there. In the commander's chambers." Tahlia wasn't ready to call Ophelia by her new title. "She didn't see me, but I watched her leave a back room and head toward the living area with a knife in her hand."

He lifted an eyebrow. "You're certain?"

"I am."

"His death could have been from natural causes, and it could have happened an hour or more after you saw her there."

"What about the knife? And why didn't she come forward when we were there? Also, you would think that Commander Gaius would have spoken more carefully if he'd known she was just in the other room and fully able to hear us talking about her."

"Well, perhaps he thought it wasn't a bad thing to bring up her struggles. Maybe she was ashamed of having her father protect her in the way he did, by asking us to refrain from courting."

"And the knife?"

"Ophelia is never long without a blade to toy with. She is always flipping one or fiddling with the hilt of the Laqqaran dagger she wears at her belt."

Tahlia hadn't noticed that, but, of course, she had only met Ophelia fourteen days or so ago. Besides that, Tahlia's focus had been on Marius more than anyone else.

"Will you question her about it?" she asked.

Marius stilled, his gaze going oddly vacant. His body appeared frozen; he wasn't even breathing. Just sitting there, staring at nothing.

"Marius?"

No response. Her heart gave a heavy thump. She stood, leaning over the table, and knocked over her cup of water. Ignoring the pooling liquid, she reached for his hand.

He rose quickly and he blinked at her like he was just waking up.

What in the name of the Old Ones was happening here? "Marius, what is wrong? Are you feeling all right?"

"I..." He rubbed a hand over his face as water dripped from the table onto the wooden floorboards. "I think so, but..."

Tahlia came around the table to stand in front of him and reached for him again. His arm fell to his side and he looked at her wide-eyed.

"You're scaring the hells out of me. What is going on?"

He stepped back, alarm glaring in his eyes. "I can't. I don't." He gritted his teeth and a growl emanated from deep in his throat.

"Did I upset you? Is this about Gaius? Should I call a Healer?"

Breathing out slowly, he shut his eyes then opened them again. "Tahlia." His voice was low and his words cracked here and there. "I need you to leave."

"What? But—"

"Go."

The command hit her like a kick to the heart. "I will, of course, but you're worrying me."

"Now, Tahlia. Leave." His lips tilted downward, and he fisted his hands at his sides. "I'm sorry."

He was torn. But about what?

Tahlia held out her hands. "All right. I'm leaving. Just promise to send for me, or anyone, if you want to talk. It's fine to show emotion even if you are High Captain, you know. But you want to be alone. I understand that." She gave him what she hoped was a supportive smile.

She walked backward out of the chamber and he shut the door without another word.

In the corridor under the flickering sconces, she stared at the door's carvings as her pulse pounded and her chest ached with the hurt of his rejection.

Was he trying to create distance between them emotionally to honor Gaius's last request—to stay apart until Ophelia was steadier? But the way he'd gone so still... Was it grief? It could shake a person and turn them inside out, certainly. Still pondering, she turned and started down the winding stairs, heading for the quiet wooded spot just behind the keep. She needed to think.

That had to be it—grief had him acting mad. Understandable. Time would help, and she'd give him all the space he required. He deserved to be supported in whatever way helped best, and she'd make sure he received that support. Even if Ophelia was up to no good...

CHAPTER 10
TAHLIA

That evening, the great hall's massive hearth snapped and crackled with flames as servers distributed pancakes fried with honey and sesame seeds, freshly steamed mussels from the river covered in a fermented fish sauce, the pale cheese common in the Shrouded Mountains, and, of course, bread.

Fara was annihilating an entire loaf on her own when Tahlia found her at a seat near the fire.

Tahlia leaned toward Fara and raised an eyebrow. "I can come back if you two need a little alone time."

Fara gave her a withering look. "You riders are mad for getting on the backs of dragons, but I will say, the bakers up here are far more talented than the ones in the valley."

Accepting a plate from one of the servers, Tahlia had a seat beside Fara. The mussels were hot and the sauce was strange but deliciously biting. She enjoyed half a pancake, then washed it down with watered crystal wine.

"Are you going to eat that?" Fara pointed to the other half of the pancake.

"No, please take it. I don't want you nibbling on my fingers if you get hungry at midnight."

"Where have you been all day? How did it go with the High Captain?" Fara glanced at the two squires sitting opposite them, but Tahlia didn't think they were too concerned about anything Fara and Tahlia might discuss. They seemed fully engrossed in their small game of three dice.

"I needed some time to ponder." She'd spent hours walking the trails that branched from the keep and out of the walls to the pine forest surrounding the castle grounds.

"Whoa, I haven't heard that one from you before. This must be pretty bad."

"Well, Marius is definitely struggling with the death," Tahlia said, keeping her voice to a whisper.

Fara nodded. "But did he listen to your, um, to your information?"

"He did, but he wasn't himself. I'll have to talk to him again later. Maybe after the funeral and a few days to get his head on straight."

"Might take longer."

"It might, but I think he needs some space right now."

Fara licked her fingers. "My parents would have died seeing me do this. I am really starting to enjoy life up here in the peaks."

Tahlia patted Fara's shoulder. "I'm glad. I would hate to be up here without you."

Tahlia tried to eat more and push her worry aside while Fara feasted, but Marius's stony face kept flashing through her mind's eye. She tapped Fara with an elbow. Fara lowered a large wooden spoon of honeyed oats and glanced Tahlia's way.

"Yes?"

"Sorry to disturb you and your next true love, but I'm going to the stables. I just want to check on the Seabreak."

"Want me to come?" Fara asked. "I can apply that salve to her left wing again if you think we should." She set her spoon down and wiped her mouth on one of the linen napkins folded at each place setting.

"No, I'd rather go on my own."

Fara smiled and went back to her oatmeal. "Don't get lost."

"I haven't yet."

"Those stables are wild. You could walk around in the passageways for ten years without finding an end."

"You'd probably get roasted before a decade passed," Tahlia said, trying for a lighter tone.

"Most likely." Fara snickered. But she snagged Tahlia's sleeve before she could leave. "Seriously though, watch out for..." She glanced around them. "For that one person."

She meant Ophelia. "I will."

This wasn't a ridiculous warning like many of Fara's cautionary comments. If Marius decided to tell Ophelia that Tahlia had seen her, even if he intended no harm, Ophelia would go after Tahlia. Who would everyone believe was at fault if she and Ophelia ended up in a fight? Their new commander, that was who. They'd have no choice.

No one—save Marius—would risk their bonded dragon for Tahlia. She was too new. She didn't even blame them. No, she had to find proof that Ophelia was involved in her father's death.

Had she killed him? Did Tahlia really think that of the female?

She chewed the inside of her cheek as she slipped from the great hall into the foyer, heading for Ophelia's chambers. She didn't like fibbing to Fara, but she didn't want her worrying.

Stars sparkled across the stained glass of the windows and reflected off the crystals embedded in the stone walls. She crossed the foyer and started up the side stairs.

Had Ophelia killed Gaius? Maybe. Who else had access to him? The other knights and Remus. But this was Ophelia. Evil Ophelia. Yeah, she was the best bet. Before she could repeat that thought to anyone, she had to find proof.

She hid in the darkness at the edge of the corridor that split off toward the bedchambers, the kitchens, and the various meeting halls. Riders and staff passed by, most of them solemn and quiet due to Commander Gaius's death. Once the area was empty of people, Tahlia slipped down the hallway that led to Ophelia's rooms.

The sconces' yellow light drew Tahlia around a tight corner, up another set of stairs, and past a new tapestry showing the wedding of Queen Revna and King Lysanael. The Unseelie King had been stitched into the scene even though everyone knew the two males hadn't made peace until well after the pictured event. Unseelie monsters' eyes glittered with gold thread, and the Unseelie King's skin was shown to be a deep gray with a scattering of dragon scales here and there. Tahlia shivered and kept on. Riding dragons was glorious, but being a dragon shifter? That would be madness.

Ophelia's door, another oaken beast of a thing, was carved with swirls of clouds and stars. Tahlia leaned against the wood to listen. If she was found, what would she say? Perhaps something about condolences. Yes, that would work well enough.

Footsteps sounded down the corridor, and Tahlia's heart shot into her throat. She lunged for the opposite side of the hallway and concealed herself behind a row of hooks and hanging cloaks. Ophelia approached, her mouth bunched and her brow furrowed. She removed a key from her belt and unlocked her door.

Once Ophelia disappeared, Tahlia moved to follow.

Thankfully, Ophelia hadn't locked the door from the inside and the oaken entrance swung open with a creak. Tahlia froze, waiting, hoping she hadn't been heard. The smell of the apartments was odd. Smoke, but not regular candle smoke. This scent was harsher. Hiding under that, a sickly odor hung in the air. Illness? Rot? Mold?

A bang and a shuffle indicated that Ophelia had gone farther in and was moving something large and heavy across the floor.

Tahlia dared to lean around the corner of the entryway. Ophelia's back was to her. She was kneeling and dragging a rectangular carpet into what seemed to be a random spot in the middle of the living area.

Ophelia paused in her redecorating mission and started to peer over her shoulder. Tahlia ducked back and held her breath.

"Lue, is that you?"

Lue was Ophelia's squire.

Sweat rolled down the back of Tahlia's neck.

The sound of Ophelia's boots and the splash of water from farther away let Tahlia relax. She peeked around the entryway wall again and saw Ophelia at a wash basin near a round window. She was cleaning her hands. Tahlia caught a flash of the back of Ophelia's left hand. A slash of gray-black charring showed.

If Ophelia was expecting Lue soon, Tahlia needed to go. She turned to leave, cracking the door open a bit more. Keeping every movement slow and sure, Tahlia made her way into the corridor, then she scurried back the way she'd come.

The sconce near the corridor's tight turn had flickered out. Tahlia ran straight into something.

"I knew it, you little beast," Fara whispered. "Let's get out of here while we're still breathing."

Tahlia rubbed her shoulder where the buckle of Fara's side-swept half-cloak had hit her. "What do you mean?"

"I knew you weren't off to the stables. You don't possess the ability to stay out of harm's way."

"This hallway is safer than a labyrinth cave system full of dragons."

Fara glanced at Tahlia, frowning as she walked on. "Ophelia is the worst kind of monster."

"You're not wrong. But I did see some odd things."

"Like what?" Fara asked.

Tahlia hurried down the stairs with Fara at her side. The sound of conversations trickled up from the foyer.

"The person in question was moving a rug."

Fara faked a shiver. "Horrifying."

Tahlia smacked Fara's arm with the back of her hand. "The place smelled so strange. Like someone had been sick there for a long time. And the chamber smelled like smoke."

"Just because Ophelia has an ague," Fara whispered as they crossed the foyer to return to the great hall, "keeps too many candles lit, and enjoys redecorating doesn't mean she murdered her father. Although I'm here for throwing insults her way regardless. Just not out loud."

Tahlia eyed the crowd in the hall, searching for a certain grouchy High Captain. "Something is off here. I just know it."

Fara reached for the milk and egg puddings sitting in a tidy row on a sideboard. "Well, for now, it's nothing a tiropatina with pomegranate seeds won't fix."

The desserts were fantastic and no one bothered them when they retired to bed, but Tahlia didn't sleep a wink. She hadn't seen Marius the rest of the evening and she could not shake the feeling that she should be working harder to uncover what in the hells was going on.

CHAPTER 11

TAHLIA

At the front of a mile-and-a-half-long line of townsfolk, the Order of the Mist Knights donned full regalia for the funeral and Blessing Procession. The sky still hadn't fulfilled its promise of a storm, but the clouds shifted and curled above the knights. Tahlia hadn't earned any purple tassels for her white riding leathers yet, but she was given a circle of golden laurels like all the other knights. They stood side by side with their squires adorned in dark blue across from them. Tahlia had filed in behind Titus and Ewan, hoping that she'd get a chance to check on Marius with a private whisper, but he had arrived later than the rest and had taken a spot at the very front of the line.

Marius had been late. Marius. The male who had his own water clock, custom-made in the valley and probably worth a small fortune, on his bedside table. The male who was always fifteen minutes early to training sessions and who arrived a half hour before mission takeoffs.

She leaned forward to peer at him. He glanced her way, making her heart triple-beat like she was some lovesick adolescent. Dark circles hung below his stormy eyes and he drew back his lips, showing his full Fae fangs as he looked her way. He wasn't angry but frustrated for some unknown reason. He seemed insistent on gaining her notice. She would be sure to grab him after this was over and see what was going through his mind.

The heralds' trumpets sounded and Marius straightened. The other knights blocked the view of him, so she stood at attention too, ready to give respect to Gaius.

A masked male wearing Gaius's livery drove a gilded cart with the casket lying in the back. Black roses, snowy mistbloom, and the commander's golden laurel circlet sat atop the casket. Tahlia's heart cinched as the casket passed slowly in front of them. Gaius could have further fought her presence in the order, but he had accepted her at the queen's behest. Since entering the order officially, Tahlia had never been treated as less by him. He had been a good male, a great rider, and a strong leader. She truly wished he would have an afterlife fit for the Old Ones.

The trumpeting stopped and all turned toward the Tombcarver, who had obviously been at work since the announcement of Gaius's death. The Tombcarver stood in front of the death monument and read aloud the words he'd carved.

"Commander Gaius Maximus Aeneas, defender of the Realm of Lights and son of the mountain. In death as in life, may you conquer evil and hear your name echoed in the clouds."

The knights knelt, Tahlia following as best she could, then they scooped a handful of the churned dirt beside the cobblestones of the road. She had been wondering why there was a row of earth piled along the pathway. The knights set their handfuls of dirt against their chests and spoke the commander's name as one.

"Gaius, we mourn you."

Tahlia hadn't been taught the funeral process, so she was late to speak and kept her voice as solemn as possible. She glanced at Marius. Unshed tears glimmered in his eyes and her heart broke for him. She longed to pull him into her arms and let him tell her all the stories about the man who had been a father figure to him for so many years.

The rest of the day passed in a quiet blur of conversations with Maiwenn, Fara, Titus, and Enora. At sunset, Tahlia and Fara went to the stables to check the Seabreak's wing. She'd injured it two days ago. Nothing serious, and the injury hadn't hindered her flying, but Tahlia wanted to keep it that way by consistently salving the area and making certain the dragon stretched that wing to keep it from going stiff.

The Seabreak's head emerged from the cave-like stall as Tahlia and Fara approached. The dragon blinked her glittering eyes and let out a puff of black smoke. Joy lifted Tahlia's heart at the sight, a sensation she always had in the presence of...

A name rang like a gentle bell in her head and shivers danced down her spine.

Vodolija.

"What's wrong?" Fara asked.

Tahlia reached out to smooth the top of the Seabreak's cyan-blue snout. "Vodolija?"

The dragon met her gaze and dipped her head. Tahlia's heart squeezed and she coughed, grasping at her vest. But the feeling subsided, and, oddly energized, she took a deep breath.

Vodolija stared at Tahlia, and together, their souls sang with victory.

The bond was complete.

Tahlia grinned and pressed herself against the dragon.

Fara whooped and raised a fist. "You found her name! The bond is whole!"

"I heard it in my head like she spoke it to me."

Wonder hung on Tahlia like a second cloak. She took a plain pancake from her pocket and fed it to Vodolija. The dragon nibbled the treat, then licked Tahlia's palm for the crumbs.

"I have no idea if there is a meaning behind it," Tahlia said.

Fara hummed and tapped her pointy chin. "It sounds like a northern coastal name."

"Agreed. I'll ask Marius about it." A weight settled on Tahlia's chest.

Like he'd been summoned, the High Captain himself strode by and made her breath catch in her throat.

"High Captain!" Tahlia raised a hand, hoping he would act like his normal grouchy, stern self. She wished for that odd mood he'd been in to be gone.

Marius turned, his face only partially illuminated by the one sconce on the wall. His gaze was pinched and his lips moved like he was about to utter something important, but he just bowed his head briefly and greeted them. "Lady Tahlia. Lady Fara."

Fara headed into the stall. "I'll see to Vodolija's wing."

Tahlia stepped closer to Marius. "Are you all right?" He looked like he'd had two pounds of goblinbloom shoved down his gorgeous throat. "I'm here if you want to talk. Or to fly. We could just go for a bit and clear our heads?"

His eyes shut for a second. "I can't. I have... I must leave."

"Leave? Where to?"

"A personal mission."

"I'd be happy to come along."

"I wish that I could welcome you, but I can't."

He extended his hand, then recoiled in the same way he had before. What was going on with him? Was he angry with her in addition to feeling grief?

She looked left and right to be certain they were alone. "Marius, you can tell me anything. And if you want space, I'm completely fine with that. Just talk to me. You are hard to read on a good day. Now it's like the greatest mystery in all the realms just trying to figure you out."

"I'm sorry. I just can't." His throat moved in a disjointed

swallow like he was holding back an unnamed emotion. "Stay here. Please keep this mission secret."

An invisible fist gripped Tahlia's heart and squeezed it mercilessly. The poor bastard. Gods, she wished she could fix this somehow. Make him laugh. Or at least give even a flicker of hope in his dreamy-as-hells eyes. "But, Marius, if you need help in some way..."

His eyes grew hazy and he turned his head, facing the wall to the side and behind her. He rubbed the back of his neck and cleared his throat, his focus then returning to her. "Keep on flying. You will be a legend someday."

She opened her mouth to say something, anything, but he quickly walked away into the dimly lit corridor, presumably heading for Ragewing.

Fara peeked her head out of the stall. "What was that all about?"

"Marius had tears in his eyes."

"Poor fellow. He really cared for the commander."

"Yes. It was so sudden."

"There's a *but* in your tone."

Tahlia chewed her lip. "He isn't acting like he's just grieving. He said he has a personal mission to go on."

"Right now?" Fara frowned.

"I think so. That's odd, isn't it?"

"It's not out of the question," Fara said, "but the timing is strange."

Tahlia shrugged. "Perhaps Ophelia is ordering him to go somewhere, some last request of her father's?"

Fara's eyes narrowed. "Or she is pretending it is."

"I'm going to follow him." Tahlia entered the stall and patted Vodolija, indicating she should move closer to the saddle that sat on the narrow wooden shelf embedded in the stone wall. "Such a gorgeous lady," she murmured to the dragon. She dropped a quick kiss on one of her shiny, shiny scales.

"Will you ask your unit to join you?"

"No, why?"

"Because they are your unit. Your loyalty to one another is tighter than family."

"They don't trust me enough just to go along. They'd ask questions I don't have answers to. Besides, what about all your warnings?"

Tahlia's heart ached painfully at the thought of losing Vodolija. She ran a hand down the dragon's scales and breathed in slowly, just enjoying being in the dragon's calming presence.

"I meant that it could be deadly to accuse Ophelia in front of the other units, the staff, Bloodworkers, or Healers. Your unit isn't going to report you." Fara looked at Tahlia like the very idea was unthinkable.

"You didn't see Claudia and Justus at the tavern. They don't like me. At all. Claudia is tight with Maiwenn, who as we both know loathes everything about me."

"Why didn't you tell me more about that night? I'm here for you, Tahl."

Fara's eyes had softened, and Tahlia's spirit railed against the pity in their depths. Maybe it wasn't pity, but it sure felt like it.

"Because honestly, I don't love whining about people not liking me. It makes me feel... I don't know, Fara."

"It makes you feel weak and you hate that."

"Wow. Yes, fine. It does."

"But just because you feel that way doesn't make it true. You aren't weak because you care about what they think. Being upset about the time they're taking to trust you doesn't make you lesser."

Tahlia's skin itched and she wanted this conversation to end already. "Well, regardless, I can't risk it."

"You have to face them, Tahlia. I'll beat them into a pile of broken bones with nothing but my indomitable rage, then they'll have no choice but to listen."

A low laugh tripped from Tahlia, and Fara scowled.

"But seriously, if you're ever to build that trust," Fara said, "you need to lean into them and tell them the truth. I am the danger alarm between us, remember? So if I'm telling you it's safe to talk to them, it must be, right?"

"Maybe if we'd been flying together for longer than a handful of days, yes. But now? Not a chance. I'm not wasting time arguing when I can just go and figure it out myself."

Fara helped Tahlia maneuver the saddle onto the dragon's back. Order saddles differed from horse saddles in that they had an extra seat behind the main one. Riders could take on injured folk or fellow riders whose dragon had been incapacitated. Sometimes riders used the additional spot for a bedroll or bag. Also, dragon saddles didn't have large pommels and were fairly low profile.

"Well, then, stubborn face, I'm going with you," Fara said.

"What?" Tahlia never thought she'd see the day Fara wanted to ride a dragon. "You can't do that and you know it. Squires don't ride dragons."

"They do in some instances." Fara glanced at the Seabreak, her eyes a little too wide for the confidence she was pretending to have. Tahlia knew well how scared Fara was of flying on dragonback.

Tahlia squinted at her. "You actually want to ride Vodolija?"

"No. Not even a little bit," Fara said.

The dragon twisted and eyed Fara cooly. Fara gave her a nervous smile, all teeth and Fae fangs.

"But if she'll allow it, I'm riding along." Fara straightened and put her hands on her hips. "As a proper friend, I can't let you head off into who knows where on your own, following a scary male who doesn't want you there."

Tahlia's heart turned to pudding. "Aww. You are the dearest friend." She hurried over and gave her a quick hug before going back to helping Vodolija slide on her bridle. "But Fara, Marius isn't going to hurt me."

"Normally, no. But he's acting off."

"He is. He heard me use Vodolija's name, but he didn't even mention it. We've been talking about Vodolija and my bond with her a good bit, so that seems like strange behavior." A shiver of said bond link traveled from Tahlia's heart and branched into her arms, a delightful sensation.

Vodolija nickered and eased herself against Tahlia gently.

"If he's being different than he has been the entire time you've been here, then you have no idea what's really going on," Fara said. "It could be one of a million horrid things! I can at least watch your back and give you some rest at night to sleep. Or whatever. Squire things like that."

Tahlia chuckled. "Squire things. Right. Well, Vodolija might not want you on her back. What do you say, my friend?" she asked the dragon.

Vodolija lifted her head and jerked it down again.

"Wow, all right. She says yes," Tahlia said, giving Fara a wide-eyed look. "You're certain about this?"

Fara grimaced. "No, but also yes."

"What about the million things that could go wrong?"

"There always are that many, really. Another day, another potential moment to die in a flurry of mistakes." Fara shrugged.

"That's the most Fara response in the world."

"Thank you."

Tahlia shook her head as they used the rope to fasten the girth under Vodolija's belly. Fara put out the stall's one torchlight, then they waited, still and quiet in the dark stall, until Marius and Ragewing passed by.

As they followed in Marius's footsteps and left the stables, the sky dimmed, clouds wrapping the stars and moon in black. The scent of rain blew past Tahlia's face. Ragewing was a slash of movement far above Dragon Tail peak.

"We have to move now, or we'll lose them."

Vodolija bent low and allowed them both to mount, Fara

sitting behind Tahlia. Fara's whispered curses weren't exactly calming Tahlia's already frazzled nerves. She'd only escaped punishment by dragon fire a handful of days ago, and here she was, breaking yet another rule, ignoring a direct order.

The Seabreak coursed into the sky and Tahlia prayed to the Old Ones that she wasn't making the biggest mistake of her life.

CHAPTER 12

TAHLIA

"This is officially the worst idea you've ever had," Fara shouted over the pelting rain and thunder.

Tahlia glared over her shoulder. "I told you not to come. This is your idea. Not mine."

Fara buried her head between Tahlia's shoulder blades, which was comical because Tahlia was so much smaller than Fara. "I couldn't let you go alone. You know that!"

"Yes, you could have."

Fara began to argue again, but lightning cracked, and she screamed instead of finishing her sentence.

"Stop digging your fingers into my sides," Tahlia said, turning so Fara might hear over the storm.

"It can't hurt you. You're wearing leathers!"

"Your fingers are worse than arrows. Stop it!"

Fara detached her vicious grip, then wrapped her entire arms around Tahlia's middle. A breath gusted from Tahlia.

"I need to breathe to get us there alive, Fara."

"I'm going to kill Marius. I'm going to strangle him until he is dead and then kick him after."

"That's ridiculous," Tahlia said, the wind biting her cheeks and eyes. She was soaked through and shivering.

"He deserves it for dragging us into this mess."

"No, it's ridiculous that you think you can kill him."

"Shut it, Tahl. Seriously!" Fara groaned as another round of thunder started up.

The storm eventually relented, and the sun pierced the blanket of cloud cover, but there was no sign of Marius or Ragewing. Tahlia had completely lost them in the dark and driving rain.

"What are we going to do? Can Vodolija scent Ragewing at all?"

"I think she still has an idea of where they are because she feels sure of herself and isn't trying to land." Being bonded to a dragon was amazing...and mysterious. Tahlia wasn't certain how she knew what Vodolija was thinking, but somehow she had a sense of it.

They flew on, the sun drying them out nicely as the wind finished the job. Only stopping twice for Vodolija to drink from the river and for a bite to eat, they covered a lot of ground.

As they rose into the air, letting Vodolija's better vision spot and trail Ragewing and Marius, Fara made a growling sort of grumble near Tahlia's ear.

"Other than the fact that I'm completely disobeying a direct order, what is bothering you?" Tahlia asked.

"If I had to guess, we are almost to the Kingdom of Spirits," Fara answered.

A chill rolled through Tahlia. No one dared to enter the lost kingdom. Old tales of vicious spirits and dangerous ghosts had given the land its name.

"I read about a rare plant that only grows in this area. It has blood-colored leaves and was used ages ago to help Fae bond with dragons."

Tahlia wanted to listen to her, but there was too much at risk to have a chat about plants.

“Would we even be able to cross the border of this ghostly place?” Tahlia asked.

There was one story Tahlia had heard at a tavern that involved some magical barrier between the Kingdom of Spirits and the rest of the Realm of Lights. Technically, the lost kingdom remained part of the Seelie Fae kingdom and under King Lysanael and Queen Revna’s rule. It existed within the Veil. But no one went in and came back to tell new tales.

“I hope not. It would be madness to try. Why would Marius even want to enter? Surely Ragewing won’t allow it. Dragons are many things, but stupid isn’t one of them.”

Vodolija growled, her body rumbling under Tahlia.

The Kingdom of Spirits. What could be in that area that involved the order?

THAT EVENING, moonlit mist billowed around Vodolija’s wings, the thick gray blocking everything except a strange distant light on the ground below. It shimmered like a ghostly gold version of those phosphorescent larvae that glowed in the creek during summers at home. It was definitely creepy, but shivers of excitement ran down Tahlia’s back. She hadn’t joined the order for easy days in the sun. She’d risked all to experience this type of adventure.

“I hope you can tell where they are,” Tahlia said to Vodolija, leaning over a bit as Fara hissed prayers that might have been less prayish and more curseish to every Old One and god she could think of. “Because I have no clue.”

Fara sighed. “Please just lie to me and say everything will be fine.”

Vodolija tossed her head and flew onward, showing confidence. Not that dragons ever deigned to show humility or ever admitted when they were wrong.

Tahlia grinned over her shoulder. “I think that’s what the head toss means.”

Fara rolled her eyes. "She could be saying she is about to dump us and go home."

Tahlia laughed even though fatigue pulled at her. It had been a very long day.

The cold air bit at Tahlia's cheeks. The temperature had dropped since sundown. She lifted the cowl she wore over her leathers and fastened her cloak's three extra clasps, drawing the wool tightly around her chest and shoulders. Fara gave her a hand and offered a pair of leather gloves. Tahlia accepted them gratefully and held the reins in her teeth as she tugged them on. Fara cursed the entire time.

Vodolija dove suddenly, Tahlia sucked a breath, and Fara shrieked.

Wings spread wide, the dragon soared toward the ground or whatever was below. The mist and the night continued to hinder Tahlia's view. Would they be far enough behind Marius and Ragewing to keep their presence a secret? If the wind blew the other direction, Ragewing would surely scent Vodolija. Tahlia gripped the saddle's pommel and tightened the muscles in her legs and stomach to prepare for a rough landing. The Seabreak hit the ground even harder than Tahlia had guessed she would and she nearly lost her seat. Fara did. She went tumbling over a wing and landed with a wet smack on the ground.

"Fara! Are you all right?" Tahlia hissed in a whisper as she dismounted.

Fara's chest moved in three quick breaths, then one steadier one. "Yes, I'm well. Thank you so much. Please remind me to absolutely never, ever get on a dragon again. That experience will fill my nightmares until the end of my days." She cursed creatively. "I forgot about the ride home. Kill me."

Ignoring Fara now that she knew she was well enough to whine, Tahlia squinted into the distance.

Beyond two dark hills, a large shape and a smaller one walked side by side toward that glowing light. It was Ragewing and Marius. Had to be, right?

Tahlia untied her bow and full quiver from the back of the saddle, her boots squelching in the mud. "Let's go."

Fara got up and straightened her belt and dagger. "Lead on."

Tahlia strapped the quiver of blue-fletched arrows to her back and started forward, Vodolija beside her with scaled head low and wings tucked. Tahlia nocked an arrow just in case it wasn't Marius and Ragewing, but the closer they got, the more sure she was about her guess.

Fara was pale, or as pale as someone with purple skin could be, and she was too quiet.

"Please whisper a warning of impending doom now and then so I know you're all right," Tahlia said quietly.

"We will all leave here with foot rot."

"There's the Fara I know and love."

What would Marius do if he saw her here? Would he demand she return? Probably. Would she follow that order? She'd pretend to, but no. Marius wasn't like this, someone who just flew off recklessly into dangerous scenarios. He thought things out. He made plans and followed the rules. This secret trip to a region known for its deadly spirits made no sense whatsoever. Marius had lost his handsome mind and Tahlia was going to get to the bottom of this. Besides, she wouldn't abandon him here. Even with Ragewing, the spirits in this forlorn kingdom of old might be too much for him. She wasn't going to leave him just to follow his rules or anyone else's. If she managed to save Marius or solve this problem he was having, it would be worth the consequences.

Vodolija, Fara, and Tahlia walked between the two hills. Marius and Ragewing stood at the bottom of a slope. A break of rowans hid most of Ragewing; only his head stood out above one of the smaller trees.

Like the gruesome teeth of a buried giant, five standing stones set into a rough circle marked the entry to the kingdom. Even though the Kingdom of Spirits was technically in the Realm of Lights and held by King Lysanael and Queen Revna, the old boundary markers had been left in place for safety. No one wanted to stumble into this haunted place. Well, no one but Tahlia's possibly less-than-wise adventurous side.

So for the thousandth time, Tahlia wondered why in the name of all that was holy Marius, a notorious by-the-book type, was calmly strolling up like he'd been planning this reckless excursion for ages.

Ragewing and Marius passed by the standing stones and the mist spun around them, hiding them completely.

"Come on, Vodolija. It'll do no good to sit here and chew our nails over the HC."

Vodolija bunched the scales that served as her eyebrows and huffed smoke into Tahlia's face.

"Okay, maybe you aren't chewing nails, but I do not like how he is acting. I really, really don't."

"That makes two of us," Fara said.

As they made their way to the standing stones, a sound rose on the breeze.

CHAPTER 13

TAHLIA

Fara grabbed Tahlia's sleeve. "No. Nooooo. Please make it stop, Tahlia."

As they walked between the standing stones, the sound increased in volume, the noise a humming or howling... The notes nearly melded into a dark melody, but just when the sound started to follow a pattern, it broke apart like a dropped glass.

The stones' presence weighed on her—in the way an Unseelie monster's energy pressed on a Seelie. It felt like the whole area had eyes and the kingdom was watching her.

"Maybe the stones have some old magic still spilling from them?" Tahlia asked in a whisper.

Vodolija growled quietly, indicating she wasn't thrilled by the feel of the stones either.

"Walk faster." Fara sped up, hurrying out of the stone circle and into the Kingdom of Spirits.

The mist split as they entered the kingdom. Mountains tore at low clouds, snow highlighted sharp peaks, and complete darkness indicated deep crevasses. No bats squeaked, no birds chirruped to announce the approaching dawn, and not even the sound of flowing water or the smallest of creatures rummaging through the scrub broke the eerie quiet. Even as the light paled their surroundings, the ground remained black. A slick mud covered most of the area with thick patches of moss-like islands in the morass.

Fara whimpered and held up her fists like she would hit her way out of this.

"I don't think you can punch ghosts, Fara."

The silver stars bled into the milk-white of dawn. The humming and howling finally faded away.

"I can try."

Shaking her head at Fara, Tahlia squinted to see Marius and Ragewing. They wound through a stretch of flat land. Tahlia, Vodolija, and Fara wouldn't be able to keep their presence a secret for long; there weren't any trees for cover anywhere nearby, and the new day exposed their position.

What was she going to say to Marius? She had to get him to talk, to tell her what he felt about everything—them, the commander, the order. She had to crack him open and get him to spill his secrets. Maybe it was presumptuous to think she was the one who could help him, but the way he'd distanced himself so suddenly pointed to a connection between whatever was making him act oddly and their relationship. Yes, their relationship, or the lack thereof, was involved somehow. She just knew it.

Tahlia, Vodolija, and Fara journeyed on, stopping now and then to nibble on the bread and dried meat Fara had brought along. Tahlia had a waterskin, which she shared with Vodolija, but they would have to find more water for the dragon or she'd begin to suffer from dehydration. Dragons were tough, but two days of no water would be detrimental. Tahlia was glad she and Vodolija had trained hard with the order and toughened up over the last two weeks, because this place pulled the energy from her limbs. It was likely doing the same to the dragons.

"Do you feel more tired than you should be?" Tahlia asked Fara as she packed away the remnants of their latest snack.

"Definitely. I'm being slowly drained like I'm the skin of water and there's this invisible giant who—" Her words fell away and her arms, which she'd stretched out to demonstrate the size of the giant, dropped as she looked at Tahlia.

Tahlia shook from restrained laughter as Fara glared.

Fara swore and made a rude gesture with her hand. "Screw you, Tahlia."

"I love you, friend."

Fara growled. "Yes, yes. Sure." She tromped off, muttering about death and revenge.

Tahlia went to Vodolija's head and patted her snout gently. The dragon blinked at her like a big cat and tilted her head, the spiraling horns there barely missing Tahlia's face. She smiled and kissed Vodolija's cheek.

Fara was walking backward slowly, eyeing them. "Did you just kiss a dragon? I had thought I saw you do that out of the corner of my eye earlier, but I thought surely I was mistaken."

Tahlia shrugged. "Doesn't every rider kiss their dragon?"

"Ha. No. I'm going with a firm *no*. They aren't cuddly."

"They can be." Tahlia rubbed her nose against Vodolija's snout. "I think she's tired. Should we find a spot to rest?" Tahlia looked from Vodolija to Fara. "I worry about losing sight of them even though these flatlands appear to go on for miles more."

Vodolija started forward, gently bumping Tahlia and letting her know she didn't need a rest.

"I guess not." Tahlia shrugged and followed Fara, Vodolija stepping slow and steady beside her.

They continued on for hours. Time moved differently here.

Night unfurled over the kingdom, blanketing them in silver starlight and shadows blacker than the darkest paint. It was as if the dark here drew in the light, allowing no starlight to penetrate its depths. The sounds began again, a low howl, then a hum of what sounded like a chorus of people. The hairs on her arms rose. But even though it was terrifying, this kingdom was incredibly interesting and the furthest thing from boring.

Vodolija bumped her roughly and nodded toward her own back. She wanted Tahlia to mount up.

Tahlia waved Fara over and they did as suggested. Relief coursed over Tahlia the second she hit the saddle. They could be airborne in moments if that howling turned into a real threat.

The scent of steel and rain wafted through the air, and Vodolija's head whipped to the side. Tahlia unsheathed her dagger, her heartbeat speeding up. Past a bush heavy with faeberries, a shimmering golden light blurred and wavered.

"What was that?" Fara tightened her hold around Tahlia's waist.

Grunting, Tahlia gripped her dagger and leaned forward in the saddle, squinting to see the anomaly better, but it was only a smear of inconsistent light. Vodolija growled, the sound vibrating through Tahlia.

"Hold, darling. Wait."

The light went out. The scent of metal and ozone immediately disappeared.

Vodolija shook like she wanted to rid herself of the whole experience, then she launched into the sky before Tahlia could order her not to. Fara let out one shriek as they flew into the starlight, the dark below like an ocean teeming with monsters.

"We have to go back home," Fara shouted over the wind.

"We can't. You made your decision to come. I'm not leaving Marius."

"He's very big. Whatever in the hells that was, well, he can handle it."

"You don't know that."

"Do you have any guesses on what made that noise?"

"Ghosts?"

"Please. Let's just go back and you can get all your fellow riders and return and save the day."

"I wish, but that's not how it would go. We left without permission. We would get kicked out if we were lucky, and Marius would be punished as well. Plus, there's a murderous commander in charge now and she isn't exactly my best friend."

Fara let out various agonized noises and set her head against Tahlia's back. "We are going to die."

"No, we aren't. You will be able to tell your grandchildren about this grand adventure."

"Don't wish children on me! Can you even imagine how worried and protective I'd be about them?"

Tahlia snorted. "They would have no lives at all."

"That's the truth. But they would be alive."

Tahlia chuckled despite the cold fear spreading through her bones.

Whatever had made that noise wanted to be heard. But why? To draw Tahlia, Fara, and Vodolija closer to inspect? To ask for help? They would never know if they didn't land.

"Let's go down, Vodolija," Tahlia said, knowing somehow that the dragon could hear over the wind and understand her. "We have to face this."

The dragon dove and Fara argued the whole way down.

CHAPTER 14
TAHLIA

"I think Vodolija is unhappy. You're asking her to go back to the creepy ghosts," Fara said into Tahlia's ear. "She's diving. Showing aggression. Maybe she wants us off her back so she can go home. I should have stayed home with all that bread. Why am I even here?"

"I might need your fists; plus, who else will make sure I pay attention to every little problem?" Tahlia teased.

If the sound had been a ghost, or ghosts, why had it alerted them like that? Was it curious? Was it even cognizant of its actions? Had it once been a person or was it a creature made of forgotten magic?

There was nothing like this in the rest of the Realm of Lights, certainly. No stories of such spirits except those that came from this broken kingdom, and those tales were sparse and lacking any real information. At least the thing hadn't attacked or injured them. That was a relief.

Perhaps none of the spirits were able to affect the living or had no motivation to do so. But if that were true, then why did border folk often find the bodies of travelers who had ventured too close to this land? The corpses found were described as having skin turned to gold with boils going up and down their arms and not a drop of blood in their bodies. The look of the dead had many proposing the idea that whatever evil had befallen the kingdom had something to do with Mistgold Fae—the families who had ridden dragons for centuries and who had that golden sheen in their blood.

Why did travelers come here anyway? For the same reason Marius had? If so, what was that reason?

They climbed a small rise, then spotted Marius and Ragewing a good ways off, seated at a sparkling fire.

Well, if they could stop for the night, so can we.

"That's bold," Fara said, standing beside Tahlia and gazing down toward the fire. "They're telling everyone they're here. Why isn't Marius more concerned?"

Tahlia shrugged, hiding the bulk of her worry. "Let's keep out of their eyeline."

She led Vodolija back down the rise. Soon enough, the fire Tahlia would make would be visible, but they could remain hidden for a little while longer.

Fara shivered as she helped Tahlia gather fallen limbs and broken sticks from the scattered trees growing here and there. A stretch of dark-leafed trees broadened into a full forest a stone's throw away, and though Tahlia worried about taking on Fara's habit of fearing everything, she wasn't about to go traipsing into the woods. Not after hearing that sound earlier.

Once they had a pile of wood, Vodolija set it ablaze and settled beside it. She trilled with satisfaction, obviously enjoying the heat. Tahlia sat on a small boulder beside Fara and they shivered together.

Fara wiggled her mud-slicked boots. "My feet will never be the same. I'll be tottering around like a hag years before my time. I hope Marius appreciates my hobbling." Her lip curled, showing a fang.

Tahlia removed her riding gloves and held her palms toward the flickering light. Vodolija lifted her head and sniffed the air.

"If you want to hunt," she said to Vodolija. "We're good here. But I do have some dragonbread if you want to stick around..."

The dragon growled low in her throat, and Tahlia chuckled. Vodolija hated that stuff.

Vodolija bowed her head, stood, then walked toward the forest. Tahlia appreciated that she was being careful that her takeoff wouldn't blow out the fire. Vodolija launched into the sky, her sea-hued wings spread as wide as a ship's sails. She was so lovely.

When traveling, the knights always brought dragonbread in case hunting wasn't possible or pickings were slim. A fist-sized serving of dragonbread could sustain a dragon for a full day, sometimes more depending on their activity level and how much they'd eaten recently. The dragons never seemed to savor the special meal, but they ate it when they had to. Marius had said they loathed dragonbread as much as younglings did their daily mineral drink, a supplement that Fae children in the Shrouded Mountains had to imbibe because of the lack of nutrients in their diet during the long winters.

Fara took some dried meat from their bags and heated it over the fire. Tahlia had eaten the stuff during training. It was pretty disgusting, but if you warmed it, it at least felt more like real food. The feeling finally returned to Tahlia's hands and feet as they dined on their meager feast. Tahlia kept an eye on the darkness beyond and the forest. Gods, she was tired, more than she should have been.

The noise of wings had Tahlia on her feet with her bow drawn and an arrow ready in a breath.

Fara had picked up a rock and was poised to throw it.

The shadow above materialized into a dragon Tahlia knew as well as she knew her own.

Ragewing.

The large Heartsworn landed a stone's throw from the fire, and

Marius swung out of the saddle and slid to the ground. He looked like a living storm.

Fara sucked a breath through her teeth and took a step back.

Tahlia's heart lurched into her throat. He had a cut along his cheek and the blood there had dried to a dark slash. She longed to touch it, to tend to it, and to ask him how he'd hurt himself. It was so odd to feel like comforting a male who appeared virtually made of solid stone.

Ragewing shook out his scarlet wings, blowing Marius's hair. Marius's gray eyes caught the glimmer of the fire and he fisted his hands as he strode toward Tahlia.

She gave him a wide smile. "Fancy meeting you here."

"Knight, you should not be *here* at all."

Oooh, using his captain voice. "I realize that, but neither should you. In fact, I am pretty sure you disobeyed a direct order."

His nostrils flared and his jaw worked. He looked Tahlia up and down, his gaze like a sweep of his hands. She swallowed and tried not to remember being pressed against this male with nothing between them but desire and joy.

"Lady Tahlia, you will return to the castle. That is an—"

"Hold on." Tahlia returned her arrow to the quiver and set her bow on the ground near the food and supply bags. Then she met his angry gaze. "Look. Hear me out, High Captain. Something is up with you."

"Lady Tahlia..." Fara wrung her hands and looked at Tahlia like she was a madwoman.

Ignoring her for the moment, Tahlia eyed Marius. "If you tell me why you're here, I'll take off. I swear it." She held a fist to her heart. "But I'm not leaving you here where there isn't a single living soul without hearing a solid reason for your little adventure."

"It's none of your concern."

All right, that actually hurt. She fought the urge to press a hand to her stomach. "It is my concern. *You* are my concern."

His eyes bunched at the edges and his throat moved in a swallow. "Tahlia, please. There is something you don't know. I can't..." He broke off, coughing and clearing his throat. When his gaze turned back to her again, he was grimacing as if in pain.

"What is wrong?" She stepped toward him.

He lurched backward and glanced to the side, his lips drawing back like he was in pain. "I am sorry for everything. But you must leave. I can't put you at risk too."

"So you admit you're putting yourself and Ragewing at risk by coming here."

"I'm not an idiot, Tahlia."

Fara snorted. "Could have fooled me," she whispered.

He glared at her and she turned away, suddenly very busy with tidying their supplies.

"It's not exactly a holiday spot," Marius said, a tone of wry humor in his voice.

"Was that an attempt at a joke, High Captain?" Tahlia grinned, thrilled to see him thawing if only for a second.

He rubbed his face with his hands, then dropped them and glanced from Fara to Tahlia. "You will leave once Vodolija returns. That is an order."

"Why?"

Tahlia stepped toward him. He dropped back fast like she was a sword aimed at his jugular. Her heart sputtered. His rejection hurt worse than any damage steel could do.

"I can't..." He growled in a very dragon-like manner and stared at the sky. "I order you to go back to the Shrouded Mountains immediately. To Dragon Tail Peak." His chin dipped down and his eyes found hers. "If you disobey this order, you will be put on probation for a time that I will determine once I return."

"*If* you return. Did you hear that sound earlier? The howling? Do you have any information about it or about this place?" Maybe if she pursued a different line of questioning, he'd give her a clue as to what in every god's name he was up to.

"I saw two spirits when they were singing, for lack of a better word. They mean no harm. Ragewing and I are as safe as we can be considering the scenario."

"What is the scenario exactly?"

His jaw worked, and his teeth clenched. "I..." Shaking his head, he looked at the ground.

"Fine. Don't tell me about your secret mission. Do you actually know you aren't about to be killed by whatever kills everyone that crosses that border or are you just telling me that to get me out of here?"

"I can't lie."

"Oh, right. I tend to forget that because you full Fae are so tricky."

Fara gave Tahlia a narrow-eyed glance.

"This conversation is over," Marius said.

But was it? "Just let me stay one full day. Then I'll go."

"No. Leave. That's an order, Lady Tahlia."

"Marius, I can see the way you're torn. In your eyes, you seem as haunted as this kingdom."

She lifted a hand, longing to stroke the rough line of his jaw, to feel his hot skin under her fingertips. He moved back another step.

Tahlia chewed the inside of her cheek. "Fine," she said, walking away. "If you're going to be ridiculous, I'll just ask the more sensible of you two."

She went to Ragewing and looked up into the dragon's scarlet face.

"Do you think we should be here? Or would you like to grab Marius and fly the hells out immediately before we end up as pale as the blank page, dusted in golden boils, and deposited on some border folk's farm?"

Ragewing's head swiveled and the dragon studied Marius.

"No," Marius said, shaking his head. "We are not leaving."

Ragewing snorted a puff of black smoke and sat back on his haunches.

"You're headed for that glowing light, the shimmering bit of stuff between those mountains, correct?" Tahlia wasn't giving up yet.

"Yes." He shook his head like he had a bug in his ear. "I mean to say, it's none of your concern. Please go."

"Please? But it's an order? Make up your mind, High Captain Marius."

The steel in his eyes hardened and a thrill shot through her at his dangerous beauty, idiot that she was.

"Tahlia." His voice went stony. "You are pushing me to consider punishments I'd rather not order."

"Do tell. What type of punishment is there for a person who saves your life?"

"You are not saving my life."

Fara brought a strip of dried meat to Ragewing, who accepted it with a grunt.

"You don't know that," Tahlia said. "Something haunted and wild could attack you right now and I'd be here, wielding my arrows and—"

"An arrow for the ghost?"

"Can't punch them either from what I hear," Fara mumbled.

Tahlia almost snarled at Marius. "Perhaps my strategy needs amending, but it could happen—I could end up saving your life here, Marius, and wouldn't you look such a fool for wishing me gone?"

"We may be off the books for this journey, but I am still your captain."

She saluted him. "I'm here and ready to obey."

He snorted, the edge of his lips twitching. "You don't even know the meaning of the word."

"I will learn as long as your orders involve me acting on your behalf here in this incredibly lovely disaster you've dragged us into."

"Tahlia, all jesting aside. You truly must—"

Vodolija landed beside Ragewing, cutting off whatever stale warning Marius was about to dole out.

“No deer to be found?” Tahlia asked the Seabreak.

A purring sound stuttered in the back of the dragon’s mouth, a noise Tahlia had learned to interpret as pouting.

“Did you find any fresh water?” Tahlia asked Marius.

“Yes. There is a creek not far away. Trees shield it from view, but if you look closely, you’ll see it.” He glanced at the flames. “We were flying back from it when I spotted your fire.”

“Eh, don’t look down your nose at me,” Tahlia said. “You made a fire too.”

“Unlike you, I am experienced. I deal with multiple threats regularly and have done so for years.”

“So you’re resorting to insults to get me to leave?”

“I’ll do whatever it takes,” Marius said. “It’s not safe for you or Lady Fara to... It’s... Tahlia.”

He looked ready to explode. What was going on with him?

Holding out her hands, she said softly, “Marius, one day is all I ask. One day, then I leave with no more insults or begging or punishments required.”

She longed to make a flirty joke about the punishment, but he had made it clear he wasn’t interested in anything like that at the moment. Though it cracked her heart into pieces, she wasn’t about to keep pushing him on that front like some jerk with her head up her arse. She only wanted to know why and what was wrong with him. She wasn’t sure she could refrain from *all* flirting, but at least she was trying.

“Fine. I give up.”

His growl of frustration usually pleased her, but in this case, it only smashed the pieces of her heart into shards that cut her through and through. There was definitely something very wrong with Marius and she was going to figure it out.

CHAPTER 15
MARIUS

He was going to rip a tear in the world. This damned curse was the most frustrating experience he'd ever had. Pacing while Tahlia and Fara built up the fire, he tried to recall deciding to fly here on Ragewing. But there was only the moment with Tahlia in the stables, then... Then nothing. A fog. Darkness where memories should have been.

He went to Ragewing and set his head against the dragon's side. Ragewing blew gently into Marius's hair, tugging it from its leather tie. The warmth of the dragon was more comforting than sitting by the fire with the females. They had arranged two fallen logs near the flickering tinder. But here, with Ragewing, Marius didn't have to look at Tahlia's sweet mouth and pert nose or see the hurt in her dark honey eyes. Ragewing wrapped him in a wing, blocking the restless breeze of this dead kingdom. He could still hear the distant hum and howl of ghosts though. They were in the forest but, thankfully, seemed to be content to remain there. At least, for now.

In the dimness of his wing enclosure, he dragged the tip of his boot in the mud. He was just so tired. Damn Ophelia to the seven hells. Forever. Longer. He was going to strangle the female no matter what the consequences.

The toe of his boot made a line and brought to mind the notes he'd seen on Ophelia's desk when he'd visited her. Notes about runic magic.

Wait. He straightened and Ragewing, noticing his change in mood, uncovered him.

"I can draw it in the dirt!" Marius hurried over to Tahlia and Fara, hope making everything seem brighter.

He stole a stick from the fire, not caring that the end was red hot and smoking. Crouching, he began to write in the mud.

"Marius? What are you doing?" Tahlia leaned forward, her jasmine scent filling his nose and alerting his body to her nearness.

He scooted back and kept on writing.

Ophelia cursed me with illegal ancient magic. If I touch you, you will die. I don't recall why I came here, but now it feels as though the answer to breaking the curse lies in this terrible land. The curse won't allow me to speak of any of this.

Well, that was what he tried to write. But instead of those words, his scrawling only produced unreadable combinations of letters and symbols.

Standing, he shouted in rage and tossed the smoking and muddied stick into the darkness beyond the fire. Facing away from the others, he shuddered and swallowed against his tight throat. The rolling hills and fog-laced land stretched into the night, seemingly endless and dangerously barren. Ragewing let out a grumble and the ground trembled slightly under what must have been a stomp.

"You promise to leave tomorrow, yes?" He couldn't turn back around to look at Tahlia. It was too much. He felt as though Ophelia had snapped his ribs, reached into his chest, and removed half his heart. The other half belonged to Ragewing and it beat sluggishly, dying a slow death on its own.

"Maybe."

"Ah, right. You can lie." He hadn't intended for his words to hold the ire they did, but he was just so damned irritated with this curse.

"Easy now, HC. Don't treat me like Maiwenn does. I'm not lying to you."

"You said you would leave after one day. You already lied."

"I didn't say after which day."

Fara snorted. "Now, that is the Fae side of you talking there."

Marius ran his hands through his tangled hair and whirled to face the females and the dragons. "I'm sorry I'm behaving like a madman."

"Not a madman," Tahlia said as she stoked the fire, "just like someone with a big problem who takes it out on everyone around them."

A pang of regret hit Marius's already severely injured heart. "I said I'm sorry."

"Show it." Tahlia met his gaze, her eyes burning.

"HC?" Fara whispered.

"High Captain," Tahlia whispered back.

"Oh, right," Fara said.

Tahlia stood, and though she didn't come closer, she felt closer to Marius somehow. "You said you care deeply for me, yes?"

Fara's eyes widened, then she rose quickly and went to the dragons, muttering about poultices.

"I did. I do," Marius said, the curse creeping up his throat again to snare his tongue. His feelings for Tahlia were tied to this dark magic. Of that, he had no doubt.

Tahlia's eyes shuttered briefly as if his words were a balm. He took a slow breath. He should have been saying that and more to her every moment they were together, back when he still could speak freely. He'd thought they had all the time in the world.

"So," Tahlia continued, "how do you expect me to leave you here like this? I feel for you as much as you feel for me. Possibly a great deal more."

"Not possible."

Her lovely dusky-rose-hued lips formed a sad smile.

"I can't watch you die for me," he said.

"I'm a Mist Knight. You probably will watch me die at some point."

"That's for the order. For the realm. I won't have your life shortened because... I can't..." Shaking and baring his teeth, he fisted his hands until his knuckles nearly broke the skin.

Tahlia lifted a hand. "Eh, breathe. I know what you mean. Because of whatever is going on with you specifically."

"So you agree to leave tomorrow?"

"Not at all."

He threw up his hands and paced a circle. "Of course."

"I understand what you're saying, but I don't agree with it. If I were in your place, would you stay for me? Would you and Ragewing risk all for me?"

He halted. "You know I would."

"I didn't realize that."

"Well," he said, tongue burning as his desire to tell her about the curse and the cause rose again, "you do now."

"Don't expect any less of me than you do of yourself. Don't degrade me like that."

"I, Tahlia, I..."

"You were trying to tell me about whatever is happening by drawing in the mud, weren't you?"

"Yes." Pain shot down his throat.

"We will figure this out. Now, why don't you sleep and I'll take the first watch. Fara, will you take second?"

"Aye."

Tahlia nodded, looking like she was the highest rank here and enjoying the feeling of leadership. A reluctant grin tugged at one side of his mouth.

"I won't sleep, but I'll try." Marius hated this, but he couldn't argue. He would do the same if he was in her boots. "But first, I need to wash."

Her gaze tingled between his shoulder blades as he walked down the sloping, mossy ground toward the small creek. He had heard that once you choose your mate, you become incredibly sensitive to their presence. Shaking his head, he hoped he hadn't doomed her. She should be with someone who wasn't wrapped in a madwoman's snare. Someone kind who laughed more than he did. She deserved joy. Not this mess. But jealous pangs hit him as he imagined such a pairing. No matter what, he wanted her for himself. Even while he hated himself for the emotion.

After washing his dirt-smeared hands and face, he did his best to wash the mud from his trousers. When he returned to their camp, he settled himself across the fire from Fara, and Tahlia took up a spot on the nearest log. She gave him a sweet smile as he stretched out on the sturdy old bedroll he always brought on missions.

"This roll smells like the disgusting sausages Titus loves," Marius said.

Tahlia and Fara chuckled.

"Can't wait to try one," Tahlia said. "Do you think we will be called to attack soon?"

He knew she was attempting to help him imagine a future when they were past this experience.

"I do. Very soon." Likely, they'd miss the first call. What would the other riders do when they realized Marius, Tahlia, and Fara were missing?

Gods, he hoped he'd see his friend Titus again and with his own mind intact and Tahlia on his arm. He drifted into musings, his thoughts floating away like sparks in the wind.

CHAPTER 16
TAHLIA

Tahlia bolted upright on her bedroll and whipped her head toward where Marius had been sitting when she'd finally given up and fallen asleep. He was still there. Phew. She hated the idea of sleeping while he was up, but she and Fara had both been far too tired to stay awake.

"How are you feeling?" she asked Marius over Fara's snoring.

The dawn was just over the horizon and the sky had begun to lighten.

Marius looked at the last dregs of the fire, the smoke rising around him like he'd been on fire too. "I'm fine."

"Sure."

He had the look of a man who'd been hit on the back of the head by something very heavy. Like someone who had memory issues from an injury.

"I am," he insisted.

"No missing pieces from your watch? No lapses in memory?"

"Not that I can recall."

He was hiding something. It was obvious in the way he wouldn't look directly at her. "What's bothering you, then? I mean, besides whatever is going on with your ability to tell me things and this whole dark adventure."

"My hands are dirty."

"Who cares? We are miles from anyone who might change their opinion of your tidy arse."

"I washed them before sleeping. Now look at them." He splayed his fingers and she walked closer to look.

Dirt lined the spaces between his large fingers and his nails held a line of mud too.

"Hmm. Well, it is muddy here. Maybe you just picked something up? Like your bedroll?" He had already packed it away apparently. "Perhaps you didn't notice when it was full dark. Or you tried to write more in the mud when you were out of it? Anyway, I'm awake now, so if you want to return to the creek to wash up, it's certainly fine with me."

He turned and grabbed a parcel wrapped in waxed linen. "Eat this. You and Fara. I already had my share."

When he lobbed the package, Tahlia caught it neatly and opened it up. A square of honeyed bread dotted with pieces of fig sat inside. Tahlia's stomach growled.

Marius walked away, Ragewing trailing him.

"What is that?" Fara was suddenly sitting up and wide awake.

"Oh, just a little treat Marius has offered us." Tahlia handed a corner of the bread over.

Fara gobbled it down, groaning in ecstasy. Tahlia laughed and they worked their way through half the square.

"I'm going to give the rest to Vodolija."

Fara grumbled but nodded and began to tie up her bedroll.

Fog crept across the dark green and gray landscape, the tops of the distant trees poking up through the misty white like fingers from a shallow grave. A chill wrapped around Tahlia, but it didn't alarm her. This place was haunted and she would have been more worried if she hadn't felt the chill. At this point, fear and fretting were the norm.

Vodolija stood over a cluster of large and mossy stones. She eyed a ferret-like creature that was darting between the rocks and nibbling greenery.

"How does that wee thing not even notice the massive predator staring down at him hungrily?"

The Seabreak grunted, a dragon's version of a shrug. Then she moved, her head lashing out like a great arrow, and the ferret was gone.

"Ew." Tahlia turned away to let the dragon finish her breakfast. "I was going to offer you a bit of honey and fig bread, but you seem to be just fine."

The dragon bumped her back and she spun to see expectant eyes.

"Fine. I suppose it can be your dessert." Tahlia opened her palm and Vodolija nibbled the bread with the tip of her smooth, scaly snout.

"She's going to take a finger someday," Fara said from behind.

"I don't know. I haven't seen any riders missing fingers. Oh, wait, I do think there was someone who was missing a thumb."

"Exactly. With you being part human, you'll probably be the next victim."

"Gee, thank you for that."

"Just warning you. Not saying I want it to happen. I'm not Ophelia."

"She doesn't just want my finger. She wants my life."

"Fair. Then maybe I should have said I'm not Maiwenn."

"Accurate."

Fara laughed sadly and offered Tahlia a steaming cup of what smelled like pine needle tea. They drank in silence as the fog circled Vodolija and their view of the slope that led to the creek.

"He's been gone a while," Fara said.

"Not really. Let's pack up and be ready to move on when he returns." Tahlia said, leading Fara back to the fire.

"What is the plan exactly?" Fara finished her tea, shook the cup, and tucked it into the middling-sized satchel they'd brought along with the smaller ones they could affix to themselves if needed. They also had a larger bag tied onto Vodolija.

"I am really not sure," Tahlia said. "I guess we'll try to get Marius to return."

"And if he refuses?"

"We'll follow him wherever he feels led to go."

"So we are putting the madman in charge of the quest."

"Only way to see what's happening."

"You sound so nonchalant considering you're wandering a dead kingdom full of ghosts."

"Don't forget. You chose to come with me."

Fara bunched her lips and whispered something that was most likely a gentle curse aimed in Tahlia's direction.

Marius returned and Tahlia didn't want to admit how relieved she was to see him. Was he really fine now?

"How was the creek?"

"I spotted a ruined fortress. We should explore it."

"Why?" Fara asked. She closed her fist over her mouth. "I meant, what do you expect to find, High Captain?"

"I'm not certain, but I feel led to visit it, so if you refuse to leave, you might as well come as backup." Marius gathered his things and they tied their bags to the dragons.

"How does it feel?" Tahlia asked, eyeing him. He seemed distracted and nothing about that put her at ease.

"The pull?"

"Yes."

"Like extreme curiosity."

The craving to go to him, to hold him, to feel the heat of his body against hers, hit Tahlia like a punch to the heart. She took a shuddering breath and he looked up from checking Ragewing's girth buckle.

"Or you can remain here?" he asked softly.

Fara had moved to the other side of Vodolija to apply some

poultice where the saddle rubbed. She'd already done so on this side.

His scent wafted through the air. She fought the urge to go to him and the desire to let go of worrying about whatever was going on with him. She forced her feet to remain where they were.

"No, we are going with you."

He nodded and climbed onto Ragewing's back, his movements quick and easy. Fara came back around Vodolija and they mounted the Seabreak and readied to take off.

The dragons soared out of the fog and into the dull light of the morning sky.

CHAPTER 17

MARIUS

The tug on Marius's soul felt like so much more than curiosity, but he hadn't wanted to further alarm Tahlia and Fara. This sensation was not a tickle of interest but more like a dragon had sunk his talons into Marius's very being and dragged him to the timeworn fortress below.

To calm his own fast pulse, Marius set a hand on Ragewing's warm scales. Ragewing raised his head and grunted. He extended a wing and held off a blast of cool wind and mist, protecting Marius in a way that had him swallowing against a lump in his throat. He was so grateful for Ragewing, for Tahlia, and even for Fara and her dire warnings and inexperience. He didn't think he deserved their loyalty, but he was incredibly glad for it.

They landed amid the fog that didn't seem to be ready to lift anytime soon. Tahlia dismounted and helped Fara down.

Four stone towers stood in a rough square. The weather-eaten remains of what had once been wooden walls stretched to each one. A variety of circular stone buildings dotted the area. One appeared to be a dovecote, another a kitchen with the domed stove still intact, and a taller one in the back had possibly been a chapel.

The wind whistled through a plow someone had pulled into the old fortress and a bronze chain clanked against one of the towers. A thousand mysteries could be hiding in these ruins. Trunks of gold and jewels might be just beneath their feet.

"Ooooh, spooky. I like it."

Fara threw up her hands. "Of course you think this haunted nightmare is great. You probably want to settle in and roast marshmallows." Her wide stare slid over the wind-blown weeds growing by a forgotten well.

It was a wishing well, complete with a wooden arch decorated with constellations. Tahlia wandered over.

Marius's view of the females blurred like his vision had been marred by drink, so he squeezed his eyes shut, trying to clear the fuzziness away. He opened his eyes again and blinked. His vision was better, but not yet normal.

"Marius?" Tahlia came closer, but thankfully, not too close.

He held out a hand. "Just give me a minute."

But instead of taking a breath and gathering himself, his feet moved of their own accord. He stalked toward the well.

"Marius?" Tahlia shouted and ran up beside him.

Fara, still near Vodolija, was saying something, but the whispers of strange voices echoed in his ears. The hairs on the back of his neck rose.

"Stay back," he said, barely able to hear his own voice.

He looked down into the black of the old well, and a sense of evil slithered over his skin. Ragewing came up beside him, growling, nostrils loosing tendrils of smoke. The dragon spit sparks into the well. The bits of fire danced down and disappeared. The whispers rose, louder and louder and louder. With voices like rocks cracking against each other, they spoke in a language Marius didn't know. The sensation of evil's presence increased. A weight on his chest, on his shoulders, the foul and invisible essence turned his stomach and brought on a cold sweat that slicked his face.

Shadows burst from the well and blew Marius, Tahlia, Fara, and the dragons backward.

"Not a wishing well! Not a wishing wellllll!" Tahlia shouted, scrambling to unsheathe her sword.

Somehow the wispy essence pouring from the well had a heaviness to it. The sentient, ragged cloud of evil zipped past Marius, then down again to release a gust of wind. Marius stumbled and nearly fell. Tahlia grabbed Fara to keep her upright. The shadows whirled around the air above Vodolija's head, then dipped and shot at Fara.

Heart pounding and ears ringing with the voices, Marius lunged and put himself between the shadows and Fara. Tahlia shouted something Marius couldn't hear.

Everything slowed. The shadows were going to unmake him. He knew it. They were pure evil. He drew his sword though it was likely worthless.

The shadows split and flowed around Marius like a river of night. His hands sparked with what felt like fire. He dropped his sword. Golden light crackled from his fingertips as he spun, and the shadows gathered overhead. With no idea what was happening, he lifted his hands. The golden light snapped upward and shattered the shadows into a thousand pieces. The wind pulled the bulk of the evil apart and the voices at last fell into silence.

"What in all the realms was that?" Tahlia was panting and holding Fara's arm.

"We should leave now before whatever it was returns." Fara drew away from Tahlia and started toward Vodolija.

Marius's arms ached to pull Tahlia to him and to make certain she was well and whole. "Are you all right?"

Tahlia nodded. "What just happened with your hands?"

"I assume it's... The..." The heat of frustration swallowed him and he swore creatively.

Fara waved from her spot beside the Seabreak. "I don't know

about sons of bastard mountain goats, but I like the sentiment. Let's fly."

"We can't leave," Tahlia said. "We have to figure out what that was and how it's tied to Marius."

Marius wanted to chime in and agree, to add his thoughts, but his tongue refused, the contents of his mind straying to the curse and its unseen rules. He bowed his head and tried to breathe through his impotent anger. Ragewing came close and extended a wing over him. He set a hand on the dragon's scales and comfort flowed into him, easing his tension.

"The shadows struck out at you and Fara," Tahlia said. "That's what you saw too?"

Marius grunted to confirm.

"But they ignored me and they didn't harm you when you defended Fara. It was like you were untouchable. They didn't even seem to notice me."

"Why are you calling a cloud of shadows *they*?" Fara asked.

"I'm not sure," Tahlia said. "I sense that it was a collection of beings. Do you agree, Marius?"

He nodded, not trusting his tongue. But maybe he could tell her a few things. He had to try. "I heard voices. Did you?"

"No." Tahlia frowned and studied his face, her smooth brow wrinkling as she pondered. He loved how she looked when she was thinking.

Fara shuddered. "Please. Let's get into the sky and away from this place."

Tahlia waved an impatient hand at Fara. "This is exciting. I'm not going back to sit by a fire and wait until whatever comes at us. I'd rather meet it head-on."

Groaning, Fara returned to Tahlia's side.

"It was another language," Marius managed to say despite the tightening in his throat and the strangling feel of the dark magic on him.

A slender shadow rose from the well and slithered toward them.

"Another one!" Fara shouted.

Marius was already lifting his hands. The golden light once again flashed from his fingers and palms, chasing the last shadow. But the shadow didn't dissipate. It just hovered over them, not attacking, but not breaking into pieces like the others had.

"Is it coming for me?" Fara had shut her eyes, but she was holding up her fists like she was ready for a boxing match.

"I don't think so," Tahlia said, studying the slip of darkness.

Marius growled at the shadow. It seemed to shiver, growing more transparent. Then it zipped away.

The evil sensation that had Marius in its grip increased in intensity. It wrapped him in a shroud of confusion and the world blurred. An invisible chain latched onto his heart and pulled hard.

CHAPTER 18
TAHLIA

A humming, howling sound similar to the one they'd heard earlier started up, coming from the forest and sending shivers down Tahlia's spine.

A flash of light forced her eyes shut.

She opened them as quickly as she could.

Fara was gone.

And so were Marius and Ragewing.

Panic lanced Tahlia and she held her breath. "Where did they go, Vodolija?"

The Seabreak tossed her head, sniffed the air, then eyed the sky. Ragewing and Marius were far above. They must have taken off in a bout of mind-boggling speed. Already, they were a blur flying over the fog. How had he mounted up that quickly? And where was Fara? Had time passed somehow while Tahlia's eyes were closed against the light?

Ice flowed through her stomach.

"Fara!"

She ran through the fortress, eyes not moving fast enough and her lungs tightening with fear.

Kicking down the door of the first tower she came to, she called out, "Fara! Please answer me!"

But there was only a broken stool, moldy crates cloaked in dust, and the musty air of a land long devoid of life. As she searched the other three towers, she replayed the last moments in her head. The humming. The light. Had the light been related to the illumination that had shot from Marius's hands when the shadows attacked? She didn't know. It had been bright, but she hadn't had time to see the hue of the illumination.

Back in the open area, she lifted a hand to Vodolija. "Did you see anything?"

Vodolija grunted at the ground. But there was nothing there.

"What is it?"

Tahlia circled the area, but not even a footprint marred the muddy spot. Only dirt and a scraggly plant with thick blood-red leaves. Vodolija bumped her from behind, urging her closer to the spot.

"I'm so confused. We don't have time for this. We might be able to spot Fara. We'll search for Ragewing and Marius afterward since a dragon is easier to spot than one skinny Fae female."

Vodolija tossed her head and sparked fire.

"Don't be angry with me. I don't understand."

The dragon lowered a wing and shoulder, allowing Tahlia to climb up into the saddle, but she was obviously perturbed. She blew a spout of flame, bright in the dark.

"Please. We can figure out whatever you're trying to tell me later. Let's get up high and see if we can spot Fara. She can't have gone far." Or been taken far.

A shiver grabbed hold of Tahlia and shook her hard. Had the ghosts of this wild place taken her? And if so, what would they do to her?

Vodolija took off and Tahlia studied the land beneath them. She tapped the dragon's neck, indicating she should fly over the forest. It was too dark to see anything really, but what else could she do? It wasn't as if she could just leave Fara. Her palms grew damp and she fidgeted with the reins. The air was wet and cold and that first shiver of fear had turned into a constant, uncomfortable trembling. Trees, trees, and more trees. There was no sign of Fara anywhere.

"Fly toward Ragewing!" she called out to Vodolija. "We'll get him and then come back for Fara."

Why had Marius taken off without warning? Had he seen Fara stolen by something? Or was he leaving for a different reason entirely? Gods, Tahlia had more questions than could be answered in one dark night. Panic seared her nerves and made her lower herself on Vodolija's neck. She longed for comfort, for heat, for the ability to turn back time and keep Marius from leaving in the first place. She should have fought with him, demanded answers. Anything to keep him from whatever this was. Then Fara would have been safe at the keep too instead of only the gods knew where.

Tahlia silently prayed for her friend as Ragewing and Marius came into view.

The wind whipped Tahlia's cloak around despite its many clasps and she fought to keep her teeth from cracking as they chattered violently from both worry and cold. Vodolija flew into a bank of ragged clouds and Tahlia lost sight of Marius and Ragewing.

"Damned clouds!"

She squinted and stood in the stirrups, trying in vain to see more than mist and inconsistent light. If she lost them, what was she going to do? Vodolija's body rumbled with a trilling purr and Tahlia resumed her seat.

Tahlia was aware her mind wasn't operating at a top notch level. Panic pinched at her confidence. "I'm trying to be calm. It's not easy."

The Seabreak snorted and blew a cloud of smoke. Tahlia set a hand on her warm scales and kept her eyes peeled for any sign of them. A scream of fear and frustration built inside her chest, but she bit it back, gulping down her worry and trying to remember that she was a Mist Knight. She could handle this.

When they broke through the cover, Tahlia spotted Marius and Ragewing.

She exhaled and finally stopped gripping the reins with her right hand. She cracked her knuckles and spoke to Vodolija.

"They're landing. Do you see them?"

The glowing light flickered, the odd shine emanating from a caldera. From where did the glow originate? Random spots on the ground?

Vodolija soared down toward the rocky formation and landed a few feet from Ragewing. Marius had leapt from his dragon's back and was tearing at the muddy earth with his hands. Tahlia dismounted, keeping an eye on their surroundings. The air vibrated with something unnameable—magic? Or something under the ground? No, it was more than a physical disturbance in the area. This barren spot felt raw and wrong. The golden light flickered over Marius's hands, reminding Tahlia of... Of what?

Then Marius shouted, his words unintelligible. Ragewing roared and stomped his feet as if agitated. Rightly so. Vodolija nuzzled against Ragewing, then swung toward Tahlia and pushed her with the edge of a wing. That red-leafed plant grew here too.

"What is it with you and this plant?"

She strode away, hurrying to Marius's side even though she wasn't sure this was the right move. What was he digging for?

The golden light created a shimmering border along oddly shaped stones set into the dirt. No, this wasn't a rock formation.

They were bones.

But not just regular bones. The one Marius was attempting to dislodge was a femur, but it was longer than a dragon's. Much, much longer. A gnarled skull sat halfway out of the ground and a twisted spine looked like it was about to crawl out of the mud. Ah, and there were hands. Very large hands.

Tahlia shivered violently.

These had to be the bones of a giant.

Giants had existed outside of old children's stories? Well, here was evidence that they certainly had. Were these bones related to why the Kingdom of Spirits had become the nightmare that it was? Had a huge monster ravaged these lands? But the bigger question was why Marius was attempting to dig up the giant's bones...

Wait. He had been wondering about his dirty hands when they'd camped. Had he already been here?

Swallowing her fear, she started to put a hand on Marius's shoulder. He swung around and fell back. His eyes were wide, and his temples glittered with the same golden light that flickered across his hands and along the half-buried bones.

Tahlia stood frozen, the bitter taste of fear on the back of her tongue.

"Don't," he growled, his voice low and his eyes vacant and glimmering with gold light. "Lady Tahlia..." He didn't blink. It was like he wasn't himself at all.

"Marius, what are you doing?" The urge to shake him was nearly overpowering, but he obviously didn't want her to touch him, so she held the hilt of her gladius instead.

He bent his head, shook it, then stood. When he raised his chin and his eyes met hers, the golden light was gone from his head and hands. The odd illumination continued to glimmer around the bones.

"I, I don't know." He looked like a wild animal about to attack.

"Ragewing, please pick up your rider," Tahlia said, still facing Marius in case he lost his mind and did something crazy.

CHAPTER 19
TAHLIA

Ragewing didn't hesitate. He lifted into the air, then snatched up Marius in his front talons and began flying out of the caldera. They disappeared behind the rocky walls of the bowl-shaped area.

Heart thumping like mad, Tahlia ran to Vodolija. The dragon eased back, lowered her head, and snorted at the red-leafed plant again.

"Fine!" Tahlia plucked a bunch of it and held it high. "Are you happy now?"

The Seabreak moved her jaws.

"What does that mean? We are going to lose Marius and Ragewing. We don't have time to chitchat, darling. What is that motion? Eating?" She eyed the plant that was half crushed in her hand. Did Vodolija want her to eat it? "Why? What is this plant?"

The dragon nudged her belly, then blew smoke over her face.

"Fine. Whatever. If I die, I'm going to haunt your tail for eternity." She bit off a small piece of leaf. Cinnamon and anise danced over her tongue, which wasn't too horrible really, but it was dry and difficult to swallow. She finally managed it. A tingling spread across her forehead and down the back of her head. She cleared her throat, tongue stinging slightly.

She held out her hands to Vodolija. "Happy now?"

I am, actually.

Tahlia fell back a step. Had she just...

Yes, that's me. Vodolija. Your bonded dragon and the one who loves you best of all.

The Seabreak trilled and lowered her shoulder and wing.

"What in all the realms? How did this happen? Am I losing my mind like Marius seems to be?" Tahlia eyed the plant again. "How? Why?"

We should probably take off sometime this year, Tahlia.

That was her dragon. Talking to her inside her mind. She couldn't seem to move.

Snap out of it, rider! Get on my back and let's get to the males.

Stuttering nonsense, Tahlia did as Vodolija suggested and soon they were airborne. "You love me?"

Of course I do. I wouldn't risk my life for you on this mad quest if I didn't.

Tahlia's heart warmed. This was incredible! She rubbed the smooth deep blue stripe of scales beside the saddle. "Do you know anything about what happened to Fara or where she might be? And what do you think is wrong with Marius and why is Ragewing putting up with it?"

I don't have any more information about Fara than you do. Although, if you recall, she is the one who told you about this plant that allows us to speak to one another. Remember?

Oh. Yes. She had mentioned blood-red leaves and something about bonding with dragons. Tahlia could strangle herself for not listening better to her friend.

I have to find her, Vodolija. Tahlia's blood felt like the icy water of the high mountains.

She was there and then she was gone, Vodolija said. *There was a delicate presence around us when she disappeared though. Perhaps a ghost? As for Marius, he has a foul energy to him. He needs time with the clear crystals.*

They cleared the caldera. Marius and Ragewing were not too far off.

"I thought the crystals only help dragons."

I think you know very well that they also affect Fae. Even half-Fae.

Tahlia's cheeks flushed. "How did you know about that?"

I have been slightly linked with you since the first day I chose you.

"Really? Is that how all dragons and riders work?"

You're thinking of the new commander and her dragon.

"I am."

He will not bond with her fully, but they are linked tentatively. He thought she would grow wiser, but she has only become more evil.

"I believe she killed her father."

You're probably right, but the dragons don't know. Well, her dragon won't communicate with the rest of us. He hasn't since you joined the order.

Tahlia poised herself to remain balanced in the saddle as Vodolija soared toward the ground, aiming for Ragewing and Marius's landing spot beside a small river. He had dismounted and started walking toward the water.

"I have so many questions, but they will likely need to wait. But, umm, can I call you Lija for short?"

Yes. I quite like that.

"Do you know Ophelia's dragon's name?"

I do.

"But you can't tell me."

I will not. It is against our ways.

"I understand."

You spoke to me through your mind a moment ago. Did you notice? Lija said.

"No. I did?"

Yes. Try again.

Can you hear me?

I can. Speaking like this might tire you at first. But you will grow used to it.

Thank you. For being patient with me.

Of course. You are my chosen rider.

Warmth battled with the cold fear in Tahlia's chest.

Lija alighted on the mossy ground and Tahlia hurried to climb off. She went to where Marius stood looking into the water.

"Marius? Are you all right?"

He was staring at the reflection of his face. "I can't..." His lips pulled back and he lifted his head, growling in frustration.

He is cursed. You know that, yes? Lija said.

Cursed? "I know he is hurting somehow and that something was wrong. What type of curse? Who cursed him and why? What can I do to help? Why won't he talk to me about it? Is he unable?"

Slow down, rider.

"Sorry."

"Who are you talking to?" Marius asked. He continued staring at the water and his rippling visage. "I... I don't know... Where..." He looked up, his eyes going hazy and gold again.

Ragewing says Marius knows Ophelia cursed him. Marius felt called to travel here.

Called? Tahlia asked Lija.

That is how it feels to Ragewing. As if some power has reached out to the High Captain and is luring him to this foul, barren land.

"Marius, we have to find Fara. Something took her or... I don't know. But she's gone and she isn't exactly an adventurer. If you can handle setting whatever you're dealing with aside for a bit, we should go look for her. Can you do that? Can you promise me you won't go back to that caldera and mess with those scary as hells bones again?"

"I don't know. I can't, I cannot seem to really... I can't talk."

"I know. Vodolija told me." He needed the same ability with Ragewing. It might make it possible for him to speak to Ragewing about the problem, at least. Tahlia searched the ground for that blood-red plant and came up empty. "I have a solution to some of this, but I can't take the time for that at the moment. I have to find Fara."

"Agreed." Marius's face was back to its stormy self and, gods, but she was happy to see it. "But then you must leave. You'll go once we find her."

"Of course," Tahlia lied.

They mounted and began to fly back toward the place where Fara had disappeared.

As they traveled, the dragons staying low, their bellies nearly scraping the clusters of scrubby trees here and there, the sound started again—a quiet howling and humming that grew in volume.

CHAPTER 20
TAHLIA

A golden light flickered below them, beside what looked like the ruins of an old castle. Marius looked to Tahlia and motioned to the light. She nodded and their dragons began to dive. Ragewing came to a stop on what had once been a rutted cart path. The two lines of expertly laid rock were now mostly covered with the greenish-black moss that seemed to grow everywhere here. Lija perched on a tumble of rounded building stones. Both riders remained on their mounts as the strange light approached. The illumination morphed into an outline of a Fae male.

The ethereal Fae had large ram horns that curled away from his pleasant-looking face. He had cheekbones like Fara's, sharp but not long. His hair and his skin were fashioned of that same golden light, as was his cloak and the simple leather boots that stuck out at the bottom of the woolen wrap. A thick torc shimmered around his neck, a traditional accessory that the Fae of the king's city still wore today.

"A ghost?" Tahlia suggested out loud to Lija. Speaking through minds was difficult. She'd had to get used to it.

Marius glanced her way, a mix of sadness, hope, and wonder crossing his features and clouding his eyes. He looked like he wanted to grab her and leave here without helping anyone do anything. Her heart surged, pushing her from her saddle and off Lija's back. But he, like Tahlia, had to know that wasn't possible.

"I think so," he said.

Tahlia found her footing off the pile of stones. Marius must have thought she was talking to him, of course, because he didn't know about the plant and all of that madness.

The ghost is quite old, Lija said into Tahlia's mind, *but his spirit is bright and full of life.*

"Vodolija says he is bright, which I'd guess means he's not a kidnapper of friends." *Fara, please be all right,* she prayed silently.

Marius dismounted and paused, hands still holding the reins. "Your dragon says?"

"Yes. That's a story for another time." Tahlia pointed at the spirit.

"Right." Marius cleared his throat and gave the ghost a shallow bow. "Spirit, we are searching for our friend, a female named Fara."

"She has purple skin, and dark hair, and is afraid of life in general. Have you seen her? Please say you have. She can't handle things like this."

Marius lifted an eyebrow at Tahlia.

The ghost floated farther away, his body partially obscured by the age-blackened remains of a gatehouse and wall. Vines grew over the stones and hung across the entrance like a curtain. The dragons flew over the old castle wall while Marius and Tahlia walked under the portcullis.

"That is why I have come to you," the spirit said. "Your friend is trapped below with the varjuline. They haven't drained her blood yet, but a portion of her spirit has been siphoned. Their feeding is accomplished through a dark, wordless magic. They glean blood and spirit from their victims and the wisps of energy and blood crawl through the very air and soak into the varjuline. They also save a portion of their victims' blood in bowls for Katk." The ghost pressed his eyes shut as if he'd seen the act and wished he hadn't.

Fear cut Tahlia again and again. "What are the varjuline?" Her voice had gone shrill. "Is that what those shadows are? We dealt with them once already. Is my friend alive?"

The ghost studied Tahlia, then Marius. "Oh, a whip. Fascinating." He raised a glowing eyebrow at Marius's favored weapon and grinned naughtily.

Tahlia waved both hands, impatient. "Please, focus. Tell us what to do."

The ghost rolled its eyes. Vodolija snorted and took a step toward the ghost.

"Easy, big beauty," the ghost said. Then he turned back to Tahlia. "Your friend still has a chance to live because she remembers her life and her center."

Tahlia exhaled, nearly falling to her knees in gratitude. Alive. Fara was alive and they were going to save her.

"That's what keeps me from becoming a varjuline," the ghost said, "which is a shadowling that exists only to feed themselves and to feed Katk. In life, I was called Trevain. Not that you asked."

A breeze that smelled like stagnant water drifted across Tahlia's face.

"Are they ghosts like you, but evil instead of oddly informative?" she asked, her hands shaking.

The ghost nodded, his partially transparent ram horns fading in and out. "As long as I retain my mind and my memories, I can withstand the call of the sleeping Katk."

"Enough talking," Marius said, drawing his sword. Ragewing flapped his wings, turning the area into a small windstorm for a moment. "We must rescue our squire."

Tahlia gave him a look, then smiled at the ghost. They wouldn't get far if they insulted anyone trying to help them. "We want to learn all about you, Trevain, but for now, can you take us to our friend?"

"I will do it for you," he said to Tahlia.

He bowed to her, then floated over a scattered floor of flagstones, moss, and earth.

An open doorway led to the remains of a staircase that descended underground. They trailed the spirit, the ghost's light illuminating the timeworn stone and the water dripping from the partially collapsed ceiling of the staircase. A corridor, as black as night, stretched out past the stairs. Marius remained in front of Tahlia, just behind Trevain.

"Stay back three steps," Marius ordered Tahlia over his shoulder.

"Aye, High Captain." She had to figure out why he was so insistent on not touching her.

The corridor opened into a chamber that smelled strongly of illness and blood.

Fara lay in the center of the room, surrounded by a cage of golden fire. They hurried inside, stopping at the ring.

"Fara?" Tahlia touched the ring. The flame didn't singe her skin, but the strange magic blocked her like a wall of stone.

Fara opened her eyes. "Tahlia?" She struggled to her feet and stared out at them through the flickering light. Her arms were covered in golden boils and instead of being the color of a rare amethyst, her skin was as pale as a shade-loving periwinkle bloom.

"You have only moments before the varjuline return," Trevain said, turning toward the doorway like he expected the villainous ghosts to enter this very second. "Though they will be less drawn to you, Tahlia, because of your human blood, there are many and they are hungry."

Tahlia unsheathed her short sword. "Move as far away from this edge as you can, Fara."

Fara did so and Tahlia swung her sword, aiming to slice through the flames. The sword passed through and Fara gasped, hope lighting her eyes. But the flames returned before she could escape.

"Damn it!" Tahlia whirled. "Marius, any ideas?"

"High Captain. Please."

"Really? You're worried about rules and regulations at a time like this?"

"This is exactly the time to remain disciplined and to follow protocol. That's all we have to rely on when so much is out of our control."

"All you might have to rely on, but rules don't always work toward an end goal." Exasperated, she waved her hands. "Just forget about that. What do we do?"

Marius stepped closer to Fara. "What happened? Who trapped you here?"

"I told you. It was the varjuline," Trevain said.

"Apologies, but I don't trust you yet," Marius snapped over his shoulder.

Tahlia gave Marius a look. "Sorry, Trevain," she said, glancing the ghost's way. "He's a bit of a grouch. He does trust you, or he wouldn't have followed you in here. He especially wouldn't have let me trail along. He's very protective."

Trevain nodded. "I know that type. The whip also says a lot."

Marius's eyes were lightning. "Will you please remain on task?"

Tahlia studied Fara, her chest caving at the color of her skin. "Fara, we will get you out of here."

Fara coughed and a spot of blood showed on her bottom lip. "Dark shadows..." More coughing interrupted her and she crumbled to the chamber's stone floor.

"Fara," Marius said, his voice stern but somehow incredibly comforting, "Lady Tahlia speaks the truth. We will free you. Have no doubt."

Tahlia melted inside. If only they could be back at the keep, feasting or flying or both. She hated seeing her two favorite people in such agony.

Fara only nodded, seemingly unable to say anything else.

"Duck your head down," Marius ordered her. He faced Tahlia. "Take my sword. It will strike a wider path. Once you cut the flames, I will lunge for her."

"You can touch her?" Tahlia asked.

Marius's eyes shuttered for a second like her words had struck him a mortal blow.

"He is only cursed to never touch you," Trevain said.

Tahlia whirled. "What do you mean? You know what's wrong with him?"

"It's insulting that your knee-jerk reaction is to think I'm an idiot just because I'm not quite alive."

"That's not," Tahlia started to say, "that's not what I meant, I—"

The ghost waved her apology away. "I know some things. For instance, Katk is trying to rise. A new champion has awakened him from his long slumber, as evidenced by the activity of the varjuline."

"I'm so confused," Tahlia said. "Let's put a pin in that for now. How can we get Fara out?"

"You'll need a really big pin for that one..." Trevain exhaled, clearly annoyed. "I have never witnessed anyone escaping a varjuline's cage."

Tahlia's heart sank.

"Then ready yourself, Lady Tahlia." Marius set his sword on the ground.

She picked it up. The hilt was still warm from his hand. She bit her lip, praying and wishing and begging all of the Old Ones to come to their aid with this whole mess.

Tahlia swung Marius's longer, wider sword along the middle of the cage. The flames sputtered and cut out and Marius moved in a blur of astounding speed, his arms reaching down for Fara. He grunted in pain and drew back just as quickly as the flames reignited themselves.

"I can't do it. They're too quick to reform."

"If they're too fast for you, they're too quick for anything in any realm. You are so incredibly fast, Marius. I mean, High Captain."

Marius's stone face gave none of his thoughts away.

"Do the creatures fear any force or being?" he asked Trevain, even though his gaze was on Tahlia. She felt his look like a hand on her cheek, and to steady herself, she took a deep breath.

"Only their master, Katk."

Marius made a quiet humming noise like he was thinking. "What does he wield?"

"Plague, of course." Trevain gestured to Fara.

"Well, I don't have experience wielding illness," Tahlia said, "aside from sneezing on folks when I have an ague."

"It's a bit more serious than that, I'm afraid," Trevain said.

Oh, how Tahlia wanted to hear Fara say something dark and worrisome. She looked awful, slumped inside the cage of flames.

"Maybe we should fight fire with fire?" Tahlia ran from the chamber, heading for the dragons.

Vodolija? Tahlia tried to speak to the Seabreak inside her head again. *Lija?* No answer. Perhaps Tahlia needed more practice.

"Vodolija?" she called out as soon as she was back in the remains of the great hall.

The dragon flew over the half-collapsed roof, then dove into the great hall, her wings barely able to work in the broken space.

Marius and Trevain ran up behind Tahlia.

She climbed onto Lija, scrambling to the saddle. "We need to get the chamber uncovered so they can try their fire on the cage."

"Worth a try," Marius said quickly.

Howling erupted outside the walls. Goosebumps ran the length of Tahlia's body.

Trevain grew even more transparent. "They're here. The varjuline. I don't know if they can hurt your dragons, but you, you must flee!"

Staring the ghost down, Tahlia shook her head. "I'm not leaving Fara."

"We don't abandon our own," Marius said.

Ragewing hovered above the ruins, wings blowing the spindly branches of a tree growing out of the wall.

"Which is why I haven't left you yet, High Captain," Tahlia said, climbing onto Lija's back.

Marius growled and showed his fangs to Tahlia, then he leapt onto Ragewing.

Black shadows coursed into the old keep, their movements like oil seeping into the empty spaces in the walls and spreading over the floor, only to crest like waves. When they peaked, their Fae-like silhouettes had heads, flowing hair in varying lengths, arms, and torsos.

"Gods, they are creepy. Lija, try frying them."

I like that plan.

The Seabreak's four wings fluttered as she flew out of the ruins and hovered beside Ragewing. Both dragons blew fire into the oily shadows, but the dark shapes fled before the fire could hit them.

"They are running from the flames, so it must hurt them," Tahlia called out to Marius. "Can you not use that power you wielded last time?"

"I will attempt it." He lifted his hands, but no sparkling magic flashed.

Damn. She guessed he couldn't control whatever that power was.

Shaking his head, he pulled his whip from his shoulder and let it whirl and crack over the area where the varjuline had gathered. They didn't dart away from the whip's end like they had from the fire, but their heads had turned.

Marius locked his gaze on Tahlia. "At the same time."

She knew what he meant. He'd crack the whip and distract them while the dragons breathed fire again.

Marius raised his arm, but a shadow shot from the group and curled around his hand. He shouted, obviously in pain.

Had the shadows learned from the first battle? Did they know that Marius, possibly because of his curse, could wield magic? Were they taking action against that power somehow?

He shook his hand, but the shadow clung tightly. His grimace told her that the shadow's touch poured agony into him. Ragewing flew higher, and finally, the varjuline dropped away from Marius. His whip hand looked paler. He put his whip in his other hand, then unleashed it with a crack.

The varjuline eyed the whip, their motions almost in sync.

"Now," Tahlia said to Lija.

Lija and Ragewing blew fire into the varjuline. They scattered, their forms ragged and bits of their essence floating into the air like clouds of ash.

"Again!" Marius commanded. He cracked the whip twice this time, once on his right and then on his left.

The varjuline howled and Tahlia's ears rang. Lija and Ragewing let loose two more streams of blazing fire, and the varjuline were no more.

"Quick, Lija, tear up the stones there. Open the place up!"

The Seabreak dove, smashed her talons into the old floor, and rose back into the air. Tahlia couldn't see beneath her mount, but Lija must have been holding a few good scoops of dislodged rock because some of the debris was missing. Fara slumped, lifeless, in the fiery cage below the broken floor.

Ragewing and Lija flew down to the next level, landing beside the cage.

Marius flexed the hand the varjuline had attacked. "On my count, flame."

"Stay down, Fara!" Tahlia hoped she would remain where she

was. She didn't want their proposed solution to be worse than the problem.

"One, two, three!" Marius called out with Trevain now hovering just behind him and Ragewing.

The flames from both dragons mingled to create a river of fire colored citrine, sapphire, ruby, and aquamarine. Fara's head lolled to one side, then she ducked again, hands over her head protectively. The cage shimmered, grew brighter, then dissolved like the creatures who had built it.

Marius leapt from Ragewing, gathered Fara into his arms, then took off. Tahlia and Lija followed close behind with Trevain streaming along beside them.

At the first area of ground covered in moss and low grasses, they landed, Tahlia and Lija quickly getting a fire going for Fara and making her as comfortable as possible considering evil ghosts were lurking about and they only had one heavy blanket between all their bags.

Fara sat up against a boulder. Marius tucked the fine blanket around her. Silver embroidery sewn into cloud-like patterns decorated the top-notch wool. He stood and turned to face the ghost.

"Trevain, do you know a remedy for what ails her?"

A small shadow oozed from the ground and Marius leapt back.

"Watch out," he said sharply. "One more."

"That's the little one that we saw the first time the shadows attacked," Tahlia said.

The shadow flew past Marius, its movement erratic, as if it was afraid. It flew into the boulder beside the one Fara was leaning on and bounced backward, trembling.

Ragewing roared at the varjuline, and the shadow cowered low.

"I have heard of too dumb to live," Trevain said, looking down his nose at the shadowling, "but too dumb to die is a new one, I must admit."

Marius lifted a hand and Ragewing let out a quick blast of fire.

The small varjuline disappeared into the mossy ground. Trevain pursed his lips like he was disappointed in the shadowling.

Tahlia knelt beside Fara and smoothed the blanket so that it lay just under her chin. "Marius brought out his rich fellow's blanket for you, Fara. Soon, you and I will have enough to buy one of these too. I mean, come on. Don't die before we get paid, all right?"

Eyes burning from unshed tears, she tucked her friend's hair behind her ear. Golden boils showed over Fara's right eyebrow and along her cheek. She wasn't as pale as earlier, but she still hadn't opened her eyes or uttered a word.

"I have never seen someone leave any of the fire cages, so I don't have any information about healing her. It's not the same as the plague that killed me. This is the plague wrought by Katk and his first champion, the plague set on those with Mistgold blood."

Tahlia tried to get Fara to drink from her waterskin, but the liquid only spilled over her unmoving lips.

"Tell us the whole story, spirit," Tahlia said. "We need to know everything."

"How about I show you?" Trevain waved his hand and everything disappeared.

CHAPTER 21
MARIUS

The world flickered back to life. Marius spun, unsheathing his sword. Fully leafed oaks swayed in the breeze, and maples spread their branches along a well-set roadway of light stone.

They were not where they had been.

"What magic is this, spirit? Where are we?" He knew he shouldn't have trusted that Trevain fellow.

"Where is Fara?" Tahlia asked.

Tahlia was panting and wide-eyed with anxiety. Marius longed to grab her and hold her tightly. But of course, he couldn't or she would die. He remembered Ophelia's words in painful detail.

"Be calm, my lady," Trevain said, making Marius want to shake him. "Fara remains nearby, but not exposed to this dimension. You are in a version of my memory."

He looked very pleased with himself that he had brought them there.

Marius glared. "Return us to our squire or suffer the consequences."

"Time doesn't pass in the living world while we are here. Calm yourselves," Trevain said.

"So nothing is going to happen to Fara?" Tahlia asked, looking to Marius.

Marius gave her a shrug and focused on the spirit.

Trevain shook his head. "She must have some blood that isn't heavily Mistgold."

"Yes, she has a dash of human blood. Not like my level of the stuff, but a little," Tahlia said.

Trevain raised his eyebrows and pursed his lips. "I never thought to see anyone escape the varjuline alive. But no, nothing will pass while we are here. She will never even know we have left and the world there is frozen, so to say, while we visit my memory. Now, welcome to my home, the way it was before the dragon riders invaded."

Marius blinked. "We are in the Kingdom of Spirits?"

"We are. About eight hundred years before the current period."

Tahlia whistled. "It's beautiful. Why did it turn into such a hellish place? What did the dragon riders do? Do you mean the Order of Mist Knights?"

"This was before they called themselves that, but in a way." His gaze cut Marius as surely as a blade. "I speak of the same families that those of the order come from, yes."

Marius kept his tongue. He had heard versions of this history, and in none of them did his predecessors seem innocent. No, indeed his people had forced their way into this land and he wasn't proud of what had happened after. He didn't blame Trevain for his glare or the sharp tone of his words. But that was all the more reason to wonder why the ghost was helping them. He hated the order. Why was he giving them aid?

The verdant forests and lush farmlands shimmered until the group stood on a high hill overlooking a walled city crafted of massive rectangular stones.

"This was our capital. The jewel of our land." Trevain jabbed

Marius with a scowl. "Your kind flew here and stripped our king and queen's coffers of silver and gold. Then you moved on to our mines, our livestock, our wild animals, and so on. While you were pillaging and doing exactly as you pleased, you spread a terrible plague."

Trevain lifted his ghostly fingers in a circular movement. Rubbish piled up along the city's streets and rats ran from building to building. The city's inhabitants and those traveling outside the walls were dotted with dark splotches. Their skin looked papery and rough.

"One of us decided to sacrifice all and raise a monster," Trevain said. "Some say he accessed Unseelie power."

The Unseelie Fae lived in another realm entirely. Though the current Unseelie king had ties to Marius's king—Seelie Fae King Lysanael—the two civilizations never crossed. Only the royals visited one another and only rarely.

Trevain continued his tale. "Others claim the monster was a summoned demon. No one knows the truth. What we do know is that this male, a guild master from my neighborhood, killed his wife and slowly bled himself to death. In the wake of his offering, a giant climbed out of the earth."

A three-story structure on the western edge of the city trembled, dust lifting from its walls and thatched roof. A dark gray-green hand exploded from the thatch, followed by a massive head and body. A giant stood up, the building crumbling to ruins around him while screams erupted from the diseased masses. The monster had glittering golden eyes and just the look of him turned Marius's stomach. It wasn't that he was hideous and frightening. He was, but the true horror came from the fact that the giant felt familiar somehow.

Why in all the hells would a monster feel familiar to him? He had never once seen this creature.

The giant stepped over the castle walls and grabbed a Green-flanked Terror and his rider. The dragon went limp and colorless.

As the monster flung the rider to the ground, the rider's scream went silent and golden boils popped up along his face and arms. These new boils were like a strange mimic of the black spots on the natives of the kingdom.

Trevain waved his hand and the kingdom faded into night. "The giant's plague took revenge on the dragon riders who had invaded. None of those with mostly Mistgold blood survived. Once the giant succeeded in his champion's task, the task set on him by the guild master, he returned to sleep beneath the ground."

Tahlia grimaced. "High Captain, I believe you have seen the bones of this giant."

"I have, yes."

"Oh, wait." Tahlia pointed at Marius. "Your hands were dirty after you woke up. Remember?"

"Yes."

"I bet you returned to the bones while we were sleeping."

"This damned curse." Marius stilled. He had spoken of something roughly related to his curse. The curse hadn't halted his tongue. "I am cursed." He stared at Tahlia. "I can say it. I am cursed."

"What do you mean?" Tahlia stepped closer.

He backed up, holding out his hands. "Stay away. If you touch me, you die. Ophelia set this curse on me and I haven't been able to utter a word about it to you."

His throat grew dry and tight and his heart pounded heavily in his chest like he was sick, but he was telling her. Finally!

"Marius..." Tahlia's beautiful eyes glistened and she tilted her head. "I knew you wouldn't just shut me out for no reason."

"I didn't realize this would affect your curse in this way," Trevain said. "I guess because we are here and removed from the living world, you are temporarily free of the curse set on you by Katk's new champion."

Tahlia faced Trevain. "So Katk is the giant? What does *champion* even mean?"

"The one who raises him is his champion. Stories say that his champion may ask for one act of dark magic, but then Katk will feed on those with Mistgold blood until he is satiated or until he runs out of victims."

"That means Ophelia is his champion. But how? The monster was never on Dragon Tail Peak," Marius said. "We would have heard of that. My family and all of the riders' families would have been killed by his plague. I wouldn't be here if he had traveled into our region."

Trevain continued. "The ritual can most likely work from far away. And the standing stones and their runes keep Katk trapped here. There is some mystery as to how my people persuaded him to sleep again, but it has to do with Mother Twilight."

"Wait, wait, wait," Tahlia said. "I can only handle so much folklore and reminiscing for one afternoon. First, I want to hear more about Marius's curse."

Her gaze shot to his face, and her eyes held so much hope. Gods, he wanted to kiss her senseless. Breathing out, he focused on the problem at hand.

"So Ophelia truly raised the monster with dark magic." He shook his head. Despite the topic, his face stretched into a smile and the sensation was odd. "It's wonderful being able to speak about it. The curse held my tongue until now, it seems. But yes, Ophelia was in my rooms when I returned there after hearing about the commander's death. She rose and touched my mouth with a bloody finger. She said if I touched you, you would die. Much of my time since that moment has been foggy and dreamlike."

"More like a nightmare."

"Indeed."

"So you believe Ophelia had something to do with her father's death? Like what I was getting at when I found you and spoke to you? Do you even remember that?"

"I don't remember, but yes I do think she had something to do with the death. The ritual demanded blood and she used his."

Trevain was nodding. "Katk will be drawn to Ophelia just as you, her victim, are likely drawn to Katk."

Marius swallowed. His mind whirled with the cascading effects of the new commander of the order being the murderer of the previous. How could she bring herself to kill him? Madness. Such a mad tragedy. "I'm surprised Ragewing permitted this journey. He knew I wasn't in my right mind."

"Oh!" Tahlia smacked Marius's shoulder, her excited eyes changing to show wide-eyed terror.

She dropped back and stared at her fingers, whatever she had been about to say apparently forgotten.

And she had touched him.

"No..." Marius couldn't breathe. He turned to stare down Trevain. "How will the curse affect her? She only touched my clothing. Does that mean nothing will happen?" And that the love of his life wouldn't die before his eyes? "Don't even try your sarcasm or wry words with me right now, ghost, or I will find a way to end you."

"Calm yourself, knight. I would do no such thing," Trevain said to Marius. Then he turned toward Tahlia. "And you seem well enough."

Trevain appeared completely unruffled, which, of course, ruffled Marius greatly.

Marius eyed Tahlia's cheeks and bare forearms, watching for signs of anything deathlike. "Come now, spirit! You must know."

"She would turn to ash most likely. That's how most curses work, don't they? How do you feel?" Trevain asked Tahlia.

"Fine." She looked up at Marius and an ache spread across his chest. Reaching out her unscathed fingers, she said, "Should we try again? Skin to skin?"

Marius drew away, heart tapping madly. "Absolutely not. Are you a fool?"

"A fool for you." Tahlia smiled, a twinkle in her beautiful eyes.

Trevain shrugged. "I don't think you would suffer any foul consequences. Although, I will say, you two are using my traumatic memory realm for your selfish purposes. I can't say that I appreciate it."

"I don't give a whit what you appreciate, spirit," Marius spat out. "We must understand what rules to follow to beat Ophelia and her monster at their game."

"Well, I suppose that does make sense," Trevain said.

Tahlia was suddenly gripping Marius's hand. He glared down at her, fear stabbing him repeatedly and making his eyes hot.

Please don't take her from me, Old Ones. If you ever cared for this rider, please refrain.

"Are you, how do you, Tahlia, I..."

Tahlia grinned again and the stabbing terror halted. "I'm great!"

Marius crushed her in his arms and pressed his lips to hers. The feel of her soft mouth on his and the curve of her against him nearly had him throwing her to the ground to ravish her properly.

"Still here," Trevain said.

"Still don't care," Marius said, taking a second away from Tahlia's lower lip.

Tahlia laughed against his mouth and drew her tongue across his. His body jolted with a desire stronger than anything he'd felt in his entire life. He wanted to shelter this female, to destroy anyone who dared to threaten her, to join with her in every physical and spiritual way possible.

He smoothed a hand across her cheek and delighted in the way she shut her eyes and sighed.

"Tahlia, you are not my knight right now. You are you. I am me."

Tahlia jumped up and wrapped her legs around him. He let out a surprised *"Oof,"* but he caught her neatly and secured her in his arms. Her warmth made him growl with want. *Mine, mine, mine.*

His heart beat out the truth. She could be his mate if they both chose that path.

He kissed her hard, claiming her even though he wasn't ready to ask her out loud about their future. He was cursed. Until they solved that problem, no future existed for them. Tahlia returned the kiss, her sweet tongue curling over his and her fingers digging into his upper arms, where the vest ended and his softer tunic began. She rolled her hips against him and he gritted his teeth as longing flowed through him, deep and sure and wild.

But the wind rushed around them. The memory world's green forests and haze of long ago slipped away.

They were thrust back into the current world. An invisible force blasted Tahlia away from him. Marius tumbled, nearly ramming into Ragewing's front talons. He sat up to see Tahlia on the ground beside Fara, Tahlia's face slack with shock.

The memory world was gone and they had returned to the current state of things. Marius shook his head to clear it and adjusted his trousers. Tahlia seemed alive and well. Gods, he worried she'd be hurt. They never should have risked touching.

"I'm fine, Marius," Tahlia said, standing up and brushing herself off.

Trevain was shouting nonsense and pointing.

"Gods, what is it, spirit? Must you shriek like a frightened hen?" Marius got to his feet.

"I saved Tahlia just now, so you can offer thanks, High Captain," Trevain snapped. "Now, look to the East!"

Katk, the plague monster, walked across the old road, smashing trees and driving boulders into the earth.

CHAPTER 22
TAHLIA

The giant stalked across the landscape with varjuline curling around his legs like scary little shadow puppies. Tahlia shivered, then stood, brushing herself off.

"Marius?" Tahlia looked him up and down, watching for signs of the curse's control.

His face only showed every emotion that she too was experiencing. Want. Fear. Confusion. Desperation.

"Lady Tahlia." He also looked exhausted.

"You're still yourself?" she asked. "Tell me your favorite game to play with Titus."

"I don't think the c—" He swore and snarled, looking away. He seemed to hate it when he lost his temper, like he was frustrated not only with the curse but with his reaction to it.

"Right." Tahlia nodded. "You can't say curse or anything related again."

The giant lifted its ugly, gnarled head and roared.

"At least, he's a ways off?" Tahlia said, her tone forcibly hopeful. "Where is he headed?" As long as it wasn't toward them, that was fine for now. They still had to rouse Fara and figure out a plan. Gods, she needed some time to process what Marius had told her, Trevain's story, and, of course, the whole *plague monster who kills dragon-riding Fae is back* situation.

Trevain floated above the dying fire, just beside Fara, who still slept. "I have a guess and I don't like it."

Marius knelt beside Fara and felt for a pulse in her neck. "Speak plainly, spirit." He glanced up at Tahlia, a world of frustration and pain pinching his handsome eyes and mouth. "She is strong. I believe she is healing."

"Katk might have figured out that the standing stones are what trapped him here during his first waking period," Trevain said. "If he destroys them, he will be free to continue setting his revenge plague on Fae with Mistgold blood from here to the coast."

"Why?" Tahlia asked.

"When the victims succumb to his plague, their blood and life force feed him. That is the only way he can remain awake."

"So to put him back to bed like the naughty fellow he is, we must starve him of victims?"

"That, or whatever solution the goddess, Mother Twilight, has up her proverbial sleeve. Perhaps we should find her..." He scratched his chin. "Presenting him to his champion would work if said champion breaks the magic that woke him."

Tahlia scowled. "Why would his champion put him to rest?"

"Supposedly," Trevain said, "if the champion did not sacrifice himself or herself, the monster's reign will end when he sees the champion. Perhaps as a check on the magic's power, set by the Old Ones? No one truly knows. Only my fellow spirits whisper this truth and most of them are stark-raving mad."

Marius grumbled something unintelligible. "I don't know why you'd expect a situation like this to make sense. In my experience, dark magic follows no logical course. It's painfully undisciplined."

"That's such a Marius thing to say." Tahlia looked to Trevain. "What happens with Marius's curse in all of this?"

Trevain shrugged. "I would assume his curse will end if we manage to put Katk to sleep again."

A frown tugged at Tahlia's lips. "Assume?"

"The monster has only risen once," Trevain said sourly, rolling his eyes.

"Watch your tone, spirit," Marius snapped.

Pleasure coursed through Tahlia's body, warming her from head to toe. She smiled at Marius and was rewarded with a smile back.

"Forgive me," Trevain said to Tahlia.

Tahlia waved him off and knelt beside Fara. Her eyes opened. Red lines crisscrossed the whites and her lids were swollen. Tahlia exhaled in a rush and hugged Fara fiercely. She was as limp as a rag doll as Tahlia helped her lean back again.

"I'm so glad you're not dead," Tahlia said.

"Me too." Fara attempted to sit up once more, but she couldn't quite manage it.

"Don't get up. Not yet."

Fara nodded and relaxed, letting her eyes drift shut again. "I thought that was it for me."

"We all did," Trevain said, giving Fara a kind smile.

The experience with the memory realm had exhausted Tahlia and Marius, so they decided to rest if only for an hour or two. They asked Trevain to keep an eye out and every living being, dragons included, lay down to close their eyes for a short break.

"You're certain we can take the time to rest? He is going to be tough to catch," Tahlia said, looking in the direction Katk was headed.

"The dragons will outmatch his pace without much difficulty if they have a moment to rest," Marius said, the confidence of many years in the order making his words firm and his tone sure.

Giving him a thumbs up, Tahlia lay beside Fara and fell asleep watching her friend's purple eyelids flutter in dreams. She hoped they were dreams, anyway, and not nightmares.

. . .

A DRAGON SNOUT WOKE TAHLIA, and when she opened her eyes, Lija was staring down at her.

CHAPTER 23
TAHLIA

Tahlia and Marius readied for flight, adjusting saddles and checking bags and ties. They worked in silence to let Fara sleep a little longer.

A cough from Fara turned Tahlia around from where she'd been checking Lija's girth strap. Fara sat up, blinking.

"Feeling better?" Tahlia asked.

"I am. Yes. Well, maybe."

Tahlia brought her a skin of water. "You were right about the plant and the dragons. I ate some of the leaves and now Vodolija can communicate with me." Tahlia tapped her temple.

Fara's face lit up as she looked at Tahlia. "Really?"

Tahlia nodded. "Yes!"

Fara drank a healthy amount and handed the skin back to Tahlia. Her sluggish movements gave away the lingering fatigue of her experience.

Beside Ragewing, Marius frowned and grew still. His hands were poised over one of his smaller satchels. "What are you two talking about?"

Another cough shook Fara, and she seemed to have forgotten

about Marius's question. "We are leaving now, right? We have the High Captain, I see. Insane mission accomplished." She faced Marius. "Are you cursed? Did you break it?"

Marius grunted, and his jaw muscles worked.

"He can't tell us," Tahlia said, "but yes, he is, and no, we didn't. We still have a lot of things to do here before we can leave."

Tahlia looped an arm around Fara and helped her to stand. She was steady enough and Tahlia was thrilled to see it.

"I'm guessing these aren't tasks I'm going to be happy about," Fara said.

Tahlia smiled. "Definitely not."

"Why are you dragon riders so enamored with creative ways to end yourselves?"

Marius's lips tilted up for a second, and Tahlia's heart soared to see him doing so well. Was the curse easing off of him because Katk was awake and Marius had done as Ophelia's monster required by digging up his bones?

Trevain introduced himself to Fara and spent a few minutes filling her in on all the happenings while Marius and Tahlia tended to Ragewing's and Lija's old injuries.

"Trevain reminds me of someone," Tahlia said.

Marius raised an eyebrow. "Who?"

"I'm not sure. His face just looks like someone I know. It's odd."

Marius frowned, and Tahlia shrugged as she finished corking the unguent Fara had brought. She placed the leather-wrapped bottle in one of the saddlebags.

Don't forget to have him eat the plant, Lija said.

"Ah! Right. Thanks."

"Who are you talking to?" Marius scowled and looked from Tahlia to Trevain and Fara.

Fara walked over on slightly unsteady feet and Lija bent so she could climb on. Tahlia and Marius each gave her a hand up.

"Wait here," Tahlia said to Marius.

She searched the ground until she found some of the blood-red plant. She plucked a bit and handed it over to Marius, careful not to touch him.

His lip lifted, showing his teeth.

"Shh, you're fine," she said, "and I'm fine. I know not to touch you. Now, eat that."

"Why would I?" Marius demanded.

"Because I told you to." Tahlia winked.

Fara and Trevain laughed. Marius grunted unhappily, but he shoved the plant into his mouth and chewed. His furrowed brow cleared. His mouth fell open.

"Ragewing?" he said quietly.

"Fara and Lija introduced me to this plant," Tahlia explained. "It sparks the ability for riders to hear their bonded dragons."

Marius faced Ragewing and had a hurried conversation, then Marius went silent though he still focused on his Heartsworn. He spun to face Tahlia. "But we can't speak back inside our minds?"

"We can. But it's not easy."

It is worth practicing, though, yes? Lija said.

"Definitely. Lija said we should practice and see if we can manage it after a while."

The effects should last forever. Once the talent blossoms, it remains. The plant is rare. It only grows in this land. My forefathers once lived here, hidden deep under the land's surface, where the sea flowed through secret caves.

"That is amazing."

"I'm jealous of this new thing," Fara said. "I'll be the big person and admit it."

"Why aren't you stelling me we are going to die from eating it? I'm impressed you're merely fretting over my friendship with Lija and how it might affect ours. Which it won't."

They took off into the sky, heading in the direction Katk had gone. Clouds whisked by, the air cold and sickly sweet with Katk's disgusting odor.

"Firstly, I'm not shouting warnings because I researched the plant. That's why I even bothered to tell you about it. Its effects on Fae are established and I have that information. Secondly, well, this is all just too much," Fara said. "Once you've hit this level of emergency, there is little point in warning everyone. We all know it's likely that death is about to greet us. Will we end up like you, Trevain?"

"I don't know. I suppose it's possible, but I died from the natural plague the Mistgold Fae brought. Your kind."

"Easy, ghost," Fara said. "Don't throw accusations at me. I wasn't alive back then. Not even close. I might be half dead, but I'm more alive than you and I can find a way to teach you manners." She cracked her knuckles.

This time, Tahlia had put Fara in the saddle's main seat. She didn't want her friend falling and it was easier to keep a hold on her from the back.

"Also, why is everyone so mean to Trevain?" Fara asked. "I'm ecstatic you're here and helping us," she said to the ghost. "Without you, we would be clueless."

Trevain glowed brightly and lifted his chin, his ghostly robes fluttering in the wind. "Thank you, Lady Fara."

"Are you secure there, Lady Tahlia?" Marius called out in his Mistgold Fae voice. It echoed in her ears like drums and she bit her lip, loving the power behind it. She would save him. Somehow.

Trevain streamed along between the dragons. "You will most likely die of the revenge plague and I've seen no ghosts of those who suffered that fate."

Katk's stone-and-moss-colored head came into view over a tumble of high hills. The stench was overpowering.

CHAPTER 24
TAHLIA

"Gods save us from the smell," Fara said, adding on some elaborate noises. "I might perish from the stink before he has a chance to bespell me with any sort of disease."

"You hover here," Marius ordered, his whip already out and ready. "I'll circle him to get his attention."

"Explain to me why isn't Marius considered the monster's champion," Fara said.

Trevain nodded "Because though he dug up the bones, he didn't perform the ritual of blood sacrifice. Sounds like your Ophelia did that."

"She is not *our* Ophelia," Tahlia said. "We loathe that dog's arse."

Fara snorted. "You're demeaning dogs with that statement."

"True," Tahlia agreed. "She is worse than that. A damn nightmare with a pretty face."

Ragewing was a scarlet blur ringing Katk's massive skull. The snap of Marius's whip echoed off the rocky outcroppings along the hills. A roar blasted through the air and Fara covered her ears.

Careful now, Lija ordered as she tilted to one side, keeping Fara in the saddle.

Tahlia grasped Fara, bracing her friend between her arms as she held the low-profile pommel. The reins pressed into the skin between her fingers. Fara talked a big game, but she was trembling.

Katk reached toward Marius, but Ragewing shot into the higher clouds, disappearing from view.

Tahlia tapped Lija's neck and the Seabreak flew closer to Katk and flapped her four wings to hover. She blew one short blast of bright flame, the heat brushing over Tahlia's forehead as the wind rose.

The monster turned to face them, his eyes black holes of nothingness and his hands encircled in shadow and golden magic.

Fara shuddered. "Can we please fly away now very quickly?" she said, stuttering.

"Lija, fly!"

The dragon took off just as Ragewing exploded from the high clouds to fly beside them. They dashed toward the ruins, where the scent of Fara and the rest of them might keep Katk busy searching for victims. The trick would be to get him hooked on the blood under the ruins' broken great hall while they flew off.

They soared over the ruins and Katk stopped, sniffing the air.

He is taking the bait.

"I hope so."

The monster lifted its head and grabbed for Lija. Fara screamed and Tahlia held tightly to her as the Seabreak dodged Katk's dark green fingers. Tahlia grew dizzy with the horrible smell and the fear of his touch.

"If he even grazes your flesh..." Trevain flitted away to float beyond the old castle's outer wall.

Ragewing dove toward Katk and blew fire.

"Here, monster!" Marius snapped his whip over the creature's bulbous ear.

Katk swung around, smashing through what remained of the great hall's floor. His bare—and fully disgusting—foot was covered in blood from one of the varjuline's ritual bowls. He grabbed the bowl, and the blood spilling from the container disappeared. The blood on his foot and ground did too.

Fara whimpered. "What kind of bizarre and horrifying thing is happening here? We are definitely going to die."

Tahlia shut her eyes and thanked the Old Ones that Fara was back to her old self. "I'm guessing that's one way in which he eats."

"Ew."

Lija shot into the sky, catching up with Ragewing, and they flew away from Katk.

THEY LANDED, deciding that everyone needed some rest if they were to keep on battling Katk. Fara had fallen asleep the moment her head hit her bedroll. Trevain had claimed to have ghost business elsewhere and he'd disappeared, leaving the dragons, Marius, and Tahlia on their own.

The fire's golden light danced across Marius's proud nose and strong cheekbones. Tahlia had never known she'd be envious of light.

"What are you thinking about?" Marius asked, his voice quiet enough not to carry to where the dragons gathered beside a sleeping Fara at the second fire.

Tahlia didn't want to say what she had been thinking. It would only be torture, and as much as she enjoyed giving him trouble, this time, teasing didn't feel right. Taking a swig from the flask of lavender mountain liquor Fara had brought, she drummed up a new question. Gods, the liquor was awful.

"What's your ideal day?" she asked finally.

He looked up, an almost comical frown on his face. "I'm sorry?"

Shrugging, she plucked a piece of long grass and twisted it around her finger. "You heard me. I was just curious."

"Always so curious."

His features softened, and she looked away, his tenderness burning her heart and soul. Their situation was such a wreck.

"Tea before dawn," he said. "A book in my hands and a day of flying ahead of me."

It was mad how hard she was falling for this male. "Tea and a book? I didn't expect that."

His eyebrows lifted. "How about you?"

"Guess."

His gaze snagged on her face, the look in his eyes bracing. "You only want to be in the sky. As much as you are able. You live to fly."

Her heart danced at how well he already knew her. "Exactly."

"But you don't mind landing long enough to have some cake."

A laugh bubbled from her. "True."

"Ask me anything, Tahlia."

Her breath caught. The way he said her name... "I don't have a list like some people." She gave him a pressing look. "So I'll have to think on it."

"What were you *really* thinking when I first asked you?" he asked. "Because that was a lie."

She swallowed. "Touching you."

Glancing away, he poked at the fire with a long stick. His throat moved in a swallow, his skin brushing the collar of his vest. Tahlia wanted to tuck her head into that space and press her lips to the beat of his pulse.

"Marius, look at me."

"It's too difficult."

Tahlia blinked, watching him stir the fire as if his life depended on its heat.

"If I study the soft edge of your cheek," he said, his deep voice a low whisper, "the lift of your upper lip, the curve of your breast, your pert nose, I'll come undone... I... Tahlia, this situation will kill me if it doesn't kill you."

She could hardly talk around the tightness in her throat. "We will break your curse."

"I wish I was as sure as you."

"We will find this Mother Twilight goddess that Trevain mentioned. She'll help us."

"She is only a story told to us by a ghost," he said. "How do we even know if she still exists?"

"We have to hope."

"Telling myself to feel things doesn't make it happen."

"Doesn't it?" she asked. "Try telling yourself over and over and over. Hold to that like you hold my heart."

He finally looked up and met her gaze. The desperation in his stormy eyes sent a bolt of lightning down her body, hitting her heart and restarting it, then shooting heat to her core. She swallowed.

His focus snagged on her mouth. "Stop biting your lip. I can't handle it."

Surprise brought a quiet laugh out of her. "Really? Doing this —" she said, biting it again, "—does it for you?"

"Thoroughly."

She couldn't help but snicker.

"You find my pain humorous, do you?" A teasing tone lightened his words.

"I'm sorry," she said. "I shouldn't."

"You can't help yourself. Vexing me is your new favorite pastime."

"Guilty as charged."

His scowl broke into a grin like the sun rising after a long, cold night. The urge to leap over the fire and dive into his arms was so powerful that it actually hurt.

She grabbed the flask of lavender mountain horror and handed it to him. "Once we break this curse," she said as he took a swig, "I'll show you exactly how much fun vexing can be." She ran her hand down her chest very, very slowly.

The splash of the drink on the ground had Marius jolting out of a stupor. He straightened the flask and swore. “It’s your fault I gave half of that to the earth,” he said to her, his eyes smoking.

An idea popped into her head. “Why don’t you follow me to that little copse of trees?”

Frowning, he did as requested.

This was going to be interesting.

They left Ragewing and Lija to their sleep, then Marius and Tahlia walked to the small cluster of maples, oaks, and pines.

The slender shadows of the wood welcomed them, the wind scented with something that was fairly pleasant. Moonflower maybe? Clover? Definitely pine.

Tahlia’s stomach fluttered at what she was about to suggest. What would he say?

CHAPTER 25
TAHLIA

She stopped and leaned back on a tall, wide maple—one of the only large trees in the area. He halted a few paces back, keeping his distance for her safety. She hated that space between them with a super searing type of hate.

The light through the trees made his Fae-white hair shimmer like magic from the ancient worlds, like Unseelie magic. Marius was every bit as dangerous as an Unseelie. He could snap her neck in a breath.

"Why are you grinning like that? It's...not a comforting expression, let me tell you."

She snickered. "I like how deadly you are."

He tilted his head and lifted one moonlight-hued eyebrow. "You do, hmm?"

That deep voice sent wonderful shivers down her back. She licked her lips and noticed that his gaze focused on the movement of her tongue.

"Just why did you drag me into the haunted forest, little salty?"

"I'm not sure I love that nickname."

"Lady of the Skies?"

"Maybe one is good for a certain situation and the second for another, very different scenario."

"Ah. I will have to study your preferences once we are free of..." His lips tightened and his throat moved in a swallow.

"For now, let's say your hands do as mine do."

His brow furrowed but he held up his hands, palms toward the forest's canopy as if in surrender.

Tahlia chuckled, slid her hand down her hip, and cupped one side of her own arse. She winked.

His lips pulled into a smile and he seemed ready to chuckle, the light dancing in his stormy eyes. He mimicked the movement, grabbing his backside and smirking at her.

"It's my turn now. It's only fair," he said.

Tahlia's toes curled inside her boots. "All right, then. Let's see what you've got."

Marius's near grin fell away and his eyes narrowed as he studied her face. He lifted a hand and drew his fingers from his temple to his jaw. She echoed his hand's action, her heart beating soft and slow now. He set his hand against his cheek. She did as well and turned her face into her hand slightly, leaning into the touch. It was her flesh, but the intention was his. A shadow of a smile graced his mouth.

"You're so lovely, Tahlia. I never tire of looking at you. The way you smile. How your forehead wrinkles when you're thinking..."

He shifted his hand to slide over the spot between his eyebrows, and so she did the same, shutting her eyes for just a moment to pretend he could touch her again. To imagine they were like any couple in the Realm of Lights, courting and unrestrained.

"My turn," she said, feeling strangely shy.

She opened her eyes and set her hand against her heart. He placed his hand over his chest and he curled his fingers for a moment like he wanted to grip his heart. She drew a line from her chest to the hollow in her throat. Her pulse beat quickly beneath her fingers. Marius slid his hand up too and a sweet smile pushed at his lips. The heat of a tear trickled down Tahlia's cheek. Marius lifted his hand and brushed his cheek as if he could wipe her tears away.

"I love you, Tahlia. You know that, right? I assume you already have me figured out."

Her heart leapt and rolled and a broken laugh of joy fell from her mouth. "I had hoped. I love you too, Marius. Even if I'm not supposed to."

"That just makes it more fun for you."

She knew they were ignoring the curse for now and that he meant the fact that she was half-human and their relationship could cause further disturbances in the order.

"I do like a challenge," she said, wiping her tears away with the back of her hand and adding a teasing note to her voice.

She met his gaze and let her eyes show him that it was time to play a little more, to stop the weeping, to enjoy one another if only for this brief moment. He smiled in return, his glance going dark and hot. Want simmered low in her belly and she took a shuddering breath.

Smoothing her palm down between her breasts, she lifted an eyebrow. He mimicked the movement, his lips parting slightly and his fully slitted irises going wide.

"I'm taking over now," he said.

The growl of command in his voice made her skin flush. He continued down his torso, then swept upward to palm his chest. He drew a thumb back and forth. She did the same, inhaling quickly as the touch had her nipple rising beneath her tunic and vest. Tilting his head as if he was truly enjoying the view, he ran his hand down to cup himself. Tahlia swallowed, her face on fire and her body melting. He was very obviously enjoying this now.

With a painfully slow movement, he stroked himself and she did likewise. The pull toward him was nearly overpowering. She wanted him against her, overwhelming her in all the best ways.

Marius's hand shifted into a faster pace. Her blood going molten, she obeyed his unspoken order. She leaned back on the tree, panting as release coiled inside her.

With his free hand, Marius dragged his fingers across his mouth. Tahlia did the same but nibbled her forefinger in the process. She sucked it between her lips and he growled, his eyes shuttering for a moment. He reduced the speed of the hand at his cock, and she whimpered quietly, not wanting to slow down. Her release was building, pounding in her blood, making her knees weak. Vicious, he was, as he eased into a crawling pace. He wore a wicked grin. She wanted to lick him up and down; her lips ached with the need to taste his skin again.

"Faster, Marius, please..."

His tongue darted out to wet his lips and he increased his pace little by little. She mimicked him perfectly even as her body demanded more, more, more. Finally, her body uncoiled and shivered. Pleasure jolted through her, and he shuddered, uncovering himself momentarily.

They gasped together, and he grinned at her.

"You are the true monster in this haunted kingdom because now I only want you more," he said.

"Goes both ways, my scary, lovely captain."

"I'll be right back," he said. "You take all the time you need to gather yourself."

"Thanks."

He pressed his fingers to his lips, kissed them, then held them out toward her. She touched her mouth, feeling the smile he'd placed there. After a quick trip back to the fireside, Marius returned with the flask. They stood under the trees, drank, and talked about little nothings that meant everything.

She would save him from this. Or she would die trying. Marius was hers and no one was going to take him from her.

CHAPTER 26

TAHLIA

Trevain led them to another forest, a sun-hued gathering of trees with wildly long and spindly leaves.

"My grandmother always said this was one of Mother Twilight's homes," Trevain said, "but I have never sought the goddess."

"She's a goddess?" Fara asked. "Why would she help us?"

Right. Fara had missed some information. "Yes, and why wouldn't she?" Tahlia asked.

"Perhaps because we are Mistgold Fae and we killed everyone with our germs?"

"I'm not Mistgold."

"Great. So she'll give you a big hug and strike the rest of us down with lightning. Fun plan."

"Hush. It'll be fine. Just you watch."

"If only we all had Tahlia's bright outlook on life," Marius said.

"It's going to get her killed," Fara said.

"Not if I have anything to do with it," Marius said.

"I'm still here, you know." Tahlia raised an eyebrow and Marius almost smiled. Every time his mouth lifted like that, her soul sang.

Trevain led them onward through the forest. The leaves were healthier here than elsewhere in this ruined kingdom, but no birds trilled as they should have, and Tahlia didn't think it was simply the presence of two dragons. The trees thinned in one spot and a waterfall splashed down from a sloping creek bed.

"It's beautiful." Tahlia set a hand on Lija.

The remnants of great power lie here like dust. She is not here.

"Lija says Mother Twilight isn't here," Tahlia said.

"She can tell?"

Marius looked to his dragon. He nodded and faced Tahlia, Lija, Fara, and Trevain. "Ragewing agrees. He said that she was here long ago but has traveled to another place. Trevain, what do you think?"

Trevain gasped. "You're asking me?"

The muscles around Marius's jaw flexed. "You have shown your trustworthiness thus far. I'm trying to take you at your word."

"I'm so honored," Trevain said, his tone wry.

"Watch it, ghost. My dragon is currently wondering if ghosts like you react to fire the way varjuline do."

Trevain seemed to shrink. "If you snuff me out, you'll have no guide."

"You aren't the only spirit wandering this land," Marius said.

"Enough, you two," Tahlia said. "Let's move on. Where to, Trevain?"

He led them onward for a while, the sky's mist wetting their faces and weighing down wings and Fae limbs.

A large cluster of lush pines stood out among the dark sludge of the valley and rolling hills. Within the first row of trees, a circle had been cleared. A perfect ring of space like an invisible door hung there suspended by unseen forces.

Trevain approached the circle slowly, holding out a hand and indicating everyone should halt. The dragons landed in the rocky area in front of the small forest, mud and algae splashing up their legs and cloaking their talons.

This place feels like being underwater.

"Really? In what way?"

It's difficult to explain in your tongue. Immersed in that which is not air. Held by forces outside your control.

"Interesting. Do you think the goddess is here?"

I would bet on it.

"Do dragons have a system of gambling?"

No. I was just using phrases you Fae use. Dragons are too wise to risk money on games.

"Right. Of course." Tahlia smirked up at Lija.

"Is the dragon telling you to hush? Because that is your move here, Mist Knight," Trevain whispered, raising a chastising eyebrow.

"Yes, Mother," Tahlia snarked back.

Trevain made a snarling face at her.

"Ragewing believes we should go in first and check the area with Trevain," Marius said. "Lady Tahlia, you keep watch of Fara, and I will whistle when you should enter."

"Something about you whistling to get me to come like one calls a dog isn't making me smile, High Captain."

He gave her a flat look. "If this was a mission for the order, your comment would be ruled insubordination."

"I think we've established that when you dig up a giant ancient monster, boring rules like that go out the proverbial window."

He rolled his eyes. "I will shout for you, my lady. Does that please you?"

Trevain and Fara traded a laughing glance.

Lija's husky laughter floated through Tahlia's mind. The sound made her grin from ear to ear.

"That will be perfect. Thank you, Marius."

"I don't like this lapse in protocol."

"Go on, now. You can lecture me later."

Marius growled quietly and rode Ragewing to the edge of the strange cutout circle. Following Trevain's watery golden light, the

Heartsworn lifted each leg carefully, stepping through to the green shadows of the wood.

He is right not to disturb the magical entrance, Lija said.

What would happen if he did?

I'm not certain, but I wouldn't want us to be nearby when it occurred. Did you realize you just spoke into my mind again?

I'm getting good at this! "Huzzah!"

Fara jolted against Tahlia, nearly toppling from Lija's back. Tahlia caught her and righted her in the saddle.

"Why are you screaming in my ear?" Fara demanded.

"I just spoke into Lija's mind again."

"No, you shouted. In my ear."

"No, before that. I said something else and Lija told me." Tahlia hugged Fara. "Isn't this telepathy thing wonderful?"

"If it involves less destruction of my eardrums, yes."

"Lady of the Skies!" Marius called out.

Tahlia waved.

"If we die here, at least you two had some time to flirt," Fara said.

"Ah, Fara. Be nice. We're about to meet a goddess. She could smite you down for that poor attitude."

"Fantastic. Now, I'm worried about smiting. What is that again?"

Tahlia patted her on the shoulder. "Quiet now, squire, and remember that coming along was your grand idea."

"Sometimes I loathe myself."

Lija brought them through the circle, her wings held tightly against her shimmering body. They caught up to Ragewing, Marius, and Trevain under a bower of red flowers growing in the branches of intertwined conifers. Petals flitted down in the breeze and the forest's scents lulled Tahlia into a relaxed state. Even Fara seemed to release some of the tension as she sat up in the saddle, straining to see past Ragewing. They walked slowly into a clearing that glowed with rainbow light.

In the center of the clearing, an old female sat on a stool.

CHAPTER 27
TAHLIA

The old woman's gnarled, glowing hands moved slow and sure as she knitted red woolen yarn. A few finished pieces lay folded at her hem on the mossy ground. Tahlia's breath caught at the beauty of the goddess. The weight of the goddess's presence was akin to the sensation of Marius's attention. Like a warm cloak had been draped across her shoulders and she'd downed a cup of crystal wine.

Tahlia glanced at Marius. Was his skin glowing slightly as well? She blinked and the sparkling of his cheeks and forehead was gone.

The goddess lifted her knobby chin and regarded the group with a pair of dark, luminous doe eyes. They were larger than a Fae's eyes and glossy like an animal's. The effect should have been frightening, but instead, only wonder poured through Tahlia's soul.

She slipped from the saddle, helped Fara down, then knelt beside Marius, who had also dismounted quickly. Red petals floated down to land on Marius's shoulders. The petals caught in Tahlia's hair and snuggled into her palms like small creatures longing for a warm spot to take shelter.

"Good hearts, I greet you," the goddess said, her lips unmoving but her voice strong and clear. Her accent was not too different from Trevain's, with strewn-together consonants and slightly rounded vowels. "Come closer and we will talk."

Marius stood and turned, holding a hand out to Tahlia, less of a helpful task than a simple show of affection.

"Marius..." she started. He had forgotten the curse. She didn't blame him. The goddess's presence was enough to make one believe everything had been set to rights in all the realms.

He winced and nodded, withdrawing.

Trevain and Fara joined them, walking alongside Ragewing and Lija.

"Greetings, Mother Twilight," Trevain said. He kissed his palm, then pressed his hand to the ground near her feet.

Tahlia mimicked the show of respect, then Marius and Fara did as well. The dragons bowed their large heads, eyes shuttering in a display of trust.

Listen closely, my rider, Lija whispered into Tahlia's mind.

Oh, don't worry. I feel her power, too.

Good. I worried you might try to entertain her with your latest knock-knock joke.

Tahlia bit her lip to keep from laughing.

"You seek aid against Katk," the goddess said.

"Aye," Marius said. "Do you have advice for us?"

"You cannot fight him. Not truly. But you can trap the monster and take him to his champion. You must move quickly. If he leaves this kingdom, he will end all the Mistgold Fae."

But Ophelia was far beyond this cursed place. "His champion is in the Shrouded Mountains, in the land bordering this one."

"Then you must trap him tightly. You must be the one to do it," the goddess said to Tahlia.

"Because of my human blood?"

"Yes, little wise one. He will not seek to plague you. But if Katk creates more varjuline, they will cage you and drain you of blood and spirit to feed themselves. The varjuline are not picky about the blood they consume. They are more animal than Katk and have no reason, only instinct."

Marius frowned. "Katk has reason? He seems blind with rage and driven by his curse alone."

"He seeks to finish what his first champion started. It is his calling."

"What will happen when we bring him to his current champion?" Trevain asked.

"When Katk is released and in the presence of his champion, that soul alone may put him to sleep for good."

"And if she refuses?" Tahlia asked.

The goddess inclined her head. "Does she want to end the Mistgold Fae?"

"She is of that blood," Tahlia said.

"Ah. Then you see what will be her motivation to put him in the ground once more."

But Tahlia could just imagine Ophelia listening to them telling the story. She wouldn't believe them. She would hesitate. She would get them all killed.

An image of Tahlia standing on a field of bloodied bodies, both Fae and dragon, washed across her mind. She shivered.

The goddess tilted her head, studying Tahlia. "That is only one potential outcome."

With a pair of heron-winged bone scissors, the goddess cut the yarn, then rose and faced Tahlia. She held out the piece she'd been knitting, a length of red with braided tassels. "I made this for you, Weaver."

Palms sweating and still filled with petals, Tahlia stepped forward. The goddess tied the piece around Tahlia's hips. Sparks of magic and the lull of power cocooned Tahlia until the goddess shifted her weight and eyed the belt.

"It fits." Her dark eyes found Tahlia's. "Remember who you are here," she said, touching a spot near Tahila's heart. "Little doesn't mean lesser in your case. Cleverly made by the Fire, there isn't a piece of you that goes to waste. You are the Autumn Weaver."

"I'm what?"

Mother Twilight just smiled and tapped her chin. "When you wear this belt, you are stronger than Katk. Not in the way of hand or foot, but in the ways that matter more."

She was lovely and powerful, but perhaps not the best at practical information. "Thank you very much, goddess. How exactly do I go about trapping Katk?"

"You will know."

The clearing turned to darkness.

CHAPTER 28
TAHLIA

When the light came again, they were back on the other side of the strange circle cut into the forest.

They stood side by side, dragons, ghost, and Fae, all seemingly stunned to the same degree. Tahlia touched the woven belt at her waist. The wool was soft like any other wool. Did this thing truly have power of some sort?

Tahlia turned to Marius, who stood on the other side of Trevain. "Why wouldn't she just tell me what to do?"

"I assume—" he started, trying to see Tahlia clearly around the ghost. Then he let out a small snarl and waved at Trevain, shooing him away. Trevain gave Marius a look but allowed Marius to usher him a few steps back.

Marius's broad chest moved as his gaze slid over Tahlia's face. The urge to touch him nearly overwhelmed her.

"As I was saying, Mother Twilight most likely knows we must go through an ordeal to gain the abilities we need to succeed."

"I'm game." Tahlia rubbed her hands together, excited for the next step in this grand adventure. "Any task that will stop that giant from killing everyone on the mountain and," she said, lowering her voice, "any ordeal that will get my hands back on you, I'm more than willing to conquer."

"I have no doubt you will subdue Katk, Lady of the Skies. But you must learn to hold your tongue when we are back with the order, on missions and in training. You must learn a semblance of discipline regarding our relationship and the order." His eyes softened and heated, his warmth extending from his muddied leathers to brush over her body.

"Aye, High Captain. I will behave. Mostly."

He chuckled and shook his head.

"You know, you look even better all grimed up like this," she said, gesturing to the dirt on his cheek, his tangled hair, and the mud along his white vest and trousers.

"I'm filthy."

"I understand that you hate it, but it does something for me seeing you ruffled."

"I'm well aware." His lips turned up at one side, and gods, did she want to kiss him until neither of them could breathe...

"What's the plan?" Fara called out. She was rubbing salve on Lija's scales like the wonderful person she was.

Marius saw what Fara was up to and seemed to be having a silent conversation with Ragewing.

"Did you figure out how to speak to him in your mind?" Tahlia asked.

"I did."

We should head toward the stones, Lija said.

A chill wrapped Tahlia. *Can you tell if Katk is headed there again?*

Yes. His evil energy thrums from that direction, from the lands just before the old border.

"Lija says Katk is going for the stones again," Tahlia said. "Eh, where did Trevain go?"

Fara and Marius looked around, and Lija faced Ragewing, their gazes locking over everyone's heads.

"Ragewing says the spirit was pulled to another place," Marius said.

"What does that mean?" Fara asked, her voice getting high-pitched.

"He is a ghost. Who knows the mystery of his afterlife?" Marius said, apparently not at all concerned.

Tahlia mounted Lija. "What is your problem with him anyway? You're a little mean to the fellow."

"I'm a *little mean* to everyone or did you not notice?" His eyes sparked with humor.

"Well, yes, you're the King of Grumps, but you're more about discipline and doing what is right. You don't usually push at people the way you do with Trevain."

"I am trying to trust him, but the feeling wavers. The fact is, we don't know what his motivation is for helping us."

Once again, the familiar look of Trevain pushed at Tahlia like a memory she couldn't quite grasp. "He can't just be a nice ghost?"

"His civilization was ruined by ours. So no, I think he has an ulterior motive, and though I can't blame him for that, I won't trust much of what he says until I figure him out."

Hurry, rider, Lija said.

"Should we move?" Tahlia asked Marius. She pushed her curiosity about Trevain away.

Marius gave a curt nod, and he climbed atop Ragewing in one seamless maneuver. She'd never tire of watching him do that.

They took to the sky with Fara in the saddle's extra seat behind Tahlia. Tahlia had Fara untie her quiver from the rest of the gear. Reins in her teeth, Tahlia slipped the quiver onto her belt, then took her bow from Fara's outstretched hand. She tucked the reins under an arm.

"Thanks!" she said to Fara over her shoulder.

"It's what I'm here for!" Fara sounded like she was about to throw up despite the forced cheer in her tone.

Tahlia nocked an arrow and watched the ground for Katk.

"So that goddess was vague, wasn't she?" Fara said. "*You will know*." She wiggled her fingers.

"Yes, and what was all that about the Autumn Weaver? I like pumpkin cakes and bonfires as much as the next person, but I doubt that's what the goddess was going on about."

Fara shivered. "Probably something horrible you will have to fight."

"More horrible than a plague giant?" Tahlia asked.

"I'm endlessly surprised at the terrors that pop into your life."

"Glad I keep you on your toes."

Fara closed her eyes and sighed like Tahlia had drained her of every ounce of patience.

Marius and Ragewing led them over a valley rutted with old roads and the chewed-up remains of villages and walled towns. A river passed through the valley and ran into a quarry that reflected the dragons' shapes.

Katk's lumbering form filled the horizon.

Tahlia had to set her jaw to keep from calling out a warning that no one needed.

"Really hoping that wisdom shows up any second now," she said, more to herself than anyone else.

Fara squeezed Tahlia's shoulder. "You can do this. I can't. I will probably fall off Lija and perish. But you, you'll be fine."

"No perishing today, please."

"I wish Trevain was here," Fara said. "He knew things. He could have helped you here, I bet."

Tahlia agreed. "I hope he is all right. He's been wonderful, no matter what Marius says."

"Is he still worried about Trevain's motives?"

"Yes. The whole *ruining Trevain's civilization and killing everyone he knew* thing," Tahlia said.

Fara made a grumbling noise. "But that was ages ago. He didn't seem to be harboring a grudge, helping us the way he did."

"And that's why Marius suspects him. He was too helpful too fast."

"I'm starting to wonder if Marius is right," Fara said. "Maybe we truly are better off without Trevain."

Tahlia glared over her shoulder. "Don't you start too. Trevain is a sweetheart."

"Only you would call a ghost a sweetheart," Fara said.

Lija chuckled in Tahlia's mind.

Katk was near enough now that the stench of him brought their conversation to a halt.

"You take the lead on this," Marius called out over the roar of the monster.

Tahlia took a shuddering breath and touched the woven belt. But nothing came into her head. No ideas. Not anything resembling a plan. She had to stall.

But they had no time for that. Over the hill, the standing stones rose from the fog. Katk would be there in mere moments.

The monster swung a fist at Ragewing. The dragon blazed a full-force flame at Katk and he reared backward, dodging the fire.

A thought simmered deep in Tahlia's mind. She pushed the thought toward Lija.

Katk's shadowlings had used a cage of fire to hold Fara. Maybe that would work for Katk?

Good idea, rider, Lija said.

Glad to hear you think so. Tahlia took a steadying breath.

"Create a crescent of flame above him and we will slowly lower the elevation!" Tahlia shouted toward Marius. She prayed the dragons would have enough fire to make this happen.

"Aye!" Marius called out, his body leaning forward as Ragewing tilted upward to hover, wings flaring.

Lija, if Ragewing's fire dies, I need you to fill the crescent. Are you feeling up to this? We will have to go in close for the flames to touch and create a barrier.

We will rope him in like shepherds do to sheep. Don't doubt my fire, rider. I am here and I am ready to fight.

Lija flew close, Marius and Ragewing going in as well. If Katk reached up now, the plague would hit Marius or Katk's fist would simply smash Ragewing out of the sky. Neither sounded pleasant.

"Now!" Tahlia's throat was already raw.

The dragons blew fire and Katk wheeled left, trying to avoid the flame. The dual fires rippled through the air, hissing into the fog and sending waves of heat across Tahlia's face. Katk let out another ear-splitting roar. Ragewing's fire sputtered and went out. He and Marius dropped back and Lija shuddered as she increased her fire to make up for the loss.

Lija's body rippled under Tahlia, the vibrations making her teeth knock together. Tahlia shot three arrows in quick succession. The monster batted two away, but one stuck in the side of his neck. Gold and black poured from the wound, but Katk didn't stagger.

He must yield, Lija said, her voice in Tahlia's mind weakening and broken with effort.

Ragewing flew around behind Lija and Marius shouted, "Pull back! She's draining herself. Pull back!"

I'm not. Do not ask me to stop!

But the pain in Lija's voice pushed a cold dread through Tahlia's chest.

Lija, the High Captain has given us an order. We must.

No, I can do this...

The fire sparkled and leapt erratically. In the space between one blast and the next, Katk swung his fist. His knuckles smashed into Lija's wing. Lija shrieked, an ear-cracking sound. They spun backward, completely out of control. Fara clutched onto Tahlia's waist. Tahlia could hardly breathe.

Ragewing shot beneath Lija. He stretched a wing and caught at her broken one, steadying her as the ground came at them fast. With Ragewing's help, Lija managed to even out in the air and soar to a stop.

Katk roared and stalked toward them. Fury burned in his demon eyes.

Ragewing and Marius whirled to face the monster.

Tahlia stood in the saddle and placed hands on Fara's shoulders. "Stay with her. Do what you can." She thrust her dagger, hilt first, at Fara, who stuttered something unintelligible and accepted the blade.

With her short sword still sheathed at her belt, Tahlia leapt from Lija's back to Ragewing's. Marius turned, eyes like bolts of lightning.

"What in the name of all the gods do you think you're up to?" he demanded.

Standing and doing her best to remain so while Ragewing lashed out at Katk with talons, she nocked an arrow. She aimed and fired. The arrow zipped past Katk's gnarled ear.

"Helping you not die," she said to Marius, her words a blur and her pulse leaping. "And I'm keeping that monster's hands off my dragon!"

Her second arrow glanced off Katk's rock-hard head and fell to the ground.

Ragewing kept fighting while Marius slung his whip through the air. The whip snapped across Katk's left eye and he howled. Blood poured from the injured eye, black and gold gore leaking down the monster's broad cheek. Katk surged forward and Ragewing was driven backward.

Tahlia tumbled to the mud beside Lija, who tried to breathe more fire at the monster but only managed a flurry of sparks. Tahlia scrambled for her dropped bow, snagged it, then she rolled and shot another arrow at Katk, this time toward his softer bits.

Katk dodged the arrow and hurried forward, his gaze on the standing stones.

They were losing him. Lija was down, maybe for good. Ragewing was out of fire. Sweat trickled down Tahlia's face and she swiped it away with the back of her sleeve. They couldn't lose this fight.

"Go!" she shouted at Marius, who was staring at her from Ragewing's back like he wanted to take her up with him.

The scarlet dragon took off like a bolt from a crossbow. Tahlia threw her bow down and drew her short sword. She ran after them, feet pounding over a rise of mossy rock. Ragewing flew in front of Katk's face and lashed the clawed tip of one wing across the monster's good eye. Tahlia couldn't see everything from the ground, but Katk certainly wasn't slowing. If anything, his steps were growing longer and more sure as he came within feet of the first rune-marked border stone.

Lija, stay with Fara. Don't try to join me.

Lija's only answer was a resounding roar that bounced off the wall of rock Tahlia ran beside. Tears pricked Tahlia's eyes. Lija's pain shadowed Tahlia's side like a varjuline had latched onto her arm and between her ribs.

Marius's whip cracked. Katk whirled, more graceful than he should have been at his size, and he reached toward Marius. Marius leapt from Ragewing's saddle and landed hard. His face shone with sweat as his sword flashed. Was his leg injured? Blood poured from Katk's knee. Ragewing flew at the monster, lashing out with talon and tooth, but Katk bent, dodging the scarlet dragon's attack. The monster swiped a hand at Marius.

Three thoughts hit Tahlia's mind like quick cuts from the sharpest blade.

Katk wasn't going to miss.

Marius would die cursed and plagued with golden boils—the same horrible end as many of his Mistgold ancestors.

She was the only one close enough to save him.

Her blood singing through her veins that this was her mate, she jumped between Katk's hand and Marius, her gladius outstretched like a spear's head. Katk's hand hit her. The blade sank into his foul flesh, and she held on to the hilt. The monster shook his hand to dislodge the blade. Tahlia was thrown into the air. Her stomach lifted as she fell again. Katk batted her body aside. She slammed into the earth. Her breath left in a violent gust. But she was on her feet before the pain hit her.

Marius stumbled backward as the monster grabbed for him again. Tahlia reached out and shoved Marius back.

Their eyes met. Sorrow swallowed the storm of Marius's gaze. He mouthed one mournful phrase.

No, my heart, my love.

Katk bellowed, grabbed Tahlia, and lunged toward the standing stones.

A wave of aching pain started in Tahlia's palms, where she'd touched Marius. The sickening sensation spread into her chest, down her legs, and up her neck toward her face. A shiver ran through her. She was like an egg cracked against stone, her strength and energy spilling into Katk's sticky hold on her.

The curse crawled through her body. The monster held her tight. He stomped on the first of the standing stones and the rock exploded. A wind scented with green grass and rain touched her cheeks.

She shut her eyes. "Goodbye, Marius, Lija, Fara, and Ragewing. I'm sorry I failed."

A warmth circled her waist. She opened her eyes. Red sparks lit her torso, only partially visible within Katk's great hand. An image shimmered to life over the view of the second stone. Katk smashed the runed stone with a fist and threw Tahlia to the ground.

But the image only grew clearer.

Titus stood beside Maiwenn and Ewan. Claudia, Atticus, Justus, and Enora were there too. Then all of the riders except Ophelia. They weren't truly present though. This was only a hallucination.

Tahlia! Lija shouted into Tahlia's mind.

She realized Lija, Fara, and Marius had been shouting her name as they tried to fight Katk.

“Tahlia! Don’t give up! Fight!” Fara’s voice was a reedy plea on the wind in Tahlia’s ears.

Blinking, she pressed a palm against her pounding forehead. The image of the other riders faded. The view of Katk’s massive form and broken bits of the standing stones went black. Tahlia fell into darkness.

CHAPTER 29
MARIUS

Tahlia's head thumped against the muddy earth. Her body shook violently on impact. Panic ripped Marius's chest and his stomach churned. He climbed onto Ragewing's back, then helped Fara up and settled her in the saddle. Pale as a fading dragon lavender bloom, she didn't say a word. Ragewing would have to carry Lija and Tahlia too.

"Will you struggle to transport so many?" Marius asked Ragewing.

Stop fretting about me, Ragewing said into his mind.

I will not, Marius said. *You will be carrying us all. It's far too heavy a burden.*

We will rest along the way. I can do this, rider.

Marius prayed Ragewing wouldn't end up exhausted into death after this chase.

"Lift your arms, squire," Marius said quietly to Fara.

She obeyed, her movements sluggish. He ran his whip around both their waists so there was less of a chance Fara would fall during this difficult journey.

Marius's gaze strayed once more to Tahlia. Her eyelids were nearly purple and her mouth was slack.

Ophelia's curse had invaded her body. He'd known it the second she touched him because a cold unlike anything winter could dole out had nearly knocked him backward. It would kill her. Her death wouldn't be from plague as he or Fara would suffer if Katk got his hands on them, but the curse's own dark end. How long would she last? What could they do to save her?

Why did you do it, Tahlia?

He swallowed hard and tapped Ragewing's scales. The dragon lifted into the air.

Marius's mind twisted around her sacrifice, trying to comprehend why she had given herself for him. Didn't she grasp the fact that his life was a husk without her in it? She'd barged into his world and turned everything beautifully upside down.

With one of his taloned feet, Ragewing took gentle hold of Tahlia, then he gathered Lija around the middle. His wings beating an erratic rhythm and his scales heating under the press of Marius's hand, Ragewing launched into the sky.

The ground below showed evidence of Katk's flight. Some of the scant trees in the area had been crushed into the moss and mud. Footprints the size of Lija created a trail leading out of the Kingdom of Spirits and well into the farmlands of the Realm proper. A barn lay half-smashed and a crowd of folk ran down the king's road to the south.

And there was Katk in the distance, climbing along a foothill. He splashed down into a lake and waded through. Water rolled up and over the lake's edge to flood an inn that sat along the road.

Ragewing increased his speed, his sides heaving with the effort.

Marius gritted his teeth.

Damn you, Ophelia.

After they cleared the first of the true peaks, Marius tapped Ragewing, asking him to land and rest.

The dragon relented, the fatigue obvious in the way he panted and the labored movements of his wings. His head hung low as he circled a small clearing near one of Katk's footprints. Ragewing eased Lija and Tahlia to the ground first, then landed.

Marius untied Fara with a careful, quick movement, not wanting to startle her. She had started to shiver with shock. He dug in one of his bags and found an extra cloak. Pulling it around her, he spoke softly, trying to ease her heart with meaningless words of comfort.

"All will be well." The words tasted like something very close to a lie—so bitter that it puckered his tongue. Not even his deep mind believed they would come out of this without experiencing great loss.

He helped her from Ragewing's back. It was miraculous that both Lija and Ragewing had deigned to allow Fara to fly with them. Perhaps the fact that squires could not ride bonded dragons was out of date and the dragons had evolved in a way the order hadn't anticipated. Thinking about less serious topics such as that kept Marius from losing his mind. His fear for Tahlia was the air he breathed, choking him to near senselessness.

She is strong, Ragewing said.

There is no solution. Ophelia was clear about that. As was Trevain.

As though Marius had summoned him with his silent words to Ragewing, the ghost appeared over Tahlia's inert body. His golden glow illuminated the hollows of her cheeks. She already appeared thinner.

Marius sat Fara on a fallen tree and tucked the cloak tightly around her.

"Can he help her?" Fara asked, her voice raw and rough.

Marius looked in the direction she gazed. She meant Trevain. "I don't know. I'll talk to him."

"Tahlia really likes him. Be nice."

"I've been nice. I just don't trust him because he has no reason to be helping us. Also, I thought he would be trapped in the

Kingdom of Spirits. I wonder why he is here and how he managed it."

"Have you ever noticed how much his eyes look like hers?" Fara asked, tilting her head.

Marius left Fara and knelt near Tahlia. Trevain floated beside him. He did have a similar set to his eyes.

"Trevain, can you help her? You know what happened, don't you?"

"I do. I will do what I can to keep her in the realm of the living. I will push her spirit, nudge her, so to speak, with my soul."

"Why?"

"She is my descendant."

Marius's mouth fell open. "Did you always know?"

Trevain shook his head, his horns glittering slightly within their own ghostly light. "I had begun to guess, but... I returned to the realm between worlds and saw the truth there. Mother Twilight guided me. Her mother came from my line."

So that was why Mother Twilight had met with them. Tahlia was one of her own.

"Before you knew that," Marius said, "you were helping us because..."

"Because you aren't evil. The varjuline are. Katk is. It had been ages since I'd seen anyone not of evil spirit in our lands. Aside from a few others like me, of course. Also, I was dreadfully bored."

Marius huffed, tilted his head, and nodded. "Well, I'll take any help you can give. I don't see how my dragon will manage to get us back to the order's castle before Katk arrives there and kills them all."

Trevain leaned close to Tahlia's face, his gaze touching her forehead, her throat. He pressed his hand to his chest and then to Tahlia's. Light blinked brightly around his ghostly fingertips. "Oh, you won't be alone. The goddess's belt has called Tahlia's own to her. Look now," he said, still eyeing Tahlia.

Marius turned to see a thunder of dragons cresting the next peak, their wings dark slashes against the lightening sky.

CHAPTER 30
MARIUS

He stood so quickly that his head spun.

The order was here.

His chest tightened, then relaxed, and he let out a sigh. Mother Twilight's weaving had somehow called the other riders.

"Tahlia already sees the other riders as her family," Trevain said from where he hovered above Tahlia. "Like Fara and her dragon. And you, of course."

Marius stared while Fara hurried to Tahlia's side. Tears silvered her purple cheeks as she took Tahlia's hand. Trevain bobbed in the air beside Fara while she plucked small yellow flowers and mashed them in her palm. Did Fara have Healer training?

Ragewing lifted his head as the order landed one by one, only some of them fitting into the clearing while the rest maneuvered into the edges of the pines that ringed the area.

"What is happening, High Captain?" Titus was the first to speak, leaping from his dragon to salute Marius.

Marius studied the faces of his fellow knights. All of them had come. Every last one, save Ophelia.

Titus's mouth was drawn tight and his eyes narrowed as he took in the scene. "We all experienced the same vision." He truly cared for Tahlia; that much was obvious from the way he kept glancing at her. The two had begun acting like siblings in training and off hours, teasing and checking on one another. Marius approved of the growing bond between them. "We saw Lady Tahlia giving her life for yours when that monster lunged for you."

"It felt like a summons," Maiwenn said.

"But who called you?" Marius asked.

"I did." Tahlia's voice rang out clear behind Marius.

His heart drummed out of rhythm, and he spun. She smiled at him, supporting herself on her elbows. Warmth flooded his veins. Though she looked like a ghost of herself, she was still herself—achingly beautiful. His lovely, brave, soon-to-be mate. Hope flickered brightly in his chest. She was still sick and cursed, but maybe she could heal from this. Maybe between Trevain's help and whatever magic Mother Twilight had awoken in Tahlia , she would be saved.

"Lady Fara gave me some flowers and I feel somewhat better." Tahlia smiled at her squire.

"The curse still threatens her life," Fara said. "I can't stop that. But the *soleils guérisseurs* should slow the decline and give her more time. Albus taught me about the plant."

The other knights simply stared. There was much to explain about what had passed.

Tahlia beamed. "I'm sorry I didn't pay more attention to your interest in healing, Fara. Lady Fara," she said, correcting herself and glancing at Marius.

Marius couldn't fight the broad smile stretching his lips. He couldn't help but hope... "Thank you, Lady Fara."

Marius longed to sprint to Tahlia's side, lift her into his arms, and hide her away from the world. Just for a little while, he wanted her all to himself. To tend her wounds. To learn every bend and curve of her body. To make her laugh, gasp, moan, and sigh. He longed to see her bloom beneath his hands and in his care. She was still terribly pale and hollow-cheeked, but she was awake. Alive. For how long, well, he refused to dwell on that question at the moment.

Keeping a distance from Trevain, the knights swarmed Tahlia.

"Please help me to Lija," Tahlia said to Fara.

Titus put an arm under Tahlia's and hefted her up. Fara took up Tahlia's other arm. They walked the few steps to Lija, then Tahlia settled on the ground and set her cheek against Lija's folded wing, the uninjured one. Titus put a palm on Tahlia's head briefly, and she looked up at him and gave him a mischievous grin. He gently bumped the underside of her chin with a knuckle.

Tahlia coughed and took a shuddering breath as she gathered herself, Titus stepping back so Fara could fuss over her.

"I called you with this woven magic artifact from a goddess in the Kingdom of Spirits," Tahlia said.

Most of the knights blinked in surprise.

Light cut across Enora's freckled face as she took a poultice from her bag and held it to Fara. "A goddess gave you a gift?"

Fara took the proffered poultice, studied the bottle, then worked on Lija. The dragon grunted in pain but only glared at Fara —no fire involved.

Ewan took a water skin from his bag and handed it to Tahlia. "What happened to Lija?"

"The monster you saw, it was Katk. He carries a plague too," Tahlia said.

Morvan's jet-black eyes studied Tahlia. "And you're injured? I'm so confused. Somebody explain everything, please."

"Stay back, just in case," Tahlia said, waving a shaky hand and nearly touching Claudia's whipping orange tail.

"I don't think the curse will touch them," Trevain said from behind the group.

The knights glanced his way, their faces drawn with wary awe.

Atticus shoved his hair back between his silver horns and turned to face Tahlia. "The curse? What curse?"

Lija was trying to partially cocoon Tahlia. Titus helped by moving a middling-sized boulder out of the way. Marius flexed his hands, wishing he was the one to physically help Tahlia. But he wasn't sure if his touch would worsen her condition. Plus, he wasn't sure he could control himself if he had his hands on Tahlia just now. He'd been so lost, so desperate, when she'd given herself for his life. If he touched her again—when he touched her—it would be to claim her in full as his mate and his ultimate joy. There wouldn't be time for explanations about Katk or Mother Twilight.

"What exactly happened?" Titus asked.

Then Tahlia and Marius told them everything about this unplanned mission in detail. More questions flowed from the knights. Tahlia answered, the tentative happiness in her tired eyes lighting a flicker of hope in Marius's heart.

Trevain also explained the history of his kingdom.

"And as much as I hate to say it," Tahlia said in a slightly broken voice, interrupting him when he began regaling everyone with the architectural details of the ruins the varjuline had inhabited, "I truly believe Ophelia cast this curse."

Maiwenn grunted and chewed the inside of her cheek. "So our new commander woke this plague monster who is set on killing all those with Mistgold blood?"

Her tone wasn't harsh, only curious, as if she was confirming what she'd been told. Something in the way they'd been called by Mother Twilight's belt at Tahlia's waist had changed the way she looked at Tahlia. Somehow Maiwenn and the rest knew of Tahlia's sacrifice.

"Did something change between us? I mean, I'm glad but..." Tahlia waited for Maiwenn to answer.

"We all felt your sacrifice. Whatever you did," Maiwenn said, her gaze flicking from Marius to Tahlia, "I'm not sure what happened, but we definitely felt it."

"The sacrifice and the Call of the Weaver," Trevain said. "Our goddess, Mother Twilight, gave Lady Tahlia a belt of our people's magic. She woke its power by giving all to another. The weaving sent a beacon to those she trusts with her life."

Atticus and Claudia exchanged a sheepish grin, then looked to Tahlia with respect shining in their eyes. Maiwenn nodded at Tahlia, crossing her arms and smiling. Titus knocked his head gently against the side of Tahlia's. He was becoming more dragon than Fae, Marius thought, silently chuckling.

I agree, Ragewing said into Marius's mind.

Marius laughed out loud then. *I'll have to tell him so.*

Tahlia reached for Fara, who helped her up. "I think I can ride. Can we move now?

Fara clucked like an old hen. "You shouldn't be going anywhere. You look like death."

"Katk isn't going to wait and I refuse to be left here."

Titus nodded at Tahlia, then eyed Marius. Marius gave a nod.

"We ride now," Marius said. "Lady Tahlia, you will be tied to Titus's saddle. He will hold you fast. I trust him." He looked to Fara. "Squire, you'll be with me. Ragewing will carry Lija for the first leg, and then, Sir Atticus and Revel, you will carry her the next." Atticus's Heartsworn was nearly as large as Ragewing.

"Aye, High Captain," Tahlia said, her eyes full of a fevered desperation.

Marius swallowed, wishing there was time to pray to every Old One he'd ever heard of. She was still worried she was going to die. So was he.

"Aye, High Captain," the other knights echoed.

Marius barked more orders, falling into the comfort of routine and familiar activities. He gave Ragewing a healthy serving of dragonbread and made certain Lija had the same treatment.

"Before we take off, if you see any plants with blood-red leaves, pluck them and eat them. Once the leaves are in your stomach, you'll be able to communicate with your dragons through your mind."

Claudia rubbed her orange forehead. "I can't take any more wild revelations."

The rest of the knights had gone silent, their dragons turning their attention to Marius.

"It's true," Tahlia said, her voice sounding weak again. "I can hear Lija in my head."

"Lija?" Brutus pursed his purple lips and fisted his hands, which Marius knew was a sign that the warrior was losing patience and more than ready to take action.

"Her name is Vodolija. Lija is a nickname," Tahlia said.

Then she crumpled to the ground. Marius went cold and hot all at once, his feet moving before he could order himself to keep his distance. He stopped short, Fara's hand suddenly on his chest.

Titus was helping Tahlia up.

"We've got her, High Captain," Fara said.

Gritting his teeth, he nodded. "Let's ride. We are running out of time to try to break this curse."

Everyone mounted—Fara with Marius, Tahlia with Titus—and they were off in moments.

"How do we set things right?" Titus called out in his Mistgold voice.

The wind tore at Marius's knotted hair and blew Fara's scent across his face. She was seated in front of him, murmuring ridiculous phrases to Ragewing.

"And if you don't eat me, I'll steal anything you want from the kitchens. You look like a guy who enjoys chocolate."

Ragewing grunted loudly and increased speed to fly beside Titus and his Spikeback, Ptol.

"We trap Katk with fire and bring him to Ophelia," Marius said to Titus, using his Mistgold voice.

It felt so wrong to address another rider as simply their name. Especially one who had been deemed their commander. But he shoved that urge to be the disciplined knight away. Ophelia didn't deserve a title. She deserved death.

"If the monster touches you, you will eventually be drained of all your life energy," Marius called out. "Keep your distance and only use flame, short spear, and arrow to fight."

Ewan's Spikeback, Angus, flew just behind Titus and Ptol. Ewan had a short spear and three more tucked under his leg for easy reach. Atticus, Enora, and Ewan would have their bows at the ready.

"To your units!" Marius called.

The knights and their dragons joined their units and flew in the standard pointed formation for a long flight when speed was paramount.

If you see anything you believe is a sign of Katk, please tell me. Nothing is too small, Marius said silently to Ragewing.

How about we check that valley to the south? If I were a lumbering giant, I'd choose the lowlands over these spiking mountains.

Let's give it a go. Marius held up a hand and directed the order toward said valley.

Ragewing led the three units over a pale limestone outcropping. Farms ripe with spring plantings of onions, cabbages, and the first shoots of root vegetables spread below like a painting of a peaceful life Marius would never know. Not that he longed to be a farmer, but the idea of working alongside others without the interruption of dark magic was certainly a draw.

"She'll be all right," Fara said, twisting to speak to him over her shoulder.

"I don't know. I..."

"Ah. You still can't speak of the curse and what you know."

"No."

Fara's hair fluttered in the wind as she looked toward Titus. Tahlia was lashed to him and Ptol's saddle. It would be difficult for Titus to fire arrows in his position. Once Ptol was out of fire, Titus would need to fall back. Perhaps serving as a distraction, out of reach of Katk, but still helpful. Marius tucked that strategy away for later use.

As if looking her way had shaken her awake, Tahlia opened her eyes.

Marius took a deep breath.

"If you scowl at her like that, she's going to pass out again," Fara said.

"If my glares affected her in any way, she'd have given up on me the first day we met."

Fara laughed. "Still. Smile at your lady, High Captain. She probably needs some reassurance. It can't be fun shaking hands with Death every hour or so."

A shudder raked through Marius. "I'd rather you not joke about her condition."

"It's that or scream and cry. You pick."

"Fine. Jokes, it is."

There! Ragewing veered in a southwest direction, taking the units with him.

Katk stormed through a boggy area, dark water splashing up around his knees and gnarled trees breaking like tall grass around him.

Good spot, friend.

Marius gave orders for the units to surround him. "Once he is contained, we escort him as quickly as possible back to the castle."

"High Captain!" Titus waved a hand.

Tahlia was awake, upright, and her mouth was moving, but the wind and Katk's roars tried to cloak her words.

Titus took over for her and shouted, "She's saying there's no way our dragons' fire will last long enough to return to Dragon Tail, to the castle! She wants us to fly back and grab Ophelia."

"Absolutely not," Marius said. "You're sick, Lady Tahlia." A thought haunted him, far more frightening than any ghost or shadowling—she was not merely ill. She was dying. "Not possible!"

"I will murder you if you let her do this," Fara said, a promise in her voice that worried Marius even though she was but a squire.

"I wouldn't blame you," he said.

Then there was no more time for discussion because they were within Katk's extended reach. The dragons encircled Katk.

This had to work or all of them were dead and the order would be no more.

"Unit one blast!" Marius called out.

CHAPTER 31
MARIUS

Marius had Ragewing fall back to protect their cargo—Lija, who was roaring in frustration. Fire spilled from the rest of the unit one dragons: blue, orange, purple, and gold. Katk shrieked and batted at the riders and their mounts. The monster's forefinger clipped Titus's Spikeback. Ptol spun and his riders jerked harshly upward, Titus dropping his bow and grasping Tahlia, whose eyes were wide open.

Marius's heart thudded at the back of his throat. With every fiber of his being, he longed to be the one protecting his intended mate.

Katk surged toward them as Ptol tried to right himself.

"Unit two!" Marius ordered. "Don't expend all your fire though. Watch your levels!" They had to reserve enough to prod this monster toward home. Such a mad plan!

Taking turns, including unit three as well, they had Katk panting and lumbering in the right direction after another hour of fitful fighting. The journey would be arduous, to say the least.

"I have an idea!" Tahlia called out. She sounded stronger and her color had mostly returned. Gods, this curse was taunting them, fading and returning over and over again.

Marius could hardly hear her above the noise of fire and monster and wind.

Her energy is stronger. Her body is fighting the curse, Ragewing said. *The blooms that Lady Fara administered have helped indeed.*

Marius whispered a prayer of gratitude. *I didn't realize you could sense the energy and health of another being.*

There is much Fae do not know about dragons.

I look forward to learning from you. If you choose to share.

A deep chuckle rumbled through Marius's mind. *Some things, I will share. Some are not for Fae to know.*

I won't be like my ancestors, harsh and cruel to those around them. If you decide on secrecy, I will honor that.

And that's another reason you're my rider.

Katk groaned and stalked through the countryside, his movements prodded by the dragons' flames. He whirled and swatted at Maiwenn and her Seabreak, Donan. Katk's fist hit Donan's side, and the dragon screeched. Lija shrieked with him. Maiwenn's eyes went wide. She dropped from the saddle and fell toward the ground.

Donan let out a spine-rattling sound of agony and dove for his rider.

Go! Marius called to Ragewing, who immediately plunged.

A jagged line of boulders marked the ground below Maiwenn. Claudia and Justus shouted her name.

Marius held his breath. They weren't going to make it. Maiwenn was going to die.

Ragewing angled to swoop below Maiwenn, and Donan dove straight for her.

Katk shouted as if in triumph, and rage poured from Marius's very pores. He pressed his palm against Ragewing's shoulder. *Please. Faster.*

I'm trying, rider!

Donan roared, the sound splintering the air. Katk broke free of the dragon fire and lunged at Ptol and Titus.

Marius's entire life was being ripped to pieces, like a crumbling piece of parchment left in the sun and wind too long. He needed his knights. All of them. They were the only ones he trusted to help Tahlia, to help him if she couldn't be saved.

The rocks flew toward them and Maiwenn was tumbling like a corn husk doll, her limbs taunted by the wind.

Donan stretched out his long neck and snatched Maiwenn from the air. But they were going to hit the ground and Maiwenn wouldn't be able to handle the crash.

Under them!

Ragewing veered harshly and came up just under Donan's tipped wing. Ragewing bumped the other dragon, the rocks so, so close. With the aid of Ragewing's bump, Donan rose sharply into the sky with Maiwenn secured between his teeth as dragons did with the very young of their kind.

Ragewing followed Donan, and Marius shouted orders, "All units, stop Katk! Turn him around!"

A sheep farm appeared beyond a crevice in the lowlands. The giant was heading that way, of that Marius had no doubt. Either with the golden plague or with simple fists and feet, Katk would kill everything in sight. These folks in the foothills of the Shrouded Mountains had Mistgold blood just as he did. And he had sworn an oath to protect them.

"Three! Unit three, take the lead!" His voice boomed off a bank of clouds shifting between Ragewing and Ewan on Angus's spiked form.

Ewan raised a fist to indicate he'd heard and would do as ordered. His dark, bald head reflected the scant sunlight as Angus dove toward the giant. Brutus on his Spikeback followed close behind, flanked by Cyrus and Lucius on their Heartsworns. Their fire rippled across Katk's face and the monster dropped back, his foot crushing a bridge spanning a broad and spring-muddied river.

"Unit two! Back them up! Southward until we hit the pit, then we push him northwest!" Marius ordered. "Unit three, fall back! We will fill in there!"

He waved to his unit behind him and they circled unit three, flaring fire as unit three filtered in between unit one, flying between them in expert-level formation. He was proud of these riders. And crushed that Tahlia wasn't among them.

A dark shape burst through the scattered clouds and every thought shattered.

Ophelia. Her cheeks and chin glistened as if she had been... No, she couldn't have been weeping. Ophelia didn't cry, not even once since he'd known her. And they had seen a great deal. Including her father's death.

Had she truly killed him? Was this all her doing?

Tahlia believed that. Marius didn't want to believe it, but Ophelia had never been a good person. She'd followed orders. Well, except concerning those damned gloves of hers. She must have felt so terribly desperate to be cruel to her dragon.

He couldn't even imagine what he was thinking when he had thought to be her mate, to wed her and have younglings with her. He'd been an idiot. A fool. Ophelia was even worse than he realized. Not just cruel to a creature because of desperation. But cruel in general. She, like Katk, was a monster.

Ophelia lifted her hand, and black and gold magic spun from her fingertips like she was casting a net.

The world's edges fogged.

Marius couldn't seem to recall what he and the others were doing here, up in the air, above the creature designed to enact proper revenge.

CHAPTER 32

TAHLIA

Tahlia felt hollowed out, weak, and unsubstantial. Her strength came and went in unpredictable waves. Focusing on the battle wasn't easy as her vision blurred off and on. She was a cracked remnant of something that was once strong on the back of a dragon that wasn't hers.

But she wasn't quite useless yet. Not during her now-and-again alert periods.

Wasn't it just lovely that Ophelia showed up as her eyes opened again?

Tahlia worked the knot holding her in place against Titus.

"What are you doing?" Titus shifted his weight and she felt his breath on her head.

"I don't need this."

"The hells you don't."

She finished untying herself from him and the saddle, coiled the rope, and quickly tucked it into one of the saddlebags while Titus swore.

"The High Captain will murder me if I live through this," Titus grumbled.

"Fly over her dragon." Tahlia tried not to dwell on the fact that Lija hadn't spoken into her mind in a long while.

Titus held her tighter. "What? No."

"Yes. She isn't bonded to that Terror, so I plan to kick her arse right off the dragon's back. Let's see if that ends Marius's curse and puts that monster down. It can't hurt."

"She's our new commander."

"And she's a murderer who raises demonic monsters," Tahlia said.

"You don't know that for sure."

"If you're going to say it, at least pretend to believe it, Titus. I saw that magic. The stuff she just flung at Katk." Ophelia had thrown power at Katk, right? Or had it been aimed at Marius? "Does Marius look normal? I can't quite see what he's up to with these half-human eyes."

"He fights Katk still. Well, Ragewing isn't firing, but I think he's just pulling us back."

"Did he give that order before I woke up again?"

"No, but he is falling back." Titus let out a whistle and Ptol tipped his wings and flapped them hard. They shifted away from Katk. "And just because the Terror isn't bonded to her doesn't mean it won't whip around and gulp you down as a journey snack."

"Nah, he won't hurt me. It'll all happen too fast."

"Says the female who is currently dancing very close with Death himself."

"Hey, don't count me out yet."

Maiwenn shouted, her voice strained and reedy. Tahlia and Titus turned to see her pointing at Marius and Ragewing.

The dark magic that Ophelia wielded, which Marius also had since she'd cursed him, engulfed Ragewing's head. The dragon shook himself hard, Marius holding tight with his legs and his body tense. Marius's eyes were wide and unblinking.

"The High Captain isn't himself!" Titus called out.

Tahlia felt like she was falling. Fara still clung to him. And Lija was clutched in Ragewing's talons. "Marius! Please!"

Ragewing twisted in the air, then faced Ptol and opened his great maw.

"He's firing on us!" Tahlia gripped the edge of the saddle, knowing what was coming next.

Ptol dove.

Heat seared the air just above Tahlia's head. Cursing Ophelia's name, Tahlia touched her hair to make sure it was still there.

"I can't fight him," Titus said, steering Ptol around to come up between Justus, Claudia, and their dragons.

Ophelia laughed, a short quick sound. "What's wrong, human? Are things not exactly going your way? Attack them!" she ordered, sweeping all three units with her vicious gaze.

Her Green-flanked Terror let out an ear-cracking roar that Katk mimicked.

Ragewing angled around to aim at Ptol once more.

Katk reached for units two and three, and Ewan, Cyrus, and Enora were nearly swiped out of the air. Their dragons roared with flame, but their fire was almost spent.

Ragewing hovered in front of Ptol. Marius tapped his shoulder, and the bespelled Heartsworn opened his talons. Lija dropped into the open sky. Fara shrieked at the same time as Tahlia, whose heartbeat whirred in a deafening pitch. Then Marius shoved Fara off Ragewing.

Lija fell in a disjointed pattern as she tried to use her broken wing. Her roars and Fara's screams ripped Tahlia in two.

Trevain materialized beside her. With a grim look, he reached out a palm and shut her eyes.

Tahlia saw Mother Twilight.

The goddess smiled, her face wrinkling beautifully. She and Tahlia sat side by side in the goddess' flowered forest meadow with butterflies dancing about and tree seeds drifting through the warm air. Peace filled Tahlia as she helped Mother Twilight feed finely spun lavender wool onto a spool.

"What do you want of this life, Weaver?" the goddess asked.

"To live it in full."

"Ah, but do you? Grief is a part of living in full."

A stone formed in Tahlia's belly and she took a slow breath. "I've experienced grief."

"Yes. You're not a... Was it a *marshmallow* you told your fated mate about?" A smile stretched her ancient lips.

Surprise shrank the stone inside Tahlia's stomach. Her limbs stopped shaking and strength flowed through her hands and legs again. She laughed. "Yes. I've been through terrible challenges."

"But you must do so again. And again. It is the way of things." The goddess lifted her free hand as if to indicate the world at large.

Tahlia's belly tightened around the stone. "But perhaps not yet?" She smiled and looked into Mother Twilight's deep-set eyes.

The butterflies stilled in the air, the wood thrushes and insects halted their song, and the tree seeds hung like unspoken thoughts in the sunny space around them.

The goddess nodded at the wool in Tahlia's hands. The lavender strands flared with purple light. "You have the power to do as you see fit."

Tahlia inhaled the sweet scent of the meadow. "I do?"

Mother Twilight pursed her lips and narrowed her eyes. "Well, mostly."

"How can I save them all?"

"Hmm. Recall your first wild idea. It's you who sees the patterns you may use as you see fit. Trust in yourself. But remember, you must feel every emotion during the varied seasons of life. Pain and triumph, joy and loss, regret and anticipation. They are connected, too."

She lifted a hand, and sparkling threads of lavender, ruby red, black, and blue appeared in a flash of light. The strands of colors linked the butterflies, the tall grasses, and the branches of the highest trees, and they were tied also to Tahlia's fingers and the pulse points at her throat...

"You see them now, Weaver?"

Tahlia nodded, marveling at the threads linking Mother Twilight to her as well. They were as black as midnight, lovely and strong. "I do."

Opening her eyes, Tahlia braced for the shock of leaving the goddess' peaceful presence and heading back into battle. She ordered Titus, "Fly over Ophelia. Now."

Titus didn't hesitate this time; he pulled in a quick breath that moved them both, then urged Ptol to shoot for the Green-flanked Terror. Fire touched Tahlia's elbow and knee. Titus called out in pain but kept his seat. Ptol snarled and hovered above the Terror.

Threads of life connected every life here. The ground, the sky, the animals, the dragons, the Fae...

Tahlia leapt from Ptol's back, a jet of flame searing her back as she landed on the Terror. Ophelia was up and throwing a dagger before Tahlia caught her balance. But the threads were there, and they spoke some silent language that said where to set foot, hand, and will.

Slipping her head to the right, Tahlia dodged the flying blade. Ophelia ran along the Terror's spine, nearly falling as she reached Tahlia, but reach her she did. Ophelia slammed a fist toward Tahlia's chin. Tahlia threw up an arm and knocked the strike to the side before cracking Ophelia's ribs with a thrust of her palm. Ophelia dropped back, holding her side and heaving. Her blue-green hair fluttered around her face.

Tahlia bared her fangs. "You poisoned me, didn't you?"

"Of course I did, fool." Ophelia launched herself forward.

Crouching, Tahlia gripped one of the Terror's spikes as the dragon listed to one side. Ophelia fell to her stomach and grabbed onto another spike, the Terror's wing nearly battering her in the process.

Tahlia stood as the threads showed the Terror was about to

even out his flight. Confusion swarmed his mind, or at least that was what the threads suggested. Maybe he would circle and hover and await an attack from one of the others to do more than that. But one thing was abundantly clear...

"Your dragon is trying to get rid of you," she said to Ophelia.

"Ha! As if you know anything about dragons, human."

The dragon dipped, and they flew up for a second, both females scrambling for a hold on the creature. If she'd not been weakened by the cursed plague, she'd have had no problem, not with the threads' help. But her body trembled with fatigue again, and she couldn't get her lungs to fill with air. The Terror leveled himself once more, flying higher, the fight between possessed Marius and his likewise controlled Ragewing and the other members of the order below them. Thank the Old Ones that the other riders and dragons were able to keep Ragewing from firing on them by peppering him and Marius with attacks. Marius had his bow out though and Tahlia fought to focus on the fight going on in front of her positionally. Even though she saw the threads clearly, her heart demanded that she check on Marius and everyone else.

Forcing herself to turn back to Ophelia, Tahlia studied the female's red-tinged eyes and how her lips were pulled back into a grimace. Ophelia was just a sad, sad person.

"I can't believe you murdered your father." Anger made Tahlia's skin itch. "Why did you do it?"

"I sacrificed everything for this order and Marius." Spittle flew from Ophelia's mouth as she made it to her feet and started toward Tahlia. "You wouldn't understand that kind of selflessness, human."

Tahlia lifted her sleeve to show the golden boils that had erupted when she'd grabbed Marius. "Wouldn't I?"

Ophelia's eyes went wide. "The ritual worked." She flung a hand in Katk's general direction, but Tahlia didn't glance away.

The threads told her what she needed to know. "The monster did that to you?"

"Marius's curse did this to me when I pushed him back to save his life."

A sick grin crawled across Ophelia's lips. "It all worked. The demon, the ritual..."

"Whatever you did woke up this monster and he is determined to kill everyone with Mistgold blood. How do you see that as success?" For a moment, black spots dotted Tahlia's vision.

Ophelia laughed loudly and shot forward. Threads, black and blue, wound through the air, connecting dragon scales, wings, Ophelia, Tahlia, and the twist of wind that buffeted them. The sparkling lines showed Tahlia exactly what to do and when to do it.

Shaking slightly, Tahlia simply lifted a foot and launched the witch off the dragon.

Bellowing, Katk caught Ophelia. Golden boils erupted over her face, and she screamed. Her shrieking faded to nothing and she disappeared inside the monster's fist. He stumbled, on the verge of falling.

Katk's creator had formed him to destroy those Fae with Mistgold blood and not even the fact that Ophelia was his champion could save her. In fact, it was that very fact that had doomed her from the first time she'd done whatever ritual it took to raise him. Katk had met his champion at last, only to kill her, and with that move, end himself as well.

Tahlia winced at the tragic waste of Commander Gaius's life and Ophelia's riding talent. Dropping to her knees, Tahlia trembled as the remainder of her strength left her body. Her skin was on fire, the dragon fire burns battling to outdo the pain of the golden boils. The sounds of the fight jumbled in her ears as if she was underwater.

Rider, don't give up. It was Lija, her voice reedy and frail.

I won't. I can see it...

Atticus and Ewan shouted for Tahlia. She turned their way as she crawled to the Terror's saddle. Beside them, Maiwenn waved her arms. Her Seabreak, Donan, clasped both Lija and Fara in his talons. Trevain floated nearby and a host of spirits the same golden shade had joined him.

Every ounce of air left Tahlia's lungs. They were alive. She'd seen it in the threads, but it was impossible not to fear the worst anyway.

Then her heart drew her eyes to Marius.

Ragewing flew toward Katk, who had gone to his knees on the earth below.

Were Marius and Ragewing still held by the curse's power? Where was Ophelia?

Tahlia searched the threads and found nothing.

Had Ophelia portalled somewhere or disappeared using more dark magic?

Ragewing blazed the back of Katk's head, and even though the Heartsworn's fire was as tattered as an old cloak, hope lit a flame of its own inside Tahlia. They were fighting Katk and, hopefully, Ophelia and the curse, too.

Katk's massive body pounded to the earth. Boulders lifted from their resting spots to roll down the foothills in an avalanche. The debris cut its way messily down the land. Trees snapped like twigs and fell. In the distance, mountain goats bleated in alarm and scattered.

The ground around the giant vibrated harshly, sending more trees and rocks into the air and tumbling.

"What in the..." Titus hissed.

Black earth churned and crawled over Katk's form. A scream erupted from Katk's clasped fist. His fingers fell open to show Ophelia, limp and unmoving. The dirt smothered them both—monster and champion—and silence bloomed.

Tahlia fell forward onto the Terror. "Thanks for not killing me, pal." She patted the deep green of the dragon's scales once and darkness poured over her senses.

CHAPTER 33
MARIUS

Marius's mind cleared abruptly.

Rider, we were under the suggestion of dark magic.

I know, well, at least I know it now.

Ophelia is dead. The curse is broken. I don't feel its power around us at all now.

Thank the gods.

Ragewing wheeled around, and there was Tahlia sitting like a young one's forgotten doll on the back of the Green-flanked Terror. Marius took a deep breath and tried not to panic that Tahlia was riding another dragon, an unbonded one.

He says he will carry her home. Lija is in too much pain to argue, but I feel as if she would approve. Anything to help her rider. The Terror calls Lady Tahlia the Weaver.

You are speaking to him?

Yes, but he speaks even less than most of us dragons. He has been betrayed in the past and is closed off to any bonds.

Because of Ophelia?

That, and I think another instance earlier on in his life. He will not share more than the vague idea of that history.

Well, he won't need to carry her for long.

"We land at the lower pass!" he called out with his Mistgold voice.

The grassy dip in the mountains appeared shortly thereafter and everyone landed. Marius hurried to the Terror, hands outstretched toward the large green dragon and his head bowed in submission.

"Thank you for carrying my mate," he said quietly.

The Terror regarded him cooly but lowered his wing and shoulder so Marius could climb up and retrieve Tahlia. She was completely out—eyelids shuttered and body limp. Her chest moved in slow and stuttering breaths as if pain tried to smother her. He swallowed and carried her quickly to the spot where everyone tended to wounds. Bottles of unguents, vials of potion, and tiny bags of healing herbs littered the clover-covered ground.

Limping, Fara walked to where Marius laid Tahlia on the green growth.

"What can we do for her? Let her sleep or try to wake her with herbs?" Marius asked Fara.

"She should sleep. Her body is most likely trying to heal from the internal damage the plague wrought on her organs. I can't believe she jumped from one dragon to another. I can't believe she fought Ophelia and won."

Pride rose in Marius's chest, the joy warring with the chill of fear in his heart. "She's a wonder, my Lady of the Skies."

Fara smiled, then winced, holding her left arm tenderly.

He nodded toward her arm. "Is it broken?"

"I think so."

"Want me to help you splint it for the rest of the journey?"

"Please."

Marius did so, using a few branches he broke from a nearby beech. He then went to Lija and oversaw Maiwenn and Atticus as they applied healing unguent to the Seabreak's wing. Marius splinted the two broken places along the top of her wing.

"The lower break will have to heal as best it can. The bones are too shattered to be splinted," he said, glancing at Atticus.

Atticus nodded in agreement, and Maiwenn opened her mouth as if to say something, but she remained quiet.

Marius knew what she had been about to say. Lija might never fly again.

Swallowing that worry down, he ordered Enora and her Heartsworn to carry Lija *en talon* as it was called when one dragon toted another with careful talons.

Once the other riders were ready, Titus helped Marius situate Tahlia on his lap on Ragewing's back. As they lifted off, the units arranging themselves in the sky, Marius tucked a lock of black hair behind Tahlia's ear.

"Soon, I'll see those honey-gold eyes of yours again. I know it."

She didn't move a muscle and so he began to repeat the same phrase in his mind over and over like a chant, like one of the Druid's spells, in hopes that it was the truth.

She is too alive to die. She is too alive to die. She is too alive to die.

Ragewing remained quiet as they flew, and the journey home was ages long.

If they had broken the curse, and the plague was gone, why was Tahlia still unconscious? Had her body suffered too much damage already? It was inaccurate to blame himself, but guilt whipped his soul regardless.

The riders soared up the crest of Dragon Tail Peak. Wind pushed at their backs, chilly but scented with the first of the summer flowers. Marius and Ragewing led all three units over the two sets of walls surrounding the order's keep. They landed in the arena, and Remus was there to greet them.

Marius climbed down Ragewing's shoulder, and Remus helped him get Tahlia down. Titus hurried to help as well.

"What's the status here?" Marius asked Remus as he lifted Tahlia into his arms once more. "Speak freely around Sir Titus."

Remus inclined his head in a shallow bow. "The Bloodworkers

are meeting now. As per the order rules, the Bloodworkers took charge the moment the majority of the knights went rogue. They are deciding whether or not to send word to the king about potentially disbanding the entire order so they may start anew."

"Exactly how do they propose to kick us out when we are bonded to dragons?"

"There are whispers that Bloodworker Cavalon has knowledge of a potion that would break those bonds and allow the dragons to choose new riders."

Ragewing growled in Marius's mind.

"How do they suppose they will talk the dragons into taking such a potion?"

Remus shrugged, then ran a hand down Ragewing's leg, eyeing the dragon's dirtied talons and a smear of char along his scales. Marius didn't know which dragon had fired on them while they were controlled by Ophelia, but it didn't matter. The fight had been madness. There was no blame to set anywhere besides on the shade of Ophelia.

Gaius, I'm sorry I wasn't there, at your back, to prevent this tragedy.

The wind lifted the ends of his tangled hair and stirred Tahlia's wavy locks too. He wanted to believe it was the spirit of the old commander, giving them his blessing.

"Sir Titus, send for the Healers that we can trust. As soon as you and Ptol are ready, fly to the king and queen. Tell them what has happened here, of Ophelia's dark magic, the monster, and my curse. Inform them of what Remus has told us. Cavalon is no friend to the king."

Titus nodded and hurried away.

Marius met Healer Albus at the side door to the riders' wing in the keep.

"Tell me everything," Albus said, waving Marius into the keep.

She is too alive to die. Wake up, Tahlia. Please, wake up.

CHAPTER 34
TAHLIA

Wool and thorns cocooned Tahlia. Her lips wouldn't part because her tongue was so dry that it stuck fast to the roof of her mouth. Her eyes refused to open even a crack. She heard the rumble and lilt of male and female voices, but the thorny wool enclosed her head and ears, too. She couldn't make out any words. She longed to shout for them to take this off of her, to pull her free...

Dreams and nightmares twisted through her mind. She fell through the clouds. Lija shrieked. Fara called her name. Marius ordered someone to stand down, to back away. None of it made any sense. Her mind swam and her stomach rolled. A bitter taste hit her tongue.

Her eyes flew open. Threads of connection flickered here and there, but they were faint, like ghosts of what she'd seen during the fight with Ophelia.

Fara was there, mouth dropping open. "You're not dead! Woooo!"

Tahlia gave a weak laugh. "What's happening?" Light stone

walls surrounded her. A long window let in the soft glow of maybe sunset?

"You're home. I mean, at the order's keep."

"Is Marius... Lija?"

Fara held out her hands. "They're both fine." Her features had gone flat, her usual fire dimmed for some purpose—perhaps to calm Tahlia.

"You're not telling me something."

Taking a breath, Fara gripped Tahlia's fingers lightly. "Healer Albus is worried that Lija will, um, take a long time to fly again."

Tahlia squeezed Fara's hand. "But she will fly again?"

"He's not sure. Now, be still. I need to mix up a draught for you." Fara went to the long table at the far side of the room and banged about with a mortar and pestle. She whistled as she worked.

Tahlia closed her eyes and took a deep breath, trying to slow her heart.

Lija?

Ah, rider. You're awake.

It's so good to hear your voice. Understatement of this eon. Tahlia didn't want to bring up the flying issue. *Can you sense my Weaver magic?*

Yes, but it rests. You don't need it at the moment. I believe it will rise if you call to it.

I have no idea how to do that.

I assume whatever you choose to do to call that power forth will work, as you are its master.

Thanks, Lija. I'm just so happy you're all right.

I am angry but alive and grateful, too. But I to go into battle with you properly. Don't say that won't happen someday.

I don't think that will be a problem.

Fara returned with a tiny crockery cup and held it out for Tahlia to take. "So glad you're not dead."

Tahlia finished the cup and set it on the side table. Fara gulped a sob and lunged, landing a hug on Tahlia that could have beat every hug in history.

They cried together, laughing too, and trading words that made little sense to the world but everything to them.

A soft knock sounded at the open doorway. Fara moved away and there was Marius. A shuddering sigh left Tahlia. He was whole. His eyes were his eyes. The curse was gone. She could leap from one mountain to another. Nothing was impossible if she had Fara, Lija, and Marius.

"I can come back later if you would like more time to catch up," he said, his deep voice a warm blanket, a sparkling fire, the best wine in all the realms.

"Oh, no," Fara said, gathering her bag and a cloak she'd had draped over her chair. "I wouldn't come between you two for anything." She pointed a finger at Marius and scowled. "But you'd better not get her all riled up. She needs rest."

Marius's stormy eyes twinkled. "I wouldn't dare."

Tahlia truly hoped he would.

Fara waved a goodbye and scurried out, mumbling something about the kitchens and some fresh bread.

Striding forward on his long, long legs, Marius gave Tahlia what could only be described as a dark smile. She loved every bit of it.

"You gave me a terrible scare, little salty."

He sat on the side of the bed and she turned to her side to face him.

"I was only getting you back for all that creepy possessed stuff you threw at me."

Wincing, he reached for her arm. His warm fingers curled around her cool skin, and she swallowed. "I'm so sorry, Tahlia. Truly. I should have been far more aggressive with outing Ophelia as the villain she was."

"Yes, you should have. But I should have spoken up and demanded to be heard, too." She traced a line across his knuckles and the scars he'd gained from fighting over the years. She wanted to learn about them all. "But she's gone for good. Right?"

"She is." He leaned forward and tucked her hair behind her ear. The graze of his thumb on her cheek threw sparks down her neck.

Leaning into his hand, she breathed him in and let a tear fall down her cheek. He cupped her face in the way he had pretended to back in the forest in the land of spirits.

She savored the moment, reveling in the peace that emanated from him. "It's so good to be able to touch you."

"I confess. I'm still nervous about doing so," Marius said.

"But the curse is broken. All is well."

His jaw worked, and he looked out the window. The reflection of the clouds flew across his slitted irises. "It is. But it was..."

Tahlia rubbed the back of his hand. "It was awful. Yes. All of it. Except for that wild magic the goddess gave me."

She told him the tale of the threads and the strange vision of Mother Twilight during the fight.

Marius was shaking his head and the hint of a smile pulled the corners of his mouth. "You grow more amazing every day, my love."

She sat up and he quickly moved to help her get comfortable with more pillows than anyone could possibly need at her back. Then she couldn't take it one more second and she wrapped her arms around him in full. More tears burned their way down her cheeks. He buried his face in her hair.

"My lady. I love you so," he whispered, his breath hot on her ear.

He took her face in his hands and kissed her softly but thoroughly, his lips floating across hers and his thumbs stroking the pulse point under her jaw. His tongue darted into her mouth and her heart skipped. She pushed into the kiss, shoving her hands into his Fae-white hair.

"You can't stand that I'm properly groomed, can you?" he asked, chuckling against her temple.

"No, I can't." She laughed. "I'll always be the one to muss you up, High Captain."

"Oh, you'll have to call me commander now, I'm afraid."

She pulled away. "Really? How long have I been out?"

"A few days, but we had to act quickly. A few of the more power-grasping Bloodworkers attempted to press their case and try their hand at leading the order. We had to put a quick stop to that madness."

"How did you manage?"

"Well, it began with Fara attacking the main player in the attempted coup."

Tahlia barked a laugh. "Of course it did."

"Once we pulled her off, I knew we had to act swiftly. Fara was only doing what all of us wished to do. That female knows no fear when it comes to defending you."

"And you now, too, I bet."

"Yes, said Bloodworker made a derogatory remark about our upcoming ceremony. By the way, you need to choose where to hold the ritual. King Lysanael and Queen Revna have invited us to bond at the menhir near the Gwerhune, but they said there is also a sacred standing stone on the land the king gave you upon winning the tournament."

Tahlia held her breath. "What ceremony?"

"You're welcome to call it off, but I assumed you would want to wed me as soon as you were awake."

Tahlia jumped at him, landing in his lap, body aching and heart dancing. She kissed his forehead, nose, cheeks, chin, and down his gorgeous neck. "Yes, yes, yes!"

He laughed loud then, a sound that would have brought her back to life if the curse had won the day. Gods, he was so beautiful. The knot in his throat bobbed as he laughed, and the corners of his eyes crinkled.

"Please always laugh like that, my delicious commander." She slid her palms up his broad chest, enjoying the feel of the powerful muscle under his thin woolen tunic.

He looked down at her, eyes practically smoking. “I will do as you ask, Lady of the Skies. You are an absolute madwoman in battle, and in bed, and I am at your mercy in every situation.” He kissed her again. “But don’t tell anyone else or I’ll lose my job.”

They laughed, and it was a dream she hadn’t dared to dream coming true. They were healed, happy, and together. She refrained from pinching herself to make certain she was awake, but it was a close thing.

“So when is the bonding ritual? Do we have a date?” she asked, more than prepared to leave the Healers’ quarters immediately.

CHAPTER 35
TAHLIA

In the end, they decided to wed on the castle's grounds. It only seemed fitting for two Mist Knights to marry amid dragons and the highest peaks. Tahlia selected a cluster of crystals as the sacred handfasting site. Marius had approved of the creativity and told her that Ragewing was in full agreement. Lija preferred it as well because she still wasn't able to fly, so she couldn't travel far.

The Druid had arrived to see if he could help Lija heal. Fara couldn't stop grinning at the idea of learning under the Druid's tutelage, even though she hadn't been promised such a situation. "Try to stop me," she'd said to Marius, narrowing her eyes. Marius had replied that he'd never even considered such an act.

In the corridor outside of Tahlia and Fara's room, Healer Albus whispered to them and Marius.

"They found runes charcoaled onto the floor in Ophelia's chambers. The Bloodworkers also determined that both the former commander's and Ophelia's blood were present on a knife found in the former commander's rooms as well as on the small rug that had covered the runes in Ophelia's apartments."

Tahlia wasn't surprised. But she had more questions. Rumors were zipping about the castle, and there were a lot of hushed mentions of a ritual book. "What book is everyone whispering about?"

"Yes," Albus said, "the dark magic book. Unseelie runes and so forth. A witness saw Ophelia take the book from the library. They asked to remain anonymous."

"Don't blame them," Fara mumbled.

Marius crossed his arms. Anger rolled off him, threads of the deepest orange shimmering from his body to lace around Tahlia like a protective barrier. "So Ophelia did indeed murder her father to do blood magic."

"I believe so," Albus said. "I don't think she knew exactly what she was doing though. At least to the extent of the evil she wrought. The Druid confirmed that when I met with him upon his arrival."

Fara grinned. "I love him so much."

Albus nodded at his new Healer student. "Talented male, for certain. We are blessed to have him in the Realm of Lights."

"What about Ophelia's admission to Tahlia about the poisoning? Any physical proof for the others?" Marius asked, brows knitted.

"We found two vials of ghostmint, one full and one empty, in Ophelia's bedchamber."

"I'd say I'm surprised about all of this," Tahlia said, "but I'd be lying."

All sets of eyes snapped to her face. Her human blood would never stop making her stick out a bit from the crowd at Dragon Tail Peak.

Marius let his arms fall and the threads around him faded into that ghostly transparency they normally had when Tahlia wasn't focusing on them and when the emotions of anyone nearby weren't running high.

"I knew it, too," Marius said. "And I apologize for not pressing the issue to Commander Gaius as soon as I guessed it."

"Stop apologizing for that," Tahlia said. "I forgave you already. Let's move on to what I'm actually annoyed with you about."

Marius raised an eyebrow and pursed his lips. "If you bring up the fact that I let you sleep through breakfast again..."

Fara stepped between Tahlia and Marius as Albus chuckled.

"You'll do what?" Fara asked, fists bunching.

Marius looked to the ceiling. "I will request an extra plate of crystal cakes for the both of you while you are preparing for the ceremony."

"One thing that is, um, less conducive to our more settled state of mind here..." Albus tilted his head and studied Tahlia.

"What is it?" she asked.

"The Druid can't help Lija."

The breath went out of Tahlia, and Marius took her arm. If Lija never flew again, she would die. Tahlia knew it as surely as she knew her own name.

Albus continued, "Her wound has a strange lacing of dark magic. But he is wondering if the humans' Witch might be able to do something."

"Really?" Fara asked.

Tahlia chewed her lip. "Would she?"

Shrugging, Albus worried the edge of his cloak. "The Druid said he will ask."

"I can make a request of King Lysanael and Queen Revna myself," Marius said.

"Thank you," Tahlia said. "All of you."

They thanked Albus again for the information about Ophelia, and he left, wishing them well.

Fara linked her arm in Tahlia's. "Sorry, Commander Marius, but I need to steal your promised mate. It is time to fancy her up!"

The Witch would heal Lija. She had to.

Tahlia laughed with Fara and shook her head. "I'm already dreading what type of corsetry you have decided on."

Marius kissed Tahlia, his lips warm and firm. "My heart beats solely for our upcoming bonding."

Fara let out a dreamy sigh as Marius left the corridor. "He is still scary even though he's in love."

"More scary, really. You should have seen the protective threads humming around him while Albus was talking." Tahlia let out a breath, her shoulders finally relaxing. At last, they knew what Ophelia had done, they'd lived through it, and it was time to move forward.

"I wish I could see them. Do they look like wool?"

"Sort of."

They chitchatted happily and entered the bedchamber to prepare for the wedding.

"You look perfect," Maiwenn said as she finished cramming another mountain bluewing blossom into Tahlia's complicated braids. "You don't need more nature shoved into your hair. Not that anyone is asking me for beauty tips."

Fara shooed Maiwenn back and adjusted the blooms as well as the circlet of golden laurel leaves Tahlia wore. Fara's fingers were light and quick, unlike Maiwenn's. "They're the commander's favorite."

Maiwenn covered her mouth and her shoulders shook. "Commander Marius has a favorite flower?"

Fara whirled, glaring. "I know you can murder me with one move, but I will land at least one hit before death if you keep teasing them."

"Calm yourself, Lady Fara. I'll back off. I don't want you to stop making my evening tonic. That stuff works miracles." Maiwenn faced Tahlia. "Why are you so quiet?"

Tahlia's lips pulled into a wide grin. "I was just thinking about what Lija told me this morning."

All the riders could now speak with their dragons because Fara had made it her mission over the last fortnight to travel and retrieve an entire basket of *salvia scarletta*, the plant with blood-red leaves that connected the minds of dragons and their bonded riders.

"What did she say?" Maiwenn asked. "I'm still surprised Donan has a northern accent."

"I mean, he is a Seabreak," Fara said.

Maiwenn wrinkled her nose. "I'd thought most of them were born on the eastern coast."

It had to be odd to hear a very Northern pirate-type accent in one's head. "Lija said because Marius and I chose the crystals for our ritual that even dragons would respect our bond. That we have accidentally mimicked the old dragon ways."

Maiwenn's eyes widened. "Do they bond in a version of marriage too?"

"Many of them used to," Tahlia said, "but their traditions have changed over the centuries. It is seen as a very serious announcement of dedication now."

"Fitting, I think," Fara said. Then she glanced at the candle that marked the hours on the bronze shelf near the door. "Oh! We have to go now. You're going to be late! Commander Marius will think you're standing him up!"

"Everything is fine, Fara. Now, give me a solid hug, my old friend."

Fara leaned down and wrapped Tahlia in her spindly arms. "I love you. If you need me to strangle your mate at any point for not pleasing you, just let me know."

Maiwenn snorted. "I doubt you could complete that task, Healer. Also, is it odd being so aggressive and wanting to heal at the same time?"

"I don't feel both ways at the same time. Plus," Fara said with a slightly dangerous grin, "life and death go hand in hand."

"Aye, they do," Tahlia said. "But please don't murder anyone today, all right?"

Fara stepped back and began straightening up the vanity table. "It's up to everyone to behave properly," she said in a cheery voice.

Tahlia exchanged a glance with Maiwenn, who mouthed, *She's scary*.

Laughing, Tahlia stood and smoothed her blue-green skirts. The embroidered gold sigils—Tahlia's chosen dragon's tooth over an oak's silhouette—ran in stripes down the cascading folds of fabric. The sigils sparkled in the window's light. She wore a military-grade vest complete with draped mail and circles of bronze plating that hugged her shape. The capped and embroidered sleeves of a fine wool shirt peeked out at the shoulders. The outfit was exactly as she'd wanted it to be—reminiscent of the first riders' vests, but still having that feminine beauty to it in the voluminous skirts. And her Weaver's belt remained at her waist, the wool a bright red and humming with power.

Fara and Maiwenn rushed her out of the keep and down the narrow steps that led to the small mountain glen just beyond the courtyard. The wind from the cliff's edge swept over them, stirring fabric and Maiwenn's unbound hair. They hurried around the corner to find the other riders gathered alongside much of the castle staff, all the Healers—Fara's new associates—and most of the Bloodworkers. Titus lifted his hand in a quick wave, his eyes shining. Tahlia winked at him.

At the rocky outcropping that butted against the keep, a jagged array of crystals in purple, gold, clear, pink, and sage green sparkled. Lija, Ragewing, and several other dragons perched above, scales glittering in the setting sun.

Morning, friend, Tahlia said to Lija.

Happy bonding, rider.

Tahlia smiled up at Lija, pride swelling at the sight of the dragon that claimed a big piece of her heart.

The mottled light through the pines flitted across the crystals' varied surfaces as if in welcome. Courage, connection, and health energies flowed from the crystals. Before meeting Mother Twilight, Tahlia had only felt the crystals' power once—when a tremor in the earth had jostled the rose-hued ones and sparked the natural attraction between Marius and her. It had been intense. But now, as she watched the threads twinkle in and out of view, she recognized the hum of encouragement from the purple crystals especially. Perhaps the magic somehow knew she was nervous. She smiled and welcomed that energy in, stepping forward. Marius walked out of the shadows of the pines to join her at the crystals.

Head crowned with a golden laurel circlet like Tahlia's, Marius wore a draping dark blue cloak. His sigil showed on the bronze clasp at his throat—a partially coiled whip and a crystal cluster. A newly fashioned white leather military vest covered his broad chest and trim stomach. He wore riders' leather trousers as well as typical rider boots. He looked every inch the powerful Fae leader he was now. Commander of the Order of Mist Knights.

But more lovely than any of his raiment was the look in Marius's eyes. Love shimmered from their gray depths and Tahlia couldn't wait to start her life with this male. Already she longed to whisk him away from the crowd and into their shared bedchamber. She wanted to trade whispers in the sunset light, feel his palms warming her belly and thighs, listen to his sighs of happiness and contentment...

"Your beauty is beyond any phrase I could utter, my lady," he whispered in his deep and melodious voice. The breeze stirred his hair and ruffled his cloak.

Joy danced inside her. They had made it.

The ceremony went as planned. First, they burned a beeswax and sage candle for Gaius, asking those attending for a moment of quiet in respect. Then, together, Tahlia and Marius burned dragon lavender at the base of the crystals and detailed their gratitude for their dragons and for the mountains that housed them. Touching a fist to their temples each, they sealed their offering of herbs.

Next, they set their palms against the rose-colored crystal, and Healer Albus wrapped their hands in the braided handfasting cord. The old male spoke the holy words, and once Tahlia and Marius laced their fingers, faced each cardinal direction, and voiced their intent to mate, their bond was formed. Marius's hands were so warm and comforting. Tahlia never wanted to let go.

With a rush of light, threads leapt around their joined hands. The ties of energy sparkled and undulated like waves on the sea.

"What is it?" Marius looked down at her, wonder in his gaze.

"The threads... We are united in deep blue and gold threads of energy. It's amazing."

"You are amazing, my love, my mate."

They kissed chastely, and the crowd cheered as they swept past the gathering and headed back to the keep for the feast.

CHAPTER 36
TAHLIA

The chambers that had once been Marius's alone now belonged to them both, allowing Fara to remain in the room in the riders' wing on her own as she worked toward becoming a Healer. Off the main living area, a balcony overlooked the pine forest to the west and the peaks that flanked Dragon Tail.

Stars lit the sky and Tahlia leaned back against Marius's chest as they finished their bottle of wine. Tahlia's stomach tangled into knots. She was glad she hadn't eaten too much during the feasting and games that had run all day after the ceremony.

Marius took her empty cup. "What's troubling you, my perfect mate?"

He set his and hers on the small round table beside the railing before turning and pulling her close. His scent of cloves and stormy skies enveloped her as surely as his arms.

"Honestly? I'm nervous." A laugh escaped her. She felt whole and loved with him, but this was an entirely new level of attachment. "I'm worried you'll come to regret asking me to be your mate." Her cheeks went hot and she shook her head at herself for being silly.

He hugged her tightly and pressed his lips to the top of her head. He was just so very tall. "I'm anxious too, love."

"You are?"

"Of course. We both want this night to be special. It's more than simply having some fun."

That was true. She did feel that pressure to make this night wonderful in every way.

"Plus," he continued, "we have made the most serious commitment possible, outside of our vows to the order. Neither one of us is being flippant about our relationship. That gives this night a certain gravity."

Smiling into his chest, she toyed with the edges of his vest. He was right about all of it. "But we have a lifetime of nights spread out before us."

"Exactly. So we need not put too much pressure on this evening. In fact," he said, pulling away to look into her eyes, "if you would rather wait to consummate our bond, I can—"

"No, no, no." She curled her hands over his shoulders, then stood on tiptoe to kiss the underside of his jaw.

He hummed in appreciation. "Whatever pleases you, I will do it. Just say the word. Give the order."

She let her head fall back and he took the hint to kiss his way down her throat. Warmth shot down her body, coiling low. His fingers dug into her hips, a delightfully rough grip that sent her blood racing through her veins. While one hand slid low to ruck up her skirts, his lips claimed hers in a kiss that was in no way gentle but insistent instead. His hand found the warmth beneath her skirts, and she gasped. Letting out another hum of approval, Marius kneaded her with his knuckles. Bolts of pleasure branched through her like lightning.

A growl rumbled from his chest into hers and she linked her arms around his neck. He lifted her and carried her to the bedchamber off the living area. A fire crackled and snapped in the bedroom's hearth and shadows rippled across the curtains draping the bed. Standing beside the bed, they tugged off their leathers, then took turns undressing one another, a layer at a time.

Once they were stripped bare, he laid her on the voluminous blankets and pillows. He crawled on top of her and drew his lips across her cheek and forehead. His body pressed against hers. She peered down between them as he nibbled the sensitive tip of her ear. His stomach muscles pulled tight and the sight of him fully bared to her in all his masculine beauty had her gasping. Heat rose between her thighs. He moved down her body, mouth grazing her breasts, navel, and hips as he traveled.

"You're exquisite, stunning, completely and utterly breathtaking," he whispered over her skin, his breath tickling and teasing.

She couldn't do anything more than moan and twist her fingers in his long hair.

With slow flicks of his tongue, he stroked her center until she was trembling. He spread his hands over her lower stomach to hold her in place, and she writhed, unable to remain still. Delight shivered inside her, ready to unfurl.

"Marius, please."

"Yes?"

"I want you. Here," she said, tugging handfuls of his hair.

He chuckled, the sound deep and gravelly. In a rush of movement, he lay on top of her again, his body poised perfectly. Impatience had her bucking against his cock. The feel of his heat on hers was unlike anything else in the world. She latched onto his shoulders and tried to urge him to enter, but he held back, grinning like a dragon about to blaze an enemy.

With one hand, he took hold of both her wrists. He pinned them on the smooth wood of the headboard and began to roll his hips, still refusing to give her what she truly wanted. She let out a groan, the desire overcoming any nervous feeling left inside her. She needed him. Now.

"Marius. Take me. Stop torturing me."

"I think you quite like this punishment."

Pleasure scattered across her torso, peaking her breasts, then traveling down the backs of her legs to pebble her skin in waves.

Two could play this game. She bit her lip, stared into his eyes, and wrapped her legs around him in one swift maneuver.

His lips parted in a gasp and he winced, hissing, his fangs showing and the veins in his neck growing prominent.

"Be still," he growled, going still himself as well.

She grinned. "Why?" She rocked herself against the length of him.

Snarling, he suddenly dropped his hips and thrust into her. He drove forward again and again and again.

"You are mine, Tahlia." His voice was the storm-tossed forest. "Mine. All mine."

The bed shook beneath the fervor of his pace, and pure pleasure whipped through her body, the heat inside her unfurling and snapping, making her cry out.

Dropping to the bed, he wrapped his arms around her and tucked her up beside him. Sweat made their skin stick here and there, but everything was perfection because this love was real and it was forever.

EPILOGUE

MARIUS

In the months that followed, Marius was never satisfied when it came to showing Tahlia love. In word and in deed, both in the bedchamber and outside those walls, he did his best to honor the love of his life, his dear and perfect mate.

And it wasn't just because a certain female Healer would stab him repeatedly if he did anything less. Fara actually seemed to like him now. Perhaps even trust him.

It was because Tahlia deserved to be treated like a goddess, and he'd be damned if he didn't make up for all the trouble he'd caused early on by not acting on his heart's knowledge from day one.

Remus is concerned, Ragewing said into Marius's mind. *He smells of fear.*

Is it Lija? Tahlia's dragon still hadn't healed well enough to fly and the Witch hadn't yet responded to their pleas for assistance.

No. Something else.

The squire rounded the corner and entered Ragewing's stall. He held out a sealed letter. "This came for you. From one of the king's messengers."

Marius set aside the cloth he'd been using to polish Ragewing's shoulder scales and accepted the letter. "What's wrong, Remus?"

"The male, he..." Remus rubbed at his nose and glanced away.

The seal bore Fae King Lysanael's seal. Marius cracked it and opened the missive.

Remus met Marius's gaze. "The messenger's horse died shortly after arriving. He rode him too hard because this message is so urgent."

"Why didn't the queen ride her forest dragon here, I wonder..."

"There's word she is in Fjordbok at the moment."

The queen's home. "Ah." Marius scanned the letter, his heart dropping with each new detail. "Remus, find Tahlia for me, will you?"

"No need," a quick and perfect voice said from the stall doorway. Tahlia lifted a hand in greeting.

A wave of concern swept over Marius and he had to restrain himself from pulling her to him protectively. He swallowed and met her at the door.

"King Lysanael and Queen Revna have set us on a mission."

"Oooh." She rubbed her hands together. "Will Ragewing let me ride with you since Lija is still healing?"

Marius could tell Tahlia was ignoring the potentially lethal elements of Lija's condition. Dragons that didn't fly, didn't stay alive for long. But for now, that issue had to wait.

"This is no standard set of instructions, Lady Tahlia. Only you and I are ordered to meet with the king. It is a secret mission and highly dangerous."

She bit her lip and looked up at him. "Order me as you see fit, Commander Marius."

"I'm serious."

"Oh, I know." She wiggled her eyebrows.

Desire and frustration warred inside Marius. He wanted to take her into his arms... He gritted his teeth and forcibly cleared his mind of those wayward emotions.

"This mission involves the most powerful artifact in history. An evil human, some type of lesser king, has somehow gained the artifact in question."

"If we are headed to the human kingdom, we can talk to the Witch about Lija ourselves!"

"Possibly, yes. Especially if our king and queen approve, which they should."

"What else?" she asked, courage practically beaming from her eyes like rainbows.

As concerned as he was, he still couldn't help but delight in how wonderful she was.

"We are to infiltrate the human kingdom during something deemed a *tomato festival.* There will be costumes and a parade," he said, shuddering.

A laugh snapped from Tahlia's smiling mouth. "I'll risk anything to see you dressed up like a vegetable. Or is it technically a fruit? When do we leave?"

Marius pinched the bridge of his nose and hoped they weren't about to die after all the work they'd put into staying alive.

CROWN AND DRAGON

CHAPTER 1

TAHLIA

On Ragewing's back, Tahlia kept one arm looped around Marius's fabulously trim waist. She turned to see how close the others were following. The wind was cool and held the scents of hay and last night's storm system.

It was nearing autumn; soon the order would head north to watch the coastline for pirates. But for now, Marius, Ragewing, and Tahlia were on their way to King Lysanael and Queen Revna's vineyard. There, they would be briefed on the mission to retrieve the artifact the king's note had mentioned. It would take place during a human city's tomato festival. Tahlia couldn't wait.

The rest of the Order of Mist Knights flew behind Ragewing in three sets of arrow formations, a stone's throw from Ragewing's tail.

Titus pretended to vomit from the back of his Spikeback dragon and then grinned at Tahlia. She smiled back.

Last night while packing for the journey, they had both taken three too many shots of Maiwenn's greenblood—a batch of highly potent alcohol that was common in the Gwerhune where Maiwenn was born. Definitely a poor choice of drink the night before a dawn flight. Fara had been there, too, warning them to no avail.

"Maiwenn had best watch her back," Fara had said last night. "If you end up too hungover to begin your secret and surely terrible mission tomorrow, I'm going to rip her arms off. You just started and you can't afford to slack on your duties and she should know better than to tempt you..."

Tahlia snickered thinking about her friend. Fara hadn't tried to come along this time because she was up to her continually raised fists in Healer training. The irony would never get old. The most fighty gal Tahlia had ever met was working her way to being one of the best Healers in the Realm of Lights. Fara had sent Tahlia off with a stack of notes labeled *The only way you will survive this adventure.*

Despite today's headache, last night's imbibing had resulted in a slew of fantastic jokes about Albus, who joined in with his usual self-deprecating comments. And they'd been delightfully entertained by Maiwenn's classic impersonation of Atticus lecturing the staff at the tavern about overcooking venison.

Maiwenn waved casually to Tahlia and Tahlia lifted her hand in response. Maiwenn's dragon, Donan, let out a short roar in Tahlia's direction, a sound she was familiar with now. He was very worried about Lija, his fellow Seabreak, and her injured wing. He'd even barged into the Healer's fifth meeting on the subject when they'd gathered in Lija's stall. *Let's just say a worried dragon is not super fun to deal with.*

Tahlia focused on her bond with Lija and spoke through her mind—a power that they had awoken with Fara's suggestion of eating a certain magical plant. The distance their communication could travel was roughly a day's travel, but the range varied. Lija and Tahlia's Energy levels, the weather, and the activity of the crystals in the mountain altered the maximum separation they could have and still talk.

Lija, how were the exercises this morning?

Lady Fara is quickly becoming my enemy.

Tahlia laughed. *You don't mean that.*

Lija's growl reverberated through Tahlia's mind. *I just might.*

Nah, she's the sweetest evil genius in the world and you know it.

Hmm.

You sound like Marius.

A reluctant chuckle echoed from their bond. *Fine, rider. I will go along with your squire's exercise plan. But know this: I'll be well and flying before she can pass her Healer evaluations, and we will put this horror in our past.*

I know you will, Lija. We will get through this.

I will miss the beat of your heart while you're gone, rider.

And I will miss yours. Terribly.

Tahlia's eyes burned and she blinked back tears.

Marius leaned left and glanced over his shoulder. "I'm about to call out a kite formation."

"Got it." Tahlia clamped both arms around him and braced her thighs against Ragewing's saddle.

She relaxed and let the power of the belt that the goddess had given her rise into her heart and mind. It was like stepping into a hot spring, warmth seeping into her and reminding her that all was well. They would get Lija healed. It would be all right. She hoped that was true anyway. The threads couldn't show her the future exactly, though they did point to the outcome of her immediate actions in the physical space she occupied.

The threads of fate, action, and what she liked to think of as willpower connected Marius to Ragewing, Tahlia to each of them and to the dragon riders behind them. Certain spots on the ground or places in the air showed possible movements of dragons and riders. Somehow, the magic the goddess had bestowed on her permitted Tahlia to understand what each woolen-looking thread meant. When she wasn't suppressing her power—which she did so as not to become lazy—she used it to decide what to do at any given moment. She didn't want any of her fellow Mist Knights to believe she was taking the easy way out. Though they had all shown her respect and dedication since the adventure with the monster, Katk, she didn't think she'd ever stop trying to impress them. They were such heroes. She wanted to be like them still. Fearless. Skilled. Undaunted by challenge.

"Kite!" Marius called out in his Mistgold voice.

The sound bounced off the clouds and through her body, warming her blood for the coming fight.

Only Marius and Tahlia would participate in the mission to retrieve the artifact, but the rest of the order had been directed to escort them. On the way to the royal vineyard, the riders were to take down a band of thieves ravaging the Gwerhune forest.

"Spotted!" Claudia called out. Her orange tail whipped around behind her braided hair, and her sunset-hued skin sparkled in the midmorning light.

Her Heartsworn let out a staccato call and Ragewing answered her. They had been in the same unit for years and were as familiar with one another's calls as well as the calls of their riders.

"I see them," Marius said to Tahlia. "By the river. Can you give me a count, either of you?"

Tahlia didn't know if Ragewing had answered inside Marius's mind, but she did her own count, tallying the group of wild Fae drinking and laughing by the silver thread of water.

"I've got eleven by my count," Tahlia said.

"Eleven!" Marius shouted to the rest of the Mist Knights. "Unit Three, take the lead!"

Ewan lifted his hand and nodded his bald brown head. His Spikeback, Angus, dropped and sped forward. He and the others in his unit—Lucius and Cyrus each on their scarlet Heartsworns and Brutus on his pale blue Spikeback—passed Ragewing like bolts from a massive crossbow.

"What do you suggest, Tahlia?" Marius asked.

"Send a unit to cut them off because they're going to run, of course. Then send another unit over the far side of the river to come in low through the trees."

Marius nodded, then lifted his fist. "Good. You're learning. Down, One and Two! Three, get out ahead of them and circle back as they flee from Unit One. Two, veer past the river and come back below the canopy! Full flame, but watch the woods for spreading!"

"Full?" It was unusual for Marius to call for certain death.

"I read the report on these wild Fae. You don't want to know what they've done to terrorize the simple folk in the Gwerhune villages. Death is too kind, really, but it's what we have been ordered to give them."

"Aye, Commander," Tahlia said, dropping any feelings she was drumming up for potentially understandable crimes of those in poverty.

Ragewing dove, and Tahlia's stomach lifted into her throat. He unleashed a blaze that crackled and snapped. The thieves swore and began to run, all of them crashing into the river and heading north—as the threads had shown her. They were fast, dodging fire and leaping over boulders that turned the water into whirlpools. Wild Fae were a tough bunch, well used to doing what they had to in order to survive the dangerous Forest of Gwerhune.

"Durniad will take you all down, you spoiled pigs!" a wild Fae called out over the splashing and the sound of wings.

Ewan turned, his purple-blue eyes flashing, and directed Unit Three around to cut them off. The unit's Spikebacks and Heartsworns created a wall of light blue and scarlet.

Unit Two appeared through the trees on the far side of the river, their dragons already opening their mouths to flame and their throats glowing. All units fired on the thieves.

Their shouts and curses cut off quickly.

Dying by fire wasn't a lovely way to go, but at least it didn't have to take long.

The thieves' ashes swirled down the river, and what remained of the criminals was gone by the time the three units gathered beyond the moss-cloaked boulders that framed the banks.

Everyone dismounted and began checking tack and dragons. Smoke curled from the far bank. The forest was catching.

"We've got it," Maiwenn said, hopping back onto Donan. They hurried to the water, and the Seabreak—the same cyan-hued color as Lija—used his finned tail to douse the smoking trees and brush.

"Did you hear what that scum yelled at us, Commander?" Silver-skinned Atticus smoothed the wavy hair between his horns, uncorked his stash of water, and took a drink. He offered the water to Claudia, who took it with a nod of thanks.

"I did." Marius's nostrils flared. "If any of the rest of you heard what he said, please keep it to yourself. It's to do with our mission and we should bite our tongues unless the king and queen release us to speak about it further."

"Aye, Commander," Tahlia said, the others echoing the response.

Maiwenn and Donan landed beside them.

A stronger warmth emanated from Tahlia's Weaver belt. Tahlia touched the magical wool. "Ow."

Marius glanced her way, a question in his storm-gray eyes.

"I'm fine, but my belt is really hot."

"Your fancy Weaver belt?" Maiwenn squeezed water from her hair.

Titus's brow furrowed in a perfect big-brother-protector type of expression. "Your magic worked up there, right?"

"Yes." The belt sparkled and the light brightened.

Maiwenn stepped closer. "Whoa. What is happening?"

The dancing light flashed. Tahlia shut her eyes against the white flare of it. When she opened her eyes... Her stomach dropped.

The belt was gone.

The others gasped, joining her in shock.

Marius touched her arm and studied her face. “Do you feel unwell?”

“No. I feel the same...” The warmth was still there, but this time, it sat along her skin. She untucked her tunic from her weapons belt and eyed her stomach. A faint red pattern showed beneath her navel. She ran a finger over it. It was smooth, but... “The belt is—it’s inside my body now?”

Marius took a knee and grabbed her hips. He brought her close and his gaze peppered her stomach. “I see its pattern. Yes. Definitely. Did the goddess ever mention this would happen?”

She held her tunic up and squinted at the markings. “No.”

Lija?

Yes?

Do you know anything about my belt? It just, um, disappeared into my body.

Ah.

That sounds like you know things.

I always know things.

Yes, yes. Please, can you tell me anything?

The magic has likely grown used to you. It agrees that you are its keeper. I wouldn’t worry about it. Your power likely doesn’t want to rely on physical presence or varieties in the spiritual plane to interact with its wielder.

Tahlia exhaled. *All right. Thanks.* “Lija suggests that the magic has fully accepted me as its wielder and doesn’t want to rely on physical something blah blah something or other.”

“Your dragon talks like that?” Maiwenn asked, a hand on her hip. She blew her Fae-white hair out of her face.

Donan snorted above Maiwenn’s head, obviously standing up for Lija.

“No, Lija is very well-spoken,” Tahlia said.

Donan lowered his head and blinked at Tahlia as if to say he appreciated the comment.

“Commander?” Titus started.

Marius was still on his knee in front of Tahlia. She didn't mind his fingers on her waist.

"Yes, Titus?" Marius spread a hand over Tahlia's new inking of sorts and delicious chills swept down her body.

"If you'd like us to survey the area and leave you two some privacy to discuss this development..." Titus shrugged, his smile barely restrained.

Marius's eyebrow flicked upward and he glanced at Tahlia's face, a teasing light in his eyes as he whispered to her, "If I were king..."

He waved off his words and stood, his thumb running over Tahlia's wrist briefly as if to secretly say he wished they could have some alone time. Heat rushed through Tahlia's body and her heart beat hard. She swallowed.

"No," Marius continued, "we must move onward immediately. We will need time to go over our information once more before the royals arrive at the vineyard."

Titus bowed his head. "Aye, Commander."

The order mounted up and flew below the canopy, enjoying the sights, scents, and sounds of the Gwerhune, the mightiest of all the Fae forests. Oaks as large as King Lysanael's castle, Caer Du, reached thick arms to one another, pixies floating within their shadows. The pixies wouldn't bother anyone until after dark. They were lovely but incredibly annoying little things. The indigo pines took over as they flew onward. Needles shook in the wind of the dragons' wings, and the trees' fresh green scent rose into the honey-sweet air. Tahlia inhaled deeply.

"You like it here, don't you?" Marius said over his shoulder.

"I adore it. It's gorgeous. And exciting."

"Very true. Perhaps we can go on a holiday and explore the depths someday."

"Really? Do we get any holiday time?"

His body rumbled with a low chuckle. "Not much, but a commander can bend the schedule sometimes."

Tahlia slid her hand down his side and tickled his thigh. "I love sleeping with the boss."

Marius's laugh shook her slightly as she leaned over to peer down. A group of moss deer bounded over yellow and green mosses that matched their pelts and the growth that sprang from the buck's wide antlers. A tangle of roots boasted a cluster of towering pink flowers that grew in a long braid.

"We could bed down right there," Tahlia said, pointing.

Marius glanced down and growled approvingly.

Tahlia smiled and held him tightly. He didn't care about the flowers—she knew that—but despite his grouchy exterior, he was always kind about what she found lovely and enjoyable. As long as it wasn't something terribly reckless.

Would they be able to have some fun during this upcoming mission or would it be all risk and danger? In a perfect world, there would be a balance of both. After all, she didn't join the order to sit around knitting and oohing over flowers.

CHAPTER 2

MARIUS

The vineyard extended from the manor house into the rolling hills like a deep green wave. The flickering light of the workers' lanterns bobbed like fireflies and Marius felt silly for wishing he and Tahlia were only here for a holiday.

"Come on, slow poke!" Tahlia waved at him from the third row of grapevines, where she was dropping another cluster of wine grapes into the basket looped over her arm. "We have to beat Waith!"

It was tradition that every soul on the grounds during early fall join in on the harvesting. Marius didn't mind it one bit. This was honest work—and a calming break from the stress of dragon rider business. He wished the rest of the order could have stayed with them, but they were needed for tasks in the mountains. Training and keeping the occasional troll out of the high altitude villages would keep them busy in this fine weather.

Marius stalked over to Tahlia and took the vine knife from her outstretched hand. Her shining eyes reflected the lanterns' light and the glow of the moon. "First, you are so beautiful it hurts.

Second, we don't have a chance against Master Waith, seeing as he has been running a vineyard since before either of us was born."

Tahlia had frozen, a grin lifting one edge of that pouty mouth he longed to devour like a decadent sweet. "I love it when you use so many words at once. It's as rare as unicorns, my love."

He growled at her and turned back to the vines.

She snickered and eased the basket into the leaves to catch the grapes he cut free. Master Waith, a male with fair skin, waved a hand at them, the two stripes of gray-white in his dark hair like the imprint of former horns.

"They will be here in the morning! Just heard." Waith nodded toward a slim lad leaving the vineyards and heading toward the stables. A messenger, Marius guessed.

"So we have all night off," Tahlia said, glancing at Marius from the corners of her painfully alluring eyes.

Marius's body heated, and he shook his head at himself as he adjusted his trousers. His mate could have ordered him to do literally anything when she looked at him like that.

"Seems so," he said, his voice rougher than he'd meant it to be. His tone didn't appear to dampen her spirits, thankfully.

"I think we should visit this exact spot after everyone has gone to bed."

He eyed the ground at their feet. Soft grasses had been pressed low during the harvest work, and blue-green moss laced a patch of earth here and there. Looking back at Tahlia, he nodded.

"Agreed."

She snorted a laugh. "You make it sound like we've planned some dark mission."

Using the full power of his speed, he moved behind her and set his teeth against the side of her throat. He edged the vine knife against her throat, though he kept the dull side toward her.

"I'll make it a dark mission if you wish it, little salty."

She shivered and rubbed her arse against him. "I do. I really do."

He chuckled and went back to harvesting.

They finished the row, and Waith called out for everyone to cease their work.

"Leave a cluster on each row for good luck!" Waith shouted.

"Aye!" the workers shouted in unison.

Happy conversation and laughter rose as everyone dumped their full baskets into the great vat at the back of the first set of outbuildings.

Most of the staff gathered at a long table outside. Dishes set with sauced chicken, piles of cubed orange cheddar, and fat slices of bread weighed the entire length.

Waith collected Marius and Tahlia and escorted them inside the manor house, where another feast awaited for the higher ranked staff.

A table had been dragged into the center of the main room. Platters of bright green apples and roasted venison sat beside flagons of dark wine. Round cottage loaves baked with the vineyard's mark steamed, fresh from the ovens behind the house. Varied wheels of cheese dotted the table as well as bowls of what appeared to be grape preserves.

Tahlia clasped her hands and sighed, her head tilting to one side. "Sorry, Marius, but I'm leaving you for this table. I mean, there is so much cheese."

He shot her a look and she stood on tiptoe and kissed his cheek. Thankfully, Waith and the other workers were too busy filling crockery with wine and singing harvest songs to notice or care about Tahlia's lack of propriety.

"We truly should go over the mission details as soon as we finish here."

"You aren't suggesting we skip this feast, are you?" She gazed at him like he had told her someone died.

"No, I don't wish to be rude to the household."

Tahlia put the back of her hand to her forehead. "Oh, thank the gods!"

"After we eat. Did you read the lines about Ragewing's position while we infiltrate the city, the location and purpose of the safe house inside city walls, and about our contacts both in the city streets and in the fortress?" he whispered.

He tried not to notice the way the soft skin under her jaw pebbled when his breath skirted over her flesh.

"I read the entirety four times. Ask me anything, Commander."

"Very good." He started to throw her a difficult query, but Waith's voice cut him off.

Those gathered for the smaller feast inside the house had at last stopped yowling like pups under a full moon.

"Please sit and let us talk about the first time you tasted one of the king and queen's vintage, Commander Marius, Lady Tahlia."

The talk went on and on, but Marius wasn't so uptight as to break the conversation to continue checking on Tahlia's memory. He kept his tongue and enjoyed the bites she fed to him.

"And this cheese is called sunlight. Can you even imagine?" She tucked a sliver into his mouth. "What's it taste like?"

He chewed, savoring the flavor despite the fact that he felt foolish eating from his mate's hand the night before a mission briefing and in full view of the king and queen's staff.

"You're too slow. I'm trying it on my own." Tahlia sliced another bit of the sunlight cheese and popped it between her lips. She moaned like, well, like she wasn't just eating food.

"Gods save us, this is divine. The smoothness. The bright flavor!"

A female with curling hair and brown skin nodded approvingly to Tahlia. "My son made that," she said proudly.

Tahlia's mouth fell open. "You must be so proud."

The female grinned and refilled Marius's and Tahlia's crockery mugs. "He's only just reached adulthood and he's already working his way to mastery."

"Give him good wishes of undying love from me, would you?"

Laughing, the female walked off to join another female standing by the front door.

Marius pursed his lips. "Leaving me for a cheesemonger, are you?"

Tahlia patted his hand, then downed her wine. "At least you were defeated by the finest of competitors."

Growling quietly, Marius shook his head and finished his wine too.

WHEN WAITH and the rest of the staff had retired to their rooms in the house and in the outbuildings, Tahlia tugged Marius's arm until they were back in the vineyard. She had knotted her hair on top of her head and donned the linen shift that the staff had given her to sleep in. He wore trousers woven of the same type of linen. Both of them were barefoot, and with the crescent moon shining down on them, that fact only made him more aware of how wild he felt at the moment. His mate. A fine night. Time enough for mating.

Tahlia stopped near the vine they had worked on and turned to face him. "I've decided to wait on leaving you for the young cheesemaker until I've had my way with you."

He took her in his arms and pressed a kiss to her ear. She smelled like a goddess of pleasure—gently floral and as aroused as he was.

"Such a cruel mate I have," he whispered. "How will I survive you?"

She laughed throatily, the sound rousing his body as well as any touch. He laid her in the soft grass and braced himself over her, kissing her jaw, then the pulse point underneath. Her throat was silk. He licked and nibbled his way down to her collarbone while her hands tangled in his hair. She bucked her hips and rocked against his length.

"What if I slipped away and ran from you?" Her tone was teasing.

He was quite nearly shaking with need. "I would be forced to chase you, love." He set his teeth on her breast and growled, driving his hips forward. The pressure between their bodies poured pleasure through his blood. "You're mine, remember?" He gripped her hip and held her against him.

She moaned softly and shifted underneath him. And then she suddenly had a vine knife in her hand and was holding it to his throat.

"You will let me run, darling." Her gaze was taunting and absolutely the most desirable look she'd ever given him.

He eased away from her body a fraction.

She was up and running, laughing quietly, before his lust-hazed mind caught up.

"Oh, you are finished, little salty. I will hunt you and take you down in a way you will never forget."

Laughing again, she turned at the end of the row. He followed.

CHAPTER 3
TAHLIA

Tahlia hid behind the stand of maples near the first rows of vines. The bark was cool and soft to the touch. She leaned around to see how close he was.

Her heart stuttered. Just a fraction of his face and body was visible behind the grapevines. A low, quiet growl emanated from him. A shiver of delight ran through her. This dangerous fully Fae male with the vicious fighting prowess and the golden heart of a dragon was her mate. She had to keep reminding herself because it seemed too wonderful to be true.

And for some reason, she absolutely adored how frightening he looked right now. Her body melted with want—knees weakening and breasts drawing taut.

She fled her cover, grinning, and dashed behind the beautiful wooden structure that housed wine aging in barrels. The scent of the wine and the green aroma of the vineyards filled her nose.

Another rippling, spine-tingling growl announced that Marius was close. Tahlia took a trembling breath. She couldn't see him anywhere. Studying the shadows and patches of moonlight, she tried to see him. But—

Suddenly, she was up against the wine house wall with Marius behind her, breathing over the back of her neck. He had both of her hands pinned above her head and his other hand was rucking up her shift. Tingling showered down Tahlia's body from her scalp, down her thighs, all the way to her feet.

"Mine," Marius growled over the back of her neck.

He licked his way over her skin, and she gasped, heart pounding. With a quick movement, he twisted her shift around his hand and roughly shoved it above her waist, exposing her skin to the night air. The cool breeze was a stark contrast to the heat of his body. He pressed himself against her and the feel of him so ready to take her stole her breath. She was dissolving into pure pleasure.

"You caught me." She could hardly speak and her pulse was going a mile a minute.

"Yes, and I will claim you now." He thrust into her and held her pinned to the wall as he shuddered with the effort of trying to control himself.

She loved that he got as riled up as she did. He slid back, then drove forward again.

"Mine," he snarled.

His teeth found the place where her neck met her shoulder and he held on, almost breaking the skin. A thrill buzzed along her veins and she nearly cried out. She bit her lip, not wishing to wake the entire vineyard. Shifting again, he set a driving pace, and the pleasure inside her built higher and more powerful. The way he kept her tight against the wall, the desperation in his breathing, and the way he nipped at her skin...

He released one of her hands, seemingly caught up and lost in the moment. She moaned as desire tangled with the love she had for this male, and her pleasure peaked. She reached back, wanting to touch his cheek.

"We are not finished yet, my mate."

Breaking away a fraction, Marius grabbed her and turned her around. He lifted her so that she could wrap her weak legs around him. She was hardly a person, completely spent with satisfaction. His mouth found hers and he kissed her softly, his tongue dancing over hers and his teeth nipping at her bottom lip as he eased his way into her once more. This time, he took her slowly.

"I would seize the moon for you if you wished it. I would burn the world to ash. Ask me anything, my mate, and I will see it done."

Heart swelling past the point she thought possible, she gripped his broad, powerful shoulders and let her head fall back. He pressed sensuous kisses along her breasts, teasing her nipples with the very tip of his tongue as he moved steadily. His grip was tight on her backside, and the feel of his large hands was delightfully naughty. Need rose inside her, a sharp crescendo, then she came apart as he worked harder, his hips slamming forward.

"Tahlia," he called out as his eyes shuttered. The long, corded column of his throat moved as he took his own pleasure, his jaw muscles taut and his fangs bared.

He was the most gorgeous thing she'd ever seen.

They found a soft patch of grass within the rows of vines and he set to tidying her shift. His gaze turned to one of approval once she was covered once more. Then he sat behind her, one of his big legs bent so that she could lean on his knee, and he began braiding her tangled hair.

His whispered her name like a prayer. "Tahlia, my love, my dark soul longs for the light in yours." He dropped a kiss on the crown of her head, the warmth of his hands and breath making her shiver and smile. "I hear your heartbeat, and I want to follow the poetic sound for eternity. Your ferocity in the skies and your love of life will always be my light in the dark."

His murmured phrases about her body, his love for her soul, and his respect for her clever mind charmed her into a dreamy sleep.

CHAPTER 4
MARIUS

Morning came too soon and Marius only wanted to keep holding Tahlia against him in this warm bed. He'd carried her inside last night and the feel of her in his arms was so perfect—he could never deserve this.

A knock sounded at the door. "Commander?"

Marius untangled himself from Tahlia as she stretched and grinned up at him. He kissed her as the knocking continued. She was so soft from sleep and he longed to bury himself in her and forget the world.

Tahlia put a gentle hand on his chest. "Whoever that is will break a hand if you let him carry on much longer."

He growled but got up, pulled on his trousers, and opened the door. A young male wearing the king's livery bowed. Marius knew what he would say before he uttered a word.

"The king and queen have arrived and they request your and Lady Tahlia's presence."

"Allow us to ready ourselves."

The fellow bowed and Marius shut the door.

"So what do we wear for this? Battle leathers?" Tahlia held up one of their bags, her nose adorably wrinkled. "The villager clothing Waith gave us? I forgot my fancy cloak."

"I think we should dress in the undercover clothing, and keep your weapons to a minimum. Leave your short sword here, but take your daggers. One in your boot and one on your belt."

Tahlia lifted the shift she'd slept in over her head and Marius turned away so he wouldn't be tempted to get them killed for disobedience to the king and queen due to more lovemaking.

They met the liveried fellow outside the door and started down the corridor that most of the rooms opened into. The rest of the manor house was noisy with the sounds of staff preparing for the day—the scrape of small shovels clearing soot from fireplaces, the shuffle and crackle of new fires started, crockery clunking on hard surfaces as morning beverages were assembled, and the conversation of those long used to working side by side. The lad led Marius and Tahlia away from the ruckus and into a receiving room of sorts at the back of the manor house.

The room had a higher ceiling. A large window on one end showed the sunlight rolling down the green hills. King Lysanael stood enjoying the view, his arms crossed and his face stern. Queen Revna was pacing, hands clasped behind her back. Their crowns glittered in the window's light.

"My king, my queen," Marius and Tahlia said in unison, bowing low.

"Please have a seat," the king said, turning to face them in full.

Marius pulled out one of the six wicker chairs at the long oaken table in the center of the room and motioned for Tahlia to sit. She did so and he settled himself in the one beside it.

"In the city of Midhampton, in the human's kingdom of Saxonion, there is a human male by the name of Durniad. Though the young human high queen and her regent truly rule that city as its in their kingdom, he has seized those in charge. Through violence, he has turned the city to his dark purposes. He is a known criminal, a pirate at times, and a man who would name himself a king of sorts. The human high queen has requested our help because Durniad has supposedly uncovered an ancient artifact sometimes referred to as the Invisible Crown or the Crown of Minds."

Tahlia's eyes went wide, and she traded a loaded glance with Marius. He took a breath and focused on the king again. He had heard of this artifact, but only in passing during his early schooling. The crown had been mentioned in a list of dangerous items gone missing ages ago in a sea battle. He recalled someone deeming the artifact the Crown of Sirens. But how was this their problem? The human high queen—called high due to the fact that some areas of the human realm were ruled by lesser queens and kings that were subservient to her—was not of age, so her kingdom was mostly ruled by her regent. Fae King Lysanael and Queen Revna had aided the young queen in taking down her horrible father. They had signed an agreement between the two realms to aid one another as needed in situations determined as emergencies. This must have been one such occasion.

Queen Revna faced them, arms loose at her sides and her human eyes unblinking. Humans' rounded irises always unsettled him.

The king continued. "He will watch the parade during his city's tomato harvest festival, entertain those he deems worthy of his presence, and then, crown himself ruler of Midhampton. Maybe more."

"The fact is," the queen said, "if Durniad knows what he's doing with this artifact, he can control the behavior of every human alive. Those with Fae blood are safe, as are your dragons."

The king nodded and fiddled with the torc at his neck. "After discussing a way to resolve this situation and avoid a mass of mind-controlled humans from ransacking their own lands as well as ours, we decided to put you two on this mission. You must keep it quiet. The human high queen and her regent don't want their ongoing agreement with us to become an issue in their kingdom. Many humans still look on Fae as monstrous and deceitful, so the fact that the human high queen works with us on occasion for the safety of all must remain secret."

Ridiculous. Humans were the ones who were experts in deceit. They were the ones who murdered innocents in droves if even a small sack of gold was offered.

King Lysanael continued, bracing his hands on the back of the chair opposite Tahlia. "Since you, Lady Tahlia, are part human, you can handle any straight-out deceit required to complete this job."

Marius's stomach twisted, but he wasn't sure why. Tahlia could handle this. They could handle this together. Then why did he feel sick at the king's request?

Tahlia gave the king a quick nod. "Of course, Your Majesty."

"But be aware," the king said, "we aren't certain how a portion of human blood will react if Durniad makes use of the crown, so you'll need to stay together in case Lady Tahlia's mind is swayed."

They didn't have to tell Marius to protect Tahlia. That would be as natural as riding a dragon. He looked to Tahlia. Did she approve of this? They really didn't have much of a choice because this was the king and queen asking, but if she didn't want to be a part of this, he would figure out a way to respect her wishes. She was his mate first, a knight of his order second.

Tahlia gave him a subtle smile, showing her willingness. He shouldn't even have wondered. If there was one thing his mate possessed, it was courage. She had enough for ten riders.

Tahlia eyed Queen Revna. "We would be honored to serve Your Highnesses as well as our allies, the human high queen and her regent.

King Lysanael stood. "Good. One last thing: to ensure stealth, you'll ride your dragon to the human realm to meet with the human high queen's Witch; after that, you'll continue on horseback. The Witch will provide a glamour potion so that none of your Fae attributes shine through while undercover."

"We understand," Marius said. "Any further directions outside the written plan?"

"I ask that Ragewing hunt in the Gwerhune and leave my flock here be." The king grinned.

Marius nodded. "As you wish, my lord king."

Queen Revna studied Marius, and he stood straight, letting her see whatever she needed to in him. He would have to get used to those irises. It was going to be so strange and off-putting to see Tahlia with human eyes and his own reflection too...

"If I may," Tahlia started. The queen waved her on. "Did you consider my request that we include Lija's healing as part of the deal with the human court?"

They'd sent that request ahead of them, and Marius hoped the wording hadn't put them off. He had been rather insistent despite the fact that he was asking from royals who could do exactly as they wished and he had to do whatever they ordered.

Eyebrow lifted, the queen sighed. "We did and we ordered it, but I will tell you, that Witch is not keen on handouts."

What did she mean? "My queen?" he asked.

Touching his torc idly, King Lysanael pursed his lips. "The Witch, intensely loyal to the human high queen, demanded that the retrieval of the crown be completed to a satisfactory degree as deemed by the human high queen before she will lift a finger for one of our dragons."

"That's a bit rough," Tahlia muttered.

"But your dragon can wait for healing for a fortnight or so, yes? Or should we press her?" King Lysanael asked.

"I appreciate your concern, my king," Tahlia said, curtseying quickly. "I don't want to rock the boat between the realms if it's not an emergency. I believe Lija can wait."

"Good."

"Then it's settled." The queen gave her husband a look Marius couldn't decipher. "Your full instructions are in a sealed scroll in your room," she said to Marius and Tahlia. "We have had our staff pack the clothing our contact in the city provided, your belongings, and food, water, and coin for the trip. You leave immediately."

Tahlia traded a glance with Marius, then they bowed and curtseyed each in turn.

"As you wish, Your Highnesses," they said in unison.

Marius wondered how it would feel for Tahlia to cross the Veil for the very first time...

CHAPTER 5
TAHLIA

Riding in Ragewing's two-seat saddle, Tahlia gripped Marius's waist tightly. Marius had braided back his long, moonlight-hued hair. He glanced at Tahlia over his shoulder.

"I'm assuming you just want to hug me and aren't feeling fatigued and in danger of falling?" he said over the wind.

"You got it, boss."

"Lady Tahlia." His tone was a warning. "We are officially on a mission at this point."

She grinned against his broad upper back. "Commander," she said, correcting herself.

He touched her hand briefly, then adjusted his grip on the reins. "We're almost there."

Almost to the Veil. What would it be like in the human realm? Would it feel different from the Realm of Lights? Would it look wildly different?

"I suddenly feel unprepared for this mission."

"Just now, you're feeling that? You're a few days behind, Lady Tahlia." His chuckle shook her slightly. "We know our orders. We will go over the king's scroll again as soon as we finish at the Witch's house."

"Tell me what you know of the human realm."

"I've only been a few times, but it is less lush than our realm. The air can be positively fetid. But it is mostly breathable. The creatures are different from what we have. No forest dragons, except those taken by humans. No mountain dragons either. But they do have a very small breed sentimentally labeled pocket dragons."

"The humans themselves... I hope they are like Queen Revna and me generally, and nothing like my father." A shudder traveled over her heart, and a longing for Lija burned through her veins.

"Humans are not worthy of our trust. There are exceptions, but..." A grumbling growl vibrated through him.

Tahlia frowned, chewing her lip. She wasn't sure she liked how he had stated that. "Good to know." She decided to change the subject. "What do you know of the Witch?"

"No more than you do, I'd guess. All right, it's time. Brace yourself. The crossing will feel strange."

Threads glittered across the sky, sapphire blue and rose connecting Marius and Ragewing. Ebony and azure threads linked her to Marius as well as the forest, the trees, the animals that scurried and leapt below in the Gwerhune. A prickling sensation started on Tahlia's nose and hands before spreading to her scalp, back, legs, torso, and feet. She hadn't realized she'd shut her eyes, but when she opened them, the threads were gone.

"They're not here," she said, feeling unmoored. She had already grown used to the thread magic that Mother Twilight had bestowed on her.

"What isn't?" Marius tapped Ragewing's shoulder and seemed to be speaking to the dragon inside his mind. They began soaring in a more southeasterly direction.

"The threads. My magic doesn't work here."

"Ah. I had wondered if that would be the case."

"And you didn't bring it up?" she asked, blinking.

"You are deadly, skilled, and brave without your thread magic. It's a non-issue."

"I had planned on kicking everyone's arse easily!"

Another chuckle shook him. "I'm sure you'll still get a chance to take some foul humans out. Even if we are meant to be undercover during this mission, such endeavors hardly ever go according to plan."

The forest below held a softer green than the Fae realm's Gwerhune. It was sparser too, with fewer leaves on the trees and fewer ground-covering ferns and flowers. It wasn't ugly—more like reserved. As if nature had to watch its back around humans, so it was keeping a lower profile.

They didn't have to fly long before they circled the Witch's abode. Trees that looked to have survived a fire reached new branches toward the sky, and a collection of Unseelie portal stones—thankfully closed by the Unseelie king a while back—dotted the clearing around the house. Of course, "house" was a pretty serious misnomer. The structure's walls were like a castle keep—solid stone and imposingly tall. Slate tiles covered the angled roof.

Ragewing landed, and soon they were rapping on an overly complicated door. An iron-worked raven descended the length of the oaken slab while gears clicked and shifted. The dramatic entrance at last swung open to show a tall female with globe-like pale eyes and straight hair that reached to her waist.

"Welcome, knights." Her voice seemed to echo slightly as if she possessed a power that worked in a way similar to Mistgold blood. No one seemed to know exactly what race the Witch came from. She was like the Druid who often worked with King Lysanael—a being singular in make and beyond the pages of historical scrolls. "Come in."

She stepped back and Marius led the way into the stone cottage. A cauldron bubbled over invisible flames in the middle of the cluttered main room. Green light shimmered over the ceiling's rough-hewn beams. A colorful tapestry showing a human farm graced the wall. In the image, Unseelie monsters hid in the trees along the border. Bundles of dried lavender, yarrow, mint, henbane, and sage hung from a row of hooks. Doors leading to other chambers hid along the dark walls. Beeswax candles flickered along a wooden slab-type table that stretched along the western side. Vials supported with wooden frames, a mortar and pestle, and numerous colorful bottles crowded the table.

The Witch's gaze felt like a press to the throat—a blade's threat, not a kiss. "I have your potions," she said quietly, turning toward the table and lifting two corked blue bottles.

"Thank you, Witch," Marius said, accepting one of them.

He spoke calmly enough, but Tahlia could tell his body was coiled and ready to attack if needed. Not that he would win. The Witch was more powerful than anyone except the Druid.

The Witch handed the second bottle to Tahlia. The glass was cool and the contents looked oily. Tahlia wasn't exactly thrilled about having to drink it.

"You know," the Witch said, "your Queen Revna took this same potion when she infiltrated your realm to assassinate your king."

Was the Witch permitted to talk about the royals' sordid past? Tahlia doubted she followed anyone's rules.

Tahlia shook her head. "Such a wild story."

Marius's features gave nothing away as he stared at the Witch.

"I have adjusted the potion because you," the Witch said to Tahlia, "were once dosed with mintbane."

"You mean ghostmint?"

"The plants are the same, though their size differs, yes. I created this potion with a lower percentage of mintbane and added more of my other ingredients so it is less likely you will lose consciousness while the magic takes hold."

Stepping forward, Marius looked from Tahlia to the Witch and back again. "Lose consciousness?"

Though her stomach turned, Tahlia gave Marius a *calm down I've got this* look.

The Witch glared at Marius. "You won't feel much pain at all, but humans struggle with such concoctions. Lady Tahlia already has mintbane in her system."

"But that was a while back."

"It never leaves your blood."

"Ah. Great." Ophelia strikes from the afterlife.

"Is there any chance of permanent damage to Lady Tahlia?"

"There is always the chance that the magic will do something unpredictable. I can't promise you anything, Commander," she said snidely.

"Of course. We understand."

"You don't because you don't know the Old Language and can't work runes," the Witch said, turning back to her cauldron and staring into the depths, "but I appreciate the sentiment regardless."

"Forgive me if this is inappropriate," Tahlia said, "but would you consider traveling to Dragon Tail Peak right away to heal my dragon, Vodolija?"

"I will not heal your dragon until you fulfill your side of the agreement with my queen."

"I'd be faster and more capable if she were healed. Even if she remained hidden in a forest near the mission starting point, her presence would ease my mind and improve my physical abilities. Don't you want the most capable agent working toward your queen's goal?"

"Sheathe your silvered tongue, knight. The terms have been signed and neither of us can alter them."

Sure. The Witch, arguably the most powerful being in the world, couldn't alter terms if it pleased her. Right.

"There are things you should know about the artifact." The Witch stood over her glowing cauldron. Steam blocked half of her austere features. "We have two spies inside the city. The one who will meet you at the safe house says the crown has been stored under Durniad's fortress. Traps await you; I have no doubt." She twisted, and with her long reach, she took a small leather bag from one of the many shelves.

Marius accepted the bag, then tied it to his belt.

"Sprinkle that mixture in the room where you believe the crown to be. The magicked dust will force the crown to show itself."

"Thank you," Marius said.

"The crown can flood a human's mind fully and the wearer can order those within earshot to do anything they so choose. Be warned. I don't believe it will alter your mind," she said to Marius, "but you," she said, turning to Tahlia, "must be on your guard. If you manage to take the artifact, you will feel the urge to retain the crown for yourself; its power is alluring. Even if no one knows you have it, people will be drawn to you when it is in your possession."

A shiver trotted down Tahlia's spine.

"Midhampton is packed with people," the Witch said. "It's not a large city, size-wise, so the inhabitants are practically on top of one another."

It was Marius's turn to visibly shiver. He was not a crowd enthusiast.

"Many visit the city due to the port's heavy trade business. A couple of strange faces shouldn't raise alarms. Especially during such a popular festival. Now, I advise you to take your potions at the arranged spot where you will trade your dragon for horses. The effects should last around five days. Maybe three. It's hard to say."

"What happens if our Fae features begin to show in the middle of a crowd of humans?"

"Perhaps pretend you wear an elaborate costume? That or run away very quickly."

Marius's eyebrow twitched. "That's not exactly a true backup plan."

The Witch shrugged. "I'm not the Mist Knight. You figure it out. Or we'll all die."

"How would that go exactly?" Tahlia asked.

"Durniad will don the crown at his self-made coronation. This will not be the coronation of a lesser king, of one who simply runs the city of Midhampton. No, he will name himself the ruler of all. Don't think it's impossible, after all, with the crown, he will control every human on this continent, and quite possibly those in the islands beyond. They will come for your people. For the gold. For the crops. For the joy of overrunning your realm with sheer numbers."

The hilt of Tahlia's dagger warmed her hand. No matter what, she wasn't going down without a fight.

CHAPTER 6
TAHLIA

Tahlia flipped her shoulder bag open and rummaged around, careful not to upend the potion bottle. Before they'd left the Mist Knight's castle, Fara had given her a bundle of letters, and it was time to open the first one.

Marius had his back to her. He watched a break of rowan trees where Ragewing was hunting for lunch. They'd reached the spot where a human contact would be arriving with the horses. So far, no humans.

"What are you up to back there?" he asked, glancing at her. "Is that what Lady Fara gave you?"

"It is." She lifted the bundle and wiggled it. The knot holding the tiny sheets of scraped vellum in a neat stack was tight and hard as hells to undo. She resorted to using her Fae fang, hoping the human wouldn't show up at that moment. Supposedly, they hated Fae fangs. Granted, it was more likely the mountain dragon would be doing all the frightening during the upcoming rendezvous.

The knot gave way at last and Tahlia unfolded the first note.

. . .

Dear Tahlia

Yes, you DO need to stay away from the water inside the human city. You'll pick up a fever at the very least and/or an extra eye if you imbibe from their disgusting wells. Just watch. You'll see loads of folk with superfluous fingers and so forth.

Oh, and I forgot to tell you that a southern herbwitch is coming to visit Albus. She is the only known one in the world and we are going to experiment with what our Healers know and her specific abilities. Should be interesting! Will probably end in someone's horrific death though.

Have a lovely trip!

Fara

"What's so alarming?"

Tahlia jumped at Marius's voice. She looked up to see him studying her face like she was an unexpected roll in a high-stakes game of Tali.

"You're surprised a note from Fara is unsettling?" Tahlia asked.

Marius snorted. "I suppose not. What are we to watch out for this time? Errant Unseelie gargoyles? Possibly the end of the very world itself?"

"Nothing so exciting as that. A Healer experiment, and a strong warning that human city water is tainted with disease."

"Actually, that's a good thing to bring up. Some human cities have water as clean as ours. Others I've tried have tasted uncomfortably like feet."

"So if it smells of feet, go with wine?"

"A sound plan. How many notes did she send with you?"

"Enough for one a day for six days. She claimed we would die without her advice joining us on the journey."

Marius shrugged. "I'm glad we won't have to find out. We should be in and out of Midhampton in four days, by my estimation. Come look at this."

He unrolled a map of Midhampton and held it aloft. Inked rivers, roads, secret passageways, and safe houses showed clearly from edge to edge. Not an inch was empty of scribbles or drawings.

"Here is where we will meet up with Ragewing once we have the crown." Marius pointed to a clearing that seemed similar in size to this one, although it was far closer to the city. "Inside, we're to pose as members of the city's temporary guard."

"I recall." He had insisted she read King Lysanael and Queen Revna's mission scroll five times. She hadn't complained, but there were moments she wondered if Marius thought she was an idiot. But perhaps that was part of the regular mission process, to go over and over and over the information. The scroll had mentioned Durnaid's tendency to use elaborate schemes for his own entertainment. The crown would likely be found amidst numerous traps and there was talk of a labyrinth.

"Durniad hires numerous extra bodies to keep the peace during the festival," Marius said. "We'll head first to the safe house near Bodwin Bridge to dress the part."

Marius looked down at her and a wave of longing swept through her. She wanted his body on hers. Was there time before the human with the horses arrived?

He lifted an eyebrow. "I hate to disappoint you, but I'll not be dressing as a tomato for this mission."

"Murderer of dreams, that's what you are." Besides, he probably didn't know for sure what the uniforms for temporary guards looked like. He could be wrong.

The corners of his handsome mouth—a mouth she suddenly and immediately wanted all over her—edged up at the corners, making her heart flip. Still holding the map in one hand, he smoothed a palm along her jaw and down the side of her neck. His storm-gray and slitted irises darkened as he leaned down to kiss her.

His mouth claimed hers, his tongue exploring the underside of her top lip and making her toes curl inside her soft villager boots. His hand slid around the back of her neck and his thumb hooked the front of her throat.

"So possessive," she whispered as he licked her earlobe.

"Do we have time for this, Commander Marius?"

He only answered with a growl as he burrowed into her neck, nipping and licking lightly. The map fluttered to the ground and he backed her up against a boulder.

Ragewing landed gracefully, his tongue darting across the tip of his snout.

Marius's eyes shut briefly before he met Tahlia's eyes. "Sorry."

Tahlia kissed his delicious jawline. "The mission comes first. I know that."

He held her hand, and they walked up to Ragewing. Tahlia exhaled, trying to let go of the desire rushing through her blood. She had to focus on the mission and prove to Marius they could do this even though they were mated fully now. She wanted to show everyone that they could be a mated pair and the best Mist Knights on the mountain.

"Good meal, my friend?" Marius asked him, retrieving and rolling up the map.

Ragewing lifted his scarlet head and a low, staccato growl rumbled from his throat.

"He says he saw the human and his horses two miles or so away," Marius said, looking from Ragewing to Tahlia.

Tahlia let out a sigh and pushed a fisted hand against the knot in her stomach. "Guess it's finally time to poison ourselves."

Marius chuckled darkly.

"Ragewing," Tahlia said, "how do you think Lija is doing? I can't hear her anymore."

The dragon looked to his rider. Marius nodded, rubbing his chin in thought.

"Ragewing says she is strong in spirit, though the challenge is one of the most difficult a dragon can face."

Tahlia said a silent prayer to the gods. Lija had to survive this. They had to heal her.

The massive scarlet dragon spread his wings slightly and bowed his head. Grateful to him, Tahlia smiled and curtseyed back, some of the knot in her stomach untangling.

Marius put a hand on Ragewing's neck. "Thank you for carrying my mate again." He tilted his head, listening to Ragewing in his mind. A laugh crept from his lips and he turned to Tahlia. "He says if you'd sit still in the saddle, the job would be far less anxiety-inducing."

Tahlia stuck her tongue out at both of them. She slipped her potion free of its leather holder, then she uncorked it at the same time as Marius opened his bottle. "Well, we need to move forward with our plans, right? I think we should human ourselves before the contact arrives with our horse. So he is less frightened of us."

"Agreed."

"Time to human." She lifted the concoction into the lines of sun that broke through the trees. "Bottoms up!"

Marius nodded, raising his potion, then he downed the stuff. She did likewise.

The potion tasted like regret and maybe deer piss? Super delightful. Ugh. She turned away from Ragewing and Marius, stomach rolling.

A warm hand found her shoulder.

"Are you all right?" Marius's breath tickled the hairs at the side of her face.

She realized she was on her knees in the dirt and grass. When had she dropped?

"I've been better, but I'll live," she said.

The world tilted and she swallowed, willing her body to accept the magic.

"Lady Tahlia, talk to me. Tell me you're all right. Or expunge it from your body and we will figure out another way to do this. I will go on my own."

Holding up a hand, she bit out her words. "No. Can't ruin mission." She did her best to grin up at him.

Nodding, he helped her to her feet. "Ach, you're fine. I see that salty little smirk."

His ears shimmered and morphed, edges rounding into a human-like shape. His skin dulled ever so slightly and as he blinked, his slitted irises became circles.

"So strange," she whispered, touching the cheekbone on the left side of his face as it lost its Fae sharpness and became less pronounced.

He was studying her like she was examining him. His gaze peppered her here and there, as if he was cataloguing the changes. "Fascinating."

"Do I pass as fully human now?" *Gods above, have mercy on me*, she prayed silently. Nausea swirled inside her. It was all she could do to keep from losing the contents of her belly. Dots swam in front of her eyes.

"You don't look well. And I'm not just talking about the human features," he said.

"It'll pass."

"We're not going anywhere until it does," he said in a tone that didn't brook any arguments.

"Yes, we are. I'm doing this for Lija, and I am not letting an upset stomach get in my way."

Ragewing snorted, then took off into the air. He flew toward the darker side of the forest.

Marius watched him go. "He says our rider approaches. Ragewing will hide himself to avoid startling the horses. He told me to bid you best wishes."

Tahlia smiled. "Tell him thank you."

A human with tan cheeks and light green eyes—and of course, his irises were round—rode into the clearing on a russet-hued mare. The human had two more horses on leads trailing behind—one dun with a star on his nose and one as black as night.

"The power of the wicked is nothing to those with hearts of fire," the contact said.

Marius lifted a hand in a wave. "Fire, we have." He put his fist to his chest.

Tahlia's stomach was absolutely stuffed with butterflies. Code phrases like that just made it all seem so real once again; she was a Mist Knight and she was on a mission. It was amazing!

The human dismounted. Tahlia could tell he was male from the set of his shoulders, but she wished he weren't cloaked and hooded so she could study his looks more closely. He had a snub nose and a heavy jaw. He didn't have the sheen to his flesh that those with Fae blood had, but other than that, he appeared pretty much the same. His movements were what gave him away as human. Though he was clearly experienced with horses—he dismounted easily and gathered the mounts like it was what he did every day of his life—his hands worked in a slower, less graceful manner. The strides he took to approach them, reins held loosely, were ungainly in a way a Fae would never appear.

Tahlia suddenly worried they wouldn't be able to blend in for this mission. Their movements would give them away, surely.

The contact gestured toward the two horses he'd brought for them. "They're good creatures. Biddable. Smart. Won't startle too easily. And they're trained to return to our place when you release them. Please do so before you come out of the tree cover near Midhampton. I don't want any would-be thieves trying their hand at stealing my horses."

"Understood," Marius said, approaching the black stallion. He picked a bit of clover from the ground and held it in his palm for the horse to lip up. "Has the festival plan changed at all?"

"Not as far as I know. Your in-town contact will know more. He has your guard uniforms."

"Oh, we had thought..." Tahlia picked at her tunic.

The man shook his head. "No, you'll have official uniforms."

Oooh, maybe there would be a really obnoxious pattern at least. Tahlia grinned and Marius glared at her like she was due for a scolding.

"As for the parade," the contact went on, oblivious to Tahlia and Marius's silent discussion, "for now, it seems it will begin at Bodkin Bridge. It'll be hard to miss. They always drape it in banners. On the far side. It will wrap in an easterly direction through the oldest parts, down near the docks, then curve back to the fortress, near the other side of Bodkin. There will be stages set up along the parade route and traffic will stop to allow for the customary dances and competitions."

"What do those involve?"

"The dances are performed by anyone willing. Sometimes, an official or guild leader will push someone on stage. It's tradition. The competitions are preplanned. Jugglers tossing tomatoes. Folks balancing on one another's shoulders to build human towers. Comedic acts that the crowd votes on by cheering. That sort of nonsense."

Marius gave the man a nod that said he liked how he didn't approve of silly things like that. Tahlia bit her lip to keep from snickering. Grouchy old things, they both were.

"Meet your contact at the safe house. Dress the part. Uniforms are hidden in an armoire in the kitchen. Enter the parade. Blend in. Head to the fortress as soon as you're able and we have a couple of inside folks there to help you out. Better you than me, I'll tell you that. I don't know how you're going to find an invisible artifact."

"We have our ways." Marius led the stallion a few steps away and released his reins so he could nibble at the tall grass.

"I leave you to it, then." The man handed the dun's reins to

Tahlia, then he mounted up. "Best of luck to you!" he called out as he rode away.

Tahlia watched him until he was out of sight.

"I'm trying not to be jealous of a human male." Marius climbed onto his horse's saddle.

"It's only curiosity."

"I understand." The sides of his mouth lifted a fraction like he was trying to smile at her, but his eyes burned with worry or confusion—she wasn't sure.

They rode into the woods. Soon, they'd be entering a human city. As they sped through the shadows of fat-trunked beech trees and around tangles of thorn bushes, Tahlia made herself breathe slowly in and out. Excitement and curiosity made it incredibly difficult to keep from asking the horses to gallop even faster than they already were.

CHAPTER 7
TAHLIA

The city of Midhampton boasted a fine arched entryway flanked by two tower guard houses—more security than most Fae towns and cities, but not as many as the Mist Knights' castle or Caer Du, the heart of the Fae realm. A long string of humans made their way under the archway, stopping now and then to answer the guards' questions. A group of minstrels in silks carrying lutes, pipes, and drums were ushered through with a laugh from a heavily bearded guard. Carts holding everything from crates of chickens to trunks overflowing with textile goods rolled into the city, mules and horses tugging them along at the behest of merchants and their families. Conversation and giggling rose in the cool, briny air to mix with the squawk of sea birds.

The cobblestones beneath Tahlia's boots weren't made of the same sturdy rock as the roads in the Realm of Lights. This rock was sandy and gritty under her step. One would slide on this surface if one came to an abrupt stop. A good thing to remember if it came to fighting.

Marius's warm presence at her back made Tahlia even bolder as their turn to answer the guards' questions arrived.

"Business or pleasure?" The guard had a low voice, and his mustache did a pretty great job at muffling what sound did attempt to come out.

"Pleasure," Tahlia said before Marius could attempt the word and ruin the mission with his inability to sound like he was about to have some fun.

The guard glared at Marius, who forced a grin. A grimace? Not sure what that was.

"Where in the city will you stay?" That mustache was almost broom-like. "I hope you don't think you can just wander in and find lodgings anywhere. And there's no sleeping on the street."

Marius nodded. "We have a room at The Stag and Pheasant."

"Oh, fine place, that," the guard said, stepping back to let them pass.

The crowd jostled Tahlia as they made their way under the arched gateway. An entertainer dressed in red stripes grinned at an incredibly tall man who carried a sack. The top of the corn dolly stuck out from the sack. Two carts of ale barrels lumbered past, nearly squashing Tahlia's foot. Marius pulled her back.

"Watch yourself, now."

"There's so much to look at. And they look so strange." Humans weren't ugly, but they didn't have the grace of Fae. It hadn't just been their horse contact; they were all a bit lumbering. They appeared softer, and honestly, their smiles appeared more genuine. "I didn't expect to like the look of them," she said quietly.

The surrounding noise of parents instructing children and excited conversation amongst merchants lugging their wares made it plenty safe for her to speak to Marius.

He leaned down, his lips grazing her ear. "You have a kind and generous spirit, and I can't fault you for that."

Human pirates had killed Marius's sister. She truly hoped he didn't hate all of them because of that. Would Marius tell her if he felt differently? Even if he wished he didn't?

"If we end up needing the others, how will we signal them?"

"I would need to get close enough to Ragewing to communicate a message that he would fly back to Dragon Tail Peak."

"Can you hear him now?"

Marius squinted as they walked. "No, we're too far, I guess. I have noticed the ability is spotty outside the Veil."

The main thoroughfare rose like a scared cat's back, and the city opened up below. Orange tiles lay in neat lines along rooftops, the East Border River slid through the buildings and roads, and the scent of roasted meat and baking bread perfumed the air. Large carts filled with tomatoes sat at almost every intersection, ready for the insane ritual of tossing the red vegetables—or fruits, really—until pulp swamped ankles and dribbled into open doorways. Numerous walkways arched over crossway paths and small bridges slanted across Midhampton. One bridge in particular commanded attention. Lined with flapping banners in every shade of red, the bridge that stretched wide over the river seemed to be welcoming everyone to the festival.

Tahlia bounced on her heels before she continued onward to catch up to Marius. "We should have practiced the telepathic chatting with varying distances before this mission."

"We had no time for a proper exploration of the limits and with your Lija still injured—"

A woman pushed through the crowd and fell onto Marius with a laugh that stank of ale.

"Hello, beautiful," she said to him, her words slurring. "Want a little pre-festival fun?"

Marius gently but firmly eased her off of him. "No, good woman. I have a companion." He tilted his head toward Tahlia.

The stream of people pushed them forward. The woman disappeared in the crowd, her hand waving above a family dressed in red for the parade. Marius took Tahlia's elbow and ushered her toward a narrow side street.

The excitement of the city's inhabitants and visitors zipped through Tahlia, and she felt incredibly hopeful. They would enjoy the festival, nab the invisible crown, and be home before Fara's Healer evaluation for sure. Tahlia didn't want to miss supporting her on her first test with Albus.

The crowd pulled them along, and soon a bridge—made of rose-hued stone that glittered in the sun—spread out, arching above the masses. The street they were on passed under Bodwin Bridge on the southern side, with the river dashing about in its banks to their left. They came out on the far side, and a shout hammered the air.

"You with the white hair, halt in the name of King Durniad!"

Tahlia's heart stilled and she gripped Marius's wrist. "The Witch's potion should've been set to hide that pretty mane of yours."

CHAPTER 8
MARIUS

It was a city guard. There were humans with hair nearly as white as Marius's, but perhaps this fellow had specific issues with Fae and was more prone to jump at any chance to find one and give one trouble. Even when the Fae helped them, some humans possessed an unbreakable hate for Fae. The guard's tassels indicated officer-level ranking as per the mission details. He was alone, so they could likely evade him if he was indeed shouting at them.

"Should we run?" Tahlia whispered.

"Not yet. It could be anything. Stay calm."

She shielded her eyes from the blazing sun. "I can't tell if he is looking this way or not."

"I don't think so."

"You're sure?" she asked.

"Not yet."

"I don't like it when you're not sure. You're always sure."

"That's incorrect."

"See? You're certain I'm wrong." Her lovely fingers left his wrist, and he mourned the loss like a lovesick youngling.

The guard was parting the crowd and coming their way.

He growled quietly. "We need to work our way out of here."

"Got it." Tahlia shot to the right, going across the crowd.

It was more obvious, but it was the fastest way to shift their direction. Conversations and the general noise of the people started up again, but the guard had his gaze set on Marius and he wasn't slowing, his body parting the crowd like a prow on the water.

Tahlia was already taking a turn to join the throng walking across the bridge on the upper level, over the place where they'd just been. Marius trailed her, carefully easing folks aside as he went. This was easier for Tahlia because she was so small. She was halfway across the bridge by the time he reached her.

It was like her head was on a swivel. "Is he following us? Where is he?"

"Look straight ahead. Aim for the second street to the right. We will cross the river again at the next bridge."

"Aye, aye." She winked at him and kept on.

Finally, they were moving in sync with the crowd. The bridge sloped down to the street once more, and they skirted their way along the edges of the people. An open door beckoned from a basketweaver's shop.

"Here. This is better."

He put a hand to the small of her back and immediately wished he hadn't because the feel of her shape caused his blood to flow away from his brain, heading south. He followed her into the shop.

"Oh, I love these!" She picked up a basket and stared at it like it was a lost treasure found.

"Do you?" The shopkeeper clasped her hands. Her eyes shone with delight. "It's my newest design."

The back door was clear, straight back. He cut past Tahlia and the basketweaver and into the dark of the back of the shop. Two small boys looked up at him from the corner where they were sorting what looked like the reeds that grew on the seaside. Marius whistled once, quick and high, a sound Tahlia would notice, but most would excuse as street noise filtering in.

Tahlia laughed at something the shop woman said, and she hurried back to join him. They were out the back door in seconds.

"What did you tell her?"

"That your ex was out front."

Marius snorted and led her over the cobblestones and toward the road to the next bridge, if they needed to use it. But if they found the safe house first, they would just go there.

Only a small group of elder humans and a skinny dog walked down this side street. The turn was clear of guards so far. They slipped down the road, and at last, the blue-painted door of the safe house appeared at the end of a more crowded lane. In front of the door, a wooden gate circled a tiny garden. Marius pushed it open and Tahlia hurried through and tried the door.

"Locked," she said quietly as she smiled at a passerby. She was handling this well, acting casual and masking their need to work quickly.

With a glance over his shoulder to check for the city guard or anyone who seemed too curious about them, Marius rammed his shoulder against the painted oak. He grunted as the door banged open. They rushed inside. He shut the slightly damaged door behind them.

"Where are the uniforms again?" Tahlia asked. "I can't remember what he said about that."

"Kitchen. It's always the kitchen for some reason. Perhaps because no one tends to search kitchens. I'll check that the house is clear first. You go on." He stalked down the narrow hallway that led to two bedchambers. Nothing.

"All clear," he called out.

"I found cheese!" Tahlia's voice echoed down the hallway.

The city cottage's kitchen was small and in need of cleaning, but the armoire was exactly where the contact said it would be—against the wall beside a window that looked out on a shared inner courtyard choked by weeds that nicely blocked the kitchen from view. Tahlia was digging through a smaller cabinet and shoving bits of yellow cheese into her mouth.

"You should eat some," Tahlia mumbled over a mouthful. "We'll need energy for this mission. Plus, it's delicious."

"I have no time for cheese. The contact will be here soon. We must be ready."

"It's like you hate yourself," Tahlia muttered, joining him at the armoire.

He paused, eyeing the windows to be sure the city guard hadn't found his way here. Tahlia tugged the armoire doors open, and a mass of fur flew out.

Heart hammering, Marius shoved his way in front of her, his dagger unsheathed and ready. Tahlia grabbed his hand and pushed his weapon down.

"They're kittens!" she cried.

Blinking, Marius looked at the armoire, the kitchen floor, and then at Tahlia. Furry rodents crawled everywhere. And Tahlia was holding one and cooing at it.

"Aren't they adorable? Sweet little darling." She kissed the cat she was holding.

"Get that thing off of you. It could have one of a thousand diseases and we have work to do."

"Fara would agree, but alas, I do not." Tahlia stroked the cat's black fur and bent to pick up another of the small menaces.

One striped creature began climbing Marius's trousers, and he plucked it off. He held it aloft to study it. "They definitely have fleas, as well as claws as sharp as a youngling dragon's."

Laughing, Tahlia took the striped nightmare from him and added it to the collection currently on her shoulders and in the crook of her arm.

Marius shook his head and growled. "Shoo the small demons away. We have work to do."

"Demons." She laughed harder. "Your face right now is making this entire mission so worthwhile."

He gritted his teeth and turned back to the armoire. Lifting a basket, he searched for the uniforms. Another furred devil shot out of the shadowed back corner of the cabinet and latched onto his tunic. It smelled like a sewer rat. He detached the beast with careful movements.

"You're treating that demon awfully carefully," Tahlia said snidely.

A growl echoed from him as he passed the creature to her.

Under a stack of folded linens, the uniforms caught the sun from the window and sparkled. Marius swore.

Tahlia slid under his arm to look. "Oh. Those are..."

"Horrifying."

"Fantastic! But that's not what the other city guards were wearing."

"No, these are specifically for the parade guards, so we won't see them until we join the madness in an hour."

He pulled them out and handed her the smaller trousers, tunic, belt, and cloak. She took them with a grin that had no business here, then shouted, making him go for his blade again.

"A tomato hat!" She lifted a round sort of cap that had been stuffed between the trousers and tunic.

Could this get any worse? He doubted it.

Her hand darted toward him and she produced his hat, an even larger disaster of fabric as bright red as Ragewing's back. She hopped up and slammed the hat onto his head, then collapsed in a fit of snickering.

"You look amazing."

"Please stop talking and get dressed. The sooner we do this, the sooner I can have Ragewing burn this monstrous headgear into ash."

"But you said we have an hour before we need to blend in with the parade."

He only growled again and shook his leg to dislodge yet another furred tangle of chaos. He headed toward the hallway to disrobe, not wishing to do so in the company of the demons.

Smiling in that irresistible way she had, Tahlia joined him, and it was all he could do to keep from pulling her to him. It took every ounce of his rigorous training in self-discipline to refrain from running his palms up her smooth sides as she changed into the uniform's tunic. The bond between them hit him sometimes like this—incredibly powerful and completely out of nowhere. The feral side of him wished to cover her in his scent so the multitudes of people outside these walls would know she was his, but of course, that was a silly thought. They were humans, not Fae. But his blood didn't seem to give a shit.

"Oh, hells." He rushed toward her and pushed her against the wall as she smiled wide.

CHAPTER 9
MARIUS

"This is unexpected, Commander Marius."

Growling into her deliciously soft-scented neck, he pressed himself against her and savored her little moans of delight. His body rose to meet the challenge and he rubbed his length along her center. She gasped and lifted her hips. Pleasure coursed through Marius and his blood pounded in his ears.

Tahlia licked the tip of his ear, sending shivers of want down his neck and back. Gods, he wanted to ram himself into her with no regard for missions or crowns or humans with their heads up their arses. He longed to feel her warmth surrounding him in full.

"Another contact will be here shortly, won't he?" she asked in a breathy voice.

"Don't care," he muttered as he moved her carefully to the floor. There was a carpet lining the flat stone and it would keep the chill from her, not that he truly worried she might get cold with what activities he had in mind. "Be good, Tahlia. You want this, yes?"

He pulled away, suddenly worried he might have assumed too much. But she smiled saucily.

"Oh, yes, Marius. Yes, I do."

She helped him shuck off her Midhampton special guard trousers and his as well. Just the scent of her skin made his head swim...

His tongue licked its way down her bared stomach and she squirmed under him, her fingers digging into his scalp. Pinning her hips with his forearm, he brushed his mouth over her navel. He longed to take his time, but time wasn't something they had much of. At least one very tiny part of his mind was cognizant of that fact.

He met her gaze and she nodded, permitting him to continue. Rising up onto his elbow, he used his free hand to lift her leg. He drove into her and his body lit up with pleasure. The sensations roared through his blood. He kissed her hard and her mouth opened to him just as her body had. She felt like an after-life he could never, ever deserve. Perfectly created for their joining.

"Perfect. You're perfect," he gasped out.

Her head fell back against the floor and she cried out, bucking her hips as she found her peak. He gripped her low around the hips, his hands squeezing her fine backside, and he thrust and thrust and thrust again until his climax claimed the last shred of his mind.

Falling gently onto her, feeling the movement of her blessed lungs and the beat of her darling heart, his pulse beat out one truth. "Mine. My mate. All mine."

"Aye, Commander Marius, and you are mine as well." She kissed the top of his head as he rested on her chest.

He hadn't realized he'd said the words aloud. A smile tugged at his lips and he held her close.

A fuzzy demon approached. It mewed directly into his face and marched onto his back. Marius growled and shifted his shoulder to dislodge the kitten, but the beastly thing held on with its foul claws. It curled up between his shoulder blades.

Tahlia dissolved in a fit of laughter. "The kitten..." She could barely speak and her laughter jostled his head. "Loves you."

A knock sounded, loud and so insistent that it had to have been going on for longer than they had noticed.

Removing the kitten from Marius's back, they hurried to clean up. In the water closet at the back of the house, they dressed while the knocking continued. Tahlia tucked Fara's letters under her tunic and into the waist of her trousers. They would be hidden, so he figured that was all right. If they were captured, their potions would fade and it wouldn't matter if the letters contained information that exposed Tahlia and Marius as Fae.

"I'm sorry I dragged you into lovemaking," Marius said.

"Don't apologize. I'll go again if you're up for it."

He froze in buttoning his trousers and eyed her smiling, beautiful face. "Do not tempt me, my mate. It's this city..." Moving on to fixing his tomato hat—*save me from this day, great Old Ones*—he continued his explanation. "With all these people around you, I feel the undeniable urge to mark you with my scent."

"Even though the humans won't detect it?"

"Yes. I know. I'm a beast."

She giggled and picked up the kitten who had befriended him. "A feral beast like this fellow?"

"Not *that* bad."

Her laugh eased his nerves and now that she smelled of him, of their union, his Fae blood cooled. Not completely, but some.

When Tahlia finally opened the door, the contact—a short human man with the same stupid costume they were wearing on his portly body—blinked at them.

He scowled at their faces, which were surely flushed. "I'm no Mist Knight," he whispered as he pushed past them and into the safe house's living room area, "but even I know *that* wasn't in the plan. Also, that hat is a lot on you, my dear man."

They followed him, Tahlia snickering. "It is." Her gaze traveled up to Marius's head.

Marius shut his eyes and begged all the powers of the world to make this day move more quickly from here on out.

The contact's gaze snagged on the pile of kittens that had dozed off in a square of sunlight near the hearth. He blew out a breath. Then he faced them again. "Your disguise spell is certainly working."

The way he said spell sounded akin to someone talking about a tragedy, but that was no surprise. Humans distrusted magic, and they believed the Fae were drenched in it. That was wrong, but perhaps they viewed some normal attributes as magical when indeed they were not. Marius wasn't sure.

"There is a change in plan," the contact said.

Marius crossed his arms. "Explain."

Tahlia bent to check the knife she had tucked into her boot. "What's happening?"

"Because of an incoming storm and the flooding that will likely be a problem in the Star Quarter of the city, King Durniad shortened the parade and will present himself, wearing the crown no doubt, in the morning. He will likely be at the fortress while you are attempting the heist. Once the tomato throwing begins, go to the fortress's southern entrance. Get in and get out. Use the name Edward Newlington, and once you're in, ask them if a storm is coming. If they're with us, they'll say, 'the sky and ocean are tricky.' Oh, and I meant to tell you that as hired guards, you'll fit in best if you participate in some of the foolish activities going on during the parade and so forth. Dance a dance if you're asked onto a stage. Have a drink, not five of them, mind you, but an ale or two will be expected on a festival day."

"Even from guards?" Tahlia asked.

"Yes. The guidelines for your behavior are up for debate. It'll all depend on which captain is bossing you about at the moment."

A spark of unpleasant heat sizzled under Marius's breastbone.

"About what I would expect from humans who tolerate pirates," he said very quietly, unable to restrain himself.

The contact's gaze flicked to Marius's face, but he didn't say a word in retort. Perhaps he agreed.

"The crown is still hidden in the same place though, right? That hasn't changed?" Tahlia asked.

"As far as we know, the crown is still locked up somewhere under the fortress. You heard about the labyrinth and the potential traps, correct?" The contact removed a waterskin from his belt and sipped loudly. Sweat shone on his wide forehead.

Marius nodded as he and Tahlia packed their clothing into a sack left for them on the table. "But no details. Do you know anything further?"

"No. Only that building out one of the traps resulted in the death of Durniad's right-hand man and a few people he viewed as less important."

"Details, please." Marius attached his dagger to the uniform's broad belt, using a loop with a long metal button.

Tahlia did the same and he appreciated the fact that she remembered to tuck an extra blade into her borrowed boot.

The contact replaced the waterskin at his belt, then mopped his brow with his loose linen sleeve. "Of course, yes. But we have little time. What I was told was that Durniad commanded his team to house something incredibly dangerous down there. His right-hand man told him it wasn't a good idea. When the trap or whatever it is killed the man, Durniad claimed the advisor deserved the death for his disloyalty, then Durniad murdered those who had agreed with the advisor."

"Really nice guy, hmm?" Tahlia shook her head, her cheeks going pale.

"An absolute pig."

Tahlia nodded. "So no other clues other than generally very dangerous?"

Marius pressed his lips together. Going into this blind was

not what he had in mind. He'd thought the contact would at least know something of Durniad's wild plan to house the crown.

"And no mention of the tools they used to set up the trap or any visiting experts?" Marius asked.

"Well, now that you mention it..." The contact bent at the waist as a sleepy-eyed monster with tabby stripes trotted up to his boot. He picked it up and stroked its back—he'd get fleas for sure. "Aside from the usual engineers employed in construction that close to the sea's edge, Durniad brought in a smithy."

"A blacksmith?" Tahlia asked.

The contact nodded as he returned the kitten to the floor. "One who is known to specialize in locks, doors, custom carts for hauling livestock. That sort of thing."

"Hmm." Marius tapped his chin. What was Durniad hoping to contain? The crown, obviously. But anything else? Would there be an elaborate trap that they could trigger upon entering the area where he had the crown hidden? Or perhaps a mechanism that made it so sharpened spearheads or blades set into the walls of the structure could be loosed from outside the building if they were seen entering?

"You know, it might not be a terrible idea to attempt to get information out of Durniad's brother, Jovanyth. He drinks too much, so Durniad basically ignores his existence," the contact said. "I tried to get him to talk to me when he was deep in his cups four days ago, but a friend of his spoiled my attempts."

"Where is this brother now?" Marius asked.

The contact waved his hand all around. "He's with everyone else. In the streets, celebrating."

"We will find him," Marius said.

"But—" the contact started, but Marius held up a hand.

"Information is the key to success. What tavern does he frequent?"

"The Siren's Grotto."

Tahlia raised her eyebrows, and the mischievous glint in her eyes brightened. "Sounds fun."

The contact snorted and Marius pondered what the sound meant to him. That the tavern wasn't fun? That Tahlia was being foolish? Marius felt his lip curl, but because of the Witch's potion, his Fae fang wouldn't show and properly threaten this fellow for insulting his mate.

Tahlia tugged on his guard uniform sleeve. "Eh, Commander, are you listening? You all right?"

Marius shook off his growing irritation with the contact and forced a smile. "You were saying..."

Swallowing, the contact dragged his gaze from Marius's fisted hand to look instead at Tahlia.

"Head up this road," he said, giving directions to the tavern. He went on with little details to look for and where to go, including a trip through the city's catacombs. "There is a torch or two sitting down there from our last use of the passage. A small bag should be beside them with flint and stone. It will only take a small spark to ignite the torch because it's doused in the same stuff Durniad uses in sea battles. Do not, and I repeat, do not get any of it on your skin. You might be powerful Fae beings, but I think it would still give you a pretty nasty wound to deal with in the middle of all this."

Marius nodded.

"The catacombs might be a little damp with the tide high," the human said. "Follow the crown symbol etched into the wall on each turn..." His directions continued, telling them how to get to the Siren's Grotto exactly. He told them to join the parade once they were finished with Jovanyth.

Marius crossed his arms. "Perfect. The tomato throwing begins at the sound of the explosions, yes?"

"The fireworks, yes. You'll hear some horns too."

"Do humans detonate fireworks often?" Tahlia asked. "Our king does, but the everyday person doesn't have access."

"No. Special events only. They're too expensive for most to purchase."

"Interesting. Thanks!"

The contact started to frown at Tahlia.

Marius stepped closer and stared down at the human. "Anything else?"

He coughed. "Ah, uh, no. That's it. But take this." Turning back toward the front door, he shoved a key into Marius's hand. "I nabbed it from one of the guards at the fortress's old gate. I'm not sure what it unlocks, but it can't hurt to have it."

"Thank you."

The contact left, and after a count of twenty, they did the same.

It was time to find a drunkard and squeeze him for information. If they missed their timing to get into the fortress, they would be caught. Their potion would wear off while in holding cells, no doubt, and then they would be at the mercy of Durniad.

Marius wasn't about to let anyone capture Tahlia even if he had to give his life to keep that from happening.

CHAPTER 10

TAHLIA

Between two three-story buildings, Tahlia trailed Marius down the set of stairs the safe house contact had told them about. They found one torch and the bag at the bottom of the stairs.

"Keep watch behind us," Marius ordered as he worked to light the torch.

Watery light from the street level filtered down to Tahlia and the noise of the crowd bounced off the carved pale stones. Wind from farther into the catacombs blew lightly like the breath of a ghost. Tahlia shivered.

Marius held the fiery torch up. "All right. I will go first. Every ten steps or so, be sure to look back to check for anyone creeping up behind."

"Will do, Commander."

The plain stone walls gave way to stacks of elaborately organized skulls, femurs, and ribcages. Some skeletons were arranged to appear like they were walking along the wall. Others lay in carved-out alcoves. A massive triangle of skulls marked an archway. The right-side passage was marked with the little carved crown that the safe house contact had mentioned. They turned in that direction and more bones greeted them.

"This is wild," Tahlia said, eyeing it all by the light of the flickering torch Marius carried.

Marius made his thinking noise.

"Their bones look like ours," she said, pondering humans in general.

"But they aren't like ours at all. Our bone density is three times theirs."

"How do you know that?"

"Albus," Marius said.

"When did he teach you?" she asked.

"For a while, as a youth, I thought perhaps I could learn some Healer skills for the battlefield. Beyond basic bandaging and how to stop bleeding."

"Why did you stop training?"

"To be honest, it bored me."

Tahlia huffed a laugh. "I can imagine you taking notes from Albus and longingly watching dragons take off outside the window."

"That is an accurate imagining."

"I never could sit still for learning either," Tahlia said.

They came to a room of sorts with a high, domed ceiling and began searching for the crown carving. Five corridors branched off from the room. A particularly large display of femurs created the shape of a lion that stretched from one side of the ceiling to the other. Tahlia went to the first corridor on the right to look for the crown.

"Nothing here."

Marius was across the room, smoothing his hand over the archway on the middle corridor. "I haven't found one yet either."

Tahlia went to the second corridor's entrance. Most of the passageways were stone, but this one had a wooden lintel. Old paint showed the faded remains of a river and three large structures set around its snakelike form. Beneath the right side, a crown had been painted in black.

"Do you think this counts? It's not carved, but it's definitely a crown."

Marius joined her and studied the painted image. "Since we can't find another, I think we should try it."

They continued onward, the sound of the city above silenced by the depth of the catacombs.

Marius stopped and Tahlia ran into his back.

"What is it?" she whispered, her heart hammering.

"Footsteps."

Tahlia drew her dagger and held her breath to listen. His ears were so much better than hers. It was frustrating.

"They're coming. Two males. Humans."

The sound of whispering and quick boot steps echoed through the dimness. Two men in muddied clothing rounded the corner, faces going slack with shock.

One with a red beard recovered first. A sly grin slithered over his mouth. "Well, well. A couple of guards keeping watch on the old bones." He rubbed his hands together. "Ripe for the picking, seems like to me." He jerked his chin in the direction of Marius's tomato hat.

"I assure you that you do not want to bother us," Marius said.

The fool was too dumb to be scared of that tone and he lunged for Marius. His friend, a man with a tiny knife and only one tooth at the front of his mouth, went for Tahlia.

Marius slammed into Red Beard, knocking the man into the wall. He exhaled in a gust of curses and raised a fist to strike.

Tahlia lifted her arms and dove into Toothy's attack—one forearm at his neck and the other hitting his arm. Her left hand slid down that arm until she had his wrist held firmly with his sad, wee knife locked away from her body. She looped the hand at his neck around the back of his skull and bent him low. She kneed him in the nose. He shrieked, dropped the knife, and fell against the far wall.

Marius had his assailant on the ground, his foot on the man's chest. Marius's eyes burned with unspent fury. "Did he injure you?" he asked Tahlia.

She grabbed the tiny fallen knife, then grabbed her attacker and threw him down beside his friend. "Nope. I'm fine. Should we tie them up?"

"Yes. We can report them to our superior once we have finished canvassing the catacombs."

Ah, right. He was pretending to be a city guard. Tahlia frowned, watching how his eyes burned as he looked at them. Yes, they were terrible people, but that rage... seemed over the top. Maybe it was because she was his mate. Males did become rather insane with protectiveness once fully married and mated. Or was it because they were humans and they dared to attack them? And human pirates *had* killed his sister. He did seem to hate humans with a special level of passion.

CHAPTER 11
TAHLIA

Three different songs wailed through the streets of Midhampton. Locals and visitors alike danced the same quick-step jig, drank ale from pale crockery cups, and laughed together.

"It's marvelous," Tahlia said, doing her best to keep moving. Marius kept gently urging her forward with a hand to the small of her back.

"It's chaos."

"What would you rather be doing right now? Sitting in your chair at Dragon Tail Peak with one of your saucy novels?"

He growled over her shoulder. She glanced up at his handsome, scarred face and grinned.

"How do you know about my reading choices?"

"I'm your mate. You think you're sneaky, putting that military history book on top of your romances, but I'm not fooled."

"Well, I'll thank you not to mention my preferences regarding books in public."

"Nobody here knows us."

His breath was suddenly at her ear. "Hush, female, or I shall have to tie you up when we get home and punish you for disrespecting your commander."

"Oooh, promise?"

A chuckle rumbled in his chest, vibrating into her back as they took the third right.

The Siren's Grotto sign swung in the sea breeze.

"There!" Tahlia pointed.

Marius trailed her through the tavern's round oaken door. "Remember, they'll call us dogs. That's the term for hired guards."

Tahlia nodded. "Adorable."

Pipe smoke clouded the air inside and the voices of at least twenty patrons echoed off the low ceiling.

A hand clamped down on Tahlia's forearm. She whipped around, her hand on the hilt of her dagger. Marius came up behind the man who'd grabbed her and had set a blade beside his throat in a movement that blurred with speed. He moved so incredibly fast. And he was going to blow their cover. Unless of course, everyone here was too sloshed to notice.

The man let go of Tahlia and held up his hands. "Easy, dogs. I was only going to offer you a drink for your services today." His smile was missing a tooth, but that was probably poor hygiene, not from fighting. He was a lump of a fellow.

Marius lowered his weapon and nodded for Tahlia to relax.

"Sorry," Tahlia said, taking on a casual tone. "We've had some real idiots to deal with already today, so we're on edge."

The man chuckled and waved them to the barkeep's counter. "I can imagine." He faced the keep and handed over a few coins. "Three of your best, please."

The ale was bitter but very cold. Tahlia forced herself not to gulp it down. She needed her wits about her. Marius was only pretending to drink. She'd seen him fake it before; he tended to furrow his brow when he was actually drinking.

Knowing Marius might murder her for the recklessness but also certain they had no time to waste, Tahlia went ahead and asked a probing question. "I bet King Durniad has called in every last soul down to his own brother to watch these wild crowds."

Marius's mouth tightened to a line, but he kept his gaze on the man and pretended to sip his ale.

The man grinned and glanced toward a weasel-eyed man at a small, square table near the back wall. Had to be the brother, Jovanyth. Marius and Tahlia exchanged a look.

"Well, he isn't that desperate, I don't think," the man said. "Your accent is unusual. Where do you two hail from?"

Marius pretended to be very thirsty while Tahlia answered with their cover story. "We're cousins. Our parents were traveling merchants, so we picked up a little of everything along the way."

Shoulders relaxing, the man appeared to swallow her lie. "Ah, so that's why you sound like a Veiler."

Veiler? Perhaps that was what they called folk who lived close to the Veil.

"Oh, look," Marius said to Tahlia, his gaze going to a terrible painting at the back of the tavern. "The use of lighting in that piece is very well done."

Tahlia stifled a snort of laughter. She elbowed the man. "My cousin has a passion for the arts."

The man frowned, then shrugged. "I never thought a hired dog would care a whit for paintings..." His gaze twisted into a look stuffed with suspicion.

A woman in a very tight and revealing corset bumped into him and giggled. The man turned to face her fully and seemed to forget about Tahlia and Marius, which was a stroke of good luck. Phew.

Marius waved Tahlia toward the painting.

"Now, what do you love so much about this one, dear cousin?" she said loudly as they approached Jovanyth's table. "And how did you lie about the lighting?" she whispered, laughing.

"I closed my eyes and imagined a painting at the castle."

"Good one."

"It's not my first mission, Lady Tahlia," he whispered under the din of the tavern.

Tahlia accidentally bumped into Jovanyth. "I wonder who the artist is?"

Durniad's brother grunted and glared at Tahlia with swollen eyes. "Eh, watch your big arse, dog."

Marius's nostrils flared and he bared his teeth. He was going to blow this thing up.

CHAPTER 12
TAHLIA

Sweating, Tahlia touched his arm. He shut his eyes and his chest moved in a deep breath.

Tahlia faced the king's brother and smiled. "Here, take my ale in apologies, my lord."

"I'm no lord, but I'll take it just the same." He grinned at her, snatched the ale, and then drank it down in three swallows.

She clapped and laughed like it was the greatest feat she'd ever witnessed. Marius, who was pretending to study the painting, looked like he was about to burst from trying not to roll his eyes or beat the man to death. Perhaps both.

"I have always wanted to meet the most powerful man in Midhampton."

"That's my brother," Jovanyth said, winking, "not me, lass."

"Ah, but he would do whatever you asked, I'm guessing, and that's the best kind of power."

Marius had told her that humans cared for control above all else, and she really hoped that was true for at least this one fellow. If he was, instead, say, more focused on loyalty, this little conversation she was attempting would rankle the king's brother instead of opening him up.

Jovanyth set his mug down and pointed at her. "You are a smart one, aren't you?" His words knocked together like untied urns in the back of a mule cart. "Why don't you sit here and chat with me for a while? Or will your man there get his feathers ruffled?"

She dismissed Marius with the wave of her fingers and sat in the chair opposite the king's brother. "My cousin is perpetually ruffled, so don't even worry about that."

The anger rolling off Marius was almost palpable, but he stayed in character and began to discuss the upcoming tomato throwing with a man and a woman wearing thick aprons stained with dyes.

Tahlia leaned over the table and began to whisper to Jovanyth. "So I heard your brother has a big surprise for the end of the festivities."

A flicker of distrust shaded the drunk man's eyes, but he shook his head and laughed, the sound bouncing off the low ceiling. He rifled through a pack strung across his chair and removed a pipe.

"Where did you hear this, pretty one?"

She smacked Marius's hip, and when he turned, she stole his ale. Marius allowed it and he quickly went back to his conversation with the couple. Tahlia sipped the ale, then slowly licked a drop off her top lip. Jovanyth watched her movements like a lion preparing to pounce.

Don't even try it, pal. Marius will eviscerate you and that will ruin everyone's day.

"I don't remember where I heard it." She tipped her mug back and took a good gulp. When she set it back on the table, he was studying her a bit too closely. "Oh, yes, I do." She laughed, loud and sure as he had. As if she hadn't a care in the world. "It was from that arse-head, Domi. He's always getting his prick into private conversations."

A smile cracked Jovanyth's frowning face. "Liked by the noble ladies, your friend?"

"Yes. He's, um, how should I say this?"

"Blessedly endowed."

Not actually entertained, she slapped the table and feigned being lost in hilarity. He joined in and called for a server to bring them another round.

Tahlia met Marius's gaze for a second. His eyes questioned her, and she gave a barely perceptible nod. Yes, she was all right. It was working.

"My arrogant-as-the-sun brother has something dangerous, I'm sure. It'll be all well for him and shit for the rest of us, as usual."

"Can't you benefit being his sibling?"

"No." He took the ales from the server and handed her one. His was half gone by the time he set the mug back down. A belch rumbled from him and Tahlia forced her features to remain in a vaguely happy position. "The bastard set up a whole series of traps around whatever it is." Leaning forward, he whispered, "Even a siren. There's a damned siren down there under the fortress. Can you believe it?"

Tahlia's body froze. No. It couldn't be. "I thought..." Her mouth didn't want to work and it had zero to do with the ale.

"That they weren't real? Yeah." He barked a laugh. "I didn't think they were either until his arse returned from the north with one. She's horrifying, and that's saying a lot considering she has the body of a goddess and the face of a dream."

"She can kill with a song?"

"Saw it myself," he whispered, leaning too far to the right. He was about to fall out of his chair, the fool.

"Wait. What did you say?"

"I saw her use her song myself."

"You did?"

"Aye. One of my brother's dear engineers lunged to grab her

and before anyone realized her muzzle had slipped, she stopped his heart with three little notes."

Goosebumps ran down Tahlia's arms and she shivered.

"Exactly," he said, nodding toward her. "That was my reaction too. See, she can direct the kill and can only take one soul at a time. The man was doomed just because she exudes desire and the poor man couldn't hold himself back. Could have been me. Easy." He upturned his mug and banged the bottom as if more ale might come out if he only tried harder.

A siren. They had to face a siren to get the crown.

"Old Durny boy tried to cage her and that went really well, too." Jovanyth chuckled and shook his head. "Had to bargain with her. You see, our family has a history with the sirens..." He set an elbow on the table and leaned his chin into his hand.

Was he passing out? Right here, right now?

Marius made his way over and jerked his head toward the door. "We have to get going."

Jovanyth lifted his hand, his ale-glazed eyes half open. "Enjoy the madness and stay out of my brother's path if you know what's good for you."

Tahlia swallowed, murmured a thanks, and left quickly. Marius was right behind her when they emerged back into the sunshine. Dark clouds rolled in the distance, and thunder rumbled over the sound of the crowd.

"Don't talk now," Marius said as they forced their way through the masses toward the line of guards dressed as they were. "We'll walk the outer edge of the crowd until the parade starts, then branch off."

Ten tidy rows of pipers, flag bearers, and folk with small drums lined up. Guards dressed as Tahlia and Marius were—in the ornate clothing and ridiculous hat—created a boundary between the crowds and the musicians. People wearing fine gowns filed in behind the musicians. Perhaps the local nobility or simply the wealthy of the city? Durniad would be among them.

Tahlia tugged at Marius's sleeve. "Did you hear what he told me? Any of it?"

"Not now."

They passed three other guards.

"Fall in line," one of the other guards barked at them, making Tahlia's stomach clench with worry. His bushy eyebrows furrowed as he studied them. "You two smell like an alehouse."

Tahlia grinned and shrugged. "You can't tell me my cousin and I are the only two sneaking a drink today."

Master Eyebrows scowled, but the guard at his side elbowed him.

"Lay off, Sergee. Everything's fine."

"All right, but I'm watching you."

Marius nodded at Eyebrows. That man had no idea that he was trying to intimidate the Shadow of the Shrouded Mountains, a Fae warrior who had taken down countless pirates, enemy armies, and more. It was laughable that the fellow thought he was in a position of power. Granted, he could sound an alarm before Marius or Tahlia had the chance to dispatch him to the afterlife, and this was meant to be a quiet mission...

Tahlia marched obediently between Marius and Eyebrows, who snarled at a woman who had let her child run into the street.

The music began and all Tahlia could think about was Jovanyth's mention of the siren's song. Sure, one could block one's ears, but many stories claimed sirens had the ability to send their power into your very bones. No rolls of cloth stuffed in the ears would stop such a magic.

Tahlia recalled a little storybook she'd seen in the market once when she was maybe ten or eleven years old. The story had included some truly dismal poems, including one about a siren. The whole thing had been penned in blue ink and it stood out in her mind's eye like she'd seen it yesterday.

She sings, she lures,
You listen, you lunge,

Into the cold blue-black, you go,
She'll drag you low, low, low,
Into the sea's dark arms you flow,
Pulled to pieces,
Knocked utterly senseless,
A song, a touch, and you're a memory forgotten.

She snorted at herself, darkly amused. *Great work remembering that horror but missing Fara's birthday last year.* Oh, gods, how Fara would be sounding the alarm if she knew that a siren was involved in this venture to Midhampton.

"Almost there," Marius whispered.

"What?" Eyebrows leaned forward to frown at Marius across from Tahlia.

A tomato soared from the crowd to the left and splashed onto a piper's head.

"Eh! Not time yet!" the piper shouted, his complaint backed up by several others calling out and shaking their fists.

"All these people have tomatoes already," Tahlia said, more to herself than anyone.

"Yes," Eyebrows said gruffly. "Of course they do. Have you never been to the Tomatina Festival?"

"Not to the one here in Midhampton."

"There are no others."

"No, there's another one. In, umm, in Deigs."

The guard who'd elbowed Eyebrows made a *huh* sound. "Really?"

Another tomato flew overhead. A shout followed. Two more tomatoes dashed across the gathered humans. One smashed into a woman who laughed and wiped her face. The other hit a drummer. The drummer threw a punch at a man to his right, who hit him back.

"Get up there and get them marching again," Eyebrows ordered Marius.

Marius nodded and started off with a glance in Tahlia's direction. Without waiting for a command from the actual guards, she followed Marius.

A little girl with bright blue eyes slipped from her father's watch and ran into the parade, dashing behind Tahlia. Tahlia whirled and snagged the girl's arm. She eased her away from the pipers and the men Marius was barking at, then deposited her into her father's arms.

"Thank you, guard."

"Of course," Tahlia said.

She wanted to study the human's face, looking for differences between human facial features and Fae's, but there was no time. She couldn't lose Marius. Whipping around, she took off to find her spot behind him again.

"How did breaking the fight up go?"

"I think I bruised an arm. Accidentally, of course."

Tahlia grimaced. "It's not easy to be careful, I'm sure." He was easily three times as strong as a human male.

The music continued, and the marching carried on until the parade had snaked its way through the streets. They kept in line as much as they could until their fellow guards began to pass flasks and skins of various blends of alcohol to one another. Then order started to fall apart pretty quickly.

They came to a wooden stage, one of several they'd seen throughout the city streets.

"You two, up, up, now," Eyebrows demanded.

"Why isn't he drunk yet?" Tahlia whispered as he shoved them toward the stage.

"Because it's a mission and nothing is ever easy."

Tahlia grinned wryly and walked up the three steps to the stage, where a woman in a long red gown embroidered in tomatoes was finishing up a song about sailors, storms, and a dance that had apparently stopped a flood.

"And here they are!" the woman shouted, gesturing to Tahlia and Marius.

Marius froze, his glare admirable considering the hat currently residing on his head.

The woman grinned. "Ah, I see that he is the storm."

The crowd's noise coalesced into a great cheer for Marius.

Tahlia elbowed him. "See? I'm not the only one who thinks you are rather delightfully stormy. Also, I think we need to drop the cousins cover and play this up as a couple."

Marius turned his scowl on her and she giggled.

The woman clapped her hands three times and the crowd quieted somewhat. They came closer to the stage, holding baskets of tomatoes.

"The lass must be our dancer, then!" the woman said.

Another cheer went up, and Tahlia bowed dramatically, glad her perfectly ridiculous hat had a chin strap. She wouldn't have wanted to lose it.

She was having the time of her life.

"Let's see what you can do, Storm!" the woman ordered.

Marius stood there, as calm and deadly as he ever was. The mass of people booed him and waved fists.

"The tomatoes will come next if you don't get to work," Tahlia said to him out of the corner of her mouth.

"This is madness. We need to get back to the street and get to the goal."

"I doubt this group here is going to let us off the hook." Tahlia jerked her chin at the people in the front row. Their faces were flushed with sun and ale both, and their eyes were just crazy enough to worry about. "Stomp around and growl. You're good at this. It's just another day at the job for you, love."

He growled all right and it didn't sound human at all. A hush began to sweep through the folks gathered close. She had to do something. Now.

She began skipping around Marius. "What a lovely day at the coastline," she sang, making notes up as she went. A few people laughed and one shouted something about Tahlia's arse. She only sang louder. "A lovely, lovely morn!" Gods, her voice was a tragedy, but she had to give it all she had. "I can't imagine there ever being a terrible moment of weather with the sky like this!" She tapped the top of his head, then leaned up and kissed the end of his nose.

The crowd burst into cheers and warnings of the storm to come, even as the actual sky overhead rumbled with real thunder.

"Come on, now." She poked his ribs on her next go round.

Marius, his tunic tight across his broad chest and his eyes unblinking, stomped his foot and the whole stage quaked. He lifted his head and let out a weak growl. Good. He'd realized his last one was far too feral to be a sound a human male would make.

"Ooooh!" the woman cooed and clapped, urging the crowd to make more noise for the storm.

Marius stomped again, then lifted his other foot and did a little double stomp.

"Oh, that is scary," Tahlia said to the gathering, clasping her hands at her chin dramatically.

"Flood the town!" the woman demanded. Then she leaned close to Marius. "Lift her over your shoulder, man. You should know the traditions. Where are they getting guards these days?"

She sounded beyond exhausted with them, and Tahlia couldn't help but chuckle. Marius rolled his eyes, then lifted Tahlia onto his shoulder.

"Spin her 'round!"

"Toss her down!"

It was a chant that all the people took up. Tahlia laughed as Marius did as commanded. He pinched her leg lightly and grumbled, "You are not allowed to find this entertaining."

"Sure, Master Guard. Sure."

She laughed harder as he cradled her, tossed her into the air a bit, then caught her, all to the happy cheers of the crowd.

"Now, dance him into submission!" the people cried out.

The woman clapped her hands over her head in a steady rhythm that the city folk took up quickly. It became a deafening drum of palms as Marius set her down. She pretended to lift a make-believe dress and danced about Marius with steps that matched the clapping. The rhythm sped up, faster and faster, until Tahlia was out of breath and nearly falling into Marius. He caught her, and if she hadn't seen it herself, she would never have believed it, but Marius actually grinned. His eyes danced as surely as she had as he dipped her low and kissed her fully to the excited cries of the crowd.

CHAPTER 13
MARIUS

Tahlia kissed him back, then smiled as he helped her off the stage.

He shook his head as they made their way back to Eyebrows. "Torturous nonsense."

"Interesting way to say *fun,*" Tahlia whispered.

"Well done, you two," the guard captain with the generous eyebrows said. "Now, fill in the gaps as the parade comes to a close."

Perfect. Now they had the freedom to move about without eliciting too much unwanted attention.

"Watch for overly aggressive participants when the throwing begins," the captain added.

"Aye," Marius said, feigning obedience. It wasn't a lie to simply agree, but his heart knew they wouldn't be doing as ordered so the word still tasted like deceit—a sharp bitterness at the back of his tongue and a branching pain through his temples.

He led Tahlia through the crowd, past several docks. The sea beyond the bay was gray and it chewed at the rocky crescent that protected the docked boats and anchored ships. Following his mental map of the city, he hurried Tahlia along until they were back on the main south road, right in front of the fortress. The crowd was shoulder to shoulder, and their pace slowed to a near crawl.

The sky cracked, and it wasn't lightning. Fireblooms, fireworks, some called them. Sparks like dragon fire bloomed over the city in an array of gold, black, blue, and red. The people crowed and howled like forest creatures and the madness began.

Tomatoes. Everywhere.

Tahlia snagged a tomato from the air and tossed the half-squished thing at a random human.

"Guard," Marius growled at Tahlia, a fierce protectiveness crashing through his Fae blood. Humans could twist into monsters at a moment's notice.

The human female Tahlia had hit with the tomato turned and laughed, lugging one back at Tahlia. Fine. She seemed so happy to be involved in the chaos, but truly, they didn't have time for this. They needed to get into the fortress before the two humans who'd agreed to work with them were traded out for the new shift.

But Tahlia's laugh and her dancing eyes made it impossible for him to pull her along or complain. Though she was covered in red juice and pieces of tomato, she was so damn beautiful. He did miss seeing her Fae fangs though since they were cloaked by the Witch's potion.

With a yelp, she slipped. He shot his arm out without thinking, and he caught her, then pulled her close. Her damp uniform did little to hide her blessed curves.

"Careful, little salty. You might tempt me to ignore all of humankind just to drag you into an alcove and have my way with you."

"I wish you were truly tempted!" She laughed into his chest, then looked up at him with those lovely eyes of hers.

Even though the glamour cloaked her eyes, their true beauty shone through nonetheless.

She continued. "But I know you're dying for me to stop having fun and get back to the job."

Normally, he would never be so tempted to take his time during a mission. "I'm torn, honestly. It's the bond."

She reached up and kissed him hard, and he stepped back, chuckling and surprised. A human male careened into them. Marius slid, grabbed at the corner of a building, but fell to his arse anyway. Tahlia reached for him and landed sideways on top of his chest. Both their stupid hats were gone, thank the gods. She laughed again, and her body moved against his, scattering his thoughts. The sun broke through the churning storm clouds for a moment. The light behind her head made her look like a goddess. He kissed her, allowing his wilder side to satiate itself somewhat. He ran his fingers through her sticky hair.

"You taste like dinner," she whispered against his tomato-drenched mouth.

Another chuckle tripped from his lips as they helped one another up all while getting pummeled with yet more tomatoes. A man with a dramatic beard and mustache reached out his hands to aid them. Marius shook his head, but Tahlia took one hand and shook it.

She should have been more wary around humans.

"This is so fun. I love your town," she said to the man.

"Glad you could make it!" The fellow nodded, then went back to participating in the melee.

Marius paused in tossing tomatoes to watch Tahlia as she stared at the crowd. Something dark churned inside him. Why did he feel terrible about her enjoying herself?

Well, firstly, because they were on a mission. That made good sense. Also, this frivolity was probably ruining their schedule. What else though? She appeared to truly appreciate the company of humans. She didn't seem fazed by the fact that they were generally weak-willed, and disloyal, and evil.

Did she possibly prefer human company?

He pulled at the neck of his tunic and tried to step away from the humans up against his right side.

Would Tahlia long for this feeling after they left this place?

Would he ever be enough for her?

Surely, she didn't prefer humans. He shook his head to clear it, then waved a hand to get her moving.

She thrust two more tomatoes into the crowd, her face lit with joy, then she faced him, smiled, and hurried to his side.

"Do we need to search this soup to find our hats?" she asked, eyeing the mash of tomatoes under the feet of everyone around them.

"If you do nothing else for me for eternity, please forget about the hats."

Snickering, she started toward the fortress with him at her side.

This was strange. He was feeling so... He wasn't sure. So wrong? Ill?

Normally, her smile broke apart the clouds that tended to gather around his heart, but that dark feeling didn't fade under her bright attention this time. Instead, it grew stronger. He gritted his teeth as they wound their way to the fortress's side entrance. He had to stop feeling like this. It was foolish. She loved him and he knew that. They were mated. Bonded as surely as they were to their dragons.

The fortress loomed high above the riotous mass of people. Its walls were made of sandy-hued stone, and crenelations along the top housed archers. The archers stood quietly, watching without their bows ready. The report that King Lysanael had given Marius and Tahlia hadn't mentioned archers. This was another barrier they would have to get through.

The side door was unmarked—a simple slender rectangle of hardwood. He knocked and a small window at the top of the door slid open.

"Name?"

"Edward Newlington."

Tahlia was biting her lip, her eyes laughing at the name. Marius gave her a good glare so she'd remember they were on duty.

The small window shut with a thud.

Was it not one of their inside contacts at the door? Were they too late for the two they were meant to meet here? Marius looked up to see an archer staring down at them.

Marius breathed in and out slowly. Tahlia touched his arm as if she wanted to ask a question. But as he looked at her, the whole door swung open, and two people grabbed them and dragged them inside.

He had both humans by the throat against the small entryway's wall before a word could be uttered.

"Is there a storm coming?" he asked, using the code question.

The human squirming under his left hand tried to speak. Tahlia tapped Marius's hand.

"Might want to let him talk. Just a suggestion."

Marius nodded and loosened his hold. Slightly.

The human coughed and her freckled forehead wrinkled. "The sky and ocean are tricky."

It was the right code response. Marius released the two women.

The one on the left rubbed at her throat with a freckled hand and glared. "He's here early. Follow Maude to our room below. You'll have to stay the night and wait until he's gone," she whispered.

The second guard—a female with dark eyes like Tahlia's and very fair skin—grimaced even as she studied Marius and Tahlia with uncloaked curiosity.

"Our disguises are in place for your eyes still, yes?" Marius asked.

The two nodded.

Tahlia stepped closer, her gaze on the empty entryway and a set of doors beyond, doors that led into the fortress's central hall.

"Durniad is here?" Tahlia asked in a whisper.

"Aye. And he is in a state," the dark-eyed, fair-skinned guard said. "Stay on my heels. Walk quickly. He's feasting in his upper rooms at the moment, so we should be all right to scurry across the hall and down the back steps."

"Why can't we access the trove tonight if he is all the way up there?" Marius asked.

"Because he will want to show off his labyrinth to his cronies after he eats his weight in pastries."

Tahlia lifted her eyebrows. He knew that look—she was dreaming of pastries instead of thinking of labyrinths. He almost smiled even though they were definitely off their schedule now.

"Our disguises will fail before we can escape the city if we wait to breach the trove."

"I know. The safe house contact sent a raven to your king and queen with a request for aid."

A headache squeezed Marius's temples with alarming ferocity. He rubbed his forehead with his fingers. That should not have been necessary.

"Do you know anything about a siren?" Marius asked.

The guard looked appropriately horrified. "I don't. They kept us from the traps and didn't permit anyone to talk about them or ask questions. Ovain, one of the other guards, asked about them and no one has seen him since."

Marius and Tahlia exchanged a look.

Tahlia rubbed her tomato-coated hands together. "So it's a smash-and-grab and run-for-your-life mission now, hmm?"

"Perhaps we can go in as soon as Durniad and his friends depart late tonight," Marius suggested.

The freckled guard shrugged. "You can try, but he parties until the early hours of the morning when he's riled up like this." A shudder shook her frame and she muttered what sounded like a prayer.

"I don't want to know what a fellow like him thinks is fun," Tahlia said, frowning.

"No, you do not," Marius said. He wanted to say something about humans' general penchant for gore and power, but he didn't want to upset the guards with so much riding on their performance tonight.

"I'll get you to our room," the fair guard said, "and then I'll get you to the trove before dawn."

"Agreed," Marius said.

The guard went to the doors beyond and pushed one open. The group of three rushed through the entrance. Marius and Tahlia's clothing dripped tomato as they went.

"What about this mess?" Tahlia whispered over her shoulder at Marius.

There weren't any other guards present in the hall—only a row of painted portraits along the front of the room and an empty table stacked with small wooden boxes that were set at each place like gifts to those who would eat here later.

"I'll tidy up as soon as you're locked in," the guard said. She turned the corner and ushered them down a dark set of stairs. The scent of the sea touched Marius's nose.

"What is in those boxes?" Marius asked.

"They're tiny wooden contraptions. I'm not sure what they are," the guard said. "I only heard they were symbolic presents for visitors who would arrive tomorrow before the presentation of the crown. Something about showing off new additions. I don't know what that means, honestly." She moved onward.

Marius frowned, then nodded at Tahlia to catch up with the guard.

At the base of the stairs, the guard veered right, and they snaked their way down to a row of doors.

"The second one is mine," the guard said. "It's open. Locks

from the inside. Stay there until we come for you. No matter what you hear. I stashed some corncakes in the dresser if you're hungry."

"What do you mean no matter what we hear?" Tahlia asked.

"I have to go." The guard left without a backward glance.

Tahlia went ahead of Marius and opened the door to a small chamber. Marius quickly surveyed the space, checking for watch holes that could have been carved into the walls and if any runes had been etched into the simple bed, dresser, or desk.

"All clear." His heart was beating too quickly. Having his mate here was undeniably distracting—he could no longer fool himself that it wasn't—and though he knew she was quick, smart, and quite capable, he couldn't help wishing she was back at Dragon Tail Peak, in the safety of the castle walls.

"Are we supposed to have a change of clothes in here? I can't remember," Tahlia asked.

Marius flipped the quilt on the bed back to reveal two stacks of dark clothing. He handed one to Tahlia. "You seem to really enjoy this tomatina nonsense," he said, trying for a casual tone even though the words meant more. What exactly, he wasn't yet certain.

CHAPTER 14
TAHLIA

Tahlia studied Marius's face as she set the dark clothing on the end of the bed. She undid her belt, set it on the ground, then removed Fara's letters from where she'd stashed them—tucked neatly into her trousers. She set the letters on the bedside table near a bowl of water, a candle and flint set, and a stack of clean cloths.

When she glanced back, Marius wasn't looking her way. Something was off. His shoulders were tense and pulled up toward his ears like he was bracing for a strike for which he had no defense.

"It's throwing vegetables, listening to music, acting like fools, and drinking ale. What's not to love?"

"Humans. And it's a fruit, not a vegetable."

Tahlia's heart cinched. "Marius, look at me."

"If you need help with washing your hair, I'm happy to—"

She tugged at his arm and finally he met her gaze. "Of course I'm enjoying this festival."

"You are enjoying being around humans."

"So? I'm half-human. What do you expect?"

His throat moved in a swallow and he held her gaze. "Full humans are terrible creatures."

Her chest caved, and she set a hand on his tomato-stained tunic. "Marius..."

"I mean," he said, looking away, "generally. Not all of them."

"You still believe that nonsense after choosing a mate with their blood? After working with a queen who is human?"

His lip curled. He turned away, running a hand over the back of his neck. He had tomato bits in his hair that she longed to comb away.

"Tahlia, I, no, I don't think I do believe humans are worse than Fae. Not anymore."

She sagged, leaning her hands on her knees. "That's basically the opposite of what you just said."

She expected him to whirl around and smile, to kiss her and apologize. But instead, he focused on the wall, his silence deafening.

"Marius, what is it?" He had to be thinking of his sister and how human pirates were the ones to end her life. But those humans were bad ones. There were horrible Fae too. He knew that, but his demeanor said he was having a hard time feeling the truth of it.

"I don't know," he replied quietly. "I truly don't know. Seeing you here, among these people, it makes me angry. Maybe I am worried I won't be enough for you. That you might want to leave the Fae realm someday and live among humans. They're more relaxed than us. I know that now."

"They are a blast, honestly. Do you think they'd accept a dragon rider and her scary Seabreak?"

He glanced at her, worry pinching his gaze. Maybe her silliness had been a bad move for this intense moment.

She held up her hands. "I'm joking. Marius, I adore you. I would never, ever leave you. Just because these idiots south of the Veil know how to party doesn't mean I'm planning to make a life

was invisible to the eye but clear to the soul. Driving forward again and again, he angled himself so that he also pressed against her in exactly the right way. His hand smoothed quickly down her side to lift her leg onto his shoulder. The rightness of their fit had her biting her knuckles to keep from crying out.

"Tell me I am your mate, Tahlia," he said, quietly, his voice a snarl. His hair had fallen in a Fae-white sheet over half his face and he looked like a gorgeous, monstrous dream.

"I am your mate, Marius," she whispered huskily. "Yours. And you are mine."

Her pleasure rose to a point and exploded across her body, sending her into a moan she couldn't hold back as she rode the wave of sensation. Marius held a hand to her mouth and drove harder into her, his gaze pinning her in place as surely as his physical presence. His head fell back and he shuddered, his body spasming.

"My lady. My Lady of the Skies. My Tahlia..."

The way he said her name with such reverence brought her back to another peak of pleasure and she shattered against him as he held still and hard inside her. At the last second, he worked her again and the second peak went on and on. She couldn't breathe for the joy and delight flooding her. He dropped down beside her, took her jaw between his thumb and forefinger, and turned her to face him. Her cheeks were blazing from exertion. He kissed her cheek, chin, and neck.

With each new kiss, he whispered a word of love and dedication. "Mine. My sweet. Perfection. I am yours. Only you see my heart, own my heart, are my heart."

And even though they would be braving unthinkable terrors quite soon, Tahlia fell into a dreamless sleep in her commander's arms.

CHAPTER 15
TAHLIA

Tahlia woke in what felt like the middle of the night, though it was impossible to tell in this windowless room. A nightmare about dark waves and claws had ripped apart the peace she'd felt when she'd fallen asleep in Marius's arms. Blowing out a shaking breath, she tried to calm her heart. Swallowing her fear, she lit the candle on the bedside table and took one of Fara's letters. Lying stomach down, Marius snored lightly beside her.

Dearest feral friend who refuses to have a normal job,

How are things going? I'll assume you still have both of your eyeballs since you are reading this. That's good. You must have avoided the human water. Is their wine any good? I doubt it.

. . .

ARE they handsy when they drink? I feel like I've heard they are. If any of those arseheads say a single thing to you that you don't like, just keep a list and some descriptions. I'll visit and undo their good health with great pleasure.

I HAVE A BROKEN HAND, by the way. I hid it from you when you were prepping to leave. I broke it on Anslem's face. He is a prickbrain. I do not regret it. I won't tell you what he said because it'll only get me riled up again, and I'm trying to study.

YES, prickbrain is a word. You can look it up in the library when you get back.

YOUR FRIEND,
Fara

CHUCKLING, Tahlia blew out the candle and settled back under the blanket with Marius. She curled her body around his, soaking in the heat and solidity of him. His scent filled the air and she fell asleep with the thought that someday soon she'd be surrounded by Fara and the other knights, that Lija would be healed, and all would be well.

TAHLIA WOKE to Marius gently shaking her arm. He stood over her, dressed and ready.

"It's time," he whispered.

Behind him, the guard with the dark eyes stood waiting, lines forming between her eyebrows.

After a quick chug of watered wine and gobbling down another corncake, Tahlia followed Marius and the guard out of the room and into the corridor. The dawn's first gray light slid through archways in the passageway. The place was quiet as a tomb, but that was a good thing. It meant King Crazy was likely asleep and his cronies gone for the time being.

The guard stopped at the end of the third corridor they'd hurried down. This one bent sharply to the right. "Down there. Third door. You can't miss it."

"And our two are in place?" Marius glanced at Tahlia, then looked her up and down as if cataloging her breathing, stance, and general level of preparedness.

The guard breathed out, then pursed her lips. "As far as I know, one is on duty. Hopefully, both, but we couldn't ask because there wasn't any clear moment to do so without raising suspicion."

"Understood," Marius said.

"May the Old Ones bless you," the guard whispered quickly before heading off.

Keeping her steps as light as possible, Tahlia trailed Marius through the shadows that the fire from the wall sconces tried to shatter. Golden runes glimmered above one of the doorways. The entrance was housed in an alcove. This had to be the one. The guards were likely right on the other side of the heavy oak.

Marius turned the doorknob.

A guard with a beard rushed out, opening the door outward and slamming it against Marius.

"Filthy Fae spies," the man hissed as he lunged for Tahlia.

Marius was pinned to the alcove wall.

Tahlia bent to grab the dagger from her boot. Pulse flying as fast as Lija on a clear day, she shot upward, jamming the blade into the bearded guard's throat. Gurgling, he dropped, and Marius slid out from behind the door and began dragging him into the room they'd just opened. The other guard, the one presumably on their side, looked from Marius to Tahlia, then grabbed the dead guard's leg. He helped Marius hide the body behind a row of boxes.

The guard shoved his shoulder-length red hair out of his face, then tugged a linen cloth from his belt and started back toward the door.

"I'll get the blood cleaned up. That guy was such an arsehole. Glad to see the last of him. Durniad was his hero."

"How did he know about us?" Tahlia cleaned her knife on her trousers, then returned it to the sheath sewn into the inside of her boot.

"He was your man until last night."

"Oh?" Marius's face was flat, emotionless as he knocked on the green-painted flagstones that made a half circle at the next door—the entrance to the labyrinth. What was he thinking? Did he not trust this guard?

"Yes, he was down here late last night," the guard said, "and when I showed back up this morning, he said Durniad had changed his mind. That he had it all wrong and that I had better get back on the right side of things or he'd kill me too. Didn't manage that now, did you?" The guard snorted and laughed.

"Do you think Durniad used the crown on him?" Tahlia asked.

Marius found the right stone and pushed one side. The stone tilted, and Marius reached into the space below it.

The guard shrugged. "It's possible, I guess. But Durniad is a great public speaker. He can charm anyone—even those he is about to kill in cold blood."

"It's a wonder he thinks he needs the crown," Tahlia said.

Marius made a *hmm* sound as he pulled a sack from the hidden spot on the floor. Tahlia joined in and they found lock-picking tools, small squares of linen, a tiny crock of grease, and a palm-sized book. Tahlia took that one up and flipped through the old vellum pages.

"Unseelie runes?" What in the world were these doing here?

Marius cut his eyes to her, telling her to keep quiet. "We are good here. Will you watch from the outside and give us a shout if anyone is coming?"

"I'll do what I can. I hate Durniad. Good luck to you."

Marius tipped his head at the human male. They divvied out the items their contacts had provided, tucking them into the leather pouches at their belts, in boots, and wherever else things would fit well enough.

"I feel like a walking craftsman's market," Tahlia said.

The weight of the rune book and the little lock pick hammer were too much for the loose waistband of her trousers. She tightened her belt another notch to keep the lot of it from falling to her ankles.

She glared at Marius over her shoulder. "No chuckling. Small but fierce, remember?"

He used to chide her for even wanting to be a dragon rider because of her size. She'd proven to him that she was a fantastic flyer and fighter despite her petite build, but sometimes, he still smirked at her inability to reach the top shelf in their chambers at Dragon Tail.

"We have no time to lose," he said, pushing through the labyrinth's door. "Time to figure out these traps. Stay close. I don't want any more blood spilled if we can help it."

His voice sounded strained. She frowned as she followed him into complete darkness.

"Should I not have killed the bearded guard?" Her question bounced off the walls, walls that felt close.

"You did the right thing. He was going to snap your neck. There wasn't time for anything else. I've seen humans snap necks for lesser crimes than espionage and theft."

Torches set high into the walls around the room flickered to life, and Tahlia blinked against the sudden brightness. She took a breath, nodding to herself about what Marius had said. That was what she'd thought—that the killing was necessary. It wasn't her first time killing, but the act certainly wasn't the norm for her day. Thankfully, the experience with Ophelia and the monster Katk had warmed her up to violence.

The firelight showed a high stone ceiling above them and head-high walls at either side of them, close-set and quite obviously the labyrinth itself.

"We're already inside," she whispered, her stomach flipping with the knowledge that anything could come at them at any moment. She got out her knife again and savored the feel of Marius's powerful presence in front of her.

"Yes, and I assume we have stepped on a plate of sorts that triggered the lighting of the torches."

"How would that work?" Tahlia asked.

Marius made a grumbling noise. "Mechanisms that are worth a king's sum, I'm sure."

"Have you seen anything like this before?"

"No, but I've heard stories of the old kings and queens who ruled here," Marius said. "This wild setup isn't purely of Durniad's mind. This place was built ages ago. Before I was born. Durniad has simply fancied it up for us."

Fancied it up. Tahlia snickered. Marius was beginning to sound like her.

"How kind of him."

Marius harrumphed. "Indeed."

"So we have no idea what we're facing here, aside from the siren, right?" Tahlia's throat was dry as bone dust. She swallowed and fought a cough.

"We know there are traps. More than one. I would assume the siren wouldn't be the first."

Tahlia grinned wryly. "Ah, thinking like a madman, are you?"

Marius's left eyebrow flicked upwards. "One must see through the eyes of the enemy to know his next move."

“Perhaps the first two traps will be simple for us since we’re Fae.”

“Perhaps,” Marius said. “Perhaps not. We don’t know if the guard we took out talked to Durniad about our plan.”

“I don’t love how much we are clueless about in here.”

Marius growled in the way that meant he agreed.

“Do you realize you have five different growls in your vocabulary?”

He made no response except to shake his head and exhale.

“One tells the recipient to back off. Immediately.” Tahlia pressed a hand to her chest. “I love that one.”

“You do?”

“It’s delightfully scary.”

“You are very strange, my gorgeous mate.”

Tahlia couldn’t fight a smile. “Another of your growls indicates frustration with the situation at hand. Most would curse and swear in place of that growl.”

“How much longer is this incredibly informative lesson going to last? We need to focus, little salty.”

“Growl number three is for me.”

“Oh, yes? How so?”

She stepped closer and ran a hand up his thigh. He stopped, looked over his shoulder at her, and growled as the torchlight flickered in his eyes. Her body grew as hot as the flames lighting the labyrinth.

“Yes, that one.”

He started walking again, shaking her off. “It’s impressive that we can feel lusty at this dire moment.”

“Well, you know what they say about newlyweds.”

He frowned, eyeing her. “No, what do they say? Is this a human saying?”

“Oh, no, I don’t think so,” she said. “I don’t remember where I heard it.”

"Eh, why don't you walk beside me? I don't like you out of my sight like this."

"All right." She came up next to him and he lifted her hand. He sniffed her knuckles. "What is it? Oh, the blood. From the guard. I didn't get it all off."

His steps slowed, and he stared at her blood-stained hand, his gaze distant.

"Marius, what's wrong?"

CHAPTER 16
MARIUS

A memory of his sister flashed through his mind. She was screaming as a human cut her down outside their home. The human pirate slashed at her again and again and...

No, that wasn't a memory.

It was how Marius had imagined her death all these years. She had been killed in that way, so the report said. But he hadn't witnessed the crime. If he'd been there, he would have defended his sister and it would have been the human's head on the ground instead of hers.

"Marius?"

He blinked the vibrant imagining away to see Tahlia's eyes. Well, they weren't her eyes, exactly. The Witch's potion remained in place, rounding her irises. This was Tahlia's human face, her human eyes. This was what Tahlia was without the half of her blood that was Fae.

His stomach rolled and he turned away, gasping. Gods, what was wrong with him? What did that have to do with anything? Why was he having pseudo-flashbacks?

"I'm sorry. I'm..." He gritted his teeth and faced Tahlia. "I had a memory, or no, a thought about my sister."

"The one who was killed by pirates."

"Aye. I only had the one." He cleared his throat.

"Are you all right? What can I do to help?"

Marius's heart melted. She was perfect. "There's nothing you need to do. Obviously, I have very complicated feelings regarding being around humans. I'm also wound up because that guard tried to kill you. It's difficult being on a mission with you as my bonded mate. "

She grabbed him around the middle as if they weren't in a madman's labyrinth with only the gods knew what facing them very shortly. He wrapped his arms around her and breathed in her scent. After a count of three, he released her.

"I can't be this selfish. We must move on, and I need to stop being foolish. You are a knight and I am your commander. I can't let myself falter."

"You are allowed to have feelings."

"Not on a mission," he said.

"But what if said emotions motivate you to fight to the best of your ability?"

He growled. She made a decent point.

"See? You agree. That's the agree growl."

"Please stop cataloguing my sounds."

"Hmm. I don't know. How about you let me if I let you take notes on my noises when we get home," she whispered, her tone sending all his blood south of his belt.

"Focus. Please."

"Yes, sir."

"That's better."

They walked on, the labyrinth taking them down neat ninety-degree turns and the torches giving just enough light to see.

A bang and a shuffling sound broke the silence. Tahlia immediately whirled to press her back to his so they were facing opposite directions and ready for a fight. He was glad to know her training had sunk in so effectively already.

"What is that?" Tahlia kept her voice to a whisper.

A rumbling shook the walls around them.

"Perhaps the storm they said was coming has landed."

"Hell of a storm."

"They do see some rough ones similar to those up north of us on the pirate coast." The moment the word *pirate* was out of his mouth, he wished he hadn't spoken it. He wanted to wash that imagined memory from his head and crush the dark feelings it grew inside him.

Tahlia resumed her spot beside him until the labyrinth narrowed—the first thing to change about the place. She stepped behind him. "Still want to lead?"

"Yes, I'm guessing any attack will come from where we haven't yet been," he said.

"You're the—"

Her word slurred into a gasp and Marius spun to see the floor under her give way. She disappeared into the black space below.

Heart locked in ice, he lunged for her, but he was far too late. A stale wind blew up from the hole in the floor. On his knees at the opening in the ground, he searched the darkness, but he couldn't see a thing.

"Tahlia!"

No sound. No answer.

He couldn't move. Breathing was a forgotten skill. His heart wasn't even beating.

If she was...

He pressed his eyes shut and shook his head. Forcing himself to breathe and think, he opened his eyes again.

"I'm coming down," he said into the dark.

A quiet snarl made him lift his head to look down the labyrinth's path.

No, it couldn't be. Gods, save him and Tahlia both.

CHAPTER 17
TAHLIA

The dark was like a second skin, so tightly woven and pressed against Tahlia with not an inch of wiggle room. Not even the hole she'd fallen through was visible. Where was the torchlight? Pain reverberated through her bones like the storm's thunder had crawled inside her body.

Grunting, she tried to sit up. Her fingers found a spongy surface. She tore a handful of whatever it was away from the solid ground and sniffed it. Moss. Not moss like they had in the Realm of Lights and the Shrouded Mountains, but something grittier and less leafy. Definitely moss though.

"Thank you, moss. You saved my life."

Without the heavy coating of the stuff, the hard earth would have cracked her skull in two. She was glad to have Fae strength. A human with no Fae blood would have been destroyed by that drop.

She looked up, not that the dark was any different up than down. Longing to call out for Marius, she opened her mouth, but then thought better of it. What if there was something down here and her shout made it attack? What if she was now in an area where Durniad's guards would hear her? Maybe that was why he wasn't calling down to her. But then again, if she was close enough to hear him, she'd see the torchlight.

Gods, what *was* this place? Was there a spell on the space that turned it into total darkness? Or had she somehow fallen so far as to be out of view of the hole and Marius?

Shaking the moss from her fingers, she began to check the extent of her injuries. A big lump on the back of her head. Her right ankle wasn't grand at the moment—hopefully just a mild sprain. She wasn't a healer, so she couldn't exactly fix it herself.

She spread a hand over her torso. Her shirt had come untucked and had ripped on one side. A cut bled lightly over her ribs. Her ribs were sore, but not broken, she didn't think. Oh, Fara's letters had slipped out of her waistband and the small belt bag that held the lock-picking items and a few odds and ins had torn away.

Getting onto her hands and knees, she felt around the ground. The scent of the sea wafted across her face and she stilled.

A breeze meant an escape.

While crawling on the ground like a sad little bug wasn't her favorite activity, she stuck with the hands and knees set up because she was dizzy. Standing up only to fall again would be the height of stupidity.

Something crinkled under her fingers.

Fara's letters! Hope flooded her. Just the idea of having Fara's writing with her now was a blessing. Her bag and the rest of her stuff were a shuffle away. She tied the pouch around her stomach, making do with the torn edges of the strap. Adjusting her belt over her tunic again, she was as put together as she could be, considering. The cut on her side flared with pain, but there wasn't much to do about it now, so she continued toward the direction of the sea breeze.

What was Marius doing? Would he try to come down here to get her? She hoped not. Fear gripped her mind, and she crawled faster, determined to fight its hold on her. If only she hadn't lost her Weaver magic when she'd crossed the Veil...

Maybe she could find it, activate it, whatever. But how?

No, she'd find the opening where that breeze was coming from. She'd get through it and somehow get back to Marius and the search for the crown.

And then a very hard surface cracked her against the head. Her brain felt like it was about to pour out her ears.

"Ugh."

She rubbed at yet another lump on her head, then looked up. Reaching up a hand, she wiggled her fingers in hopes of feeling the sea air.

A breath of the outdoors danced over her fingertips and she scrambled to her feet. Dizziness pulled at her, but she braced herself against the wall that had so unjustifiably attacked her.

"The least you can do is hold me up, wall. This is your doing."

Hmm. Was she woozy? Why was she talking to a wall?

Running her palm up the rough stone and patchy moss, she found a hole. She could fit exactly zero parts of her into said opening.

Dammit.

She sat down to cry. Because honestly, she needed to get it out of the way. Her head was killing her. Maybe if she wept for a bit, she'd have the mind to work up another plan.

Pressing her hands over her eyes, she let the tears roll.

"I refuse to have a pity party, but this is decidedly not knight-like, this whole falling in a hole to die alone and filthy thing."

A prickling sensation spread across Tahlia's scalp and into her ears. She shivered. What in the...

"Tahlia?" A quiet voice, like someone very far away, echoed in her ears. "Tahlia."

Tahlia sat up straight, her eyes going dry immediately. "Who said that?"

The voice was familiar...

CHAPTER 18
MARIUS

The minotaur launched itself at Marius, who shook himself and began to run.

A minotaur? Even more than sirens, he'd thought minotaurs were a thing of imagination. At least the bottom half was human. Surely he, a full Fae, could outrun it. But what then? Keep running until it tired, go for a kill? But how long would that leave Tahlia beneath the labyrinth? He had to get to her. This place was making it incredibly difficult to remain logical. None of this seemed real.

He longed for his dragon and his whip as well, but as he had known for quite a while now, longing didn't kill the pirate or monster or minotaur.

Action did.

With the grunting bull creature not five steps behind him, he turned sharply and made to speed past it and run in the opposite direction. If anything, he had to keep his hold on where Tahlia had fallen. They had to have passed it. Why hadn't either of them fallen through?

Roaring, the mythical beast gave chase and Marius kept a keen eye on the path.

But the hole wasn't there. All the stones were smooth, unmarred and unbroken, as if Tahlia and her drop had all been in his imagination.

He whirled and kicked toward the minotaur's chest. His boot made contact and the creature howled, dropped back, and made to lunge, but Marius was faster. Marius drove his blade into the bull-headed thing's eye. Hot blood gushed over his hand, but the minotaur shook and pierced Marius's shoulder with the tip of a horn. Pain spread out in a web over Marius and he grunted, angry. He tore the knife from the minotaur's eye and jammed it into the beast's neck.

The minotaur disappeared.

What in the name of all the gods?

CHAPTER 19
TAHLIA

"You know who this is, you fantastic idiot," the voice said. "I can't believe this is working!"

Tahlia's tears returned and brought loads of company. "Fara!"

She slapped her hands over her mouth, worried her shout would bring out something she didn't have the balance to fight right now.

"What's working? Am I hallucinating?" Tahlia whispered.

"No, it's Fara! Lija and I are with Healer Albus and an herb-witch from the south."

Tahlia's heart lurched and her eyes burned with tears. Lija. Fara. She grasped at her tunic, her pulse pounding like her heart might beat right through the fabric.

"Fara," she said, voice cracking. "I want to know everything, but currently, I'm stuck in a very deep, probably cursed hole under a madman's fortress. I might die." An unhinged laugh bubbled from her. "Like soon. Lija, I miss you. I hate being so far from you. Fara, can you make it so I can talk to Marius?"

"Hello, rider," Lija said.

Her voice was low and soft, comforting but edged with desperation. This wasn't like the experience of speaking mentally; this was like Lija was nearby and Tahlia could simply hear her. So fascinating!

But despite the joy of this magic, Tahlia could easily tell that Lija wanted to hide how poorly she felt. Not being able to fly truly was bringing her down.

"I'm going to finish this thing and get you healed, Lija."

"I believe it."

A tear tracked down Tahlia's flushed cheeks. "Fara, can I contact Marius?"

"He isn't with you?"

"No. Only I fell. And for some reason, I can't even see the hole I fell through nor can I shout up to Marius. If up is even truly up here..."

"Gods, that sounds terrifying. All right. Hold on."

"Can this herbwitch heal Lija?"

"No, she tried. She says she isn't very powerful and her talent sits mainly in communication so she was thrilled to find this rare herb that facilitated this due to your soul bond with Lija and—"

"Fara. Please. I don't know how much time I have. Marius is assuredly desperate and searching for me, which will make him vulnerable to attack. For all I know, he is dealing with a siren right now."

Fara swore creatively. "I thought sirens had gone extinct."

"I thought they were never real."

"Hold on, sorry. Just a minute," Fara said.

The sensation of the magic they were working rushed over Tahlia's scalp again.

"Try now," Fara said, her voice going in and out.

Saying a silent prayer, Tahlia took a breath. "Marius?"

There was a grunt of surprise, then silence.

"Marius, it's Tahlia. Fara and her gang are doing some sort of communication magic. It's really me. Ask me anything." If it was even working... What if it wasn't him she was talking to?

"Tahlia." His voice flooded her with warmth from the top of her head to the very tip of her toes. "Where are you? Are you hurt? Are you able to communicate with them and with me due to your Weaver magic?"

"No. It has to do with Fara and Lija. I'll explain later. I fell into a dark cavern of sorts. There is a small hole in the far wall down here, and I smell the sea. Sadly, I can't see the hole I fell through. I think this is a cursed or spelled area."

"Agreed. I can't find the broken path you fell through on this side either. There are Unseelie runes everywhere in this damned fortress. Idiot humans messing with powers they can't possibly understand."

"Yes, yes," she said. "Berate them at your leisure once you get me out of the very scary hole, agreed?"

"I would begin working on that if I weren't currently on top of the labyrinth wall, trying my best to find a minotaur that apparently is capable of portalling from one place to another as he sees fit."

"I'm sorry. What?"

"You heard me correctly. Half-human. Half-bull. Disappearing and potentially reappearing. Even grouchier than I am, if one can believe that."

Tahlia laughed darkly. "I'm glad you've adopted my whole humor-in-the-face-of-death practice. Do you have a guess on where the minotaur is right now? I can't believe we have to deal with not one, but two mythical dangers on the same mission. This is too much. I want a raise."

Marius growled. "I heard a noise in that direction," he said pointing farther into the labyrinth. "Could be the minotaur. But something is very off here, Lady Tahlia."

"So many somethings are off."

"I'm going to attempt to kill the minotaur, and then I'll drive through the damn floor and get to you."

"Sounds lovely. Happy hunting, dear," she said, hoping her teasing tone covered the fear inching up her back like a horribly large spider. She took a shuddering breath.

Marius's grumble faded into the recesses of her ears as Fara's voice came through once more.

"Did it work?" Fara asked. "Did you cut him off yourself?"

"I think so? I have no clue how this is working."

"The herbwitch said something about intention and need."

"Fine. Whatever. Can she tell me how to get my Weaver magic back out here past the Veil?"

"Let me ask," Fara said.

Tahlia frowned into the dark. "Are you eating?"

"Just a crystal cake. Look, I need energy to help you, all right?"

Tahlia snorted and shook her head, but she wasn't irritated. She was just so glad not to be alone in the dark. She took another deep inhale of the sea breeze and tried not to panic about being stuck and about Marius battling a bull-man.

"Have you tried meditating to try to get your weird little lines back?" Fara asked.

"No, my head is just now clearing from the hard hit when I fell, and there hasn't been time for it in the chaos of this city. You should see the humans, Fara. They're so relaxed and always laughing."

"Well, you're seeing them during a festival."

"I think they're like this though. Full of jokes and not nearly as uptight as us Fae."

"Us Fae?"

"You know I always felt more Fae than human," Tahlia said.

"Do you still feel that way?" Fara asked.

Tahlia chewed the inside of her cheek. Maybe not. Maybe she did feel more of a natural connection to these humans. "I'm not sure. Let's move on to this meditation idea."

"All right. So in Healer training, they taught me that slow, steady breathing actually lowers your heart rate and helps you think more clearly. Perhaps that would help your magic?"

"I'll give it a go. Will you stay with me?" Tahlia hated that she sounded so needy, but losing a chunk of her pride was nothing to being alone in the dark.

"We aren't going anywhere," Lija said, speaking over Fara shouting, "Of course!"

A smile pulled at Tahlia's lips, and she sat up. "Any tips on how to do this?"

"Sit with a straight spine if you're able," Fara said. "How are your injuries at the moment?"

"I'll live. All right, I'm sitting. What else?"

"Breathe in for four counts, hold it for four, release it in four counts, then pause for four, and begin again. Close your eyes."

"It's so dark. It won't make much of a difference."

"It cues your body to relax because everyone closes their eyes to sleep."

"I can sleep with my eyes open," Lija said, her voice sounding a little farther away than Fara's now.

"To watch for predators," Tahlia added, feeling a glimmer of Lija's pride through their bond. "I felt your pride, Lija! Maybe this aural connection makes it possible for us to examine one another. Can you tell if I have any serious internal injuries?"

Lija made a low growling sound and Tahlia knew what she was thinking. "I sense pain," the dragon said, "but nothing that will stop you from getting out of there and back home to me."

Tahlia chuckled. "Spot on." She closed her eyes. "I'm going to begin now. I hope I'm facing the place where I fell so maybe something will come to me and show me how to escape. It's tough to tell direction down here."

And it was tough not giving up. Tahlia swallowed and breathed in slowly.

Hold on, Marius. Just stay alive.

CHAPTER 20
MARIUS

Marius crept down the top of the labyrinth's wall, keeping his steps completely silent. Breathing sounded a short way down the labyrinth. It had to be the minotaur... Unless there was another massive mouth-breathing monster down here. It was possible, but he certainly hoped it was just the one beast.

The tops of the minotaur's horns showed above the third turn past where they had been fighting. Marius's heart lifted. It was injured. He could finish the job now and go back to helping Tahlia.

But that was odd... The air didn't smell of blood. The beast had definitely been bleeding from the eye wound. At least, the fluid had been red like a basic creature's blood, and it had smelled as such at the moment. Perhaps the minotaur was capable of more than portalling from one spot to another.

He took as deep a breath as he dared, not wanting to alert the creature in this tomb-like silence. There was an occasional noise, like a bang and a murmur, far off, but that wouldn't cover Marius's sounds this close to the minotaur.

He crept closer, closer still. The beast's scent—like any barn animal's homely smell—touched Marius's nose.

Marius leapt from the wall and rammed his blade into the base of the minotaur's head. The creature shoved backward, crushing Marius between beast and wall. Marius swore, pain lashing through his spine. With a mighty roar, the minotaur shook itself. Marius held on, eardrums buzzing and cracking with the minotaur's noise. The agony of being crushed grew to a point that seemed deadly. Shouting out in desperation and frustration, Marius pushed the blade in further. The minotaur dropped. Exhaling a gust of pained breath, Marius fell with him, but...

The minotaur blinked out of existence.

Marius snarled and lifted his weapon. There wasn't even a speck of blood on the blade. It was madness! His mind whirled and he gritted his teeth. What was happening here? What was he missing? He'd thought the traps would be primarily physical until the siren, but this...

Wait.

The siren. What were sirens capable of exactly? In the stories, they were so beautiful that those attracted to the female form were drawn into the water the sirens inhabited. Some tales claimed sirens were half-fish while others said half-bird. All had elements of song to the myth, and many included illusions. He assumed the siren would make herself appear as the victim's most desired form, but perhaps there was more to the creature's powers. Perhaps a siren could make him see a minotaur and fail to see a hole in the floor.

He hurried back to where Tahlia had disappeared. Kneeling, he felt around for any break in the stones, anything off at all. The path was smooth though. He reached farther, then his hand dropped, and he nearly tumbled through a break in the labyrinth's floor. There it was. As plain as the sun in the sky, though this was black as night. He could see the ground, wet and rough.

"Tahlia?" he called out as loud as he dared.

He didn't wish to alert the siren if his guess was correct and she'd been the one creating the illusion. If she found out he'd broken the magic, surely she'd be angered and perhaps she'd come for him. He needed time to help Tahlia.

Praying, he called for Tahlia again, this time a bit louder. Should he drop into the hole himself or would that be ruining their chance at success here? He looked around, wishing he had something—anything—that could serve as a rope. He could rip his clothing into strips. *Yes, that might work.*

Or should he leap into the hole?

He could see the ground at the base of the hole, and even with his Fae blood, he wouldn't be able to handle that drop without risking injury. No, he had to be smart here and not let the feral side of him panic for fear of his mate. He bridled his growing alarm and put his meager plan into practice, calling out for Tahlia between his quick ripping and braiding work. He only needed the lower half of his trousers. They were double-layered.

A great howling echoed through the labyrinth, raising the hairs on Marius's arms. What was that? Gods, they had to get this job finished and get out. Who knew what other horrors awaited them in this terrible place?

He went back to fixing the rope, constantly debating whether he should make it thicker or longer and which would help her more.

After a few minutes of braiding, he finally finished. He removed two of the blades he had stashed in his uniform and knotted each end of the rope around one of the sheathed weapons. A space about a hand's wide had opened up between the cobblestones that made up the labyrinth's floor. He wedged one blade into the space, securing the rope. Tugging, he tested the blade and knot's position to see if it would hold Tahlia. Satisfied, he dropped the other end into the hole.

"Tahlia! I've lowered a rope down. Can you hear me? Tahlia?" He dared to call out a bit louder this time.

Then his ears began to buzz. A song filled his head. Chimes. Bells. A voice so clear and full of mourning that tears burned his eyes.

"What are you doing, Fae male?" a light voice asked a few steps down the labyrinth's path.

He turned but could only see a shadowy silhouette. But she was the one singing.

"I fashioned a rope," he answered, not at all concerned.

"Why?"

"To help Tahlia free herself." His head swam, and he rubbed a hand over his face quickly to try to clear his mind.

"Hmm." The melodious voice sounded closer though the speaker didn't appear to have moved. "Come with me. You won't need to worry about rope or her with me."

"But she needs me. And I, her."

"I doubt that. Come," she sang. "Come with me."

Each time she sang the words *come with me,* a breeze fluttered through Marius's half-bound hair and the scent of brine filled the air. He remembered a day long in the past, a day that honestly he might have invented, something that wasn't a true event and only real in his imaginings. But in this makeshift memory, he stood beside his sister, hand in hand, and they stared at the sea. There were no fires in the cliffside fortress or pirates firing arrows from their quick ships. Only the rolling waves, a soft wind, and the scent of sand and sea. It was before he had known much about the world at large, back when everything felt safe.

"Come with me, Marius," she sang, the song unfurling in his blood and making him feel as light as air.

Pleasure and anticipation danced through his veins. He looked up and realized he was standing instead of sitting beside the hole where Tahlia had fallen. A figure stood beside him, her eyes trained on a pointed archway opening to a low roof that hung over a sloping stretch of black sand.

"How do you know my name?" he asked, turning to face the figure.

Swiftly flowing water covered every inch of her skin. He looked her up and down, unable to stop his lips parting in shock and wonder. No, the water *was* her skin. Beds of kelp, coral shelves, and schools of fish lived in her skin. The scale altered from one moment to the next with the fish and kelp looking miniature now and then full scale somehow. He shook his head, dizzy with the impossibility of what he was seeing. Her watery flesh held in a heart as bright as a gold coin and lungs as red as rubies. She was made of the sea's treasure—both natural and lost in shipwrecks. The female was gorgeous, but his mind couldn't comprehend her in full.

His gaze slid to her face. "Your eyes..."

They were topaz—copper and sea blue. It was like they laughed at his wonder, but how could eyes laugh like that? The sound of her voice chimed in his ears. He growled in frustration, but the song crashed into him anyway, turning everything to bliss. A soft hand tugged at his hand, and the black sand was pleasantly gritty beneath his bare feet.

When had he removed his boots?

When had he left the labyrinth and decided to follow this female made of sea and treasure?

"Come with me," she sang again, and that breeze and those feelings once again swept across him and burned his worries into ash.

All worries and every thought besides the sea melted from his mind as they left the dark and sandy corridor and approached the easy waves of the shoreline. He sighed and went with the being into the ocean, delighting in the feel of the cool water lapping at his knees. They walked slowly until the water was chest-high.

"Be still," the female said.

He obeyed, and she passed a hand over his face.

Then she pulled him under.

CHAPTER 21
TAHLIA

Tahlia was free from the dark hole and back in the labyrinth.

But Marius was gone.

Damn. If she had her Weaver magic, she might be able to track him. But she'd tried the four-count breathing as Fara had instructed, in and out, with all the ridiculous holding and everything. But no magic had sparkled over her head or eyes or whatever. No, she'd found a rope though, and she was out of the hole. She assumed Marius had made the rope out of his clothing because his scent had drawn her through the inky darkness to the rope's braided fabric.

She lifted her nose, trying to scent Marius again, to see if anything led her the way he'd gone. But no, her nose was good, but not full-Fae-blood good.

"I really hope I don't run into a minotaur right now. My ankle and ribs are still killing me. At least my head is feeling better."

Lija's voice mumbled through Tahlia's mind. Tension tightened Tahlia's shoulders and neck. She couldn't stand to lose her aural connection to Fara and Lija when Marius was missing.

"I couldn't hear that," she said quietly, hoping the mythological beasts roaming this madhouse wouldn't be alerted. "Can you speak up or toss some more of that herb into the mix?"

"Rider, do you hear me now?"

"Ah, much better, yes."

"Lady Fara is threatening the visiting herbwitch."

Oh, no. "Why?"

"She said if this connection fails before you catch up with Marius, she'll, and I quote, 'String your yarrow-scented intestines over the castle walls.'"

Tahlia bit her lip to keep her laugh quiet. "Tell her to behave. She might ruin her chances at becoming a full-fledged Healer if she does too much eviscerating."

Lija's chuckle was music to Tahlia's ears.

Wait. "I heard music while I was climbing out. Did you hear any of that? It was very faint. Felt off."

"I didn't," Lija said.

"Me neither," Fara said, her voice coming back and overlapping Lija's. "And don't you worry about me and my situation back here. Not your business, you wonderful, death-wish-having maniac. You are my priority."

"Thanks, Fara." Her heart warmed and she walked farther into the labyrinth. "I think that space under this labyrinth was cloaked in a spell because I couldn't even see the opening I was climbing out of until I was nearly free. And the music..."

A chill swept over her. "Oh, no."

"What is it?" Lija asked.

"The music I heard," Tahlia said, "I bet it was the siren."

Fara was swearing before Tahlia had finished her sentence. "... and that cock-brained arse with—"

"Fara. Calm down. Please. I need to think. If Marius was here setting up the rope for me..." Tahlia absently touched the two blades she'd untangled from the rope's end knots. "And the siren appeared." She exhaled slowly, trying to feel anger rather than fear. "Well, I guess we know where Marius went."

"I can help," Lija said. "I've lived near sirens. Long ago, during my youngling stage."

"I had no idea. I thought you were born in the Shrouded Mountains like the other mountain dragons."

"I was born near Dragon Tail Peak, but Seabreaks usually visit the sea to swim before reaching adulthood. It's a rite of passage."

"Fascinating." Lija's information helped Tahlia keep her panic at bay. "Tell me more."

The labyrinth met the wall of the massive chamber then turned to the left. In the wall, an opening the size of a double doorway shimmered.

"Wait. There's a magical opening here. It could be a portal. It's definitely been created with magic."

"That will be her entry to the sea. Sirens can remove stone like a splash of water clears mud if they are motivated to do so."

Black sand lined the ground beyond the hole in the labyrinth wall. Two sets of footprints marked the sand. One was a slender barefoot print about the size of Tahlia's foot and the other showed what had to be Marius's boot print. The sound of the ocean whispered down the sandy, cave-like corridor.

"All right. I'm following footprints. I'm fairly certain one set of these is Marius's."

"Whatever you do, rider, make certain the siren doesn't see you. They won't smell you in the water. Their sense of smell is one of their weaknesses."

"That's very good to know."

The sand crunched beneath Tahlia's feet as she hurried down the black sand and into a breeze that grew saltier with every step. The corridor opened up to a rocky beach. Pale cliffs towered behind Tahlia and the foamy waves lapped the shore at the toes of her boots. The waves were growing larger and wilder, like gray hands clapping and grasping at the lowering clouds. Lightning cracked overhead and thunder shook the beach as the smell of rain filled the air.

"I don't see them anywhere."

"She has taken him under already?" Lija asked. Voices spoke in the background.

"Yes. Unless I'm wrong, and he hasn't been swayed by her at all. Maybe he's back in the labyrinth. Yeah, perhaps I should head back inside and make sure he isn't just around another corner or two."

"If she has claimed him, you have very little time to catch up to them before they disappear for good."

Tahlia gritted her teeth and fisted her hands. "But he isn't currently drowning if he's down there with her, right? Please tell me that, at least."

"No, she won't let him drown before she entertains herself with him."

And then she spotted Marius's boots. A chill rocked her and she bent halfway, bracing herself on her knees. Swallowing against the lump in her throat, Tahlia tried not to panic.

"All right," she said, her voice shaky. "I'm going in. But it's not as if I swim regularly. I wish you were here, Lija. For many, many reasons."

"I do too, rider. I do too. Now, shake that despair off your shoulders, knight, and look around the shoreline for a palm-sized stone that has been smoothed from years of seaside existence."

"Why?"

"I'll explain as you search," Lija said.

The beach was a sea itself with pebbles stretching for a mile, maybe more. "Any palm-sized stone?"

"Yes. If it doesn't work the first time, we can try until it does."

"Try what?" At Tahlia's feet, a smooth, light brown stone reflected another strike of lightning. She picked it up. "Got a rock for you, my mysterious dragon."

"Good. Do you have a blade?"

"Several."

Lija's chuckle was dark and full of promised vengeance on those who went against them. "You'll need to carve four runes on the stone."

"But I don't have magic. I have no Unseelie blood." Some Seelie Fae did have Unseelie blood and were just recently being open about it. After discovering the link between Fae King Lysanael and the Unseelie realm, the stigma had faded somewhat. Only the humans' Witch and the Fae's Druid could do full magic in this realm—the world of Seelie Fae and humans.

"This is sea magic and you are bonded to a Seabreak, rider. Trust me."

"Do the other knights know about this magic of yours?"

"They've seen some of it in battle with Donan and Lady Maiwenn, but they know enough not to ask too many questions about dragon business."

"Understood."

Lija began detailing the lines and shapes of the runes Tahlia had to carve. They went one by one, Lija explaining and Tahlia etching the magical symbols as clearly as possible on the stone.

"It's finished," Tahlia said, feeling shaky for a thousand reasons. The rain was cold. Marius was missing. Durniad would be claiming the crown and using it to wreak havoc on the entire world in a bit. She had injuries that burned and pulsed with pain. Oh, and she was about to hunt a siren.

"Sit as Lady Fara instructed you earlier. Hold the stone over your chest."

Tahlia didn't argue, but she did take a minute to strip off her boots as well as to remove her belt and Fara's letters. When she was in position with the stone against her chest, she checked in.

"I'm ready."

"Imagine that I am beside you and your hand is on my scales. Pretend as though we breathe in and out like we are the same creature."

A warmth traveled down Tahlia's head, shoulders, and chest. Her lungs, mouth, and nose tingled like they were going numb.

"Do you feel the magic, rider?"

"I do."

"Then you can enter the sea without worry for air. Leave the stone on the beach and let us begin our hunt."

Tahlia waded into the chilly, storm-tossed surf. The cliffs curved around the beach like a scythe. The tide tugged at her legs.

"Will the runes also help me swim in a storm like this?"

"You're stronger than you realize. Your bond with me has altered your body and your blood."

The water deepened and Tahlia began to swim. Maybe she truly could find Marius and help him escape the siren. Maybe Lija wasn't being insane.

"How does this hunt begin?" she asked, trying not to let fear roll over her like one of the sea's massive swells.

"Stop lollygagging and get on with it. Dive in, rider!"

"Bossy, aren't we?" Tahlia did as Lija ordered.

The water enveloped her and she parted her lips. Would she drown? No, Lija would protect her. She knew that.

Tahlia opened her mouth and inhaled. Her lungs expanded, pressing against the pain in her injured ribs. But the rune stone worked. She was breathing under water. Miraculous. But could she speak to Lija like this? She hadn't been able to speak inside the mind as she and Lija usually did. Communicating out loud had been an intuitive decision that had held. But maybe...

Can you hear me, Lija?

Tahlia swam forward and the water parted around her limbs like she'd been born a fish rather than a half-Fae. Wow.

"Can you see any bubbles as if something large is exhaling into the water?" Lija asked, her voice quiet but clear in Tahlia's ears.

Hoping this was going to work, Tahlia opened her mouth to speak. "Can you hear and understand me?" How could she?

Tahlia's words were strangled by the water and she couldn't pronounce anything correctly.

"Well enough, rider. Well enough."

"Good. I see many bubbles."

"Keep swimming, my lady Tahlia," Lija said. "Look for a trail of bubbles in the shapes of feathers."

Feathers? Tahlia kept her eyes open, shocked that she could see clearly. Granted, the flash of lightning and the twist of the water altered the look of the sandy ocean floor, the waving kelp, and the two schools of fish—one silver and one poppy red—that swam by. But still, the details of a round coral bloom showed clearly despite appearing one hundred yards or so away.

She reached out her arms and kicked her feet in the cool water, her eyesight far sharper than it had ever been under water. The sea floor dropped, and a break of seagrass with bright gold flowers that shimmered with their own illumination ran in a curving path along the deepest cut in the ground. At the end of the seagrass, a line of elongated, soft-looking bubbles danced through the water toward the surface.

"Found them," she said as best she could with water chilling her mouth and salting her tongue.

"Good," Lija said. "The entrance to her lair is likely decorated in a way you won't miss."

"I don't like the sound of that."

"A fitting attitude when dealing with sirens. She is extremely dangerous, rider."

"Let's say I make it into her lair—what do I do then? I assume hand-to-hand combat isn't my best choice of action."

"No, unless you can break the hold she has on Marius. You two could probably best her physically. But not just you. She'll use him to get to you. And that's if you manage to surprise her before she can sing to you."

"So I am susceptible."

"Maybe less so because you find males attractive, but her power remains a definite threat."

"This whole *saving Marius from an evil female* is getting old, if I'm honest."

Lija huffed, dark amusement coming through their bond. "Let's hope you are saving him and not just tossing yourself into the tragedy."

Tahlia blew out a mouthful of bubbles. "Yes, let's hope for that," she said wryly.

They weren't so deep that light didn't penetrate the water here. Flashes of lightning danced through the salt water and helped Tahlia see.

She said a silent prayer and swam forward.

CHAPTER 22
MARIUS

The moment the ocean water hit Marius's face, his mind cleared. He swore viciously inside his head.

He'd been fooled by a siren.

They swam onward through a deep valley under the sea. He didn't dare alert the siren that he was aware of himself. How was he breathing down here? He had no recollection of leaving the labyrinth or arriving at the seaside.

The siren wasn't singing now. If she started up again, would he lose his senses? Maybe if he recreated his state of mind when his head cleared, he'd be able to do it again should the need arise. He recalled the chilly water and a bolt of protective desire for Tahlia. Their mating bond was powerful and the thought of her had forced the siren's magic from him. Were sirens aware of that? Considering he hadn't even realized sirens existed in today's world, he certainly didn't have a broad knowledge of their behavior, strengths, or weaknesses. This creature swimming beside him was an unknowable enemy. The worst type of opponent.

He longed to look around and make certain he knew the way back to shore. Not that he had a single idea on how to breathe under water long enough once he fought the siren and broke whatever magic she was wielding to keep him from drowning.

"Welcome to my home, Fae."

Her chiming voice threatened to pull his mind under again. He imagined the feel of Tahlia's cheek on his palm and the heat of her kiss. The siren's influence faded.

The inconsistent light of the storm above sent flashes of illumination through the water. They swam through a curtain of dark red kelp and into a cave with a wide opening on the far side. Sea creatures like snails gathered in clusters on the cave walls, their shells glowing as gold as the coins that made up the siren's heart. Something pale on the ground caught Marius's eye and he looked down to see a path of bones.

It was only his training that kept him from reacting and giving himself away. Some were the tiny bones of fish, their spines still intact. But others...

Human skulls, long femurs, and the unmistakable cages of ribs littered the lair.

Fear sliced across his thoughts, but he found the calm within him as he always did in terrible scenarios, and he schooled his features before she looked at him again. He had to get out of here. Now. Durniad would be coming for the crown soon. Tahlia had to escape the fortress before she was caught. He knew her enough to be certain she'd be searching for him if she managed to free herself with his rope. His fingers began to curl into fists, but he relaxed them and kept his gaze on the siren.

She eased him toward one of the cave's walls, singing as her palms pressed into his chest. Memories of his family flooded his mind; then there were memories that weren't real. He had no brother. Who was that? He visualized Tahlia laughing and the soft touch of her hand in his. The siren's manufactured memories faded from his mind's eye.

The siren plucked a pale orange berry from a plant growing along the cave's roof. She placed it between his lips.

"Eat this, Fae male. You will feel very good indeed if you do."

Her words, not sung exactly but lilting and song-like, warmed his ears and he relaxed more than he needed to.

Tahlia. Tahlia, my mate, he repeated silently to himself.

What would this berry do to him? Kill him? Put him to sleep so she could dine on his innards without a fuss? Gods, this was horrendous.

But what choice did he have? If he fought her, she might be stronger than him. Or she might negate whatever magic had him breathing here.

The siren parted his lips. "Open up, Fae."

Heart racing, Marius rammed his forehead into her nose. Blood bloomed around them, and he shot toward the lair's entrance as the siren shrieked. Her noise made his ears ring painfully. Swimming as quickly as he could, he breathed like some sort of magical fish, using his mouth, nose, and lungs still. Her magic hadn't broken with his strike.

But he knew without looking that the siren would be on him in moments despite her injury. He hurried, swimming as quickly as his limbs allowed.

He swam right into another person. Grunting, his eyes focused and...

It was Tahlia. No, she couldn't be here. He gripped her arm and started swimming again as the siren's screams came closer. If she began singing, they were through.

Tahlia jerked away from Marius. What was she doing?

Trust me, she mouthed, holding a finger to her head.

What did that mean?

CHAPTER 23
TAHLIA

"Cut yourself!" Lija shouted into Tahlia's ears. "The sea needs your blood."

"What? No time!"

"Come on!" Marius attempted to snatch Tahlia's wrist, and she dodged him, swimming in place an arm's length away.

The siren was swimming toward Tahlia and Marius and although she was bleeding profusely, she was still speeding through the water as quick as a lightning bolt.

"Gods, her skin... She's beautiful. Horrible, but gorgeous and impossible..."

"Rider! Cut! Now!"

Tahlia blinked, pulled her nearest dagger, and sliced the top of her forearm. Blood snaked into the churning water and lightning flashed overhead. Thunder boomed through the ocean.

"She's still coming at us, Lija!"

The siren opened her bloodied mouth to sing.

"Wait," Lija said. "Don't try to out-swim her. She'll just catch you faster. Wait."

"Tahlia!" Marius looked ready to explode.

Tahlia's blood drew into a perfect sphere and pulsed like a heart. "It's doing something, Lija."

The siren's song filtered through the water and Marius began swimming back to his captor.

"Marius! Stop!" The water muffled Tahlia's voice.

"Draw the following rune into the sphere," Lija ordered.

"You know what it looks like?"

Marius stopped swimming toward the siren and pushed back toward Tahlia, rage and shame etched into his features. The siren swam in big circles toward them now, as if she was preparing for a kill like a shark. Her smile was a bracelet of diamonds, her flesh like the sea captured under glass. She was stunning.

"Rider! Focus!" Lija shouted into Tahlia's ears. "Draw a straight, vertical line, then a left to right downward, diagonal slash. Add a crescent on top like a dome and one dot inside the crescent."

Hand shaking, Tahlia did as instructed. Marius stared, his gaze going from her face to the blood and back again. He was frantic and she could almost feel his panic in her chest, thrumming side by side with her fear.

The thunder rolled again, but was it thunder?

Shadows curled from the distant deep blue and from around the coral and rock that shielded the siren's lair.

"What is happening, Lija?"

The dragon's quiet little laugh usually meant someone was about to suffer in exactly the way she wanted them to.

Eels with bright red stripes and jagged teeth shot from the shadows and swam for the siren. Sharks slipped through the water and opened their great maws as they closed in. Where did they come from?

The siren shrieked as she kicked out at a shark's nose. An eel wrapped her wrists and tugged her away from Tahlia and Marius. Another shark bumped her in the back and she whirled, or at least she attempted it, looking more like a broken marionette.

Tahlia set her gaze on Marius, then began to swim toward the surface. He was right beside her in a blink. His eyes said he had numerous questions; hells, so did she.

"Lija, what was that all about? Are you a dragon or maybe a goddess and you've been pretending to be a dragon like the others on the peak?"

Lija chuckled. "Dragons of the sea are more tied to the Unseelie realm than other dragons. We have access to the old magic. Not power enough to best any, but we have tricks hidden between our scales, rider."

"I can see that. I can't wait to hear more about this once we are out of this place."

"Do you know where the crown lies?"

"Not yet, but we are close."

"I wish you all the luck, Lady Tahlia," Lija said. "The communication herb has burned away, so Lady Fara and I will no longer be in contact."

"See you soon."

She walked up the shoreline with the sea tugging once more at her legs. Marius was right beside her. He smoothed his wet Fae-white hair away from his face and squeezed the water from his tangled locks. Drops ran down his inked torso and the muscles of his stomach.

"How are you communicating with Lija?" he asked.

"How did you know?"

"Because that was Seabreak magic," he said, "the likes of which I've only heard about in old stories."

Tahlia twisted her hair and the ends of her tunic, and water splashed onto the stones near her feet. "You've never seen Maiwenn's Donan do anything like that?"

"Similar, but not that powerful. He's never raised an army to defend him from enemies, that's for certain."

Marius wrung the seawater from the loose remains of his

ripped trousers while Tahlia put her dry socks and boots back on. Pride in Lija swelled in Tahlia's chest.

"There's an herbwitch at the castle and she helped Fara and Lija communicate with me via my bond with Lija."

"And then talk to me via our mate bond?" Marius found his boots and removed the socks tucked inside.

"Exactly."

Raising his eyebrows, Marius nodded and grunted in approval. Once they were as ready as they could be, he grabbed Tahlia and kissed her hard.

"I'm glad you're still here to ruin my focus, Lady of the Skies."

She nipped his bottom lip and gripped his narrow, delicious, male hips. "Back at you."

They hurried back the way they'd come. The siren's portal remained, shimmering and dizzying. They entered the labyrinth and took a right.

"The minotaur was an illusion. But it was an illusion strong enough to kill," Marius said as they walked on, drawing their blades and shaking or wiping them dry as best they could.

"The siren's doing, I guess?"

"Yes. Did you not feel swayed by her?" Marius asked.

"I did somewhat, but Lija was able to bring me back to myself."

"Thoughts of you are the only reason I was able to strike out at her."

Tahlia's cheeks warmed. "Glad I could help."

The labyrinth went around and around until it reached an arched wooden door with a small, simple brass knob.

"I suppose we're headed in there? The crown is probably sitting right in there on a fine pillow with some magical light illuminating it for us, right?"

Marius lifted one eyebrow and growled.

"Yeah, I didn't think so," she said. "Let's get whatever this nightmare is about to be over with. I'm ready to leave this crazy place."

Marius kicked the door open and Tahlia nearly leapt out of her skin.

"Did the door knob insult you?"

He pushed the broken remnants away and walked forward into the chamber. Tahlia followed him. The room was a twenty-by-thirty-foot dusty enclosure. Footprints ran in a crescent shape around a raised platform crafted of dark wood. On top, a box large enough for three crowns boasted a seashell-shaped lock.

"That has to be it, right?" Tahlia asked. "Or is this another ruse?"

"We won't know unless we try it. Can you still communicate with Lija? She may know something about such a lock."

"Because of its shape."

"Aye."

"I can't talk to her anymore, I don't think. She said the herb-witch ran out of the rare plant that allowed us that link. I'll try though just in case."

Marius nodded, and from the small bag at his belt, he removed the key the contact had given them at the warehouse.

"Lija? Fara? Can you hear me?" Tahlia closed her eyes to focus, listening for any sound, any whisper.

Sighing, she opened her eyes and shook her head. "No go."

Marius jerked his chin in understanding. "Tell me immediately if you notice anything amiss when I put the key in place."

"Do you think that's the right key?"

Chewing his lip, Marius lifted his eyebrows. "There's a solid chance it is. That contact has worked in Spycraft since he was a child. It's in his family."

"You know them?" Tahlia asked.

"I've heard of them."

Glancing around the room once more, he lifted the key to the seashell lock. His shoulders moved in a breath and he inserted the key. The lock clicked, the sound loud in the small and silent chamber. The walls had to be incredibly thick because not even the sea's crashing was audible here. The seashell fell open and the corner of Marius's lips tilted up in a half grin. He removed the lock and Tahlia took it from him, tucking it into her pocket. He lifted the box's lid...

Another box sat inside with another lock, this one in the shape of a fist.

"Think the little key will help us one more time?" Tahlia removed it from her pocket and stuck it into the fist. "It fits!" She tried to turn it, but the lock didn't give. "Damn. I was hoping it would be that easy."

"Easy?" Marius stared at her, wide-eyed. "A collapsing floor, a bespelled darkness, a minotaur, and a siren, and you call that *easy*?"

"We made our way through it all, didn't we? I only have some sore ribs and an angry ankle."

"Maybe you have a terrible concussion. I don't think you're clearheaded at the moment."

Tahlia grinned and smacked his arm. "Shut it, you big lug."

Marius pursed his lips and lifted the box carefully. "Maybe it's time for a blunt approach."

He slammed the box onto the floor. Tahlia gasped as the wood splintered as the door had. There was nothing inside the box. But then again, the crown was invisible.

Marius took the concoction the Witch had given them from his pouch, uncorked it, and sprinkled the floral-scented blend over the mess of what had been the second box. The air glimmered as if it was under water with the sun shining on ripples of seawater.

"Is it not working or is the crown not in here?" Tahlia fisted her hands.

Durniad would be here soon, if their information was accurate. Sweat beaded on her upper lip and she swallowed while Marius bent to squint at the sparkling area.

"Look." He pointed near a broken corner of the box.

Fingers of a dark metal appeared out of the Witch's shimmering magic. The tines came together with sapphire circles and bronze leaves, and soon, the crown showed itself in full.

"Can you just pick it up?" Tahlia asked. "Is the crown's power only activated if you put it on?"

Marius exhaled. "That's what King Lysanael said."

A shuffling sounded behind them. "Is that so?"

Tahlia's heart iced over.

Durniad.

CHAPTER 24

MARIUS

As fast as he could, Marius set the crown on his own head and got between Tahlia and Durniad. Magic shivered down his back and along his jaw. The cooling sensation traveled along his throat and into his chest.

Durniad's smug look had fallen and his eyes looked ready to pop from his meaty head.

"You see the one who should wear the crown wearing it now," Marius said, not knowing what in the hells he was doing, but desperate to escape with Tahlia. He had been ordered to avoid bloodshed if possible. But with Durniad flanked by four large guards, the crown was the only way they could leave without a great deal of damage and a high body count.

Tahlia's hand found Marius's back, and he was glad he wore no tunic because he could easily feel that her fingers didn't shake. She wasn't afraid of the power he held at the moment. His mate truly trusted him.

Durniad blinked quickly, then he and his guards stepped aside.

Marius started down the labyrinth with Tahlia behind him.

"This is great!" Tahlia whispered. "Oooh, tell me to do something. I want to see how it feels."

"This isn't a game, Lady Tahlia."

"Aw, come on, Commander. Make me run or say the alphabet backwards."

"Your ankle is injured."

"Actually, it's good now. My ribs and head aren't great, but I'm fine. Do the alphabet one. Wait. I know I'm not capable of that. What if I explode when you order me to try?"

"You are far too excited about the prospect."

"It's fascinating!"

"Spontaneous combustion would compromise our mission."

"You're so Marius, you know that?"

He frowned. "Why would I be anything else?"

A shrieking shattered Marius's thoughts.

They whirled to see the siren dragging herself through her portal behind them.

Tahlia swore in a Fara-like manner—some curse involving monkeys and testes. Marius agreed with the sentiment if not the communication style.

The siren had lost an arm. Her watery flesh had gone blood red. She looked like a true nightmare now, her jeweled eyes gone cloudy and her mouth ripped at one side.

"I will have my revenge." She rushed them—moving faster than anything Marius had ever witnessed—and snatched Tahlia's belt.

Marius's body went tight with battle readiness. The siren wavered on her feet. The surge of activity had depleted her somewhat. She was weakened.

The siren hauled Tahlia backward, the creature's arm laced around Tahlia's neck. Opening her mouth of coral and shark teeth, the siren prepared to bite down on Tahlia's shoulder. Panic threaded through Marius's every bone, tendon, and muscle.

"Get off me!" Tahlia snarled, grabbed the siren's arm, maneuvered her hips, and slammed the siren onto the floor. "Ugh. Your skin feels so bizarre." She shook water from her hands and grimaced.

The creature howled and slowly raised herself back up.

Tahlia drew her two daggers and slashed at the siren's gut, but the creature evaded her and hissed.

"Leave. Go back to the sea," Marius demanded.

"That crown has no power over me," the siren whispered.

Her power must have been diminished by her injuries because her voice didn't seem to affect Tahlia or him at all.

The siren lashed out with her fingers. Each watery digit ended with a claw made of some dark coral that leaked a foul, green substance that would poison Tahlia if she made contact. Marius knew that somehow. The scent of the stuff made the hairs on the back of his neck rise.

A rushing sounded. Tahlia glanced at him, keeping a blade between her and the siren.

What was that sound?

The siren's arm became a small torrent of rushing water, and the siren encircled Tahlia's neck, choking her and pulling her close.

"Stop!" Marius lunged forward with his dagger outstretched, but he couldn't do anything without further threatening Tahlia's safety.

Tahlia was choking, her eyes panicked and her cheeks red. A shout sounded behind the siren and Tahlia. Durniad tore Tahlia from the injured siren's arms.

"Get me that crown, siren, and you get your revenge," Durniad said.

"You want to release her," Marius ordered. The crown's power shivered down his spine and throat.

Gaze going blank, Durniad did so, but the siren's entire body turned into a rushing wave and drove Marius to the ground. He leapt up again, but the crown was gone from his drenched head.

The siren reformed. Tahlia slashed the siren's waist. Water

gushed from the wound. The creature hissed and snared Tahlia's hair. Shouting in pain, Tahlia dropped her blade. The siren yanked Tahlia out of Marius's reach. He froze. The siren's abilities were an unknown. He had to stall and figure this out. Tahlia's face said she too was trying to work out a strategy here.

"Why are you working with him?" Marius asked the siren, truly baffled.

"His great-grandsire killed my mother's enemy. My mother created that crown and I owe him a blood debt."

Damn. Marius couldn't twist that to their benefit.

With a cocky laugh, Durniad placed the crown on his head. "Drop all your weapons," he ordered Marius.

To keep up their ruse that they were human, Marius dropped his daggers while the siren dragged Tahlia toward the portal. Marius could not, would not, permit the siren to take her. His body hummed with rage.

"Take me," Tahlia said, her tone casual. "I'll call up my ocean pals to rip your face off the second we hit the water."

"Not if I bind your hands so you can't make runes," the siren said.

Tahlia laughed. "That's what you think. I'm not the creature you think I am."

The warped grin on the siren's injured face fell, and Durniad frowned, his brow furrowing with confusion.

A tingling zipped along Marius's ears, jaw, and down his whole body. He watched as Tahlia's ears grew back into their regular pointed shape and her irises returned to their slitted, Fae form. He touched his ear, and yes, the Witch's potion had reached the end of its time limit.

The siren hissed and shoved Tahlia to the ground. Her cheek hit the ground hard and she groaned, immediately trying to pull herself back up.

"Stay on the ground, woman," Durniad said, not realizing she was part Fae. Would the amount of Fae blood she had be enough?

The siren fled through her portal. The shimmering opening fizzled like water on a hot stone and then it disappeared entirely.

"I don't know what your backstory is with the siren," Durniad said, "but I don't care. I think I'm ready for some entertainment. My grand plan takes off very soon, so I don't have all day."

Tahlia glanced at Marius and remained on the ground as if the crown did hold sway over her body. Was she faking like him?

Marius was a living storm of indecision. Durniad hadn't yet noticed Marius's ears and eyes. Should he attack Durniad and his men in hopes of grabbing the crown and releasing Tahlia? Or should he keep still in case Durniad truly did control Tahlia? The makeshift king could order her to ram her own head into the wall and end herself.

Swallowing the bitter taste of fear on the back of his tongue, Marius stared at Tahlia. He hoped for a wink only he would see or some other indication. But Tahlia remained still. Her gaze stayed on him, but her look told him absolutely nothing.

"King Durniad!" one of the human's guards rushed toward Tahlia.

Marius started toward him, fuming.

"Stay," Durniad ordered.

Marius held himself back as the guard moved Tahlia's hair away from her ear.

"What is it?" Durniad spat as he studied Marius with a look that said he was deciding how to torture him.

"Her ears. She's Fae." The guard lifted his head and eyed Marius. "Him too."

Durniad stepped forward, getting closer to Tahlia, who lay between him and Marius. "Hmm. Now why would the Fae be involved here? And how is my crown controlling them if their blood isn't human?" His delighted grin made Marius's skin crawl. "Perhaps I should rework my grand plan and make it even grander."

He set his foot on Tahlia's lower back and she grunted, likely her ribs paining her. Gods, Marius was going to kill Durniad very, very slowly when the right moment came. He savored the thought of it.

"Maybe they're half-breeds like Syonia," the guard said.

"Ah." Durniad clicked his tongue. "That would explain it. Let's test this out, shall we?"

Marius growled.

"Oooh, you are protective of her. She is your friend? No, I think she is more than that. Don't Fae mate for life?"

"They mate casually, but they mate in another way for life," the guard said, his distaste for Fae apparent in his sneer.

The feeling was mutual. Marius felt another growl building in the back of his throat.

"That's what my Veilbury cousin told me anyway," the guard said.

Durniad nodded at his knowledgeable guard. He removed his foot from Tahlia's back. "Stand, half-breed."

She did so with odd, jerky movements. So she was actually controlled by Durniad. The magic of the crown obviously wasn't as overpowering on her as it was on the full-blooded humans. Marius weighed his ideas and how that could help them. He had to get her out of here before Durniad did something truly terrible. Marius knew he could take the guards and Durniad, but while Durniad had the crown, Tahlia was in serious danger. He didn't dare attack. Not yet anyway.

Ragewing, if there is any way you can hear me, please let me know. We are in a tight spot and I might have to throw caution to the wind and ask you to charge in for a rescue.

There was no response. Damn the distance between them.

What could he do? Marius ground his teeth and bared his fangs. Durniad glanced his way and paled slightly as he adjusted his crown.

"Easy now," Durniad said to Marius. "Don't go feral on me." He faced Tahlia.

Marius could only think to stall the madman, to give himself some time to come up with a plan.

"King Durniad," Marius said, "why do you want this crown? Why this elaborate protection? What do you want of life?"

"Such big questions from an intruder. Listen, no one else has the stones to take what we, the people of Midhampton, need. We were the first human city to have art and high-level architecture on the continent. The first to begin trade with the east and north. We deserve to thrive and use this gift Fate has set in our laps. I do this for my people." He fisted his hand and pounded it once against his barrel-like chest. "I was born to be their king and to bring them back to the top of the world. There will be no starving in our streets. No mistreated children or people worked to death. We will be as fat as pigs and as wealthy as our kings of old. We will be the center of civilization again and all will come to us for advice and to raise their level of living."

"No one could fault you for lack of confidence," Tahlia muttered.

"Do not speak, either of you. Unless I demand it."

Marius acted at not being able to say another word, opening his mouth and pretending no sound would come.

Durniad eyed Tahlia with a detached look. "Break one of your fingers," he commanded.

Marius's stomach dropped. His entire mind focused on murder. He would bleed this man dry.

Tahlia's lips pressed tightly together. She gripped her left pinkie finger and Marius held his breath.

CHAPTER 25
TAHLIA

The urge to follow the madman's command was like a terrible itch under Tahlia's skin. She set her jaw, refusing the crown's demand, pushing it away like her thoughts were giant palms in sand made of magic. *I am Tahlia. I will not go down like this. I refuse anyone else's will being imposed on me. I have my own mind and I will use it.* She chanted that inside her head. The magic shivered over her, but its influence weakened. She released her finger and glared at Durniad.

With a shout of pent-up rage, Marius launched himself at Durniad. He drove a fist into his throat. The crown went flying and freed Tahlia's body. She spun and hit the nearest guard with an elbow to the temple. Drawing her dagger, she watched Marius snag one of his blades from the floor in a blur of incredible speed. They cut the guards down, but Durniad rose behind them. He went for the crown that had skidded across the floor. He placed it on himself.

"Guards!" he called over the labyrinth. "Kill my enemies!"

A rush of boots sounded at the beginning of the labyrinth and soon guards were pouring into the walled space. Their eyes were glazed and their movements frantic as they came with swords, fists, and even objects that were never meant to serve as weapons—a set of manacles, what appeared to be a hair comb from one man's pocket, and a scroll one fellow brandished like a knife.

The guard who had helped Tahlia and Marius earlier swung a book at Tahlia. She ducked, set her head on the woman's hip, and grabbed the backs of the woman's knees. The guard went down with a grunt.

They couldn't maintain this level of fighting. The walls beckoned.

Tahlia kicked a man's stomach, throwing him back. She jumped off the back of a staggering, mostly collapsed guard whom Marius had hit and leapt onto the top of the labyrinth's walls.

"Up here!" she called down to Marius.

He bent his knees and jumped up beside her, and then they were running, dodging arrows, and leaping over sloppily tossed daggers.

The doorway into the chamber was empty. All the occupants within hearing range of the crown's influence must have already entered the labyrinth.

"What's our plan?" Tahlia asked as they jumped down and fled the chamber.

"Run like those cakes you love are at the end!"

Tahlia cackled as they swept up the stairs and ran out the side door of the fortress. There weren't any guards anywhere. The larger street they came out on was still flowing red with tomatoes, and people were dancing and playing pipes and lutes everywhere. Mugs were lifted and toasts shouted as Tahlia and Marius wove through the mess of humanity.

"We Fae should take a page from their books," Tahlia said loudly as they came to a meat pie cart that had been overturned in the ruckus.

Marius grabbed her wrist and turned them down an alleyway that headed roughly toward the city gates.

"I'm serious," she said, glancing at his scowling face. "They aren't worried about appearances. Only fun, fun, and more fun. Our kind could use some more of that."

She didn't feel odd saying our kind because she had been raised in the Realm of Lights as a Fae and had always considered herself Fae even though she was half. But looking around at the humans, she realized this was what she'd been missing. This pure and simple embracing of joy. This was part of what it meant to have human blood.

"Less talking. More running, Tahlia."

A now familiar voice carried on the wind, the words strung out as if shouted from afar.

"People of Midhampton, stop the white-haired Fae male and small half-Fae female if you see them. Use whatever means necessary to bring them alive to me."

The command held no spark of magic that Tahlia could feel, but that was likely only because Durniad hadn't directed the order at her. Or was it because she had fought the magic earlier and managed to break its hold?

"How does he know you are full Fae and I'm half?" she asked.

"I moved easily against him," Marius said. "Your movements were clearly hindered. I'm thinking he is simply very good at making judgment calls."

Marius led her to the edge of the main street with Bodwin Bridge in the near distance. The entire mass of humans dropped their hands to their sides and their smiles fell into flat looks of magical obedience.

They started toward Tahlia and Marius.

"Well, this is just fantastic. What's our new plan? Because running for cakes seems a tiny bit completely impossible at the moment."

They backed up as three men and a woman neared them, one with a pipe extended like a blade and the other two with hands outstretched.

Grimacing, Tahlia moved back another step and glanced over her shoulder, probably to check for more humans approaching. Thankfully, that side was clear.

"This would honestly be hilarious if they weren't trying to beat us up and hand us to an all-powerful madman," she whispered.

Marius grunted, his gaze darting to the buildings surrounding them. "Let's climb."

"Don't have to tell me twice." Tahlia grabbed the closest down-spout and began scrambling up the side of a tailor's shop.

Using his full Fae strength and agility, Marius jumped onto a low balcony, then reached up to swing onto a second balcony above that one. Soon, they were both on the roof, looking down at the nightmare this day had become.

The people of the city lifted their heads as one to watch Marius and Tahlia. Durniad stood on one of the many temporary wooden stages the city had erected for the festival. The crown shimmered on his brow and he lifted a bronze speaking tube to his lips.

"Climb, you idiots!" Durniad shouted. "Shoot arrows at them if you can. Just don't kill them. Not yet!"

"Can they do that? I mean, with half-human blood, I can't do what you did on those balconies. They are fully human; surely they can't scale this..."

Her words faded from her tongue as a slender brown-haired human man began to climb the building next to the one they were on. He used the jutting spots of plaster and planks of wood support to rise higher and higher. Slowly but surely, more followed the man. They would be overrun in a matter of minutes.

"Marius. Listen. I broke the crown's hold on my mind by reminding myself who I was. I pushed the urge to obey the crown away. Maybe I can help everyone do that too?"

"They're human. You have Fae blood. You were able to do that because of your Fae blood."

"I don't think so. I think it was my human blood fighting something that threatened its freedom. Humans enjoy doing exactly what they want to do."

"And Fae don't?"

"Fae are more instinctive. Don't you agree?"

Marius tipped his head to one side and shrugged. The movement meant he saw her point but didn't love it.

"I'm going to talk to them." She stepped even closer to the front edge of the building.

Marius was right beside her. "They will be here in a moment. We must figure out a way across to the building behind us. Just there. Then perhaps we can find a way to the city wall and down."

"And maybe I'll sprout wings. Come on, Marius. We are completely toasted here. No chance unless I make this work."

"Tahlia."

Tahlia paused, the tone in his voice tugging at her heart. "What's really wrong? You're acting off." She spoke quickly. They were about to be overrun with attackers, so there really wasn't time for this, but... "Something is bothering you. I mean, aside from all this." Waving her hand around, she indicated their current situation.

"You don't realize how simultaneously weak and evil humans are."

That actually hurt a bit. "I think I do. I am half one of them."

He shook his head like there was a bee in his ear. "You're not truly, though. When they killed Bellona..." His throat moved and his eyes shuttered briefly.

Her chest went tight and she gripped his forearm. "Oh." She finally understood what he'd been dealing with during this mission. "Marius, you know, deep down, that the humans are good and bad and everything in between. Just as the Fae are. We are all faulty and kind and cruel and beautiful. We are all complicated creatures."

He exhaled roughly, his gaze going to the ledge. "We can talk more when we aren't in mortal danger."

"Agreed." Not waiting for him to say more, she lifted her arms. "Hello, humans! I am half-human and I've enjoyed watching you embrace life in all its messy glory. Break the hold Durniad has on you by reminding yourself that you are you and you have the freedom to do exactly as you see fit. Find your center. Imagine pushing Durniad's magical influence away from you."

A few here and there blinked and frowned as if they were hearing her, but not quite understanding. She repeated her words.

"No tyrant will control us! No tyrant will control us!" She shouted the phrase again and again and soon the festival-drunk crowd was echoing her, joining in on the chant, their faces clearing of enchantment and showing anger as they turned to face Durniad.

Marius stood beside Tahlia, his mouth parted in shock.

Tahlia squeezed his hand. "They are not the villains here. They are victims."

Nodding, Marius stared and stared.

Durniad shouted at his guards.

Tahlia squinted at a shape some guards appeared to be pulling from a space between two buildings. "What is that?"

Carted on two large wheels, the contraption had wooden arms and a complicated system of ropes.

"I'm not sure, but that is definitely a giant crossbow bolt," Marius said.

"Aw, is that for us? Durniad, the gift giver."

"I doubt it's for us, actually." Marius turned and looked into the cloudy sky.

As Tahlia lifted her face, a thrilling blend of hope and fear shot through her veins.

CHAPTER 26
MARIUS

A scarlet shape too high and far away for Marius to see clearly plunged from the cloud cover.

"Ragewing!" Both he and Tahlia shouted the dragon's name as he flew toward them.

You called, the dragon said inside Marius's mind. He tucked his wings and began to dive.

I didn't realize you could hear me. Watch out for the ballista. I've heard they can launch a bolt higher than a three-story building. Marius hated that he was about to witness the firing of a weapon the order had only talked about in wary whispers.

Ready yourselves, Ragewing said. *I'll fly low between the building you're on and the blacksmith's forge.*

Behind them. *All right.*

Try to get onto my back so I can tuck in my legs.

We will.

It made more sense because *en talon* transportation would be a nightmare with flying projectiles coming from the ground.

Tahlia didn't ask questions; she followed Marius as he ran over one of the roof's shingled peaks and toward the back of the building.

The ballista had Marius wondering if Durniad had known all along that the Mist Knights were working with the human high queen against him, or at the very least, had realized the possibility. Sure, the ballistas were good for fighting encroaching ships in the harbor, but on this side of the city, the weapons were only truly good for taking down dragons.

Below, the humans were still fighting the crown's power. A terrible sound rose over the murmurs and shouts of the crowd. The sound was like the twang of a bow but so much louder.

Ragewing spread his wings slightly and angled himself to fly along the edge of the buildings down the back street. A bolt the size of a small tree shot through the air and narrowly missed the tip of Ragewing's right wing.

"Watch out!" Tahlia cried.

The dragon roared and people screamed, running like rodents along the street below. Not rodents, Marius corrected himself. Humans. Good ones who were like Tahlia and Queen Revna.

Ragewing zipped toward them.

"Now!" Marius's heart climbed up his throat.

He and Tahlia jumped onto the dragon's moving back.

Tahlia sat behind Marius, her voice in his ear. "We can't leave yet, can we? Try to lie, I beg you."

Ragewing's scales were hot. He had been flying hard or he was stressed or both.

"We have to get the crown," Marius yelled toward Ragewing's ears.

"Damn all-powerful artifacts. Always ruining our day," Tahlia said, the wind snatching at her words.

Marius slid a bit because Ragewing wore no saddle. He still had part of his reins on—a leather strap that reached across his back and joined under his front legs. Marius grabbed hold of the strap.

Flying higher, Ragewing left the cover of the buildings and rushed toward Durniad.

And straight toward the ballista.

Tahlia laced her arms more tightly around Marius's waist. "I hope they take another ten minutes to reload that evil contraption."

Men were pulling at the ballista's twisted ropes while Durniad commanded them to hurry.

"Hold on to his spikes now, Lady Tahlia," Marius said, allowing his training to kick in and drive his worry away. He became the cold warrior, the Shadow of the Shrouded Mountains. "You're not struggling against the crown's power, are you? I don't want you leaping from Ragewing's back when I least expect it."

"I've conquered it. I can feel its influence, but I can fight it pretty easily now."

"I love knowing that."

He edged his way down Ragewing's side, keeping one hand on the strap and dropping his other arm low to ready himself.

"You're going to lift it right off his head?" Tahlia asked, laughter in her voice.

Gods, she was fearless sometimes. "Aye." He longed to ask Ragewing to lift the man and drop him from the clouds, but killing Durniad wasn't part of the mission unfortunately and they'd already broken enough of the rules to get themselves into a load of trouble.

Ragewing flew low. The men tipped the ballista and readied to fire. Durniad's face purpled as he shouted to his men.

A wicked grin tugged at Marius's lips. He leaned low on Ragewing's side, then swiped the crown.

"Be glad I let you keep your head, Durniad!" he shouted.

Ragewing sped sharply toward the open sky, climbing so quickly that Marius's breath caught. The twang of the ballista sounded.

Ragewing shrieked. The scent of dragon's blood filled Marius's nose and they began to tumble downward.

I lost her! Ragewing shouted into Marius's mind.

The city's structures sped closer and closer.

What? Marius whirled and his body went rigid.

Tahlia had disappeared. Blood flowed from Ragewing's tail.

CHAPTER 27
TAHLIA

Tahlia slipped through the sky end over end. Her view of Ragewing and Marius blurred, but the blood flecking out from the top side of Ragewing's tail was unmistakable. The bolt wasn't visible, but it had surely been the cause.

She hit the water hard. Cold enveloped her, but she couldn't be mad. At least it was water instead of cobblestone or one of Bodwin Bridge's spikey torch posts. Lungs burning, she swam toward the surface. She broke through at last, gasped, and looked up to check on Ragewing and Marius. They were no longer tumbling, and they had flown toward the city gates.

"Get her," Durniad commanded from the bank side.

His guards did as ordered, splashing into the drink after her, but the people of Midhampton were less than thrilled with the day's events.

The crowd shouted at Durniad.

"You tricked us!"

"We won't be shoved about with dark magic!"

Some were simply confused.

“What is going on?”

“Was that really a dragon or part of the magic?”

“Are you Unseelie, Durniad? Are you Fae?”

“Someone bring him down here to explain himself!”

Flustered, Durniad ignored the yelling and focused on Tahlia. She couldn’t exactly remain in the water and no doubt Ragewing had to leave the city and find someone to patch him up. So she thought she might as well go along with the guards.

She swam over to them. “Fine. You have me. But be aware, fellas. The big red boy up there isn’t the only dragon I know. And I’m pretty sure Big Red will return fairly soon and he will be powerfully angry.”

The guards grabbed her under the arms and hauled her out of the slanted riverside. To their credit, though they paled at her warning, they held her tightly and didn’t make a sound to give away their fear.

“Listen, I’m half-human. I am a lot like you. You can see this Durniad arsehead is a complete wreck of a person, right? Why follow him? The crowd is behind us. Let’s overthrow him right now. It’ll be fun!”

“Shut it, woman,” the guard on her right snapped.

“Don’t act like you’re not thinking about it,” she whispered as they dragged her toward their fool of a boss.

Durniad’s dark blond hair stuck to his sweating forehead. He pointed at Tahlia with a thick forefinger. “I have a delightful surprise for you, my dear.”

“I seriously doubt my reaction is going to match your expectations.”

“No, you don’t understand.”

“I don’t comprehend you? I agree.”

The madman chuckled and came close. Tahlia could break out of these guards’ sad little hold on her arms, but it would be smarter to wait for a better moment to escape. Granted, said adventure would need to happen before they locked her into a dungeon somewhere or lopped off her head or whatever sick stuff Durniad had planned for her.

"I am going to make you my queen."

Tahlia's mouth fell open. She nodded slowly and exhaled. "I have news that's going to disappoint you, good sir."

He frowned, then one of the guards holding Tahlia said,"She's mated to that Fae male on the dragon, my king."

Durniad waved off the man's words like they were annoying gnats. "We aren't in the Realm of Lights now, are we? We are in the human world. I can be her human husband. We will wash that Fae side right out of her."

"Why in the name of all the gods would you want to wed me? I loathe you. And let's get really honest here. I could kill you. Pretty easily."

A laugh boomed from Durniad as they started down the steps of the festival stage. Durniad must have ordered more guards into the streets because the crowd was breaking up now under the strike of clubs, swords, and fists.

"You entertain me, lady. Now, what is your name?"

"Why don't you call me whatever you like since you seem to think you're a god."

"I am rather like one, aren't I? Fully in control of my fate despite setbacks. I am unbeatable even without the crown."

"Are you though? Because my mate isn't finished with this fight. I can promise you that."

He chuckled again—a disgusting sound that included a sort of wheeze—and led his men forward. Tahlia didn't tug at her captors, but instead, she let them carry her along, giving herself some rest. She'd be slipping away shortly and she needed the energy to run and climb.

"Well, if I am going to be your sweetheart, maybe you could give me some food? I'm starving."

"Of course!" Durniad smiled at her over his thick shoulder.

"You'll have everything you want. You'll be a queen. We will reign here on the off-seasons."

"Off-seasons of what?"

He lifted a hand. His sleeve fell back and a pirate's inking showed—this particular rendition being a skull and a sword. "Pirating, of course."

"Ah, yes. I forgot you don't restrict your arseholery to land-based situations."

"Such a naughty tongue."

"Please don't make a disgusting joke. That's such a droll, villain thing to do. Be more creative."

The madman's shoulders shook as he laughed. "I'll have to sharpen my wit for you, my dearest."

"Well, listen. This has been fun, but I have things to do and places to be."

Tahlia dropped her weight. The guards grunted and their holds on her arms loosened. She slammed her elbow into one guard's groin and spun to knee the other's stones. Whirling, she lunged away from them and the three who had been walking behind them. She smashed into the smaller of the three, sending him into the taller two, and then she was running.

Down the road. Through the guards beating the hells out of the crowd. Around a cluster of angry men and women brandishing kitchen cutlery at Durniad's men.

"Keep that up!" she shouted, trying to encourage them. "I'll come back with a dragon or two and help you out!"

They cheered her as she climbed a downspout and headed for the rooftops. The sun blazed onto her head as she jumped from building to building. Shouting erupted from the streets she leapt over. More guards. The city walls were only three roofs away. She could do this. She'd climb down the walls, fight whom she had to, then run into the forest and find Marius and Ragewing. Unless they found her first, which would be even better because that would mean Ragewing was patched up enough to fly them to the Witch's house to deliver the crown and end this wild mission.

With the last big jump, Tahlia landed on the city's three-Fae-wide protective wall. She smiled, hope making her feel like she could best ten of these guards with one hand tied behind her back.

Twisting, she fell from the wall and darkness swept over her before she could see what had struck her.

CHAPTER 28
MARIUS

Ragewing growled as Marius knotted up the sad excuse for a bandage on the top of the dragon's wound. He'd been forced to use the bottom half of his trousers and part of the leather strap that usually stretched over Ragewing's shoulders as an additional part of his rein system.

Not so tight, Ragewing hissed inside Marius's head.

It must be so you can fly back and not risk bleeding out.

Rider, I can't fly into Midhampton to rescue Lady Tahlia and you know it. As much as I wish I could, they will have me down and we will only end up giving them more captives.

We must. I'm sorry, but we must. They'll kill her. Marius's entire body hummed with pent-up violence. It was unthinkable what that madman might be doing to her. If she'd even survived the fall. No, he couldn't imagine she wasn't alive. If he did, he'd go as mad as Durniad.

They won't.

You don't know that.

She's a valued member of the Fae realm. Durniad knows not to risk angering King Lysanael and Queen Revna.

Does he? Because he spends his autumns ravaging the northern coast. His pirate crews have led attacks that we have fought against, Ragewing. He is not cowed by anything even if it would be wise to back down.

This is different. He is greedy. We know that. He will want to use Lady Tahlia's life to get something from the king and queen. And perhaps from his human high queen as well, if he can work an angle that makes sense.

Marius fisted his hands so tightly that his knuckles cracked.

You'll break a fang if you grit your teeth like that.

Glaring at the dragon, Marius battled the impotent rage storming inside his heart and soul and mind.

Breathe, rider. Breathe and think. Be cold. Store the anger for later and plot. You can do this. I'm with you.

His mind whirled, panic lancing through his thought processes, jumbling potential plans with random imaginings of ripping Durniad's head from his body. He closed his eyes and set a hand on Ragewing. The dragon's side moved steadily in and out as he breathed, and Marius matched the rhythm, inhaling and exhaling slowly.

What do we have to use? Ragewing's question was quiet and calm. *Materials. Allies. Environment.*

The crown. Two blades at my belt. Our main contact is likely stuck in the city, but perhaps he'll be able to do something to help Lady Tahlia. We have your fire if we can get you into the air for at least a little while. The Witch isn't too far for me to reach on foot if you must rest.

I can fly to the Witch's house. Will she help us? Ragewing shuffled his wings and adjusted the lay of his tail, wincing and flashing vicious white teeth.

I would think so. This is her queen's mission, after all.

But we have the crown already. Will she care that we left a knight behind?

She doesn't have to know we have the crown, Marius said. *The crown's power worked in two ways from what I saw in the city. If a human is within earshot, they can be heavily influenced. And the influence seems to spread like an illness, catching from one to the next.*

The magic most likely manipulates a person's energy, then, Ragewing said.

I'm not sure I fully understand any of its magic.

Ragewing let out a plume of fire smoke, which he often did when thinking. *Me neither.*

Let's say I enter the city again using the crown to control the humans as I go, Marius said.

Ragewing's body was very warm, as if he was ready to breathe fire. *Will it matter if they stop up their ears? Because I would assume Durniad will be giving orders to do that if it blocks the crown's influence.*

Marius nodded. *I think that would keep the crown's magic from working except in those cases when it already has a human under its control and that human nears the one with stopped-up ears. The virus, so to speak, of the crown's control would spread regardless.*

So stealth would be in order. Durniad could hurt Lady Tahlia if he sees you coming.

Yes, Marius said, *We would have to attempt to sneak in again without being recognized...*

Ragewing grunted and shifted his weight, adjusting the way he rested on the ground. *But you don't have any more of the Witch's potion to disguise yourself.*

No. Let's visit her and see if she will help us once more. We'll pretend we don't have the crown.

Perhaps you should hide the crown here somewhere, Ragewing said, *so you can deceive her more easily since you truly won't have the crown in hand.*

Good idea. But I think I'll simply hide it outside the Witch's house. I don't like the thought of leaving this powerful artifact unguarded here in the woods.

He unbuckled his belt, slipped the leather through the artifact, then put the belt back on, securing the crown to himself. He could remove it upon arrival and hide it in the greenery near the Witch's abode.

CHAPTER 29
TAHLIA

Tahlia opened her eyes for the third time since she'd fallen from the city wall. This time she was less dead so she actually felt the injury in her side.

"Ugh. Kill me."

The room was bright because the evil sun was shining through a high window. A bandage wrapped around her torso, a bit of blood staining the linen.

A female human approached the cot she was resting on. "Never saw someone with Fae blood heal in front of my eyes. Amazing."

"Glad to entertain. Why don't you stab me with another little something and we can both enjoy the power of magic all over again?"

"Oooh, would you be willing?"

"Kidding, woman. I was kidding."

She bit her lip and had the grace to look ashamed. Gods, Tahlia wouldn't be able to murder her in order to escape. She was too sweet.

"Is Durniad around? Where exactly am I? What happened?"

"You were shot with an arrow. It didn't pierce anything important."

"I count skin as important."

"Ah." She shook her head like Tahlia was silly. "King Durniad will be here shortly. You're in his fortress."

"The same place where he stashed that horrible crown and tried to kill me the first time?"

"Probably, yes, although I wasn't privy to all of that business," she said chirpily.

Tahlia shut her eyes. She definitely hadn't healed fully in front of this woman's eyes because with every heartbeat, pain lashed at her side.

"Tons of guards outside, huh?" Tahlia asked, hoping to tease some information from the Healer.

"Of course. The king wants you to stay put on account of your upcoming nuptials."

"You think I should marry him?"

The Healer glanced at the closed door and grimaced. "No. I do not."

Tahlia snorted. "Great. Then can you help me escape?"

"I wish. But I just landed this job. I used to be a tanner's wife."

"You left him?"

She grinned widely. "He died."

Tahlia laughed. "I guess he deserves that vicious joy on your face?"

"Completely."

"You remind me of my friend, Fara. She's a Healer too. Maybe a person has to be vicious to sew folks up all day."

"You do, yes. Or you'd be weeping or puking or both during every shift."

Tahlia nodded. "Now, about that escape..."

"I could look away maybe while you check out the window up there..." The Healer raised her pale eyebrows.

Tahlia twisted, wincing, and eyed the window in question. "It's forty feet up with nothing to climb to get there."

"But you're half-Fae."

"I hate to burst your bubble, but we can't leap that high. At least, I can't."

"Too bad your dragon isn't here. I heard you're a Mist Knight of the Shrouded Mountains."

Of course she knew who they were. Ragewing had completed their already-pretty-much-blown cover situation. King Lysanael was not going to be best pleased. But Tahlia wasn't going to worry about any of that until she got out of here still breathing.

"What about that door there?" Tahlia jerked her chin at a slender wooden door in the corner of the room.

"That's a privy."

"Perfect." It would dump into a body of water, hopefully.

The Healer helped her up and walked her to the door. "I'll leave you to it unless you call out, all right?"

Nodding, Tahlia entered the privy. This wasn't going to be fun.

"I hope the humans and Fae alike appreciate my sacrifice here."

They had managed to take the crown from Durniad. The mission was at least successful in that regard. Marius would try to come back for her. She had no doubt about that, but would he have any support? They'd already created a fantastic mess and sending someone back in would only make more waves. The human high queen and her regent didn't want this snatch-and-grab job to point to them at all. So perhaps it would make sense to return and rescue her so Durniad wouldn't have her to question?

Well, Tahlia wasn't waiting on Marius. She was leaving. Now.

Even if she had to deal with a privy.

She lifted the wooden seat and squinted through the hole carved into the stone floor. Several stories down, a narrow river ran quickly along the fortress's base, no doubt heading for the sea. She blew out a breath. Could she fit through that hole? Would she break her body further if she landed wrong? Lots of questions. No answers. And she wouldn't figure it out mulling about in here.

Wishing she had her boots and bemoaning the fact that they'd stripped her of her weapons belt, she sat backwards on the privy's seat, held her feet together, then launched herself down, down, down.

The carved hole out of the fortress hit her spine as she fell awkwardly. Pain shook her and she tried to straighten her legs again, working her position so she'd land feet first in the water.

The river's embrace wasn't for the faint of heart. The cold and the strike of the surface made her cry out in agony, her side flaring with pain and her back shrieking with what was going to be a mighty bruise. Carrying her past the fortress, the river gurgled around her ears. She spread her arms wide to keep her head above water.

She could practically hear Fara's voice in her head.

Can't believe you jumped into a privy and the refuse river with a hole in your side? And how many times have you fallen through the air today alone? You truly do want to perish horribly, don't you?

Tahlia's thoughts tumbled along with the river, her cheeks flushing though her body was cold from the water. She hoped she wouldn't be suddenly dumped into the sea. She'd really had quite enough of the ocean for the time being.

The river widened and shallowed. She swam toward the edge. A stand of trees blocked this part of the river from the city streets beyond. No one was around. Finally, she was having some good luck. With shaking legs, she lumbered out of the water.

Her nose caught the scent of something familiar. She looked up into Durniad's smiling face.

"Damn it."

A FEW HOURS LATER, they had her rebandaged, dressed in a trailing pearl-colored gown, and standing beside Durniad at an altar dedicated to a goddess Tahlia knew nothing about. A man droned on about commitment and care, and she rolled her eyes for the ninth time.

"Remember," Durniad whispered, his lips at her ear. "Smile and do as you're told and you'll live. If not, I'll hand you over to my guards. I like to watch."

"Classy." She drew away from him.

A sneer curled his lip. "Say one more word like that. I dare you." His voice was barely audible. He gripped her hand and attempted to crush her fingers.

He wasn't nearly as strong as he believed himself to be.

Well, the plan now was *murder*. She'd end this fool's life tonight in their wedding chamber and it would be a good deed done for anyone and everyone he'd ever met. Forget the human and Fae relations, screw the agreement between King Lysanael and the human high queen. Tahlia had had enough. She'd spit this monster like the pig that he was, then fight her way out of the fortress. Maybe Marius would show up at some point and help out. Maybe not. But no matter what, she wasn't giving in to this idiot.

CHAPTER 30
MARIUS

Ragewing flew over a forested stretch of land between Midhampton and the Witch's house. Marius breathed in the cool evening air. He turned to check Ragewing's bandaged tail. Some would think the injury wasn't as serious being near the end of his tail rather than higher up, but that wasn't true at all. The tip of a dragon's tail helped them cut the air and steer their way through the wind currents. Every part of Ragewing worked to make him deadly in the sky, able to turn tight arcs and whip around to fire on attackers. When one element of that flying system was disturbed, especially the tip of the tail, the dragon suffered in the area of agility, response time, and stamina.

Attempting to be more like Tahlia, Marius tried to think positively. Ragewing was flying steadily with no wobble or sense of pain through the bond. He was quiet, but he usually was. Nothing out of the ordinary there. He didn't speak to Marius unless he had something important to say. Marius respected that.

They soared over a cluster of sycamores that waved their branches in the gusty breeze.

I smell a dragon.

Marius's body coiled, ready to take action. *Where?* He wished he had more than just a couple of blades.

I can't see him, but he's there. I sense his presence and his scent is reminiscent of the Gwerhune.

That was King Lysanael's forest, the wood that lay south of Caer Du.

A dark shape materialized about one hundred yards away. Ragewing snarled and let out a warning shower of sparks. It was a forest dragon—black in color and capable of an invisibility glamour. On the dragon's back, Queen Revna lifted a hand in greeting.

"My lady queen!" Marius echoed the gesture and tapped Ragewing, asking him to land.

Ragewing and Arkyn, the queen's forest dragon, flew in descending circles until they landed in a small clearing dotted with gold and red mushrooms.

Ragewing bowed his head to the queen as Marius dismounted.

Marius bowed low. "To what do we owe this meeting, my queen?"

She hopped from her smaller dragon and gave him a smile. Queen Revna's smiles were honestly a bit frightening. She had Berserker blood from Fjordbok and had worked as the human king's assassin before meeting Fae King Lysanael. It was a romantic story that even the cold-hearted could be swept up in.

The queen's ice-blue eyes studied him. "Please, stand, Commander Marius."

He did so, and Ragewing rested on his haunches beside him.

"Your contact from Midhampton sent a message via his trained raven. You've made a mess of this mission, you know."

"I apologize. It has been challenging to say the least. Durniad has taken Lady Tahlia captive." Marius kept his features blank, trying for professionalism even though he longed to tear the damned world apart for his mate.

Queen Revna's lip curled. She was human, so she had no fangs to bear, but she'd obviously picked up the mannerism from King

Lysanael. "That man needs to die. I will go with you back to Midhampton and we'll use Arkyn's invisibility to enter the city. You are still in possession of the Crown of Minds, yes?"

Marius nodded and took the crown from where he'd buckled it onto the back of his belt. He offered it to her.

"No, you keep it," the queen said. "I'd rather not have something on my head that I can drop while fighting or flying. Being Fae, you have better reflexes than me. We can infiltrate the city, and while we remain invisible, we can use the crown to covertly retrieve Lady Tahlia. By the way, you're handling this with surprising self-control. Lys would be frothing."

Ragewing grumbled quietly and Marius set a hand on his side.

"Oh, I am internally frothing, my queen," Marius said. "Unless you order me not to, I will kill Durniad."

The queen's eyes softened as if she could empathize with his protective feelings. But only a former assassin would give him that look when chatting about murder.

"I'm fine with it," she said, "but you must make it look like a heart attack or an accident. And Lysanael can't know about it. He must be free of any responsibility of this mess due to the agreement."

"Understood."

"Lady Tahlia won't talk under duress, correct?" the queen asked. "She's been trained?"

"She has. And she is the bravest female I know."

The queen smiled, and this time it was less frightening and more a show of genuine approval. "She certainly impressed me when she faced that Green-flanked Terror."

Marius bowed his head. "I will pass on your praise when we have her safe with us."

"Do you know where they are holding her?"

"My only guess would be the fortress, but where within its walls, I don't know."

"What is your protocol in these cases?"

"The captured knight will attempt to reach open air to prepare for rescue. We aim for balconies, rooftops... That sort of thing."

Hands on hips, Queen Revna nodded. She tapped one finger against her hip, thinking. "All right. We fly toward the fortress. I've seen a map and shared it with Arkyn, so we should be good to go. We'll circle three times to seek her out. If we don't find her that way, we will land on the rooftop and come up with the next plan based on the level of security on the grounds."

It was wonderful having a queen that knew how to handle a situation such as this. Queen Revna was no spoiled royal, raised simply to dance and embroider. She was a warrior queen with a vicious and strategic mind.

"How close must Ragewing and I stay to Arkyn for the glamour to cover us?" he asked.

"If he's feeling strong, you're fine to fly beside us at a comfortable position. He's grown stronger with the care he's received in the time I've been queen. If he is injured, or if we continue on for over two hours, you'll need to be closer. Fly right beside, above, or below us as best you can." The queen leaned over to eye Ragewing's tail, and her brow knitted. "Is he injured?"

"Yes. Durniad has a ballista and a bolt nipped the top end of his tail. He was bleeding pretty badly, but thankfully, the wound has clotted. He isn't at full strength or agility, but he's close to it."

And I wouldn't let you do this without me, Ragewing said into Marius's mind.

Marius glanced at Ragewing, who was giving him a loaded look that said *do not underestimate me.*

Even wounded, you remain the most powerful dragon in the world, my friend.

Correct.

Marius wanted to grin, but his heart ached too much for Tahlia, for the chance to eviscerate Durniad for daring to set a finger on her.

"A ballista? You mean a large crossbow-type weapon?" the queen asked.

"Aye, my queen."

Grimacing in Arkyn's direction, she sucked air through her teeth. "Hope you're ready for this, pal," she said to the black dragon.

Arkyn huffed and raised his head high as if insulted she would even ask. She rolled her eyes and rubbed the smooth scales under his chin.

"All right, I think we are good to move on," she said.

Marius's frustration and anxiety over Tahlia eased somewhat as they flew, fully invisible to all, toward Midhampton's walls. The heat of Ragewing's body and the familiar feel of riding the wind calmed and cleared Marius's head. Even though they were invisible, Marius could see the others as usual.

A fog rolled in from the direction of the ocean. The blanket of ghostly white reached them, blocking Queen Revna and Arkyn from view.

Don't worry, Ragewing said. *I have their scent. We remain within the boundary.*

The city appeared out of the night's fog like a beast waiting to spring. Not one, but three ballistae stood on the walls, bolts loaded into place and three men at each one. The weapon in the middle swiveled suddenly, turning so that it pointed over the city itself instead of at the forest.

They would have to watch for them from every aerial direction.

We're coming, Tahlia. Marius wished for the hundredth time that he could communicate with his mate the same way he could with Ragewing. *Hold on, little salty.*

CHAPTER 31
TAHLIA

Tahlia followed Durniad into his bedchamber. A massive bed with curtains occupied the far wall. A table stood to the left of the door, wine pitcher and goblets readied for them. Woven in yellows and blues, a circular carpet covered the wide floor planks. Beside the bed, three windows looked out on the courtyard. A downspout ran along the left side of the window that hung closest to the large bed.

The guards shut the bedchamber door, leaving Tahlia alone with Durniad. Yet another mistake on their part. The first error they'd made was allowing her to take a quiet moment in the feasting hall before the guests arrived after the ceremony. She'd stashed a nice little eating knife between her breasts.

Durniad faced the tray sitting on the side table. "Would you like a glass of wine, my bride?"

"So many glasses." Tahlia removed the elaborate veil Durniad's assigned handmaidens had braided into her hair. Tossing it onto the floor, she drew Durniad's attention away from her, then she pulled out the knife. Keeping her hand against her side—the side facing away from Durniad—she held the weapon flush against her wrist with the hilt in the palm of her hand.

Durniad turned and handed her some wine. She took it and drank it down in one go. The burn was lovely. He finished his, his gaze roaming about her face and body, then set both their glasses back on the tray.

"Do not fight me, Alanna."

"That isn't my name."

"I have decided it is." His tone was brusque. He appeared to have mastered his impatience since their earlier spat, but the pulsing vein on the side of his forehead said his calm wouldn't last. "This is all very simple. Do as I say, and you'll live as a queen. I will treat you with care and appreciation."

"As long as I go by the name you prefer," she said. If she could get him to rush her, his weight alone would help her pierce his chest or throat.

He sniffed and studied her face like he was trying to read her intentions. "And do exactly as I instruct. I won't bother you often. I am a busy man."

"Busy claiming titles and tyranting along the coastline?"

His eyes narrowed, and that vein grew even more pronounced. "I don't believe *tyranting* is a word."

"If you get to make up names, I get to make up verbs."

"Kiss me, my bride. Kiss me, and let your new life begin. Or you can try to stab me with that little knife of yours and die trying."

So he had noticed. Hmm. He didn't attempt to disarm her, so she decided to move the conversation for the moment.

"How are you going to get the crown back?" she asked. "Or do you not really need it?"

His face flushed, and the vein practically waved at Tahlia. *Ew.*

"I will make a plan to retrieve the crown from that monster as soon I as receive word from my allies. Tell me where he will take the crown and I'll see to it that you have free time every day to walk wherever you please."

"I assume he'll destroy the crown the moment he is able."

Some of Durniad's bravado slipped as his eyes bugged out. "What?"

"He's not like you."

"What do you mean?"

She shrugged, her heart beating quickly now. "He's not attempting to be a god."

"Then he's a fool."

"Who are your allies?" Steeling herself for what was about to happen, she worked to even her breathing.

Durniad drew his fingertips along Tahlia's collarbone. She fought the urge to puke the wine he'd given her right back at him. Maybe later.

"Well, Alanna, my allies are many. First, we have the Witch. Ah, I see you know of her. Of course you do. Yes, she is on my payroll. The Eelsmen are another ally in my pocket."

Tahlia swallowed a bitter taste on the back of her tongue. The Eelsmen were a group of northern pirates known for the way they used prisoners as bait for the midsized kraken they caught for prize money.

"I also have a group of wild Fae working for me in your Fae king's forest. They're just there to stir up trouble and cause distractions."

"I have bad news for you on that one."

He frowned and ran a finger down her arm, toward the hand holding the knife. "Explain."

Tahlia grimaced. "Unfortunately, we set them all on fire."

"You did what?"

"With our dragons. You do remember the dragon element to this whole equation, right?"

His face went purple, and his hands went for her throat. Bracing her feet firmly on the floor for balance, she jabbed the knife between his ribs. He dropped to the floor, gasping and yanking on her dress.

He tried to yell, but she had nipped him in the lung. "Guards! Please..."

"My name is Tahlia, you prickbrain," she said as she flipped the knife and dragged it across his throat.

The door burst open, and five guards spilled in. Tahlia turned and ran for the windows, wishing she wasn't wearing a damn dress even though it was actually very pretty.

One thought spun through her mind as she balled up the skirt of her dress and punched through the window glass. She'd killed yet another person and she was totally fine with it. She climbed out the window while the guards shouted and followed. Well, that bastard deserved death as much as the pillaging thieves in the Gwerhune and Ophelia had, and she wasn't about to waste any energy on being upset about spilling his blood.

CHAPTER 32
MARIUS

Marius glanced at Queen Revna and Arkyn. The evening fog swirled around the black dragon's wings and the tiled roofs they flew over.

I realize we are unseen, but can they not hear us, rider?

Ragewing tipped to the right to avoid clipping a pointed tower that appeared to have some ritual purpose. The humans were gathering at its base with candles and were singing in a melody that brought to mind promises and the length of a life.

They were singing of a bonding.

Marius's stomach turned and he squeezed his eyes shut. The city was celebrating the wedding of Durniad and Tahlia.

And suddenly, Marius felt as if he was a living flame, roaring heat rising from the tips of his toes to the tips of his pointed ears. There was no word for the level of this righteous anger. For this outrage. The way he felt could only be encapsulated in a tremendous warning snarl, a sound he could not make at the moment. He would ruin their covert entry and only lessen the chances he could rescue his mate.

Breathe, rider, Ragewing whispered into his mind. *We will have her with us soon and Durniad will be dead, his blood easing the pain in your soul.*

Marius wanted to thank Ragewing, but gratitude was as amorphous as the fog. He couldn't grasp it to pass it on and so he just held to his dragon and leaned into the fact that they were bonded and Ragewing knew exactly how Marius was feeling.

When they reached the fortress, Marius waved a hand at the queen and pointed to the structure. Bowers of dark greenery showed between the plumes of wispy cloud. The humans had decorated the structure for the wedding, stretching lengths of braided flowers and leafy branches from window to window. Banners of bright red matched the festival's last tomato remnants on the cobbled streets below. To think he and Tahlia had laughed together not that long ago. It felt like a lifetime had passed. Each moment she was inside that fortress with a male who believed himself mated to her was another lifetime again.

Damn this fog! He was fairly certain Tahlia wasn't on any of the window balconies or on the roof. But could he be sure?

Queen Revna motioned for them to circle the rooftop again and Ragewing followed orders.

Marius shut his eyes and inhaled deeply, seeking his mate's beautiful scent, but it wasn't there. The fishy odor of the river, the refuse of a large population, and the soft aroma of the flowers and greenery were the only scents floating through the mist.

A crash sounded, glass catching the scant moonlight as it flew outward from an upper-floor window.

There! Marius shouted into Ragewing's mind. *Hold!*

Ragewing hovered and Arkyn did likewise beside them. A figure in a dress appeared on the downspout, then crawled over the lip of the roof to stand on the slant of rounded tiles.

Her scent was both a balm to Marius's heart and a fuel to the fire eating him alive.

Tahlia lifted her chin, looking for them. She slipped, her skirts flipped up on one side.

Marius's heart stopped.

As she tried to right herself, her foot shot out. She grabbed the tiles with a hand and stood again.

He exhaled, his head swimming. "Hold out your hand!" Marius shouted.

She started in surprise, then did as he asked, holding her arm out straight and bending her knees. Though she had to be wondering how they'd managed to be invisible, she knew what they would attempt.

Guards climbed the downspout as Tahlia had. They would be within reach of her in seconds.

Go, please, as we have practiced, Marius said to Ragewing.

The scent of blood rose in Marius's nostrils and he gritted his teeth. His mind was a whirlpool. He couldn't smooth the path of his thoughts.

Ragewing and Arkyn rose up, then swooped low to circle tightly around the fortress's roof.

Marius leaned as far as he was able down Ragewing's side, then he gripped Tahlia's upper arm while she took hold of his. He helped her scramble up behind him, and the sound of fabric ripping found his ears as she settled in the back section of the saddle.

"Whose blood is it?" He inhaled her scent.

"Take a guess," she whispered, her tone bright.

He smiled as the fire that had been consuming him eased into a delightful warmth. "Spoken like a seasoned Mist Knight." He reached down, grabbed one of her hands from his waist, then kissed her knuckles as they flew toward the city walls. "Whether King Lysanael agrees or not, you have done your human side a great favor in ridding this city of that vile soul."

She sat up suddenly, and the hair that had fallen from her intricate braids whipped forward in the chaotic wind from Ragewing's wings. He glanced at her. Her gaze was pinned to Queen Revna and Arkyn.

"Her dragon is the reason we are all invisible, right? Not a Witch's spell?"

"Yes. This is Arkyn's magic."

Lifting her shoulders, she wiggled, which did delightful albeit inconvenient things to his body. "How exciting!" She clamped her hand over her mouth.

They kept their voices quiet as they soared over the moonlit city. Though they couldn't be seen, they could still be heard.

"Before I escorted Durniad's sorry arse to the afterlife," Tahlia murmured, "he claimed to be in league with the Witch herself as well as the Eelsmen."

"I seriously doubt the Witch would give him the time of day. But the Eelsmen..." He grunted, thinking. "We'll deal with them in the next moon. It matters little whom he was in league with anyway since he is gone."

"So are you finally finished loathing humans?"

The hesitation in her voice punched a hole in his heart. "I don't loathe everyone in Midhampton and I certainly don't loathe you."

She held him tightly, and her body moved as she took a deep breath. "Well, I am glad to hear my mate doesn't hate me."

The tear in his heart ripped open further. He took her hand again and nipped at her palm. "You know what I mean." Gods, she smelled wonderful, and he couldn't wait to ravish her properly.

Through the plumes of mist, the ballistae on the city walls whipped around to face them. Those manning the weapons looked around like their heads were on swivels, so Marius was fairly certain they remained invisible.

Queen Revna eyed Marius and pointed up.

Ragewing, prep for a launch.

On it.

CHAPTER 33
TAHLIA

Ragewing shot toward the very moon itself and Tahlia nearly swallowed her brains. The queen's black dragon did likewise—the flying part, not the brain eating—assumably because remaining close kept them all invisible and they needed to get out of range of the ballistae. The cool night air bit at Tahlia's cheeks and she grinned widely, restraining herself from whooping with joy.

The dragons leveled out until the city was a fogged gathering of stone that appeared to be the size of a fisted hand. They flew quickly past the walls and over the nearby forest.

"We are visible now!" Queen Revna shouted over the wind, her words barely audible.

Tahlia knew how that felt. Their voices weren't powerful like Marius's and the other Mist Knights.

"To the Witch's abode, my lady queen?" Marius asked, using said Mistgold blood power.

She nodded, and the dragons flew onward into the night. Tahlia couldn't decide what was more exciting: Marius's divine body against hers—she shivered with delight as he gripped her thigh with one of his perfectly large hands; the success of their mission—if one didn't fret overmuch about the murdering; or the fact that the Witch was now responsible for healing Lija and soon she'd be in the skies with Tahlia, flying high and heading for battles with pirates.

"How much trouble will I be in for killing Durniad?"

"No more than Ragewing and I will be for exposing our identities."

"I hope we get to share a dungeon cell at least." Tahlia slid a hand over Marius's leg and stroked the inner side of his powerful thigh. Oooh, she loved those thighs.

Marius growled low in his throat, the sound he made when pleased but also not able to approve. It was one of her favorite sounds.

AT THE WITCH'S HOUSE, Ragewing and Arkyn landed. The queen remained on her dragon's back, but Marius dismounted and bowed. Tahlia followed, taking Marius's hand. An owl hooted from the peaked roof of the Witch's abode, and a chill ran over Tahlia's back. She ripped off the remainder of the dress's skirts, glad that she'd slipped some loose sleeping trousers underneath before she'd been "married" to Durniad.

Queen Revna cleared her throat and looked around, as if she was expecting someone. "Well, this is where I leave you. I was never here. You never saw me," the queen said quietly, and then she and her forest dragon flew away.

The branches of the oaks overhanging the Witch's house waved in the wind of Arkyn's wings. Marius looked at Tahlia; he was chewing the inside of his cheek as if deep in thought.

"What was that all about?" Tahlia whispered.

Marius grumbled. "She was helping us in an unofficial capacity, so we must pretend that she never did. We'll give the crown to the king. He doesn't need to know details."

He unbuckled his belt and handed her the crown. It was invisible in spots; the Witch's concoction was wearing off.

"But we will have to tell him that we killed Durniad, right?" She turned the crown over in her hands, studying its shine and weight. "And that the humans saw Ragewing."

"I suppose so," Marius said. "We wouldn't want to hold anything back that would come out later. They need to know a portion of the challenges we encountered and the changes in plan we were forced to enact."

As they approached the Witch's door, the heavy piece of oak and metal swung open on its own. Tahlia leaned around Marius to look at the strange blue lighting of the house as she trailed him inside. The Witch and King Lysanael stood at a cauldron in the center of the room. Sparks flicked from the black pot like little stars. Scary little stars.

Tahlia bowed and Marius joined her in the movement. The whole place smelled like danger, and it did absolutely nothing to soothe Tahlia's nerves.

Though this mission was over, it felt like a new one had already begun.

What would the king do when he found out that she and Marius had compromised information and pretty much negated the entire agreement? Could the king remove them from the order of the Mist Knights? Technically the king and queen were in charge of the order, even though he took little action in the day-to-day activities and lived far, far away from Dragon Tail Peak and the heart of the Mist Knights' operation. He could put them to death if he wanted to, but the king didn't seem like an unfair male.

Tahlia gulped and wiped sweating palms on her dress. She truly hoped her guess was accurate.

The Witch opened her mouth to speak, but King Lysanael cut her off. She gave him an irritated look, her eyebrows flicking together and her cloudy eyes darting left and right.

"Lady Tahlia," King Lysanael said, "I would like you to report in full what progressed in the city of Midhampton. I see that you have the crown."

Why was he asking her to report and not Marius? As Commander, Marius was the one responsible for reporting to the king. A thought shimmered through Tahlia's mind. Oh. It was the fact that she could lie. Though Queen Revna had acted as if the king knew nothing of their escapade, obviously the two were exchanging information of some sort. Perhaps the king was aware that some information would have to be altered or withheld. And so he had asked Tahlia, hoping she could do the job using the human half of her blood.

Hoping she was doing the right thing, she detailed most of the happenings, but left out pieces of the tale here and there to avoid angering the humans and the Witch who loved the human high queen like a daughter.

The back door of the Witch's house opened, and Tahlia thought Queen Revna had returned. But instead, a slight young girl who couldn't have been older than fifteen walked in. Behind her, a tall woman with silver-shot hair pulled tightly back and wrinkles at the edges of her eyes entered. This was the human high queen and her regent.

Marius inclined his head, not bowing as far as he did for King Lysanael, and Tahlia mimicked the movement. The Witch bowed to no one. The king nodded his head respectfully, a shallower nod than Marius's or Tahlia's.

"Thank you for saving my people," the young queen said.

Her voice was sweet with the newness of youth, but it was steady and strong and gave Tahlia the idea that someday she would be a good queen.

The regent merely pinched her lips together and glared at the king, Marius, and Tahlia in turn.

"And where is the crown?" the regent asked.

King Lysanael lifted it up. "Right here."

The regent's eyes glittered with the look of one plotting something unpleasant. "What are we planning to do with it?"

"Destroying it, as we discussed," the king said, his voice calm but packed with power.

Clasping her hands at her waist, the regent gave the young queen a simpering smile. "Are we sure that is the best course of action? With this crown, we could solve a great many of the world's problems."

"Could you?" the Witch asked, her voice haunting and quiet, though every ear heard it clearly, Tahlia was sure. Anytime the Witch spoke, it was like one had no choice but to listen.

The tension in the room increased so much that it almost felt as though the air buzzed. She blew out a breath, wishing she could tell a joke to lighten the mood.

King Lysanael handed the crown to the Witch. "Destroy it. Now. As we all agreed." He looked over his shoulder at the young queen, ignoring the regent entirely.

"Yes," the young queen said, not a quaver in a single syllable.

Tahlia liked her very much. She smiled at the queen and gave her a nod. The queen grinned back.

The Witch held the crown over the cauldron. "I prepared its destruction. Now, stand back."

She dropped the crown into the steaming mixture. Bright, green light flashed and Tahlia winced, shutting her eyes. When she opened them, red stars filled the air—pinpricks of floating lights that for some reason she didn't want anywhere near her. She shifted her feet to avoid one that floated near her shoulder.

The Witch chanted sounds that were likely magic words and the red stars stilled. The stars shot toward the cauldron. A crack sounded from the bowl's steaming depths. Tahlia held her ears as they rang.

The Witch eyed the cauldron, which had stopped steaming and was only popping lightly. "It is done."

The regent blew air through her nostrils and turned away, her jaw set, while the young queen nodded approvingly.

"Thank you, Witch," King Lysanael said. He turned to face the queen. "Now, I must relay some changes my knights had to make to the plan."

Tahlia stood straight as the king detailed the appearance of Ragewing, the town's response, and then finally, how Tahlia had been forced to kill Durniad.

"I will consider whatever corrections you have in mind to rectify the peace in your town of Midhampton. How can I help?" the king said, crossing his arms and giving the young queen an encouraging look.

The regent whispered into the young queen's ear, but she was foolish if she didn't think King Lysanael and Marius couldn't hear every word. Tahlia couldn't quite catch the whole statement, but she heard her name in there along with *donation*.

Shaking her head, the queen looked up at King Lysanael. "I'm glad to be done with Durniad. I will simply address the city and declare that we had an agreement with your kingdom. There will be rebellion because of it. A knot of folks there are staunchly set against the Fae. But I will deal with that. You have done us a great service, and I'm glad your knights and your dragon, Ragewing, weren't mortally harmed in the completion of this mission."

"How did you get Lady Tahlia out of the city after the killing?" the regent asked, nearly cutting off her queen.

Marius's eyebrow lifted. "If I may, King Lysanael?" he asked, wanting permission to address the regent.

Tahlia bit her lip. How was this going to go? Gods, she was sweating. She was a damned fountain.

King Lysanael nodded. "Of course, Commander Marius."

Marius spread his hands wide, palms up. "We were the recipients of luck, really."

He couldn't lie. How was he going to keep Queen Revna and Arkyn out of this tale? Why had he offered to speak up?

"A thick fog rolled in that night. Ragewing and I used the cover to evade the ballistae. As my king explained, Lady Tahlia had escaped the guards and climbed to the roof. We simply picked her up and fled before the fog had completely lifted."

"Luck." The queen grinned and studied his face. "A great tale for the ages. I look forward to sharing it with my children someday."

The regent glared but held her tongue.

Tahlia exhaled. Ah, the deceit of simple omission. Of course, Marius was wise enough to keep it simple. She was, once again, so incredibly grateful for him. And for Queen Revna, Arkyn, and Ragewing. She didn't want to imagine what would have happened to her if she'd been stuck in Midhampton with Durniad's blood on her hands. His guards hadn't just been city guards. They were pirates playing roles and Tahlia knew exactly how rough pirates played from the tales Titus and Maiwenn had told her.

"Will you tell me about the city's defenses?" the queen asked, eyeing Marius.

Marius looked to King Lysanael, who nodded. "Well, they have at least four ballista machines..."

He went on about the weapons, approximate numbers of guards, details on the city walls, and so forth.

One thing they hadn't brought up was Durniad's claim that he was allied with the Witch and with the Eelsmen of the North. The Witch didn't even flinch at the news of Durniad dying, so Tahlia doubted he had been telling the truth. Perhaps he had only said it to see how Tahlia would react considering he knew the Witch had dealings with the Fae from time to time.

Should she bring it up? Probably not. She fiddled with her ripped skirts as she pondered. Why didn't more of her Mist Knight training involve how to handle reporting like this? What if she got Marius into trouble by not mentioning Durniad's supposed enemies? Maybe she should just interject. Marius was about finished. She didn't want King Lysanael to mistake their silence on this for any sort of treasonous behavior.

"Also," she began.

Marius looked at her, his usual scowl not giving anything away. She hoped this was the right move.

Tahlia cleared her throat. "Durniad claimed to have allies in the Eelsmen of the North. He said he was in league with the Witch, too."

Marius's face went very blank, as if he was hiding how he felt about her reporting these details.

King Lysanael's mouth parted as if in shock. He whirled to face the Witch. He didn't approach her. His movements were stilted as if he was plenty wary of the scary lady.

"Can you explain Durniad's suggestion of your involvement?" he asked her.

"You have no right to question our Witch," the regent snapped.

The young queen looked from the regent to King Lysanael, obviously unsure on what to do.

The ceiling flickered with blue light, almost like lightning. "Are you accusing me of being disloyal to my queen?"

"You sided with us against her father not so long ago," King Lysanael said.

Tahlia remembered a bit about that story, about how the Witch had hidden the young queen from her father, who at the time had been king. That tale was tied into the one about how Queen Revna had met King Lysanael.

"I did so to protect souls that the former king had in his grip. That situation had changed and your Druid tested the truth of my heart. You recall that day, I'm certain, King Lysanael."

"I do. I wish our Druid was here to mediate."

The great Fae magician was very ill, or so the gossip said. He had once helped the Realm of Lights with many great tasks.

The queen clasped her hands in front of her. A large seal ring on her thumb reflected the light of the scones on the walls. "Well, I trust the Witch, and Durniad is dead, so what does it matter?"

"I suppose it doesn't," the king said quietly. "I offer my apologies, Witch, for questioning your loyalty to your queen."

"Thank you." The Witch watched the king with her haunted eyes. Could she truly see in the way those with normal eyes did?

"As for the Eelsmen," Marius said, watching the rulers as if he wasn't certain he was permitted to speak, "they likely have every criminal on every coastline at least halfway in their gold-heavy pockets, so that's nothing shocking."

Everyone agreed, and the Witch stepped forward. "If you are prepared to travel, I will meet you at Dragon Tail Peak in two days' time."

Would Ragewing take the Witch on his back too?

The Witch's head turned toward Tahlia, and Tahlia swallowed.

"I will travel by way of a portal created only for my body," the Witch said.

"Ah, magic. Of course," Tahlia said, then she buttoned her lip. She hadn't meant to speak that out loud.

The young queen grinned at Tahlia. Tahlia rolled her eyes at herself, which made the queen laugh out loud.

Tahlia wished she could tell Lija that they would be home soon, and the Witch would be showing up in some surely fantastic manner forthwith.

The mission was finally over. Hopefully, Lija would be flying within the next few days.

EPILOGUE

Tahlia

"Huzzah!" The hall echoed with the Mist Knights' cheers, the staff's praise, and the roar of the dragons gathered in the courtyard outside the open doors.

On the dais at the front of the hall, Fara and the two others who had tested alongside her raised the scrolls that named them official Healers of the Peak. Seated on one of the benches at the long, food-heavy tables, Tahlia shouted so ferociously that her throat burned. She didn't care. She couldn't have been happier.

Lady Fara looks five feet taller, Lija said into Tahlia's mind.

Tahlia turned on the bench to see Lija peering through the right-side doorway. *She does! Do you want one of these?* Tahlia lifted a pink crystal cake and wiggled it.

You know that I do, rider.

Tahlia chuckled. She jogged over to meet the dragon at the door. She held out the cake and Lija basically inhaled the sweet treat.

Marius stood beside Fara and Albus on the dais, his hands raised to quiet the chaos. "All right. That's enough. Now, eat the food you've been given and let's enjoy our pre-pirate raid rest period."

The crowd erupted in cheers once more. Plates and cups banged and clanked around the hall as toasts were made. Platters of rosemary roasted venison, pitchers of crystal wine, and deep bowls of noodles with cream sauce were passed from person to person.

Tahlia gave Lija a quick scratch under the chin, then returned to the benches to meet Fara for dining. Atticus was already there, as well as Enora and Justus. They toasted Fara again, also praising Tahlia for her secret mission work. Jokes were told, flirting commenced, and fun was had all around.

Fara gripped Tahlia's hand tightly. Her eyes shone with unshed tears. "Thank you for finishing up that secret mission nonsense and getting back here in time."

"I wouldn't have missed it for the world."

"Unless you had contracted an ague or even the plague." Fara's face fell. "I forgot to ask. You did avoid drinking that human water, right?"

"Shh, you're not supposed to know we were beyond the Veil."

"Whatever. Tell me. I need to know." Fara lifted Tahlia's chin and examined her throat. "Your lymph nodes might be swollen." She prodded her throat roughly and Tahlia coughed and pushed Fara's hands away.

"Well, they are now anyway. Leave me alone. I'm perfectly fine."

"Except for your weird Weaver scar."

"It's great actually. Now I'll never lose the belt. It's part of me."

"Has your magic returned in full?"

"As of this morning. I think I just needed a good night's rest inside the Veil's range."

Fara nodded, but her brow remained furrowed. "If you say so. But I think you should take some time with the crystals and Lija. We have yet to determine how much they can heal a Fae, but they do improve mental clarity and energy levels. We tested it!"

She shoved a sage-green cake into her mouth and kept on talking. Titus, Ewan, Claudia, and Maiwenn found seats nearby. They began discussing the coming trip north.

"Tahlia, you ready for another adventure or do you need some more of Maiwenn's greenblood?"

Tahlia pretended to be choking. "Yeah, no. I'm good to go when it's time without any of that poison, thanks very much."

Titus snorted a laugh and began rolling dice while the others talked about potential pirate landing spots.

"Care for a midnight flight?" a deep voice said behind Tahlia.

She shivered with delight and turned to see Marius looking down at her with eyes that promised more than flying. He wore a black tunic that matched the inkings that peeked from the neckline and over one shoulder. His trousers were tucked into the soft boots he preferred when they weren't on a mission or training, and he wore a braided belt with one small dagger sheathed near the brass buckle. Scowling, he tucked a hair behind her ear and she swallowed, heat already pooling low in her belly. His jaw flexed as he took her in, his gaze like a hand smoothing down the side of her neck to her breasts. Her body pulsed with want. Gods, the way he could affect her with just a look...

"Fara, I'll see you in the morning. All right?"

Fara nodded, waving an icing-covered hand at her, then continuing her line of questioning aimed at Ewan. "But don't you think you need a Healer with your units?"

"You'll fall off during fighting."

"I'll show you falling off." Fara started toward Ewan, and

Tahlia started to grab her arm to hold her back, but Maiwenn stepped in and snagged the back of Fara's tunic.

"I've got this, Tahl. Enjoy your time off," Maiwenn said.

Tahlia gave her a smile. "Thanks."

THE NIGHT WAS clear and absolutely bursting with stars. Lija spread her four wings wide and soared above Ragewing. Marius glanced up their way and Tahlia's heart sputtered as she imagined what might be going through his mind at the moment.

Lija made a content, rumbling sound deep in her belly, which vibrated through Tahlia.

Ah. I'm finally myself again, the dragon said into Tahlia's mind.

Tahlia leaned forward in the saddle and ran a hand down Lija's neck. *I'm so relieved. I was truly worried about you.*

I was worried too.

It's brave of you to admit it. Normally, dragons were too arrogant to be open about their feelings of vulnerability. It was a rare feeling for them in general, so they had little practice.

That Witch stank of Unseelie power, but I can't say I'm not eternally grateful.

Tahlia huffed a laugh. *I was glad to see her go. I don't think she likes Fae or dragons, honestly.*

No, she does not. But at least she honored her word and healed me when others could not.

Agreed.

Ragewing said he would like to drop you and Commander Marius at the Starwing Cave while we fly over Goblin's Pass.

He always wants to see the most barren of places.

Lija laughed. *He likes the dramatic vistas.*

You don't mind?

No, because right after we're going to swim at Steaming Aspen.

Steaming Aspen was a high mountain lake fed partially by hot springs, so it remained unfrozen year-round. *Oooh, that will be fun. You'll have to take me next time.*

Will do, rider.

Lija and Ragewing swooped low over the gray pebbles that marked the path up to Starwing Cave, a popular spot for mated Fae to visit on special evenings, and soon Marius and Tahlia were hand in hand on the ground.

They watched their dragons soar into the stars.

"She's doing very well. I'd have thought she'd be too fatigued for such an adventure tonight," Marius said. His thumb rubbed the knuckle of her forefinger, and she felt like a fool with how the simple act made her cheeks heat.

"She's the best."

Marius chuckled in full then, a rare and lovely sound that she treasured.

"Is this your first time here?" he asked as they walked under a low arch of stone and into the cave.

It was oddly warm for a cave. She parted her lips to answer, but no sound came. The cave sparkled with teal, rose, and golden light.

"They're butterflies!"

The luminescent creatures fluttered along every inch of the rough stone walls, their light reflected in the occasional puddle of snowmelt.

"They come here to rest before finishing their migration south for the winter. The magma inside this peak runs close to the floor of this cave and so the area remains far warmer than the outside."

Tahlia let go of his hand and spun, taking it all in. "It's absolutely beautiful."

Marius walked ahead of her, then he stopped and gestured to a tumble of smooth rocks. Golden moss cloaked the ancient stones, and runes had been carved into the base of them.

"What is this all about?" She touched one of the runes and a shiver of magic danced up her arm. The threads she sometimes saw with her Weaver magic became clear, connecting the runes to one another, to the butterflies, and to Marius and her.

"They're blessing runes. Nothing too powerful, but set here long ago by the gods as a gift to Fae couples. Come," he said, holding out his hand.

She took it and he drew her to him as he sat on one of the mossy stones. She straddled him and bit her lip at how happy he already was to be here with her.

Shifting her hips, she pressed into him. A jolt of sheer pleasure made her gasp. "I see you have more than sightseeing on your mind, Commander."

He smoothed her hair away from her shoulders and began nibbling her neck. His body was so warm and her core pulsed with want.

"You are an astute observer, Lady of the Skies."

His tongue flicked over her collarbone, and he gripped her hips, easing her more firmly against him. He raised his hips and pleasure rode across Tahlia's center. She exhaled next to his ear and he snarled lightly into the space under her jaw.

"I want to see how little movement it takes to satisfy you," he said, his voice incredibly deep and gruff, as if he was having a difficult time controlling himself.

She was panting, and honestly, she didn't care how easily he aroused her. It was fantastic. "That's just mean," she said breathily, teasing.

He licked her throat in one great sweep, but he refused to move even as she wiggled in the vise of his hands on her hips. Again, he licked her—this time over the hollow in her throat while he growled possessively. The feeling of his tongue, his chest vibrating with his growling, and his cock so hard on her most sensitive spot were too much. She dug her fingers into his shoulders and rocked against him. Desire grabbed hold of her and shook her hard. Exquisite pleasure burst from her core, then outward.

"Now," she said, catching her breath and trembling, "this time you need to earn that."

He took a fistful of her tangled hair and chuckled into her temple. "As you say, my lady."

Drawing her tunic off, he dusted her with kiss after kiss. With slow and careful movements, he eased her onto her back. The moss was soft and smelled faintly sweet like jasmine and vanilla. She let him disrobe her completely, and once they were both unclothed, he lay on top of her and kissed her thoroughly. The way he moved his mouth over hers and how now and then he bit at her chin and lower lip with his fangs... Ah, it was perfection. She was swirling with desire, completely drunk with it by the time his hand slid down her stomach to cup her right where she wanted him to. His fingers knew exactly how to draw pleasure from her as he slowly increased the speed and enthusiasm of his stroking and pressing and rubbing. She was delirious with it and moaned his name, utterly out of her mind. He rose up on one elbow and entered her in one great rush. The fullness... It was the most glorious feeling.

"My lady of the skies," he whispered huskily against her forehead as he thrust forward hard.

Another explosion of pleasure built inside her and she grabbed at him to pull him closer, savoring the scent of him all around, everywhere.

He drove into her mercilessly and nipped at her breasts and brought forth an array of stunning sensations until she thought she would simply die right there of delight. But before she could come undone, he had her leg up high and had turned her onto her stomach, his body still linked with hers. She wasn't sure how they had even accomplished it, but she wasn't complaining.

"I love you, Tahlia," he said, his breath hot on the back of her neck as he thrust deeply inside of her. "I love you so very much." His body brushed along her back, their skin lightly sticking. "My soul aches with it."

She laced her fingers into his as he drove them toward ecstasy. "I love you, Marius. With everything I am."

"I love you exactly as you are," he said, and she knew he was talking about her human blood. "I would never change anything about you."

He could barely speak and she knew she couldn't utter a word. The fullness of him and the way he knew exactly how to touch her here and there as he moved unstopping, never failing… The pleasure was more than she thought a person could experience. Her flesh went hot, and he sped up, and the world dissolved into a glittering, beautiful storm of their bond.

The threads around them shivered as Marius eased his way onto his side and curled himself around her. It was as if their love affected the magic as it did their hearts and souls.

"You were created to be my mate," he whispered into her ear as the butterflies glowed and sparkled around them and the sweet scent of the moss danced through the breeze. "I'm certain of that. And I was created for you."

She turned and cocooned herself into his massive body, delighting in the feel of his warm skin and the beat of his heart. "I thought I was only climbing the mountain to fly dragons. Lucky me, snagging a true mate in the process."

STORM OF FLAMES

CHAPTER 1

TAHLIA

Smiling like the madwoman she knew she was, Tahlia held to Lija's reins as they crashed into the waves. The deep gray-blue enveloped them in a cold, salty embrace. Because of her access to Lija's Seabreak magic, the experience was absolutely glorious. Power tingled down her limbs. She could have seen clearly, but the whitewater from their entry blocked her view.

Where was the shipwreck Marius ordered them to find?

Lija untucked her four cyan-blue wings, spread them out, and began to glide effortlessly through the water.

Ah, now this is what I've been craving, rider, Lija said inside Tahlia's mind. *A nice dive and swim in the morning. Isn't it lovely down here?*

The bubbles cleared somewhat and Tahlia looked around. *It is. Just perfect.*

Golden ribbons of the dawn's light danced through the water. A coral shelf in bright orange and stunning pink housed three varieties of fish in yellow, black and white stripes, and silver.

Do you see any wreckage? Tahlia asked.

Not yet.

Down here, Tahlia had two types of magic working for her.

Her Weaver magic showed how all things were connected and how one action might affect the environment and those beings in said environment.

She also had the benefit of Lija's Seabreak power. Before they'd submerged, she'd used her bond with the dragon to create another runestone on shore. With that in place, breathing down here was as easy as it was on land. She could see too, although she'd fashioned some goggles to protect her half-human, half-Fae eyes from the salt water. Just for the comfort of it.

Like all dragons, Lija possessed a second eyelid which protected her from fire, But unlike non-Seabreak breeds, she possessed a third too—one that made being in the ocean as comfortable and clear as being above the water.

Around a stack of orange coral, a tumble of dark brown shapes appeared.

There! The wreck is just ahead and to the south, Tahlia said.

Got it.

Lija swam faster and soon they were circling the shipwreck that Marius had ordered them to check out. If they could find either the eel and skull flag or a pirate's corpse with that same symbol inked in his or her skin, they would know this was the Eelsmen's second ship, the one they were currently hunting. Some of the folks in the coastal village had told them about the ship sinking during the last storm, the storm that had battered the Mist Knights as they'd flown north just three days ago.

The ruined main hung over the cracked deck like a massive broken finger, a school of blue and yellow fish shaped like spears darted through an opening in the hull, and the helm spun as if a ghost turned the rudder.

They swam closer, skimming the remains of the deck, then slipping below decks. Well, if one could call it that. The whole thing was cracked open like a nut. Telltale signs of kraken.

Tahlia looked over her shoulder to peer at the dark blue behind them, just in case. It would be amazing to see a kraken, but maybe from the sky instead of the sea.

There's a body. Snagged on those hammocks, Lija said. *I can't get any closer, but you can.*

Tahlia lifted off of Lija's back and swam toward the dead pirate. He'd been a burly villain with big arms and tree-trunk legs. She hovered, not wanting to touch him and hoping against hope that the water's soft current would turn him so she could view the inkings on his forearms and wrists. She nudged the body with her foot. Gods, she wished she was still wearing her boots. But the water would have ruined them, so she was only in her small clothes and goggles. Not even Lija's saddle was down here with them. The salt water wasn't good on leather.

Giving the pirate another push with a toe, she managed to flip him sideways. His left arm showed a kraken. So he was certainly an Eelsmen. Only they wore such inkings. Aside from pirating, they caught and sold kraken oil on the black market. It certainly wasn't allowed by any king or queen's laws even this far north.

She twisted in the water, trying her best to breathe normally, and squinted at his right arm. Ah, three eels slithering into the shape of a flower. That had to be specific enough information. She swam back to Lija and climbed onto her back as she moved her wings delicately in the cool current.

Are we finished? Lija asked.

I think so. Do you know what eels in the shape of a sea rose means?

No, but Commander Marius will.

They moved quickly through the water and away from the shipwreck. Tahlia kept an eye out for kraken and sharks.

Don't fret so much, rider. I will sense them before you see them.

Lija built up speed as they approached the surface. She blasted through and Tahlia gasped as the sea magic faded from her lungs and blood to let her breathe air once more. Lija flapped her wings hard and rose into the blue sky.

The rest of the Order of Mist Knights stood waiting for them on a sandy beach beneath a row of willowface palms, trees with broad purple leaves that swayed to their own rhythm rather than with the wind. The beach belonged to no one because the whole little island sat in a strip of ocean deemed ungoverned and free to all—which just meant pirates reigned here. Thankfully, the place was empty at the moment. But that was why they were all perplexed.

Marius's gray eyes glittered as he took her in. She was soaked though, of course, so he had plenty to eye. He stepped forward, partially blocking her from the others' view in a markedly possessive move. She didn't bother fighting the grin that slid over her lips.

Clearing his throat, Marius seemed to gather himself. "What did you find, Lady Tahlia?"

"No flags. One body. A barrel-chested fellow with a kraken inking and one with three eels tangled up to form a sea rose."

Marius's eyes widened and he turned to Ewan.

In unison, they said, "Captain Darkmirth."

CHAPTER 2
TAHLIA

Partially blocked by Lija's wings, Tahlia discarded her wet underthings and put her riding leathers and boots back on.

Titus frowned and looked out over the waves. "If his ship is down, where are the others? He couldn't have been killed that long ago if the reports on land were accurate. I'd have thought his men would have been here, sounding the mourning horns."

"Mourning horns?" Tahlia asked.

Marius stared toward the open ocean and Tahlia knew he was doing his best not to sneak a peek of her getting dressed. "They blow brass horns the dawn after a fellow Eelsmen's death, usually within sight of where their man went down."

Tahlia strapped her weapons belt back on, then wiped a bit of salt from her chin.

"But they can't possibly do that when their fellow pirate died during a sea battle, right? Because then they'd be all 'Eh, we are right here, being sad and vulnerable. Why don't you attack us again while we aren't ready?'"

Titus inclined his head. "The Eelsmen don't lose to anyone except kraken."

"And kraken go deep after a kill, so they're not a threat immediately after destroying a ship or taking a life," Maiwenn said.

Tahlia shivered and Lija echoed the movement.

Have you ever encountered one? Tahlia asked the dragon.

Yes.

Tahlia waited for more detail, but Lija just gave her a look that said she didn't care to reminisce. Maybe she'd get it out of her by the fire after this mission was over.

Marius was pacing. Not a great sign.

"What if it was a random storm?" Ewan looked toward Marius, his dark eyes shining with curiosity. "Like that waterspout, we dealt with two years back."

Enora blew out a breath, her freckles standing out as her already fair face paled. "That was a nightmare."

Atticus nodded his horned head and muttered something about water getting into places it should never be.

You'd have no trouble in a waterspout, rider, Lija said.

Why?

We would escape under the waves, down far enough to flee the storm.

I don't think either of us would want to leave our fellow knights and dragons.

Surviving is the first step to helping others escape.

Tahlia rolled that piece of wisdom around in her head.

"I don't think it was a storm," Marius said.

Fara tromped out of the berry-heavy shrubs under the willow-face palms. "Could the whole crew have contracted a plague and the Eelsmen sunk the ship to put the men afflicted out of their misery?"

Growling, Marius continued pacing. "There's not a chance they would give up a ship like that for a mercy killing."

Tahlia gave Fara a smile. It was great to have her here. Fara had persuaded Marius to let her come on the argument that they should always have a Healer in tow for these pirate escapades.

Back at home, she'd said, "From what I've heard, you continually suffer from reduced numbers due to injuries a Healer could fix fairly quickly."

"But what dragon would take you?" Titus had asked Fara.

"Lija will," Tahlia had answered, and then the rest of the strategy had smoothed itself out rather easily.

Fara couldn't go underwater with Tahlia and Lija though. She wasn't bonded to the dragon and didn't have access to the power that permitted the use of runestones or the strength and seaworthiness, for lack of a better term, that had developed in Tahlia over the last weeks. Lija and Tahlia had practiced their abilities in the bodies of water near Dragon Tail Peak, hardly taking the time to eat and sleep. But in the sky, Lija was fine with carrying Fara and the risks were minimal.

"But perhaps plague was part of the story," Claudia said, flicking her orange tail this way and that as she picked at a piece of dried meat. She offered some to her dragon. "The captain grew ill and lost his mind and ended up skewered on the rocks. That coral shelf out there is set into some viciously sharp rocks if I remember correctly."

"It is." Marius eyed Fara and then Claudia. "Regardless of how the captain went down, we need to know where the Eelsmen are now and who is leading them. We must know our enemy to fight them efficiently."

Maiwenn adjusted Donan's saddle. "Donan is saying that we could do a flyover of the island and to the northeast. He is plenty rested for the job."

"We will all go," Marius said. He paused and looked up at Ragewing, whose chest rumbled. Tahlia knew they were speaking through their bond. Marius faced everyone once more. "Ragewing agrees. Let's mount up, knights."

"Aye, Commander!" everyone said in a quick chorus.

Fara climbed into Lija's double saddle and Tahlia sat in front of her. "Less squeezing my guts out of my eyeballs this time, all right?"

Fara pushed her forehead against Tahlia's back. "I'll do my best, but I can't promise anything."

Tahlia patted her friend's hand, the hand currently crushing her ribs. "Lija's got you. Don't worry."

Fara snorted. "Sure."

"Once again, your idea."

"I know. Shut up."

Tahlia leaned her head back to bop Fara's. Fara snarled and then Lija bounded forward, jumped, and took off.

"I can feel your silent scream in my back, Fara."

"Deal with it!" she shouted into Tahlia's vest.

Soon they were soaring over the pale blue, the rounded mountains of green, and the black rocks typical of this area.

Glassy rock like that is *called obsidian,* Lija said. She'd been teaching Tahlia about the north off and on during the mission. She jutted her snout toward a tumble of stone covered in holes. *Those are hag stones. The obsidian can be used for weapons if handled by the right Fae craftsman.*

I'd love a blade like that. It looks far more evil than adamant.

Lija chuckled. *You are so bloodthirsty now, Lady Tahlia.*

Only toward the ones who have earned some serious wrath.

Of course, rider. I know your heart.

At first, Tahlia felt childish when Lija had talked about her heart. Like she was too naive perhaps. But after a while, Tahlia recalled the horrible way some souls acted in this world, and she stopped worrying about whether or not she was "adult" enough. Screw the people who looked down on a determined sense of wonder and a joy in righting wrongs. She was who she was and she didn't give a rat's ass who didn't like it. Her dragon loved her. Her mate loved her. Her fellow knights loved her. The rest of the population could deal with it.

The island's coasts tightened like a fisted hand and the sea grew choppier.

That's Ketch's Strait," Lija said. *Named for the hangman, I believe. Pirates name many things they hate after the hangman.*

Because that's how the locals put them to death when they get their hands on them?

Exactly.

You'd think they would name more hated geographical oddities after us riders and you dragons. The order has slain more pirates than any locals, right?

Yes, but they don't want to admit that. Pirates are too arrogant to give us the satisfaction. They find dark humor in the locals getting the best of them on occasion.

A strange sense of humor.

Agreed, rider.

Beyond Ketch's Strait, Marius and Ragewing led the units northwest and a scattering of islands appeared, bridges stretching between them and docks reaching into multiple sandy coves and natural bays. There were at least six large ships docked around the cluster of islands. All of them looking like pirate vessels. Their decks were not scrubbed clean like the locals' official ships. Dark flags, too far to see clearly, waved occasionally in the breeze.

CHAPTER 3

TAHLIA

Lija grumbled and the sound vibrated through Tahlia's legs.

"What's wrong?" Fara asked, her voice shaky.

"The Eelsmen aren't here. None of these are theirs," Tahlia said.

Fara took a nervous, uneven breath. "Are we still going after them?"

I doubt the commander will order it, Lija said. *We have to focus on the Eelsmen, as per our order from the king. We can only take them down if their presence directly affects the Eelsmen or if we witness them harming the local communities. Ragewing tells me we are going to land on the farthest island, out of sight of these pirates.*

Tahlia relayed the information to Fara, who thanked her with a weepy voice.

"It's so much worse than I remember," Fara whispered.

Fara had ridden with them during the days of fighting Ophelia and Katk.

"Why do you think that is?" Tahlia asked.

"Probably because I've been studying serious injuries. Now, I am fully aware of what happens when we fall off."

Reins held lightly in one hand, Tahlia laughed and gripped one of Fara's arms—the arm laced so tightly around her middle that she worried Fara was going to break a rib.

All the dragons increased their speed and dropped to lower altitudes. Fara whimpered and Tahlia patted her arm.

The wind was warm on Tahlia's cheeks as they flew, and for the hundredth time, she marveled at the strip of land and sea that received such pleasant autumn weather this far north. It had to do with the air over the ocean to the west or something like that, and it only grew cold here during the last month of the calendar year. She didn't understand what Marius had tried to explain on this front, but regardless, she was happy to feel good in her sleeveless tunic and leather vest.

Marius and Ragewing led the order to a sandy landing spot surrounded by trees that looked like pines. Instead of green needles, these had orange and red pin-like leaves.

From Ragewing's back, Marius lifted a hand. "The dragons may water themselves at the river that flows through those trees there."

Tahlia knew he was only giving such detailed directions because she hadn't been here before. The rest of the knights were well acquainted with the spot.

"Knights, please remove their tack and take time to clean your weapons as needed. After this short respite, we will send a few volunteers into the closest village to see if anyone knows anything about the Eelsmen's location and who is leading them now."

"I volunteer," Tahlia said as she slid off Lija's lowered shoulder.

Lija purred with approval at Tahlia's courage. Tahlia rubbed her neck, then started unbuckling the saddle's girth strap.

"I will go myself as well. Anyone else?" Marius asked. He already had Ragewing's saddle off and was working on the reins.

"I'm up for it, Commander," Titus said.

Maiwenn and Fara lifted their hands.

"I'd like to go," Maiwenn said.

Marius nodded assent. "We'll have to strip off these vests at the least and don our cloaks as well."

Thankfully, they'd brought extra tunic tops and summer-weight cloaks that wouldn't be too out of place.

These island villages are used to travelers, so you won't be as noticeable as you might think, Lija said.

"Well, this is incredibly convenient," a deep voice said from the colorful pines' shadows.

Marius withdrew his whip, ready to strike. The knights had their short swords out or bows drawn in an instant. Tahlia held her blade and stood in front of Fara. The dragons lifted themselves up, and fire crackled in their bellies and throats. Black smoke plumed from every dragon's nostrils and out of some of their mouths too.

Stay close, rider, Lija said, her voice tight.

A tall male with gray skin, and short, messy black hair strode into the sandy clearing. His fingers ended in long claws.

Fear shot through Tahlia like a crossbow bolt. An Unseelie?

"Who is he?" Fara asked in a whisper.

Marius swore, and Tahlia rebuckled Lija's girth. Then with her free hand, she pushed Fara to remount.

Why in the world was there a full-blooded Unseelie in his high Fae form here? A buzzing sounded in Tahlia's ears. This was bad. Very bad.

CHAPTER 4
FARA

Fara scrambled onto Lija's back. She didn't need to be told twice and Tahlia's urgent movements were command enough for her.

She didn't know who this was, but clearly, he was Unseelie. While the Seelie—Fae of the Realm of Lights—had light peach, brown, blue, silver, orange, purple, and more colors within their population, Unseelie only had gray skin. Likely from living in their dark, mysterious realm. It was a place pretty much unreachable by Seelie Fae, with the exception of King Lysanael and Queen Revna.

Why was he here? Who was he? It wasn't as if all Unseelie were evil. The Seelie used to believe they were, but Fara's people had been proven wrong when Seelie King Lysanael discovered he was related to the Unseelie king. But that didn't mean this particular male was trustworthy. No, in fact, he looked like the farthest thing from trustworthy.

Unseelie held unpredictable magic, unlike the Fae of this realm. Fara had always been frightened of their power. It was the stuff of childhood nightmares. Snakes and insects gathering to do their bidding. Weather altered by a whim. The ability to shift their physical form. She shuddered.

Fara set a hand on her pounding heart as she took in his clawed fingers and the easy way he walked forward like there weren't a load of arrows and blades aimed at his chest. He was as tall as Marius, but that's where the similarities ended. His blue-black hair was braided and came to the nape of his neck. A strange sensation crept over Fara's skin—like the drag of talons over her flesh.

"Tell me why I don't truss you up like a pig and have my dragon light you up right this second," Marius said, still holding his whip ready.

"Curiosity," the male said. His voice was like thunder, resonant and threatening despite his simple words.

His voice was fascinating. She wanted him to speak again just so she could pin down what was unique about it. He could probably sing well if he decided to.

She pressed her eyes shut, annoyed with herself. She wasn't thinking clearly. This was an emergency and she should be more logically minded if she was going to join in on missions.

A massive scar ran across the Unseelie's throat and down one arm. His short-sleeved vest pulled tight at his chest. His thighs were more pronounced than most males'—the muscles large like he did squats for a living.

The Unseelie cocked his head and studied each of the knights and dragons before his gaze landed on Fara. She felt his focus like a cool breeze dancing over her cheeks, down her chest, along her legs... His eyes glittered, and she swallowed against a sudden lump in her throat.

"I am the new leader of the Eelsmen," the Unseelie said.

CHAPTER 5
TAHLIA

Their captain? Tahlia put a hand on Lija's warm, scaled leg. Sparks danced around the Seabreak's snout, her fire barely contained.

It has to be a trick, some ruse to confuse us, Lija said.

Well, it's working.

"Why are you in this realm?" Marius demanded of the Unseelie, edging closer to Ragewing, who growled low and rumbling.

Tahlia's Weaver threads shimmered to life, connecting Marius and her, the dragons and their riders, their potential flight… But there was a chaotic vibe to the magic and it was impossible to read.

Why was there a strong connection between the stranger to Lija?

She glanced sideways to study it…

Oh, so the thread didn't link the male to Lija, but to Fara. A chill crawled down Talia's back. Did he pose that clear of a threat just to Fara? She couldn't read its intent, its purpose, its root. Gritting her teeth, she narrowed her eyes and tried to make the magic smooth itself out and show its workings. Why would—

The Unseelie male cut through her thoughts with his gravelly voice. "That part isn't any of your business."

"I believe it is," Marius said, his voice eerily calm. He was at his most dangerous when he looked and sounded so very, very calm. "I come here by order of Seelie King Lysanael and Queen Revna."

"It's not their business either." A very punchable smirk twisted the Unseelie's mouth. "I just wanted you to see who you would be up against for this year's round of fighting. It's only fair to warn you that the Eelsmen now have a ridiculous slew of magic at their disposal."

Lija's body rumbled with a low growl. *On my back, rider. We are leaving. Now.*

We can't. Marius hasn't ordered it.

He could cast a spell and kill us.

Maybe he's going to kill Fara. Tahlia's mind whirled as she pondered the threads and what they meant. She gripped her sword and whispered a prayer.

Marius knows that, she said finally to Lija, *and he isn't signaling to take off.* Tahlia watched his hand—if he fisted his free hand and shook it slightly, he wanted them to mount up and take off immediately.

What are the rules of Unseelie magic? Are there any limitations?

The runestone magic we use is the same that most Unseelie high Fae can work.

He can do any type of rune magic? Tahlia was having trouble breathing.

Yes, unless his veins are diluted with Seelie Fae or human blood. But he appears fully Unseelie with that gray skin of his and those claws.

Tahlia swallowed. Again. Her face ached from clenching her jaw.

CHAPTER 6
MARIUS

Marius's hand twitched, almost giving the signal to take off. But this Unseelie—what in the name of the gods was he doing in this realm?—was a wild card. What if he had already enacted rune magic that would kill them as soon as they left the ground?

"Why are you in this realm? What do you want? We can petition King Lysanael to return you to the Unseelie realm if that is your goal," Marius struggled to keep his tone even.

"I have my own passage, thank you very much."

His own passage? Was there a forgotten portal here like the one they found in the southwestern human lands? That one had been destroyed.

"What is your goal?"

"You're boring me, Commander Marius."

How did he know his name?

"I'd have thought you would be more interesting," the Unseelie said. "Too bad."

He grinned with his wickedly long fangs, teeth that were far more animal than Fae, and Ragewing growled in full.

The Unseelie snapped his fingers. Two things happened simultaneously. The air exploded in a cloud of glittering black and indigo, and a sapphire-hued smoke slithered over the ground, heading toward them.

"Fly!" Marius shouted, already leaping onto Ragewing and checking if Tahlia was climbing onto Lija. She was, thankfully.

They drove into the air, the smoke and glittering magic chasing their tails. Marius twisted in his saddle. The Unseelie stood below, amid the magical chaos, smiling in a way that made Marius's blood boil.

What power is that? Ragewing asked. *And which way should we head?*

I have no idea. I know very little of Unseelie magic. I was hoping you could tell me.

I have done my best to steer clear of Unseelie, although I have met three Fae with both Seelie and Unseelie blood who were decent folk. I don't hate them outright, but they don't make me very comfortable, you could say.

Marius laughed without humor. *You could definitely say that.*

He looked to Tahlia, who met his gaze. She didn't often show fear, but it widened her eyes now and he hated to see it. Wise, though it was.

Marius commanded the order to fly back to the beach where they'd started from in case the Unseelie had patrolling boats near him, past the Ketch Strait.

As they landed and dismounted on the beach, Fara's swearing drowned out all other sounds.

"We have to annihilate him." Fara's voice was strong and unhurried, but her hair had slipped from her braid and her purple skin had flushed to a deep plum. "He is certainly going to do it to us if we don't. He's the Eelsmen captain now? I can't even believe it. Have you ever fought a full Unseelie?" she asked Marius.

"Slow down, Healer. Let us all talk calmly. We will figure out a plan."

The riders gathered around him, their dragons facing out of the circle to keep watch and to defend if some magical attack tried to surprise him.

"Does anyone know of a portal that may have been forgotten?" he asked the group.

Before King Lysanael shut the drumstones, which had served as a rough portal, many Unseelie monsters and folk had accidentally fallen into the Seelie realm. But since the closing of the stones, Unseelie were a true rarity in this land and the surrounding kingdoms as well. Yes, some folk had a touch of Unseelie blood—some distant ancestor who had a roll in the hay with an Unseelie in their high Fae form—but Tahlia had only met two in her entire life traveling about the Realm of Lights.

Ewan rubbed his bald head with increasingly exasperated movements. His purple-blue eyes narrowed. "Not me."

Maiwenn perched on a boulder and kicked the sand at her boots. "I have no idea."

"Could we send a raven back to Dragon Tail and have one of our Scholars look through the old scrolls for any mention of a portal up here?" Tahlia suggested, glancing at the cage on Titus's Spikeback. Two ravens cawed from inside, trained birds that were well accustomed to these missions.

"It's a good idea," Marius said, proud of his mate's ability to think under pressure. "Will you take care of that Justus?"

"Aye, sir."

Justus and Titus set to writing a note on the waxed parchment they'd brought and securing it to one of the ravens' legs.

"We must assume we can't simply shove him back through the portal from whence he came," Marius said.

"Please start pacing. Your stillness is making me nervous," Fara said.

Tahlia's forehead bunched. "We need to know what he is capable of."

Atticus crossed his silver-skinned arms and set his gaze on

Tahlia. "Anything. He can likely do almost any type of spell if he has the knowledge, the time in the moment of action, and the will to draw the Unseelie runes for it."

"How can we negate this magic?" Titus asked as he watched Justus release the raven into the wispy clouds slipping through the blue sky.

"We must surprise him at every turn," Marius said. "We must act fast enough that he isn't able to draw whatever rune might hinder our attack."

"Maybe we can approach him from the far northern coast of that island. No one comes down from that direction," Claudia said.

Atticus and Enora nodded.

"True," Marius said. "But there's a reason for that. This lovely warm breeze isn't present when you cross over the Kniving Sea. We don't have the clothing for that trip."

Justus fed a crumb of dragonbread to the raven who hadn't been sent on the messaging errand. "We might have to do it anyway."

Tahlia raised two fingers. "We have a pair of Seabreaks. Let's make use of their magic and stealth. Maiwenn, our mounts, and I could approach from under the water and distract them as the rest of you come from the north."

Maiwenn raised her eyebrows. "Not a bad idea."

"Maybe Lija and I can call up the sea creatures like we did in Midhampton."

"You were in Midhampton?" Maiwenn climbed off the boulder, staring.

Ah, Tahlia, he thought, grinning and covering his mouth with a hand. When will you learn proper knight behavior? Mission information was always on a need-to-know basis.

He cleared his smile away. "Forget she said that. You heard her wrong. But yes, that is a fine idea. Will you ask Lija how she feels about this? And Maiwenn, will you speak with Donan?"

Tahlia and Maiwenn nodded and looked to their dragons, speaking through their bonds.

"Does dragon fire affect Unseelie like it does humans and us?" Ewan asked.

"I believe so," Marius said.

"So we flame him the second he's in range," Atticus said.

"At first thought, yes, but he will expect fire."

"Then how do we end him?"

"With bloodiron."

"I forgot about that stuff," Maiwenn said.

Bloodiron was often used by King Lysanael before the portals were closed, back when Unseelie monsters were tripping into this realm every other day. But in the Shrouded Mountains, they rarely had use for the material.

Maiwenn finished whatever she was telling her dragon and met Marius's gaze. "Donan is good to go with the underwater surprise distraction attack."

"Same with Lija," Tahlia said. "She's excited about it." Tahlia's grin was far too wide for this deadly situation they were in.

Ewan rubbed his bottom lip and frowned. "But how are we going to get bloodiron? Only the king's guard has it and they don't have much, from what I've heard."

This would be tricky, but... "I would be willing to bet that we can find it around here on the black market," Marius said.

Tahlia wiggled her eyebrows, and Marius shut his eyes, shaking his head. She was undoubtedly imagining insane disguises.

"No hats this time," he muttered in her direction.

He was rewarded with a small chuckle that gave him hope somehow in this impossible situation.

They set to planning a trip to the nearest port town, Queen's Coral.

CHAPTER 7
TAHLIA

Queen's Coral was a bee hive of activity—traders, buyers, sailors, and pirates flitted from cart to tavern, from brothel to dock. Tahlia couldn't help but love it a little bit. Except maybe the brothel part.

"Have you been here before?" Tahlia asked Marius, who was hooded and glaring daggers at every human that passed by.

"I have not. Only flown over it."

"You might want to glare less. You catch more bees with honey in this hive." She laughed, enjoying linking up her earlier thought with the idiom.

Maiwenn gave her a questioning look and she waved her off.

They passed under a clutch of chittering birds whose long, blue tails hung from the branches of a tree with bright pink leaves. The tree's shadow fell over them and eased the heat of the sun on Tahlia's head.

Marius's boots kicked up some of the sandy ground. They hadn't lined their roads with stone, instead, the pathways were simply sand and smooth pebbles. "None of us have been to this town. Remember, no names. No dragons. Only the money we will pay and the amount we need."

Tahlia nodded and checked in with Lija. *How are things?* They'd left their dragons in a humble cave system with the rest of the riders.

It's not a luxurious hideout, as you well know.

Sorry about that.

I am fine dealing with hardships during missions. I know what dragons of the order are expected to endure, and I do it with fervor.

You are loyal and brave and I would ride no other.

Tahlia could feel Lija's satisfaction with her response. The bonds between riders and dragons fed the creatures' souls. Old stories stated that unbonded dragons died younger and often suffered from melancholy—many refusing to eat until they wasted away. Tahlia was so glad she and Lija had found one another and that the dragon's broken wing was healed. They were blessed, for sure.

But rider, Lija said, *I'm unhappy because you are keeping something from me. You are greatly troubled and I can feel it quite keenly through our bond.*

Tahlia exhaled. *I saw a thread connecting the Unseelie directly to Fara.*

What did the thread say would happen?

It doesn't always work like that. I can see possibilities pretty clearly on a normal day, but this day, it's not normal at all. The threads were chaotic and unreadable. I could only tell that certain people were bonded and that if we took off, we would elicit a violent response from the Unseelie. The threads also showed a powerful connection between Fara and him. I think he is going to try to kill her.

Try?

Tahlia's heart skipped two beats. *I can't even imagine the male being capable of the deed. I just can't think like that, Lija. No. He won't win. He can't take her from me.*

Slow your thoughts, Lady Tahlia. We are in this moment and nothing is happening to her right now. She is right here beside me.

All right. Good. Good.

I'm looking at her now, Lija said. *I see her cautious eyes, her healthy limbs, and her smooth, plum-hued skin. She is well and unharmed.*

Tahlia took a stuttering breath. *Thanks, Lija.*

You're welcome. Now, don't you keep such burdens of information from me next time. I am here to help you shoulder such weights.

Thank you. Tahlia sent a bolt of appreciation and love through the bond. Lija returned it and the sun seemed to grow brighter.

Marius stopped at a blacksmith's forge with Maiwenn and Tahlia taking his back to watch for anyone suspicious. In the workshop, a human with slightly pointed ears—half-Fae like Tahlia or just born a little early?—clanged a hammer or whatever they called those things onto a strip of dark metal. It was impossible to tell what the item would become.

"Good morning," Marius said, sounding less *good* and more *get what I need immediately.*

Maiwenn and Tahlia traded a look, and Tahlia stepped forward.

"Master Smith, forgive the intrusion. We need to purchase a good supply of bloodiron. Arrow tips. Blades. Spearheads. Whatever you might have to sell us. We can come back at another time if you would like."

Marius raised his lip, and the always observant Maiwenn kicked a nearby table of tools to distract the smithy from seeing Marius's Fae fang. It would be better if the smith thought they were humans. There weren't many full Fae up here on these islands. Along the coast, yes, of course, because that was part of the Realm of Lights. But not here. This was beyond the water, still inside the Veil technically, but existing in its tattered edges. The divide wasn't clear-cut like it was at the southern border of the Fae realm. Of course, these folks knew of the order and Titus said that most here were appreciative of the work the order did in fighting pirates. But that didn't mean the humans trusted the order. And sometimes, they likely hoped some pirates escaped dragon fire to spend gold in towns like this. Needless to say, it was complicated.

The smith nodded at Tahlia and gave her a smile. But as he took in her eyes, then looked at Marius, his grin faded. Damn. He'd noticed Marius's eyes. He knew he was full Fae.

"I wish I could help you, but I only have that bit there." He lifted his chin to indicate a crate of raw bloodiron sitting against the wall. He sounded like he couldn't get rid of them soon enough.

Marius looked into the crate and scowled. "This will work. We will take the lot."

Tahlia and Maiwenn examined the contents. There were three rectangles of the metal, unformed as of yet into anything of use. Beside them was an open leather sack of arrow tips. A blade of the stuff sat unsheathed near the bag.

"How long would it take for you to use the blocks to make another three spearheads?" Marius held out a bag of gold coins to the smithy.

The blacksmith took the sack, loosened the tie, and blinked at the gold. He cleared his throat and looked up. "I can drop what I'm doing and get it done by sundown. I have three apprentices that are up to the task and we can work alongside."

It was disgusting how gold could sway someone with a closed mind against other races. Not surprising, but gross.

Maiwenn took over the conversation at that point. Her family ran a weapons shop at Dragon Tail, so she was well-versed in pricing, buying, and selling. The smith began haggling half-heartedly, his nervous gaze peppering them each in turn.

They spent the day hiding in the shadowy corner of a tavern, playing dice games and drinking rum. As the last of the sun's light departed, they left Queen's Coral with bloodiron weapons in tow, ready to find the Unseelie and end him before he could do the same to them.

CHAPTER 8

TAHLIA

Back at the temporary base they'd created on the island, Marius handed Tahlia three arrows. "Only fire them when you know you can hit him. We won't get more."

He looked tired, and she longed to fold him into her arms even though he was far too big for any of that.

Lija stood behind Tahlia, her warmth a comfort. Marius bowed his head briefly to the Seabreak and she echoed the gesture.

"So we are bypassing talks and heading right to killing the stranger," Fara said, her tone was odd.

"You're usually the first one in line for bloodshed when dangerous villains are involved," Tahlia said, keeping her voice low and studying the arrows.

The others seemed to sense they needed a minute and they drifted over to where the dragons had convened near a grass-topped dune.

Fara looked first at the ground and then at her hands. She began to wring them and shake her head.

"If you chew your lip any harder, you won't need the food I nabbed from Queen's Coral."

Fara froze, then swung around. “What food?”

Tahlia drew a small green fruit from her pocket and tossed it to Fara. She gobbled it down in the same way Tahlia had eaten her share on the ride back.

“Now, tell me what’s going on with you, Fara.”

“I just... I feel like there is more to this story than what we know.”

“Of course, there is. We don’t know how he managed to cross into our realm and we have no clue why he wants to run the Eelsmen. Though I assume it’s for gold, spoils, and females.”

“What if it’s not?”

“What if he’s a kindhearted gentlemale with some secret charity mission?”

Fara hit Tahlia on the arm. “Stop. I’m serious.”

“So am I,” Tahlia said, looking into Fara’s eyes. “The pirates are horrible to the people up here. You know that better than I do.”

She nodded.

“So why the hesitant mood about offing the dangerous magical creature who wants to lead them in their dark work?” Tahlia didn’t want to scare Fara by mentioning the thread that had connected the Unseelie to her, but maybe she needed to know.

“No, you’re right,” Fara said. “You and Marius are right. I’m being a civilian over here, fretting about loss of life in battle. I just don’t have your nerve.”

Tahlia snorted and slapped Fara’s shoulder. “Now, that is the biggest heap of bull shite I’ve ever heard. You have more guts than all of us together.”

Her purple cheeks darkened in a blush. “Thanks, Tahl, but this is different. It feels more... I don’t know. It feels more real, I guess?”

“How about we get Justus to take you back to Dragon Tail Peak? You don’t need to be here. It’s too much.”

“No, I want to help. There will be injuries.”

“You don’t have the training to deal with death and battle.”

“I don’t care. I want to stay.”

Tahlia took her hand and squeezed it. “You’re certain? Because I will make someone take you back. No questions asked. I’m sleeping with the commander, remember? I get favors.”

Fara laughed sadly. “I’ll save your favoritism for the dining hall and those crystal cakes.”

Tahlia pulled her into a hug. She smelled like the herbs she was always fiddling with these days. “All right. It’s a deal. But you let me know if you change your mind.”

“I will.” Fara hugged Tahlia back tightly, then as they broke apart, Fara eyed the bloodiron arrows.

“These will end him quickly. It shouldn’t be much of a fight if we manage to distract him.”

Fara swallowed and nodded. “I’m going to check my stores of tallow and thyme. Don’t forget to tie your hair back. If it’s doing all of that,” she said, waving fingers at Tahlia’s mess of hair, “you are doomed and me along with you.”

“Of course.” Smiling, Tahlia watched her go to her bags and rummage through them busily. There was something off here, but she couldn’t pin it down.

She studied the weight of the arrows in her hand. They were heavier than regular arrows and would require being closer to the target than she was used to. Exhaling and trying to breathe through her understandable fear, she joined the other knights.

While Marius doled out a spear and a few more arrows to the others, Tahlia cut a length of leather from Lija’s saddle, rolled it, and tied it with the thong that had been holding back her hair. Tahlia tied the makeshift quiver onto Lija’s saddle and tucked the arrows into place where she could reach them easily.

Marius was suddenly standing beside her, his hand poised on her forearm. His fingers were hot and his eyes were hotter.

“Are you certain you and Lija can handle going under the sea like this? We can come up with a different plan if either of you are concerned.”

He need not worry about us. Or Maiwenn, Lija said inside Tahlia's mind.

Tahlia put her hand over his and a sensation like sparks danced down her arm from the point of contact—he always had this effect on her.

"We've got this. Maiwenn and Donan do, too. Lija is confident."

"All right," he said, drawing even closer and rubbing his thumb over her knuckle. He lifted her hand and kissed it. His gaze snagged hers, and she was pinned by his stormy eyes. "If anything happens to you..."

"I'm a knight, remember. I've survived so far."

The side of his mouth lifted and her lips longed to press a kiss there. "You're right. I must stop coddling you, Lady of the Skies."

"Lady of the Seas, now, hmm?" She grinned up at him.

He smiled in full then. "Yes, I suppose we will need to expand my nickname repertoire."

"It'll annoy Fara even more."

Chuckling, he kissed her hand once more. He nodded then and left her to speak to Claudia and Ewan.

That Unseelie pirate has no chance against us, rider, Lija said.

You're damn right about that, my friend.

CHAPTER 9
TAHLIA

Tahlia pulled Marius aside as everyone at the tree line was finishing up with battle preparations. "Can I talk to you alone for a minute?"

"Always."

They walked away from those gathered on the beach to a spot within the tree line of thick palms and shaggy, colorful evergreens. Snails glowed lightly from wide-leafed plants that lined the animal trail into the thicker part of the island forest. The palms blocked the moonlight and even though they were on a mission, Tahlia went ahead and just hugged Marius like they were at home in their bedroom.

He kissed her hair and his chest moved as he breathed against her. "What is it, Tahlia? I'm listening. I'm not your commander right now. I'm your Marius. Talk to me."

Warmth suffused the cold spots lurking in her heart and she pressed her face into the salt-hardened leather of his vest.

"Thank you. It's the threads."

"What about them?"

“A strong one connected the Unseelie and Fara.”

“In what manner?”

“That’s the thing...” She turned and plucked a snail from a bush. Its shell was warm and it smelled like cloves. “I don’t know. Usually, it’s easy to read. There’s a possible action and then the consequence. Easy peasy. But this was different. I saw what would happen if he cast a spell. He did have that as an active thread, but that’s not the part that I can’t untangle. Untangle, get it?”

He gave her a flat look and she shrugged, her heart not in the stupid joke mood like it usually was.

“Will you explain the active thread part to me again?” Marius asked.

“An active thread is brighter. My guess is that it means the individual is seriously considering that outcome and/or action as a way forward. So yes, he thought of casting a spell, and the thread of that shone like a torch, but that’s not all. There was a secondary thread underlying that action, that spell. I have no idea what that second bit meant.”

“Because of its color? Or because it went right along with the action choice to cast a spell?”

“Both. I usually see one thread. They aren’t usually doubled up like that. And the color was odd too, really. A haunting sort of blue-black. Like a bruise or a shadow.”

“You sound like a poet.”

Tahlia smiled up at him, and his hair sparkled snow-white in the moon’s shimmer. “I sound like the goddess who gave me this gift.”

He kissed her and she parted her lips to encourage more of this lovely choice.

“Well Commander Marius, I didn’t think you were supposed to grab knights’ arses during a mission.”

“That’s correct,” he murmured into her ear, sending shivers down her back. “I’m only permitted to fondle one knight’s posterior and that one knight is you, my lady.”

"Fondle away, sir. Fondle away." She forgot about threads and Unseelie for a few moments, savoring instead the feel of his strong arms around her.

CHAPTER 10

TAHLIA

The plan was going smoothly for once.

Everyone aside from Maiwenn and Tahlia had flown farther north to come at the Unseelie from a hopefully unexpected direction. Tahlia, Maiwenn, Lija, and Donan coursed through the water, quickly approaching the place where they'd met the Eelsmen's new captain.

It's time, Lija said.

Tahlia lifted a fist at Maiwenn who nodded. They drove faster and swam toward the surface, the Seabreaks' magic hurtling water before them. The moon and stars cast nets of silver over everything.

The sea crashed onto the shore, its foaming arms seemingly reaching for the Unseelie, who was flanked by five Eelsmen. A blast of dragon fire heated the air and Tahlia, using the sea magic that her bond with Lija allowed, looked up through the splashing water to see Ragewing carrying Fara and Marius. The others followed closely in a wing pattern.

"Watch out!" Maiwenn called out, her Mistgold voice strong

despite the noise of the water, the fire, and the shouts of the pirates.

As Lija broke the surface to ride the tide her power had created, Tahlia saw the Unseelie and his men running for the forest. A swathe of ocean water swamped the slower pirates and they shrieked and began swimming even as the waves threw them toward the trees.

A dazzling, sparkling cloud of dark magic washed over the chaos, heading right for Ragewing. The power rolled like storm clouds. The bulk of it looked like a cluster of raven wings lit here and there with fire.

Unseelie magic.

The Unseelie had disappeared into the trees, whose leaves caught fire. Ragewing dashed to the side to avoid the black and sparkling fingers of the cloud, but the magic wasn't deterred. It sped up.

And snatched Fara from Ragewing's back.

"No!" Tahlia pressed her hand against Lija's neck. *Hurry, please!*

Lija growled, the dragon's muscles tensing beneath Tahlia. With a bubbling roar, she burst from the flood of water and churned sand. Maiwenn looked up at us as they left the water. Tahlia's heart crawled into her throat, and she held on for dear life. The sea dragon leapt into the air, then flew at the dark magic cloud, which was retreating toward the forest beyond the flooded beach.

Together, Lija and Tahlia zipped through the burning palms and sea oaks, pirates' shouts of pain or direction coming from both the left and the right. Tahlia ducked as Lija flew under a massive tree branch.

"Don't fret, Seelie rider," the Unseelie called out. "She is mine, and I will care for her better than you ever could."

Mine? What in the hells is he talking about?

Tahlia wanted to roar like Lija at the Unseelie, but her throat was too tight to even utter a word. Her body shook and her mind whirled. It was unbelievable, that her friend had been claimed somehow by this powerful stranger. She kept moving her lips and trying to figure out what to shout, what to do, what to ask of Lija that might help them.

A warm cascade of strength and understanding washed through her.

Breathe, rider. Feel how much I believe in our bond and in you. We will rescue her.

Tahlia's throat unclenched and she raised her chin. "She's ours!" she shouted finally at the Unseelie. "She's Seelie! You can't take her. Why do you even want to?"

If Fara had been able to speak from wherever he was holding her, she would have shouted some indignant response, but only the Eelsmen's new high captain's voice could be heard.

I can smell him, Lija said. *Easy to track. He is very fast, and he is still carrying Lady Fara.*

A crash in the trees behind them had Tahlia turning in her saddle. Marius and Ragewing had caught up. Maiwenn must have remained in the water to continue blocking the pirates' escape that way.

"He has Fara!" Tahlia shouted, her throat raw.

Marius gave her one stern nod and unfurled his whip. He looked like a vengeful god and she was relieved he was on her side. Ragewing rushed past Lija. He was obviously less fatigued than her because normally he wouldn't have been able to pass her. Tahlia knew what Marius was up to. He would come at the stranger from the side and, hopefully, they would corner the Unseelie using some natural barrier like a rising cliff face, a drop-off, or a body of inland water. It was one of the techniques they had practiced countless times during training.

Suddenly, the Unseelie was there. A cloud of his magic swirled around him as he flew with Fara at his side.

Though bile touched the back of her tongue, Tahlia forced her mind to calm and her body to be ready. She removed a water-soaked bloodiron arrow from the makeshift quiver on Lija's saddle. Nocking the arrow, she took aim. Her fingers released the bloodiron weapon, and the arrow whipped away, shooting through the trees toward the Unseelie.

What if I hit Fara?

Lija growled as she flew hard. *You won't.*

A false hand made up of dark, swirling magic grabbed the arrow and thrust it down.

"Damn him!" Tahlia nocked her second arrow as Lija zipped to the left around a cluster of palms.

She fired again. The arrow cut through a maze of thick vines, sending glowing night insects into the air with a resounding buzz. The insects blocked Tahlia's view for a fraction of a second. Then she saw the arrow disappear into the Unseelie's dark cloud.

Maybe it hit his leg? I can't see, Lija said.

I can't either. We can hope. I'll fire another. Stay on him.

Lija increased her speed and Ragewing and Marius flew over a small waterfall to join them.

Tahlia refocused on the Unseelie. Fara was limp in his arms. That bastard was going down.

She loosed her last arrow. The bloodiron-tipped projectile was nearly impossible to see as the forest growth overhead thickened. Pirates shouted far away, and the sound of Ragewing's and Lija's wingbeats were like the ticking of a clock. The arrow disappeared completely into the Unseelie's magic and Tahlia dropped back into her saddle.

"Faster!" Marius shouted.

Tahlia felt like she was watching her life end.

The Unseelie rose into the canopy. They followed, staying just out of reach of his dark power, but when they blasted through the tops of the trees, there was nothing but stars and the luminous moon.

Fara was gone.

CHAPTER II

FARA

Fara woke in a room lit by just one lantern. The room swayed slightly and the scent of salt permeated the air. Heart pounding, she sat up.

Oh no, she was on a ship.

With her stomach in her throat, she climbed out of the large bed attached to the wall and went to the three tall windows that looked out of the back of the ship. A gray and yellow beach peered back at her from not too far a distance and a large chain reached from the ship and into the sea. They were at anchor at least. But where?

The door to the cabin swung open and a scent like oud and beeswax candles swept her way. She began to turn, even though she already knew who stood behind her. Her captor, the new high captain of the Eelsmen, an Unseelie with powerful runic magic.

"Good evening," he said with that creepy low voice.

She shivered. He was awful. His skin, his clawed fingertips, his animalistic stare... "What do you want from me?"

She remembered his magic taking her from Ragewing's back, but she had no memory of anything else.

He walked fully into the room and shut the door. "I'm High Captain Teague. We will talk once you've eaten and had time to yourself to calm your thoughts."

"It's adorable that you think I could calm myself when I have zero information aside from the fact that I have been stolen from my friends by an Unseelie Fae who also just happens to be in charge of the worst pirate clan the world has ever known. Also, you can go ahead and screw yourself."

Snarling, she flashed her middle finger at him, then she pushed up her sleeves and readied to fight. He would win, but by the gods, he would hurt first.

"Ah, now, settle down, feisty Seelie. You don't want to get physical with me, do you?" His eyes glittered with double meaning, and she growled low.

In the blink of an eye, Teague was at her back and had her wrists pinned. His breath stirred the hair at the top of her head, and she shivered. She'd expected his touch to be cold, but his skin was smooth and warm just like a Seelie's even if it was the color of a winter dusk.

"I have bad news for you," he whispered.

Her heart thundered against her ribs. "Even worse than being captured by you?"

"So much worse."

"Do tell."

His lips brushed her temple and instead of recoiling like she should have, her body leaned into him. She gritted her teeth and tried to pull away, but he held her firmly against his strong body.

"The moment I saw you," he said quietly. "I knew you were meant to be mine."

She laughed. "Fated mates happen once in a century. Maybe less. And King Lysanael and Queen Revna stole that move already for our era."

"We are not fated mates, per se, but that is the nearest thing. I am a Seer of the Unseelie realm and there is a legend called Seer's

Heart. The story tells of one like me who was drawn to another, one who sparked his very soul. I have Seen you in my crystals. You have walked through my predictions like a spectator for years. Have you ever dreamed of me?"

"Definitely not. Get over yourself."

Teague continued, smirking and making Fara long for a very sharp sword.

"When I saw you on that Seelie dragon, I knew you were mine. I think you did too although you won't admit it. Even to yourself."

Her cheeks went hot. He had lost his mind—if he'd ever even had one. She struggled to free her wrists from the circle of his thumb and forefinger. "You're mad. I know no such thing and neither do you. You're cracked, is all. Let me go."

He released her immediately. She spun and slammed her fist into his nose. Well, she'd aimed there, but he'd slipped his head and her fist had gone pointlessly over his shoulder. He stepped back, head tilted, grinning in a way that made her want to set the whole stupid ship they were on aflame. Where were the damn dragons when you needed them?

"How did you grab me? What was that cloud? Was that rune magic?"

"Of course."

Her skin felt too tight and talking was keeping her from screaming. "How does it work?"

"I inscribe a rune of power on a stone and whisper my will into the old symbols. Simple." Teague shrugged.

She glared and crossed her arms. "Simple."

"Yes."

"What exactly do you plan to do with me?" she spat. If looks could destroy, he'd have been a pile of ash already.

"Marry you. Sweep you off your feet. Tempt you until you beg for my attention."

She snorted. "Fat chance of that, Unseelie."

"I think my chances are quite good." His gaze slid down her

body and she felt the look like a touch. His nostrils flared and she knew that he knew she was attracted to him even though she didn't want to be.

He began to pace the length of the cabin, which was rather sizable considering it was on a ship. Fara had never been on a large vessel like this. Oddly, she found the motion of the sea beneath her soothing. Or she would have if she hadn't been insanely angry at the impossible beast walking to and damn fro in front of her.

"I only came to this land to retrieve what is mine and to have my revenge. Once that is accomplished, I will leave. You will be coming with me."

"To the Unseelie realm?"

"Yes."

She barked a nervous, high-pitched laugh and turned to look out at the sea. They were still anchored. She could still be rescued. Right? What would Tahlia and Marius and the rest of them do in this situation? Fara had heard that in captive situations like the one Tahlia was in during the last mission, riders were instructed to get up as high as possible to make it easy on a dragon to snatch her up and return her to safety. But did that apply on a ship? Did it apply when dealing with rune magic they couldn't fully prepare for?

"This is just annoying," she said finally, focusing on his forehead instead of those haunting amber eyes of his. "I'm not meant to be with you. Please just return me to the shore. Then you can go about your fun, evil little plan. Have a grand time. Most of the people up here are criminals anyway."

"Not in the coastal villages."

She narrowed her eyes at him. "Why are you standing up for the people that you're about to pillage?"

"I'm not pillaging anyone."

"If you don't stop being so pointlessly cryptic, I'm going silent. Then see how much fun you have flirting with me, your non-mate."

He laughed loud then, bending slightly. When he straightened, he wiped a tear and shook his head. "You're wonderful. I am so glad I found you."

"You didn't find me. You stole me. And you're fully cracked in the head."

"Likely true about that last bit, but anyway, I'm not here to hurt the good people who dwell on the coastline. I'm here to ruin the men I lead and take down every last pirate in this cursed strait."

"What? So you're claiming you're on the Mist Knights' side now? That's a touch tough to believe considering you just tried to smother them all to death with a great magical cloud."

"I was chasing them away, so they wouldn't burn me alive. Can you blame me for that?"

"If you would have opened the talks with *Hello, I'm actually here to help you* then perhaps things would have progressed differently."

"Hmm. Do you believe that? If I had exposed my plan to the Eelsmen waiting for my word in the shadows and risked telling the truth to your Seelie friends, you think they would take me at face value despite the history of discord between our people?"

He had a fair point. "Things are different now. You know the truth about my king and yours."

"Aye, things are changing, but to the average Fae on either side of the divide, it's not yet a new world where we trust one another without testing the waters."

"Why are you captaining the very men you plan to destroy?"

"What better way to ruin a company than to infiltrate it and lead them to their own demise?"

"I don't know, maybe use that rune magic and be done with it in one fell swoop?"

"You think too highly of my magic. Plus, I wouldn't catch them all if I did that. I can't destroy the entire pirate infestation by taking down a few handfuls of the foul humans."

"Some have Fae blood, you know."

"Not enough for my taste."

"So you too have your prejudices."

He lifted his eyebrows and flipped a hand palm-up. "We all do."

"What's stopping me from shouting your plan to your men on deck and the ones below decks happily snoozing in their hammocks? I have Mistgold in my blood and I could shout that truth to the skies. They'd be on you before you could scratch your dark magic on your bedpost there."

"Though I hate to draw your thoughts away from my bed, fierce one, can you play out how that would work for you? Would the Eelsmen be so grateful that they granted you leave to return to your people after they bludgeoned me to death?"

"I saw it more like they would chum until they had a kraken nearby, then toss you overboard and watch the beast take you. But bludgeoning works, too." She didn't want to admit it, but he was right about the pirates. They would do exactly as they pleased with her once their captain wasn't offering her protection. She swallowed the bitter taste of fear.

The Unseelie raised his nose to the air. He could scent her trepidation. "So you do understand."

"Of course, I do," she said, relenting even though it burned her to do it. "I'm not ignorant of the stories. I am a Healer at Dragon Tail Peak, where the knights reside. I know all about this crew of yours and those of their ilk."

"Then we have an agreement. You keep my plan to yourself for now. I keep you alive and happy."

"I am not happy."

"Try this." He held out a silver goblet filled with dark wine.

"I shouldn't but..." She took the wine and drank it down. "You probably poisoned that and I'm going to die in the worst pain, but at least I'd be keeping you from thinking I'm yours."

"Why would I poison you if I want you to be my mate?"

"Because you don't truly desire me."

"Don't I? Remember that though we are different, we share the inability to lie. Besides, what would be my motivation to deceive you about being my Seer's Heart?"

"Cruelty."

He nodded and poured himself a goblet of wine before refilling hers. "A possibility, certainly, but as I've said, I have my cruelty planned and it doesn't include you."

"You don't think stealing me off a dragon's back is cruel? Because it is."

"I do apologize for that." He dipped his head and made a pretty bow as if he was at court.

"Stop with all that. I'm not going to be swayed by overdramatic behavior. I'm not some green youth."

He approached her slowly like a lion stalking its prey. His chin was set low and his eyes speared her, keeping her in place. Her body flushed with heat and she found herself biting her lip. She growled and bared her fangs.

"I know that you are not. I love the ferocity and wisdom I see in your eyes."

She snorted. "Right."

His gaze didn't waver.

"High Captain," a gruff voice said from outside the cabin door. "We have a problem."

Teague picked up something from the table and stuffed it into her hand before storming out of the cabin and slamming the door behind him.

She looked down and uncurled her fingers to see a lovely piece of bread. Damn it. She couldn't actually hate someone who gave her bread. Could she? Well by the gods, she'd certainly try. She bit into the buttery wonderfulness and began working on the nearest window to see if she could climb out. She'd always been a good swimmer.

CHAPTER 12
MARIUS

Marius's thoughts twisted around this terrible problem. He never should have agreed to take Fara along. This was his fault as Commander of the Mist Knights. Never once in Dragon Tail Peak's history had a Healer been kidnapped by pirates. He felt sick and tried very hard not to put Fara beside his sister in his imaginings of how Bellona died. That was a long time ago, and Fara was a different person.

Tahlia circled him, her scent both intoxicating and alarming—her fear was pungent. "How are we going to get her back? That Unseelie can do things we don't even understand. But we have to try. Let's go under the cover of night. The ship is still in the same place, right? No small boats have left it?"

She craned her neck looking around him and the tree cover. He'd ordered the knights and dragons to land on a small island beyond the cove where the battle had taken place. The spit of land was uninhabited and hosted thick pines that worked well for cover. After sending Enora and Ewan off to scout the Unseelie's ship, he's tasked the others with tending wounds and talking over potential solutions. They would have a full group as soon as the scouts returned.

"Let Ewan and Enora finish their work and we will make a plan. Now, you need to sit with your dragon and gather yourself. Rash behavior won't help Lady Fara."

Tahlia nodded, her movements jerky and so unlike her usual graceful way. She went to where Lija was resting with Donan. Maiwenn lifted a hand at her approach and the two began whispering about what the Eelsmen's new high captain had accomplished with seemingly no effort.

Marius was truly worried about what he might be able to do to their dragons. Could he injure them from afar? Definitely. That was surely what that cloud had intended—harm. But at what intensity? Could he kill from the beach while they flew above him? How many dragons and Fae could he influence or harm at one time? Hopefully, Ewan and Enora would return with information. They would listen to the Unseelie talk to his crew and hopefully garner a hint as to what the Unseelie's goal was or what he could or would attempt to do via his dark magic.

"If we chopped his fingers off, he wouldn't be able to carve any runes," Titus said, coming up behind Marius from the direction of the rocky inlet where they'd quietly landed earlier. His hair was wet and he was bleeding from his elbow.

"What happened to you?"

"Just a rock. That obsidian is angry stuff."

Marius huffed a laugh without much good humor behind it. "True." He lifted his forearm to show a scar from a pirate battle he'd been in years ago right in this area.

"What are the Unseelie's weaknesses?" Titus asked.

"Our bloodiron."

"Which we still have. We're down three arrows, right?"

"Yes, but with Lady Fara captured, I don't think it's wise to attack openly."

Titus murmured assent. "What if we grind the bloodiron and get it into his nightly serving of rum?"

"Who is going to manage that? Also, I'm not sure if that would be enough to kill him or wound him severely. He's going to scent the contents before he imbibes much. The Unseelie can smell as well as we can."

Titus clicked his tongue and eyed the ship where it bobbed in the placid water. "Water's calm, isn't it? Odd for this time of year."

Hmm. Marius approached the tree line and studied the ripples of the strait and the currents combing through the dark expanse. Sharp boulders of obsidian stuck up here and there like the teeth of a great, fallen kraken. The moon—nearly full—floated over the water like a spirit of old.

A realization spread over him like frost. Marius's breath left him and his head grew light.

"What is it?" Titus came forward and his gaze peppered Marius's face. "Marius, what is it?"

He used the tone for times when they were off duty and simply being friends instead of commander and captain.

"I didn't mean to alarm you, but I think I just figured out what the Unseelie is up to. I think it involves Lady Fara as well."

Tahlia popped up and nearly made him jump. He was so distracted by the horror of what he suspected.

"What involves Fara?" she asked, coming close and staring up at him in that beautiful, determined way she had.

Marius cleared his throat. "The stranger is going to offer Fara to the full moon kraken."

CHAPTER 13
MARIUS

Tahlia fell back and Marius reached out to grab her arm, Titus bracing her back with his palms too. Marius could almost read her thoughts. *Fara. Kraken. Unseelie.*

Titus was the first to break the silence. "How does that work? Have you witnessed the offering?" he asked Marius.

"This is a thing? Offering people to sea monsters?" Tahlia's voice cracked and she wiped sweat off her forehead and neck. "How can that be a tradition?"

"The northern folk used to perform the offering every full moon. Yes, I have witnessed it. Though it isn't often practiced anymore, they resorted to it during a recent year of continuous storms, asking the kraken to rise and frighten the sea into submission. It worked. The full moon kraken isn't like all the others. It holds powerful magic. No one knows when it was born into this world or if it was touched by magic through someone else. It's all a mystery. As for the ritual, I watched them bring a female they chose forward..."

"But she was human, right?" Titus asked. "This is a human tradition. He's Unseelie."

Marius took a deep breath. “Aye, but maybe he is determined to do his version of it.”

“Why?” Tahlia’s voice cracked. “Wh, what does he want the kraken to do?”

“He’ll offer her up on a dinghy, tied and painted in runes. The creature will rise and claim her and at the same moment those performing the rite will shout their request to the full moon. I don’t know what the stranger will ask.”

“He isn’t even supposed to be here. The king sealed the drumstones.”

“There is likely a portal somewhere up here, as we mentioned.”

“Don’t you *as we mentioned* me! This is Fara! We have to go. Now!”

Marius grabbed Tahlia and breaking all the rules, pulled her to him and held her. “My love. My lady, please. We all want the same thing here.”

She pressed her forehead into his chest and her shoulder shook violently as she fought a sob, not allowing herself to make too much noise and give them away. Her small but strong fists knotted in the edges of his sleeveless tunic that showed at the sides of his leather vest.

Titus pressed his lips together and watched with kind eyes. He glanced toward the others and Maiwenn looked up. Her gaze flicked to Marius, then she nodded like she knew to keep everyone busy for a moment. She turned and approached the center of the riders and dragons and began motioning for everyone to come closer to her. She would be telling them something that seemed important, keeping their attention off Tahlia and him. She was always so good at that sort of thing.

A bay owl’s call had Titus and Marius turning toward the western edge of the small island. Ewan and Enora swam up to the smooth pebbles of the beach and walked out of the sea.

“We will see what they have to say,” he said quietly to Tahlia, allowing himself just one more moment of comforting her.

She sniffed and broke away, her face flushed, but her gaze steady and serious. "All right."

Titus reached them first. "What did you hear? What did you see?"

Marius and Tahlia were just steps behind him.

Enora squeezed the water from the end of her braid. "The crew is celebrating a coming event of some sort. They say songs will be sung about the new high captain's revenge."

Ewan dried his feet on a patch of moss, then began putting his socks and boots back on. His tunic, belt, bow, sword, and leathers were there too, alongside Enora's gear and clothing.

"They say their high captain is a demon," Ewan said.

"Correct." Tahlia's tone was dark and dangerous. It was unusual to see her so serious and full of rage, but Marius didn't blame her one bit. He felt the same.

Enora turned her back to them and shucked her linen top off. She tied her leather vest on as she talked. "The captain claims he lost his father here in the north. He wants to pay back those who ended his life too soon. Nothing was said about who exactly killed him. I assume he means the humans along the coastline somewhere."

Titus frowned, bent to retrieve Enora's weapons belt, then handed it over to her.

"Has to be," Ewan said. "No one else is up here. Only the villagers, the traders, and the pirates."

Titus looked to Marius. "Could he be going after other pirates?"

Crossing his arms, Marius fought the fatigue that always crept into a knight's body after a battle. "Makes more sense that a pirate would kill an Unseelie they found than the traders doing so. The traders would have sold him for money if they were able to subdue him. The villagers would have simply avoided him at all cost. This father must not have been nearly as magically capable as his son to be killed by humans."

Ewan murmured something about superstitions that Marius

didn't care to worry about. Yes, the northern folk were superstitious; the Fae and the humans here alike would hear about the full moon ritual, no doubt, and they might come to watch. It could be dangerous, but the order had to focus on this problem right in front of them. They had to retrieve Fara before tomorrow night when the moon rose to its peak.

A clarity came over Marius as it usually did after talking out problems. He gathered the order together and announced a plan to fire on the ship that held Fara and the Unseelie. To torch the end opposite the high captain's quarters and see if they can provide enough of a distraction that Fara can get to a place where Ragewing could pluck her from the pirates' vessel.

"What if we end up killing her ourselves?" Tahlia asked, her face ashen in the moonlight.

"If we don't try, she'll be dead anyway."

Tahlia's eyes shuttered and she took a shaky breath. Then she opened her eyes again and regarded everyone one at a time.

"All right. I'm in."

The courage in her voice and her features made Marius feel like she could never fail at anything. He wished that feeling was fact, but sadly, he knew well that battles with pirates and hostages rarely ended without significant injuries or death.

CHAPTER 14
FARA

A bang echoed through the ship and the room where Fara had been spending her hours listed to one side. She grabbed the stupid Unseelie's stupid desk and it was apparently attached to the floor because it held and kept her from falling. Teague had left the door unlocked because he said they had to learn to trust one another. What a joke.

Shouts broke through the sounds of sea and crew. The smell of burning wood pricked at Fara's nose. Someone screamed, then there was a splash and another loud bang. Fara ducked like that would somehow help. She rolled her eyes at herself as she ran out of Teague's quarters and up the steps to the deck.

A pirate wearing a black head wrap threw a spear into the sky.

What in the...

A storm of dragons burst from the low, moonlit clouds. The spear slid between Ragewing and Lija. All the knights and their dragons were in on the attack and though it was terrifying to see, Fara was touched by their commitment to her. Sparks and flames poured from their mouths. Fire engulfed the ship's bow. Smoke billowed from the mainsail. Pirates had created lines to pass buckets of water to douse the fire. But the dragons swooped low, and the lines broke into chaos with the crew running this way and that, some jumping from the ship and into the sea only to be caught up by dragons and pierced by those horrible teeth. Shrieks pierced the air and Fara knew this was her moment.

She pushed past two pirates attempting to load a massive crossbow. The tilt and sway resulting from Ragewing ripping his talons into the railing made that chore impossible. Lija soared overhead, her four wings out in a low glide, and Fara waved at Tahlia as she tried to climb the lesser mast—whatever it was called. There were metal posts in the pole and it wasn't too difficult to clamber up.

But then a set of hands was on her, yanking her back to the deck.

She kicked out at whomever it was and swore. "You donkey-dicked asswipe! Let me go! I'll kick your gods-damned teeth in if you have any, you filthy pirate!"

Arms, strong and warm, clamped down on her and a voice found her ear. "Retract your claws, my pretty cat. We must get you to safety."

Fucking Teague. "Leave me alone! I want to go with them. They won't hurt me, unlike you and your pirates."

He merely threw her over his shoulder and carried her down to his quarters. Kicking the door open, he said, "I should have explained my whole plan to you already. You wouldn't be running away if I had. My apologies." Easing her to the floor, he chuckled. "I just need to send your dragon rider friends on their way with a little magic and I'll be right back."

She tried to lunge and beat him to the door, but he was as fast as a stag in the wood. There was no catching that damned Unseelie.

The door's lock clicked and the sound of Teague's boots knocked along the wood, an echo to the mayhem going on above.

Fara kicked the door viciously. "If you hurt even one of them, your life will become a nightmare that you never could have imagined! I'll find a way to make you hurt, you arrogant lunatic!"

She would never stop fighting this fool and somehow she'd get out of here. Tahlia would never give up, so Fara wouldn't either. She'd die first.

CHAPTER 15
TAHLIA

Lija let out another string of heavy fire. The crackling, curling flames licked over the decking and caught not one but two pirates' clothing on fire. They screamed and leapt from the ship.

"Two more for you, Morvan!" Tahlia called up to the black-haired Fae riding a Heartsworn nearly as large as Ragewing.

Donan flew by and tipped two of his four wings. He scooped water and tossed it over the stern, the spot where Ragewing had seen the Unseelie take Fara just moments ago. Apparently, Fara had been climbing one of the masts. Tahlia had missed it in the smoke and the action. Lija veered north and came back around to blaze the bow again while Titus's Spikeback, Ptol, let out four quick successions of flame aimed at the sails. Atticus's Heartsworn joined Ragewing and Marius in encircling the ship with heavy fire—keeping the pirates from swimming to shore or the rocks farther out.

"Come on, Fara. Find a way out," Tahlia said more to herself than anyone because there was no way for Fara to hear her.

Want me to drop you on deck? Lija asked. *You could infiltrate the captain's quarters and free her.*

Yes, let's do it.

Lija started back toward the stern of the bobbing, smoking ship. *I'll tell Ragewing.*

When they flew low, Lija hissed. *Ragewing says Marius ordered you to remain on my back.*

Fine, then land on the stern. Bust through it with your talons. We are getting our Fara.

I like the way you think, rider.

But the Unseelie burst through the belowdecks opening and lifted a flat stone into the air. A pale mist scattered from his chest and covered the ship, pirates, flames, dragons—everything in sight. All was turned to white and everything went silent. A ringing sounded in Tahlia's ears.

Ack! Rider, I have to leave. This noise...

Lija dashed away from the ship and toward the open sea, sounds of pain echoing through their telepathic connection.

Tahlia shook her head, attempting to stop her ears from ringing. The farther they got from the ship, the more the pain lessened.

Are you all right? Oh stones, Lija, your ears are bleeding!

I'm fine, Lija grunted. *Let's just get to our gathering spot.*

Tahlia said more prayers for Fara as Lija flew quickly through the night toward the island Marius had selected.

We will get you back, Fara. Know that I'm not abandoning you.

CHAPTER 16
MARIUS

On the forested island refuge, Marius and Ragewing landed and sprayed black sand into the air. The rest alighted beside them, faces pinched and some bleeding from near misses of crossbow bolts.

"Is anyone seriously injured?"

There was a chorus of negatives, and Marius nodded, his gaze snagging on Tahlia and Lija. His ears were still ringing slightly.

"A bolt glanced across her wing and that bizarre mist magic burst one of her eardrums," Tahlia said, dismounting.

"Do you have salve? Is she able to keep on?"

Tahlia nodded. "I have it." She untied one of the bags at her belt, then removed a vial. "Yes, she says she'll be all right to move again when we need to."

Rider, Ragewing said, *creatures approach under the water.*

Marius whirled away from the knights and the other dragons to eye the dark water. Under the moon's strip of white on the waves, the sea gurgled and churned like a large beast swimming toward them.

Creatures? More than one? Can you tell me anything about it?

Ragewing lifted his head to scent the air. *"Only salt water and fish."*

"This could be more of his dark magic," Marius warned the group.

Tahlia was applying the salve to Lija's wing and around her hidden ear. Titus and Atticus were tending to minor cuts on their mounts. Maiwenn, Ewan, Enora, and Justus were listening to Claudia describe her run-in with the spear-throwing pirate who had first spotted them.

The knights halted in their conversation and tending of dragons to draw weapons. The dragons rose and positioned themselves to defend their riders. Marius would never stop being enthralled with the way the dragons worked with them—that bond between souls was a true miracle.

The sea foamed and three large eel heads appeared just above the waterline. The one in the center held something in between its jagged teeth.

"What in all the names of all the gods is happening?" Tahlia's arms dropped to her side and her eyes narrowed.

Ewan spoke first. "The eels in this area are magic-touched. Perhaps from ancient gods' spells. No one knows. But this is why the pirates are called Eelsmen. They have long worked with the foul beasts to send messages to their fellows on other ships."

"Humans can work magic like this?" she asked, lifting her weapon again.

Marius walked into the water far enough to take the offered item. "This is only circumstance of power that I've seen or heard of."

It was a thick, glass vial that held a small scroll.

He nodded a thank you at the eels, who then swerved around and retreated into the moonlit sea.

Everyone gathered close as he broke the wax around the cork and removed the missive.

"What's it say?" Tahlia was practically sitting on his arm.

I HAD HOPED you would leave me to my work for just a day or so, but since you are keen on attacking me and my new ship, I must tell you the truth.

"IT'S FROM THE UNSEELIE. I'll read it aloud."

He caught them up on the first line and then continued relaying the words scrawled on the vellum.

"He says he will not harm Lady Fara, but he intends to call on the full moon kraken and act as though she is his sacrifice."

Tahlia gasped and paled.

Marius was afraid this was his plan. Why was he pretending there would be no harm done to Fara?

"His command to the kraken will be to right all the wrongs done by pirates. He believes the kraken will make the pirates susceptible to us in magical ways. Says we should be ready to fire on any that are exposed to us by the kraken tomorrow night."

"He's against the pirates he's leading?" Titus said, frowning.

"I'm lost," Enora said.

"He's lying," Tahlia said. "Wait, can Unseelie lie? They can't, right?"

"No, they are like us in that," Marius said.

"The Unseelie instructs us to fly at moonrise and wait. He swears on the name of the Unseelie king and his queen that he is not our enemy."

Tahlia turned away, her hands fisting at her sides. "Oh sure, I trust that."

"We're still going to try to get Fara back before then," Marius said. "I don't know what this new high captain is truly up to, but I don't trust him any more than you all do. Finish tending wounds. Those who are able, we fly out again in one hour.

As they prepped, a bank of clouds drew down low on the island. Everyone looked up, then one by one, they dropped to the sand and fell into a deep sleep.

CHAPTER 17

FARA

Hands tied to prevent her from jumping ship, Fara sat on a crate near the steps leading up to the stern's deck. All day, she'd been ignored by Teague and his crew as they repaired the damage the dragons had wrought. They cut out fire-eaten boards and replaced them with lumber they'd stored below decks. Some of the pirates were reworking the shrouds near the bow so they were usable. They cut away the scorched rope and knotted the loose ends to the areas that had gone untouched.

For the first few hours, she had screamed and leapt from the ship and fought Teague tooth and nail. But now, well, she'd given up—for a little while anyway until she thought of some escape.

Escape didn't feel right though. An odd feeling had stolen over her in the last hours. Each time Teague walked nearby, the feeling intensified. It was a fluttering sensation that started in her chest, then moved to her stomach, ultimately landing between her legs. She shook her head at herself. Clearly, her asinine body was physically attracted to the Unseelie. He was incredibly built and hadn't actually hurt her in any way, but he had kidnapped her. He planned to take her to the Unseelie realm somehow. He was most definitely not lover material. But that strange sensation didn't care about any of that. It wrapped her up now, the fluttering evolving into a sensitivity of sorts. She could almost feel Teague's breath as he sawed a plank at starboard. His movements were her focus even when she tried instead to watch the gulls fly or keep a keen eye out for the knights. It was as if his presence pulled her in like a whirlpool's impossible current. Part of her didn't want to escape. She tugged at the rope binding her wrists. The other part of her knew she was losing her mind.

Could he be right about this Seer's Heart thing? Panic laced cold fingers around her throat. She refused to be fated to this kidnapper who spoke in riddles. She snarled at him, frustrated and hot with confusion.

Teague left his work and walked over. He dusted his hands together, his clawed fingertips clicking lightly. "Do you need a drink? Food? You could go below and take a break from the sun if you like?"

"I need to be free, you bastard. That's what I *need*."

He grinned sadly at her and lifted her chin with one claw. Lightning shot down her body and warmth pooled in her core. Her breathing became unsteady and she hated herself for it. She jerked away.

"I am sorry you don't enjoy the bond. You will in time. Once you see what I am up to."

"Why don't you just tell me?"

He rubbed a hand through his hair. It wasn't braided today and instead dusted his powerful shoulders. "Well, it's a bizarre plan and I worry it will upset you. It's better if I tell you right before we go through with it so you'll only have a minute or two of fretting about it."

"Oh, that's incredibly comforting. It's so bad that you don't want me to know until it's bound to happen. Great."

"Perhaps, I'm wrong then. All right. Let's have a strong drink and I'll explain everything.

As the sun lowered itself against the horizon and drew pink skirts around its final rays, Teague served her a heavy pour of what smelled like cherry brandy. They were alone in his quarters though the noise of the pirates' dancing and drinking made it feel as though they weren't completely isolated.

"What is this?"

"It's not dosed with anything if that's what you're wondering."

"I'm glad you're not poisoning me, but no, I meant what type of drink?"

"It's redleaf whiskey, a local favorite."

She sipped it and the warmth of the drink smoothed its way down her throat. "Not bad."

After they took a few more sips and her limbs were feeling looser, he shut the door to his quarters and locked it.

"That's a fantastic way to start this little tale. Making sure I don't flee in fear, eh?"

"You never have anything to fear while I am with you. I value your life above mine. It's the bond."

She didn't want to think about that and how her heart told her he was speaking the truth and how much her very soul seemed to luxuriate in his words like a sleepy cat in a ray of sunlight.

How in the hells was her kidnapper comforting? Gods, she'd heard of things like this happening, captives falling for captors. She'd always thought it to be so very sad and truly pathetic. But here she was, falling right into that very trap. She downed another swallow of whiskey, hoping it would drown the physical desire for Teague that was swirling through her blood.

"Promise me you will sit and listen to my entire plan, that you won't attempt to run or climb through the window again."

That had not gone well. She didn't really fit and he ended up tugging her out, his grin telling her how much he enjoyed having his hands on her arse.

"Fine. I will listen to the whole damn thing. Fine. Yes. I promise."

He nodded and took the chair opposite hers—a high-backed velvet contraption with loads of shell carvings just like the one she was in. His elbows rested on his knees and still his head was high above hers. He wore an ivory tunic rolled to his elbows. Forearms scarred and marked with odd inkings in red, he would have made an imposing figure even without the claws, longer fangs, and those claws of his.

"Fara—"

"Did I tell you my name? I don't remember doing that."

"I heard your friends call it out when they attacked."

Fara bristled. "Go on, then."

"I will call up the full moon kraken."

Her heart hit the back of her teeth. Leaping out of her chair, she nearly fell backward over the overly ornate arm of the thing. "The kraken? I heard you wrong."

"Alas, you did not. But sit. You promised."

Fara felt her nostrils flaring. She was covered in sweat. "If you think you can sacrifice me for your wildest dreams, you are painfully wrong. I won't let my death benefit you, you arsehole. I'll find a way to end myself first if it comes to it. I can't believe you pretended—"

He rose and took her hands in his. The movement was so gentle that the urge to fight back, to pull away, didn't even cross her mind or make her flinch. The warmth in his fingers soothed her, sending waves of comfort through her arms before spreading out to all areas of her body. She exhaled slowly and met his gaze.

"My heart, you will not be touched by any monster except me. And then, only if you will it. You are safe with me."

"You keep saying that, but you make no sense."

"Listen to my plan. You've seen my magic."

"Yes. So? What is that against the chieftain of the northern waters?" Fara's great uncle had told her tales of the great kraken and the wishes he granted when the sacrifice was right.

"I will fool the kraken into believing he has already consumed you."

"How? There won't be time when he surfaces."

"I will paint you in runic magic before we summon him. The moment he sees you, the magic will act on his mind. I am a Seer, remember? I have seen this."

"What will you ask for? What is this all about?"

"I will ask it to right the wrongs done by all pirates. To avenge the innocent. To balance the scales."

"That's ridiculously vague." She gripped his fingers even though he was her captor, her nightmare, the one she had to escape from before it was too late and he enacted this mad plan. "You have no idea what such a request would do to this area. There are no parameters."

"It doesn't matter."

Would Marius get his revenge on the pirate who murdered his sister, Bellona? "Why are you so angry with the men who live as pirates? Aside from the fact that they kill and pillage and gods know what else."

Teague's amber eyes seemed to glow with grief and rage. "The Eelsmen killed my father."

"Why was he here? How? How are you here?"

"There is a portal deep in a sea cave near this island. No one knows of it, but me. My father showed me. He brought me here to see this realm. He said the world was larger than most knew and that he wanted me to know of things beyond the Realm of Night."

"Were you with him when he died?"

"I was. The pirates attacked the small boat we rented for fishing. They didn't see me hiding under the tarp stored in the bottom of the craft. Father hid me, then..." He shut his eyes and a shudder shook his frame.

"I'm sorry, Teague. No youngling should see the end of a parent."

"Thank you."

He reached out and brushed his knuckles over the back of her hand. Longing drummed through her bones.

"Now, will you trust me to paint the runes on you and go through with this?" he asked.

"I… Of course, I can't. This is madness."

"It's not. What if I prove to you what my magic can do? I will paint you and then you can test it on the crew."

"Teague, I am not going to—"

His hand shot out and pressed gently against her heart. One solid, hard beat thumped from her body and into his fingers. She lurched forward, pulled to him by some invisible force. Her breath caught and then he was cupping the back of her head with his free hand. She was tethered to him by an unseen rope that felt stronger than the one that had bound her hands earlier. It was invisible, but it held firm as she tugged backward. She should have felt panic or had the sensation of being physically trapped, but instead, that fluttering sensation traveled through her chest, down her limbs, and even to the top of her head. She wanted him to devour her and she longed to do the same to him. His scent. His hands. His warmth. Him. Just him.

"Gods, it's overwhelming," she said her voice raspy with want and joy and whatever the hells this was.

He dipped his head, his mouth so close to hers and his breath soft on her cheek. "It is. I've felt this way since I saw you."

"This strong? I can't pull away."

"I fought it. I fight it still."

"No wonder you nabbed me from the back of a fire-breathing dragon. I would have done the same." Swallowing against a dry throat, she shook her head. She didn't want this feeling. But it was the best sensation she'd ever experienced.

He drew back slowly and the bond's hold on her lessened so that she felt free to move. Her mind and soul and body still longed to be fused with him in every way possible, but it was weaker now and she was able to sit back and not touch him.

"Will you let me paint you?"

"Yes."

She could feel his thoughts somehow and sense the truth there. He needed to avenge his father and this was the only way to truly rid everyone of the pirate scourge. He was a hero, not a villain. She knew that now as well as she knew her own heart.

CHAPTER 18
FARA

Fara held very still as Teague dipped his long, black paintbrush into the special ink he'd concocted for rune magic.

"What's in it?" she asked breathily.

His knees butted against hers and the desire to climb onto his lap was nearly undeniable.

"Clay from the Realm of Night. Ink from the spotted octopus. And no, I didn't kill one. We harvest ink from these creatures when they die back at home. There's also a bit of honey and a few crushed leaves of sage because that aids the magic. At least, that's what my grandmother always told me."

Fara smiled. "I can't imagine you as a youngling, sitting and listening patiently to a grandmother of any sort."

"She was twice as big as I am now."

"What? Really?"

"Aye. Sometimes the women in our family show off a bit of troll blood."

"That's honestly horrifying."

He chuckled. "It's an old family joke. We don't actually have troll blood. We just had a few larger folks in the line."

"Oh. Right. Of course."

He slid the neckline of her tunic to one side and set the brush on the top of her shoulder. Drawing the ink in a slow circle, he hummed and murmured words in a language she didn't know. Every stroke sent wonderful tremors down her body until she was melting. Each dot and slash of the brush was like a soft kiss along her flesh. He painted his way up her neck, then over her forehead. The ink was cool and when he hummed that odd tune of his, the runes tingled lightly.

They talked as if she wasn't about to meet a kraken face-to-face. She told him about helping Tahlia sneak into the dragon rider tournament, the struggles and joys of becoming a Healer with the order, and of her time before going to Dragon Tail Peak.

In turn, he regaled her with stories of his realm, of running through mossy forests where trees read your aura and reflected it back to you, of fantastical animals she'd never even heard about, and about the night market festivities. He told her about how his family was all gone now, but that he had friends enough to suit him. He'd met the Unseelie king a few times as a Seer, and he gave that king, King Toren, advice on how to proceed with monster wrangling—it could be a real problem in the Realm of Night—and what to do with an advisor who he knew was on her way to betraying him.

Almost every inch of her exposed skin was now painted in power.

"I'll need you to remove your trousers," he said, raising an eyebrow. His mouth quirked up with mischief.

Taking a deep breath, she nodded and did so, leaving her small linen shorts on. Going to his knees, he held her knee gently and continued humming and murmuring. He painted a tree-shape over her thigh and she shivered. As he added two dots over the shape, his claws dragged over her. Her skin pebbled and her heart smashed against her chest. She licked her lips and noticed his gaze pinned to her mouth. He paused in his work.

"Maybe we need to wait on this until after I've introduced you to what our private life will be like once you give up fighting the bond."

"What do you mean?" She knew, but she wanted to hear him say it.

He just chuckled low in his throat and went back to painting. Such a bastard.

His fingers moved gracefully and quickly over her other thigh, down her calves, and then he took each foot in turn and drew runes on her arches.

"Please, stop. That tickles so badly."

He drew one claw up the side of her foot, then down to her heel. Heat poured into her core and she took a shaky breath.

"Teague, please."

She wasn't honestly sure what she was asking for. For him to stop messing with her ticklish feet? To stop painting so they could do more interesting things on his bed over there? What did she want? She knew, but she didn't know. Pressing her eyes shut, she felt him move away a little.

"We can take a break if you need it," he said quietly.

She opened her eyes and savored the look of him on his knees before her. "No, I'm all right. I am adjusting. Or fighting it. I don't know, Teague. This is just..."

He tucked her hair behind her ear. "I know, my heart. I know."

With quick strokes of his slender brush, he inked more runes down each of her arms, their shapes ending at her wrists. The tickling bristles and the soft hold of his fingers turned her into a puddle. There was a distant voice in her head that still claimed he was the enemy, but she knew that was the part of her that hadn't yet accepted the bond. There was no denying this feeling. It sang through her soul like the most beautiful and fitting piece of music. When she mixed the herbs just right and watched her patients at

Dragon Tail Peak recover, she felt a fraction of satisfaction like this. She wanted to cradle his head in her hands and study every line of his fierce face. She longed to learn about each one of his scars and why he wore a ring with a blue stone on his left forefinger. Every story of his should have been hers. Her heart had accepted him. Her soul, too. Her fearful side would need time, but she knew he would be patient with that element of her personality.

He paused, brush hovering over the tip of her chin where he'd painted a swirling rune that tingled with power. His mouth was less than an inch from hers.

"Kiss me," she said.

And he did.

Careful not to smear the runes, he set his lips to hers, nipping at her lower lip with his long, Unseelie fangs. His tongue danced across hers and desire crashed through her body in one great pulse. He tasted like cinnamon and mint and something else that was entirely him, and she never wanted to stop kissing him.

A knock at the door broke them apart.

Teague's eyes held her gaze as he said to the door, "What is it?"

"The sun has set, High Captain," the pirate on the other side replied.

Fara's heart beat frantically and Teague smoothed a thumb over the palm of her hand until her pulse evened out.

"Come in, Renyo," Teague ordered.

The door creaked open and the spear-throwing pirate gave a head bob. "Captain?"

Teague stood and stepped away from Fara. "What do you see?"

"The purple-skinned Seelie captive, but she's..." He blinked and rubbed his eyes. "No, she's gone. Wait. I..." The man grabbed his stomach and grimaced.

"You're dismissed," Teague said.

The pirate nodded and left, shutting the door as he went.

Teague turned to Fara. "The illusion isn't set for him, of course, but he lost sight of you. The kraken chief will see you, and then he will imagine he has swallowed you whole. You will be invisible to him and he will feel a fullness in his great belly."

Fara stood on shaky legs. "All right. Let's go cut out the evil of pirates for this generation, at least."

Teague smiled and the candlelight from his desk twinkled in his eyes. "Thank you for trusting me, my heart."

She gave him a half-lidded look as she walked past him and opened the door. "The bond gives me no choice, but I'll take the gratitude anyway, I suppose."

He was suddenly kissing the back of her neck. His hot breath made her shiver. "I will make it up to you, Fara of the Shrouded Mountains. I can't wait to hear everything about you. I want to know it all."

She knew exactly how he felt. Letting her head drop back onto his chest, she let out a sigh. "We have plans to make, but first, we have a sea monster to deal with. Words I never thought I'd say..."

They both chuckled and climbed the steps to the ship's deck.

IT ALL HAPPENED QUICKLY. Fara walked through the suspicious and confused pirates, who made occasional foul remarks about the Seelie. Teague acted at forcing her into the skiff they'd lowered into the eerily calm sea.

The moon rose like a lantern raised for the gods to view the whole world. Its silver beams threw crystals on the water's surface and made Teague's eyes dance.

He took her hand. "It's time."

She swallowed and did her best to feel the promise of their bond.

The kraken rose from the deep, its eyes monstrous and wet, its tentacles bubbling from the foam. Fara stilled, her heart hanging between her ribs without even the hint of a beat. The night was too quiet. The moon shimmered over the sea monster's head. Even snow and ice couldn't compete with the cold whisking over Fara's exposed skin. Fear or temperature? Both? A pattern of circles and slash marks laced the kraken's head. This was the ancient chief of the creatures that made their home far below, hiding in the black depths of the strait's crevasse. He alone possessed the intelligence, as legend states, to claim the female sacrifice and do the bidding of the Beckoner. This being would understand the desire of the Beckoner's heart...

The moon's blue-white glow danced across the water, moving like a spirit until it rested on Teague's chest.

He inhaled sharply and held more firmly to Fara's hand.

Then he began to speak in the old language, a tongue that was magic in and of itself. His tongue flicked and rolled and clicked along as he spoke his desires to the ancient monster. Each syllable uttered from his lips sent a shiver over Fara, raising the hairs on the back of her neck and forearms. The scent of sage rose into the air.

Fara held so still even though she longed to put her hand over her chest to see if her heart had resumed beating. She would be dead if it hadn't, so of course, it was. But the feeling of no pulse, no life, remained. She was a spirit herself, floating in stasis, unable to return to the living world and barred from the afterlife.

Teague spoke the last of his wish and the kraken reached three of its massive arms high.

Would his trick work?

Shaking, Fara forced her eyes to remain open. If she was to die like this, she wanted to see the bastard monster's face as it took her. She was a Healer and Squire of the Shrouded Mountains. She would not cower. Tahlia would be proud. A small smile touched her lips and Teague glanced her way, his eyes wide and a surprised grin on his mouth.

"You're a wonder," he whispered.

The kraken's tentacles wheeled up then down and the monster dove back into the water, his movement rocking the skiff violently.

Sparks of golden light flashed beneath the water's surface, curling into the depths and shooting out of the waves into the sky.

Teague held Fara as they stood, working hard to remain in the craft. Her heart was certainly awake now and hammering away inside her shaking body.

"You did it. Your tricky dark magic worked," she said.

"Don't seem so shocked. It's insulting."

Fara snorted and gripped Teague's vest with her trembling fingers. "I've known you for two days."

"Time enough to know I do as I say."

"Well, I didn't know the kraken was going to agree with your mad plans."

He looked out over the raucous waves, the whole area gurgled with activity now. "All the kraken will gather to their chief and end the pirates once and for all."

"I think we should sail behind them and enjoy front-row seats," she said, surprising herself with her courage.

A sharp laugh came from him. "You are so vicious. I adore it."

"What about the men on your lead ship?" The men were already shouting questions and giving congratulations with a tone that hinted strongly at their confusion.

"This is the Beckoner's only ship now," Teague whispered to the sea, his cadence like the spell he'd cast over the kraken.

Fara looked from his moonlight profile to the ship.

One black and glistening tentacle shot from the water, wrapped the ship, and cracked it in one quick and violent move. Screams punctured the night and Fara shivered at the pirates' fate even though they surely deserved that and more for what they'd done to the coastal villages during their lifetimes.

CHAPTER 19
MARIUS

The dragons flew low over the shoreline, watching, waiting.

Golden light highlighted ships near and far, magic gilding the pirates' bodies.

Screams and shouts joined those of the Unseelie's crew, and a pirate's body washed ashore in Ragewing's moon shadow.

Ragewing dropped down and landed beside the dead pirate, and Marius was quick to dismount. He stood over the body, the hairs on his arms rising and a cold wind whipping across his back. The pirate had a long, white beard, ice-white eyes, and fine clothing. He still wore his boots and had a sword at his belt. Hatred teemed through Marius like eels swam through his blood. He bent over to be sick on the sand.

Rider, do you need me? Ragewing said.

The other dragons hovered above, awaiting Marius's command.

Marius held up a hand and spit to clear his mouth. *No, I just need a moment. I...*

"Brother," a sweet, haunting voice said. Marius looked up to see his sister dressed in the clothing in which he'd last seen her. She remained young as if years hadn't passed since her death.

His chest caved and he reached out a hand. "Bellona." His eyes burned with unshed tears.

"This is the pirate who led those who killed me. The old chieftain has ended them all. Every pirate in every hideout. Each of those who did wrong to the people of the north and beyond. Lady Fara's soul mate, the Unseelie named Teague, worked this magic. He is to be trusted."

Marius's heart felt like it was exploding and reforming over and over again. He looked up to Tahlia, who was wide-eyed. She nodded as if in encouragement and strength filled him again.

"Bellona, I am so sorry about what happened. If I could have done something differently, I would have. I would now."

"Shh, Marius." She smiled and though her eyes were nearly clear they still seemed to sparkle with life. "Death is not the end, but the beginning of life. All is well. Enjoy your time here. Learn. Grow. Savor. I will see you when you are ready."

"I love you, sister. I miss you," he said, his voice cracking.

Ragewing sent a wave of warmth and friendship through their connection.

"I love you, Marius. You are a beautiful soul," Bellona said. She lifted her hand in farewell and disappeared in a flurry of golden stars.

CHAPTER 20
TAHLIA

Tahlia hadn't slept much after all the pirate killing and Marius relaying what his sister had told him. It was just a lot to process. At the shoreline, she and Lija splashed about in a series of tide pools to clean their faces and hands. There had been more eel messages, which would never not be creepy, and even a visit from several locals, who had sailed over to offer them baskets of fresh bread, fish pies, berry tarts, and ale galore. The locals didn't really want to hear that an Unseelie had been the hero of the day, and Marius gave up trying to explain after a half hour of arguing. The order had sat down to a proper meal on the beach, and now they awaited Fara and Teague's arrival.

The skiff slid with the tide onto the sand and Fara leapt out and ran to Tahlia. Tahlia grabbed her into a vicious hug.

"I am truly glad you aren't decorating a kraken's digestive system right now, my friend," Tahlia said into Fara's messy hair.

"You and me both, Lady Tahlia."

They shook their heads and laughed at one another before falling into another hug that turned into a dance.

Teague, Marius, Titus, Claudia, and Enora were discussing the details of what was to come while Maiwenn, Justus, Ewan, and everyone else finished up the food and talked with the locals.

Tahlia and Fara collapsed on the sand and watched the knights, humans, dragons, and the one Unseelie enjoying themselves. Lija butted her head against Tahlia's back, then trotted off to join the others. The morning sun glinted off the Seabreak's scales, making her look like she'd been covered in magic. She shook out her four wings and let out a trill as she used her tail to toss some sand at Ragewing.

Fara laughed and Tahlia leaned her head against her friend's shoulder.

"It's so good having you here," Tahlia said.

"It's fantastic to be alive."

"Teague, huh? For life?"

The Unseelie was shaking hands with Titus and laughing.

"I'm afraid so."

"You won't leave forever, right?"

"We are going back to the Realm of Night for the ceremony, then we will come back to Dragon Tail Peak to live."

"And he promised you this? Leaving his kin for this realm?"

"He did. He said his home is wherever I am."

"Impressive."

"Well, I had to talk him into it. He wanted to take me back to his home for good. I assured him that his life would be far more pleasurable if he compromised and simply visited his realm regularly."

Tahlia grinned. "I need details on how you talked him into that."

Fara's purple cheeks flushed darkly. "Mind your own business."

"As if you don't stick your nose into mine?"

Chuckling, Fara poked an elbow at Tahlia. "You know me. I love a good double standard when it helps me."

Tahlia laughed loudly at that and slung an arm around Fara.

"Just swear to me that if he ends up not being what you truly want, you'll tell me and let me help you kick his arse."

"I swear it."

"No one will ever deserve you in my eyes, my friend," Tahlia said to Fara. "No one."

Fara's eyes shone with tears. "I still think Marius could be nicer."

Tahlia grinned and hugged Fara tightly. "I'm happy for you."

"I'm happy for me, too!" Fara said.

Tahlia helped her up and they joined the group. Marius glanced her way, love shining in his stormy gaze. He'd received his closure concerning Bellona, and Tahlia was grateful. He had opened up before they went to sleep last night, his words flowing in a way they rarely did. She was so glad he felt secure enough to share everything he was feeling with her.

Yes, she was blessed beyond words. She would wake up every day and attempt to deserve her wondrous, exciting, beautiful life.

CHAPTER 21
FARA

Sitting on a velvet blanket in the shade of a willowface palm, Fara lifted the goblet and finished her wine. "There isn't enough of this to wash away last night's events."

Teague walked behind her, on his way to fetch the platter of fresh island fruits, and dropped a kiss on the crown of her head. Tingling spread from her scalp down her body. It was amazing what this male could do with such a small gesture. The maddening bond awakened when he'd painted her in runes shivered through her and everything else fell by the wayside—all her trepidation, the ridiculous nature of this relationship, the fact that he was Unseelie. She was his. He was hers. It was that simple, and the bond was stronger than anything she'd felt toward another person in her entire life.

"Not sure you've thought this far since you're a male, but how exactly do you plan to get us home? You haven't changed your mind? It is very cold there most months. I've seen bears. Wolves. And of course, the dragons can be deadly if you don't watch your manners. But you *are* coming to live with me at Dragon Tail Peak, yes? "

He sat beside her, eyes glittering with amusement though she was being quite serious. "If they'll have me," he said.

"You heard Commander Marius. He'll talk the others into it. You've single-handedly wiped out the entire pirate population."

"They will respawn."

"Yes, yes, but it will take a while, and I bet your sea monster friends won't mind taking a few more down now and then."

"That magic has faded now," Teague said, "but I will try to hope as you do."

"My friend Tahlia taught me to be optimistic."

"A rider can't be that naive, can she?"

"Only with great willpower." Fara smiled and bit into a pink and pale yellow fruit the locals called *hfnaptra*. Juice burst in her mouth and a subtly sweet taste rose from the soft texture. She moaned and took another bite before she realized he was staring at her, his lips parted and his eyes on fire.

"I'll have to bring one of those to bed with us," he said.

She laughed. "Please do."

He bit his thumb and blood beaded like a tiny jewel on his gray skin. "Do you trust me?"

"Unfortunately, I do."

"It's the Seer's Heart bond. Hold out your hand."

"More runes? Who are we casting an illusion over now? A roaming wolf? A bear? I confess I was hoping for a pleasantly boring day, Teague."

He settled himself on top of her and she leaned back, savoring the feel of her true mate all around her. His thigh pushed its way between her legs and he pressed himself against her. She ran her fingers over his hair—he'd braided only part of his thick tresses.

"You left some for me to enjoy," she whispered into his neck.

His throat bobbed and his cock twitched against her center, making her lips part as heat washed through her. His big, masculine body appeared quite primed and ready.

"You did seem to like twisting my hair between your lovely fingers," he said quietly as he dusted sand from her temple.

She indulged herself and looped a blue-black tendril over her knuckles. "Like silk."

"I'll brag about that to my friends when we visit. I'm sure they'll be very impressed."

Fara pinched his arm. Drawing her dress's neckline down, he kissed his way over one breast and then the other. Delight echoed over her skin. Under the attention of his forked tongue, her nipples hardened. He slid his hand low, under the dress she'd bought at the market they'd found two small islands over. His hot hand gave her a wonderful chill as he kissed her mouth again. His tasting of her grew rougher until he was sucking on her lips and tongue like he was pulling honey from a comb. His low purrs sent thrills along her body and she wriggled against him. The friction sent a deep throb of sensation through her and she gasped.

His hand went higher up her bare leg until the tips of his claws found the convenient slit between the legs of her undershorts. Quivering, she looked up at him.

"But your claws..."

He grinned and kissed her nose. "Don't worry, my heart. I know what I'm doing and your pleasure is my top priority. I would never hurt you. It would be worse than injuring myself because of our bond and because I simply adore you."

Sighing, she let her head fall back and tried to relax. His finger curled and his knuckles kneaded her warmth until she was desperate for more.

"Can we?"

He licked the lobe of her ear as he worked his way farther inside her body. "Can we what?"

"Oh, you know what. Stop teasing me."

His knuckles and the tongue at her ear had her trembling on the very edge of release.

"But teasing is my favorite part."

She glared at him even as she shook. “I bet claiming me in full will feel even better.”

Eyes shining like the sun on a sword, he pulled off his clothing in harried movements. He climbed on top of her in full, only a fraction of his weight on his elbows. His cock pressed against her center and she ground her hips against him. Her tension unwound and pleasure ricocheted around every inch of her body.

“Gods, yes...”

He moved slowly, letting her enjoy every last bit of her climax. Then he put her arms around the back of his neck, rucked her dress up fully, ripped her drawers away, and set himself against her entrance.

“There is more teasing I plan to do to you, but since you have awoken the more feral side of this Unseelie, I must claim you now in body.”

Easing his way with gentle pushes, he kept his eyes on hers. “Tell me how you’re feeling.”

Her face felt flushed and her body was molten. She gripped his shoulders, digging her nails into the lines and curves of him. For an answer, she rolled her hips encouragingly.

“How do you think?”

His eyes fluttered and he groaned, entering her fully. “You’re exactly right for me.”

The fullness of him sent tremors down her legs and through her core. She was already close to climaxing again.

“How...” She could barely speak as he went in to the hilt. “Teague...” The desire humming through her was insistent and pounding like her pulse. Longing to experience every bit of this that she could, she reached through the bunches of fabric and her leg to feel the spot where his body met hers. His stones were hot and she heard herself growl.

“I guess I’m a bit feral for you, too,” she said. She bit his shoulder. From the stories she’d read, she knew Unseelie were rougher in their mating.

His hand went to her throat and he placed his forefinger claw against her pulse point. He was shaking now too and only shifting slightly inside her. Gods, he was so large. It felt amazing. And they both held one another in a dangerous way, a way in which each was in some way so vulnerable. A rush of knowledge ran across her mind. Trust. That was this feeling.

"Still all right?" he asked, his voice husky.

The bond beat like a third heart between them—hot, tingling, powerful.

"Yes. Claim me, Teague. You are my heart as well."

He pulled back and she gasped. Then he drove forward again and again, starting slowly and building to a chaotic pace. His jaw was loose and his eyes were like that of a wild animal. She clung to him and matched his fervor. A knot of pleasure grew heavier deep inside her and then she was soaring, splintering, shimmering in a haze of absolute completion. Not only was there pleasure in her body—her soul was renewed and anchored. She felt safer than ever. More right than ever.

Teague halted and shook, his warmth releasing inside her and his lips on her forehead, his claw still at her throat as his hips shuddered between her thighs.

"I love you so much, Fara of the Shrouded Mountains, Healer of Dragon Tail Peak."

He held her close and she cuddled into his big arms. The sun poured its golden rays over them and she smiled into his strange Unseelie skin. His hands found hers and cupped them gently at her stomach.

"I love you, too, Teague of the Night Realm and Captain of Nothing."

He laughed into her hair and kissed her ear, her neck, and the crown of her head. "I will never deserve you, but I would like to try."

"You better or my dragon-rider friends will annihilate you."

He pretended to shudder in fear, chuckling.

"Now, you still haven't answered my question," she said. "How are we getting back? Not sure you remember, but we said farewell to all of my dragon-riding friends this morning."

The corner of his lips lifted and a dimple showed in his left cheek. "I have one last Unseelie trick to show you." He stood and held out his hand. "Come. I can't perform this magic under this tree cover."

She looked up at the palm's branches. They were easily eight feet high. "I—"

He tugged her farther onto the beach's powdery, golden sand. Releasing her, he stepped backward from her ten paces until the surf lapped at his bare feet.

He smiled, showing his Unseelie fangs in full glory, and then he burst into a plume of glittering black and plum-colored magic.

Teague was gone, and in his place, was an eagle roughly the size of Ragewing.

Her hands fisted. She fought the urge to run. His feathers were a deep and lustrous brown and his curved beak held a golden hue that changed as he tilted his head to look at her with one massive, black eye.

"You're a shapeshifter. Of course, you are." She felt like she was dreaming. Or having a nightmare, maybe. This wasn't real. "All Unseelie have an animal form. At least, that's what I was taught. But hearing it from one's tutor doesn't do this justice. You're magnificent."

She ran to him and he lowered his wing. Taking the cue, she clambered onto his back.

"I'm no dragon rider. I don't know if I can handle this."

He shook his feathered head as if to say yes, you can, silly. And then he took off.

This was magic. Love, belonging, someone to watch over her forever, and mysteries that would unfold during their life together.

. . .

Bonus Scene

(A lot of y'all have emailed or DMd me asking for this, so here you go! This is Marius and Tahlia's first love scene which happened after Bound by Dragons and before Kingdom of Spirits on the night of the feast)

Tahlia

Tahlia's stomach flipped pleasantly as she and Marius hurried into the second tack room in the dragons' cave system. Starlight poured from the three small windows at the top of the far wall. Rows of saddles, reins, and replacement pieces sat neatly labeled. A large cot had been pushed against the right side of the room, a spot for those too tired to return to their lodgings after a mission or for a rider or squire keeping watch on a sick or injured dragon. The coverlet was a thick white wool. Releasing Marius's hand, she went to smooth the bedding, wondering if the structure was enough for what she was hoping was about to happen. They had both had some ale. And maybe a little wine. But they were perfectly capable of enjoying one another. Tahlia's face flushed and her pulse skipped with excitement.

Marius had put his life on the line for her. For her. He'd stood up to the commander and that horrifying Green Terror because he believed in the dream she'd been dreaming as long as she could remember. Even though they were tipsy and being a little wild, a voice inside her heart said this was only their beginning.

Tahlia turned to face Marius, and she leaned backward on the cot. She knew she was staring, but anyone would be. Not only was he the bravest, most upstanding person she'd ever met, this Fae male was a study in sharp angles and cuts like he was carved of stone. His hair draped over his shoulders and she longed to run her fingers through the silky length of it. His scent of cloves and coming rain mingled with the leather and rock of the room. With a look that promised wicked pleasure, he took his whip from his belt and unfurled it as he stalked closer.

"Take off your clothes," he said, his voice a growl. "Now."

Sensual shivers carried across her chest and pebbled her nipples. For a second, his gaze softened and he tilted his head. She smiled, understanding the unspoken question. He was asking if this playacting was what she wanted. Tahlia felt safe with him; he'd proven his dedication to her well-being.

"Yes, I love it. Carry on, Captain."

A quick grin stretched over his very kissable mouth and then his face resumed its commanding arrangement of narrowed eyes, furrowed brow, and a slightly bared set of Fae fangs.

She giggled, low and quiet, despite his ferocity, and crawled onto the cot. Up on her knees, she unbuckled her belt, slowly pulled off her tunic and the wrap she sometimes wore over her breasts for training, and then threw all of that onto the tack room floor.

"Faster," he growled. He cracked the whip again.

A prickling sensation suffused every inch of her skin. She wanted those skilled and dangerous hands on her now, but her damned boots wouldn't come untied. Probably because she was trembling with giddiness and a little tipsy from the celebration.

He dropped to his knees, tucked his whip into his belt, and began working on her laces. His brow bunched and he didn't look up; his entire focus was on her boots. After jerking the boots free and tossing them over his shoulder, he rolled her woolen stockings down with gentle motions despite his rough act. With a few quick movements, he tugged her trousers off. She loved every second of the brusque treatment. It was tantalizing, having the stern captain so determined in his desire for her.

He rose and flicked his whip out, and the snap of leather over her head had her gasping with delight. Such a rush.

"Lie down," he commanded. "Spread your legs."

She bit her lip. “Yes, sir.”

Still fully dressed, he climbs onto the bed. Using the whip’s handle and his free hand, he spread her knees wider. Bending low, he purred against the tender crease where her right leg met her body.

“You smell divine,” he whispered.

Pleasure raced through Tahlia’s veins like some new magic. He reached his arms under her legs and encircled her thighs. His biceps pressed into her flesh, his muscles straining as he tugged her closer. He began licking his way from the crease of her leg to her hot center. His gaze flicked upward. His eyes were the steel of a sword.

“You must be still, Tahlia.”

Her name on his tongue was another spell newly born into the world. She would do almost anything to hear it again.

“Marius, I can’t possibly...”

He cocked his head. “It’s an order.”

Desire pulsed down her body in a slow rhythm of heartbeats. Her body wanted more. She wanted more.

A grin lifted the edge of his mouth and he lowered his head to resume the decadent torture. He licked—long, slow strokes, quick flashes of his tongue’s tip, and delving thrusts of the full length of his tongue inside her folds. She trembled from head to toe. The weight of a building climax hummed inside her, but he wouldn’t give her the pressure right where she needed it so badly.

“Please, Marius.”

She tried to buck her hips, but his arms were vices on her thighs.

“Be still, female. Not yet,” he whispered against the curls covering the warmth between her legs. “I will not be rushed. I’m taking my fill of you first. You cannot limit my feasting.”

The rising pleasure pressed on her, urging her to move, to find friction, but Marius only teased her again and again, his tongue brushing the secret places just next to the very spot that pulsed with need. Another warm intrusion found her slick entrance. He slid what felt like two of his large fingers into her and curled his knuckles. She turned to moan into the pillow, her body trying to crest over that nearing edge of completion. Finally, his tongue found her center and dragged wet heat over the top. Desire exploded in her core. She called out his name and gripped handfuls of his Fae-white hair. Her hips bucked uncontrollably as waves of pleasure shattered into a chaotic flurry of mind-bending sensation. He continued to stroke her with finger and tongue as she rode out the crescendo. The peak subsided finally and she blinked up to see him undressing. His molten gaze burned her in the best way.

Gods, he was just too lovely. Every inch of his body had been honed by training and battle. The scars along his pectorals only served to thrill her more because she knew he won the fights that gave them the marks. He was the Scourge of the Shrouded Mountains and he was between her legs. His black and gold inkings highlighted the musculature of his neck, shoulders, chest, and flat abdomen—all the way to his slim waist. He removed his trousers and his cock stood proud, the tip glistening and ready.

"Turn over. On your stomach. Now."

Tahlia thought it would be impossible to feel even more aroused than she had been moments ago, but she was wrong. The moment he was behind her with his weight lightly pressed against her back, his cock rubbing between the sides of her arse like it was made to be there, and his hot breath dusting over the nape of her neck, she knew she'd been wrong. She swallowed, unable to utter a word as he poised himself to thrust into her properly.

"Tell me if you want me to stop," he said, his voice low and quiet.

She shook her head and swallowed again as his hand raised her hip so he was better angled. "Don't stop. Please, don't stop."

He pushed inside her body slowly, his movements careful despite his playacting at being completely domineering.

"Are you all right?" he whispered against her shoulder. He kissed her there, his lips sticking slightly to her damp skin.

"Yes. Take what is yours tonight, Captain Marius."

He nipped her flesh lightly and drove hard inside. Pleasure jolted up her spine and reverberated through her entire body. With three more strong thrusts and insistent growls, he released within. Heat poured through her as her inner muscles quaked and squeezed his cock, her pleasure flying even higher than it had earlier.

"Fuck, Tahlia. You're..."

He shuddered and pushed once more, his huge body quivering and his breath hot on her back and in her hair. The scent of him was everywhere and she was certain this was the best feeling in the world.

They collapsed together. Holding her tightly, he murmured sweet little phrases into her ear.

"This might be even better than riding a dragon," she whispered, feeling like a dessert pudding melting on a plate.

He chuckled and kissed her gently. "Riding the captain, you mean?"

She huffed a laugh as he rolled her over and kissed her temple. "Yes, but I'd like to make sure I'm the only one permitted to do this job."

He cradled her in his arms, and she took joy in the feel of his heart beating in time with hers.

"I'd like that too."

She kissed him and he kissed her back. An exciting promise bloomed in that embrace. If she had to guess, they were going to be together like this for a long, long time.

ABOUT THE AUTHOR

USA Today bestselling author Alisha Klapheke infuses her books with unique magic, far-flung fantasy settings, and romance. Her inspiration springs from an obsession with history, years of travel, and the fantasy she grew up secretly reading during math class.

When she's not writing, Alisha teaches martial arts at her family's dojo. That may be why writing fight scenes is her favorite.

Alisha also writes spicy cozy fantasy under the pen name, Lila Appleton.

ALSO BY ALISHA KLAPHEKE

When the Weaver Met the Gargoyle

The Fae King's Assassin

Enchanting the Elven Mage

You can find many more and a guide for where to start at https://www.alishaklapheke.com/

www.ingramcontent.com/pod-product-compliance
Lightning Source LLC
Chambersburg PA
CBHW030758200726
PP18592100001B/10
9798998600517